TALL, DARK, AND DETERMINED

TALL, DARK, AND DETERMINED

 HUSBANDS FOR HIRE—BOOK 2

Kelly Eileen Hake

BARBOUR
PUBLISHING

Other books by

KELLY EILEEN HAKE

HUSBANDS FOR HIRE
Rugged and Relentless

PRAIRIE PROMISES SERIES
The Bride Bargain
The Bride Backfire
The Bride Blunder

ISBN 978-1-60260-761-3

All scripture quotations are taken from the King James Version of the Bible.

This book is a work of fiction. Names, characters, places, and incidents are either products of the author's imagination or used fictitiously. Any similarity to actual people, organizations, and/or events is purely coincidental.

For more information about Kelly Eileen Hake, please access the author's website at the following Internet address: www.kellyeileenhake.com

Cover design: Brand Navigation

Published by Barbour Publishing, Inc., P.O. Box 719, Uhrichsville, OH 44683, www.barbourbooks.com

Our mission is to publish and distribute inspirational products offering exceptional value and biblical encouragement to the masses.

Member of the
Evangelical Christian
Publishers Association

Printed in the United States of America

DEDICATION

As always, my books are dedicated to my Lord,
who gives me words and patience when I have neither.
But this particular story is for my fellow capable, take-charge
women—and the men strong enough to love us anyway.

ONE

Colorado Territory, June 1887

Dead men told no tales, but jailbirds sang aplenty. Chase Dunstan knew Braden Lyman, victim of a mine collapse, couldn't be telling anything. Problem was, no one else gave details about the accident, leaving too many questions about how—and why— those men died. The property sold with ungodly haste.

Only a need for answers brought him to the jailbird, a man foolish enough to miss their rendezvous four days and three counties back. Getting thrown in a cell didn't excuse failure.

"What did you find out?" Chase waited while his quarry paced the small room, still not responding. He waited while the other man drank a dipperful of water and almost choked. A dry throat and slippery nerves made anything hard to swallow, and the man before him dealt lies thick enough to block a bison.

But Chase knew what all good trackers knew; waiting was the longest part of the hunt. So he tested his patience against his fellow man instead of an animal until Robert Kane faltered.

"You're not going to like it." When Kane finally spoke, Chase didn't so much as shift on the hard wooden seat he'd chosen.

"That much, I can tell you plain and simple."

"That much, I already knew when I found you in a cell." Chase allowed a thin thread of amusement to reel in his prey.

"And left me here to rot." Kane kicked the wall to vent his frustration and regroup. "You could've posted bail, us being brother-in-laws 'n' all." His grumble died out when he looked up and caught Chase's unblinking gaze. Robert Kane possessed no shame—but he boasted some degree of self-preservation.

"Your brother's marriage makes you no relation of mine." *If the scriptures say a man leaves his mother to cleave to his wife, surely that includes his no-account half brother.* Chase eyed Kane. "*He was a good man, so for both your sakes, I hope you found some information worth my time.*"

He made no direct mention of his sister. Laura had seen enough hardship at the hands of their own family without allowing Kane's oily thoughts anywhere near her. There were worse reasons to send Kane to Colorado than to keep him away, but only one better. Details about the death of Laura's husband—and the mine collapse to kill him—hadn't been forthcoming.

The settlement the mining outfit gave Laura to make up for the loss of her husband wouldn't last a year. Chase would have taken the matter to Lyman, the partner he'd dealt with when working as a guide for that same outfit early on, but Lyman went down in the collapse, too. Chase's suspicions deepened when the surviving partner sold the town in record time and vanished.

Since then the only mention of Hope Falls came through a ludicrous ad folded and still tucked in his back pocket:

Wanted:
3 men, ages 24–35.
Must be God-fearing, healthy, hardworking single men
with minimum of 3 years logging experience.

TALL, DARK, AND DETERMINED

Object: Marriage and joint ownership of sawmill.
Reply to the Hope Falls, Colorado, postmaster by May 17.

The thing must serve as some sort of code. But if the mining company was involved and covering something up, they might recognize him. Chase Dunstan couldn't go poking around Hope Falls. But Robert Kane held the anonymity and logging background to head out there and look for answers.

Kane also had the bone-deep idiocy to botch it.

"If the information's good enough, will you get me out of this cell?" No longer pretending any sort of kinship, Kane began bargaining for freedom he didn't deserve. "Because I don't have to tell you anything, Dunstan. As long as I'm behind these bars, it doesn't matter to me what happens in the world beyond them."

"You're bartering with what already belongs to me." It wasn't a question. Chase didn't ask questions he already knew the answers to unless trying to appear unthreatening.

"You don't have the information; it doesn't belong to you." Kane spread his hands in offering. "It's simple business."

"Business finished when I saved your backside from that posse stringing you up for fraud. Try again." He stood up.

"The past doesn't concern me. Right now I need to know—"

"You can stay out of reach behind those iron bars. Or I can get you out and show you firsthand my opinion of men who fail me. Either way, you'll tell me what I want to know. Your only choice, Kane"—Chase leaned forward—"is how."

"All right, all right." Kane glanced at the bars as though afraid they might vanish. "Can't blame a man for trying."

Yes he could, but Chase didn't waste the breath.

"The mine collapsed—you can see where it used to be, how the mountain sort of fell in on itself and crumpled." Words started pouring from the prisoner—and lucky for Kane, they were true

9

so far. Chase had circled close enough to confirm the collapse for himself just after hearing about the tragedy.

"And the ad that got your hackles raised?" Kane started to get to the good stuff. "Sure enough, there were four women running that town. They dangled the line that three of 'em wanted husbands to keep control over the loggers."

"Four women run the town?" Chase ran the pertinent detail to ground. "The ad made it seem as though three owned it." *If any of them do, and it's not some elaborate hoax.*

"Four. Claimed that together, with the one's fiancé, they'd bought up the town and wanted to convert it to a sawmill. They chose a site and cleared it, brought in an engineer, interviewed everyone, and divided them into work teams. It's just like the ad said, Dunstan." Kane smirked. "Those women weren't ladies—no lady puts out an ad like that, and no man with half a brain would believe it. Course, most of those loggers didn't own half a brain, so they were fooled into hoping for pretty wives in the wild. Could almost see why—the gals meant business."

But what kind? Chase kept the question to himself and asked another. "Who's the fiancé—the man they claim owns Hope Falls?"

"Don't remember." Kane looked chagrined—or at least as chagrined as he could look, which meant he looked afraid of displeasing Chase. "But he was in bad shape—bedridden. The man giving orders went by Creed, if that helps. He arrived after most of us, and it looked like he only knew one of the women."

"No." Chase didn't know any men by the name of Creed, which was too distinctive to forget. Then, too, any man planning on being front and center running the town would have established his status from the start. Some truth ran through the old saying men were dogs—when it came to dominance, neither animal left room for questions. "The name of the fiancé. Now."

"I can't remember." Kane started talking fast. "Adam? Brian? Something like that. He was fiancé to one of the Thompson sisters and brother to the girl I had my eye on."

"Word is you had more than your eye on her, and you got caught." Chase cast a glance around. "Was she a widow?"

"No, a miss." Kane scowled. "Now there was a girl who didn't belong in the backwoods, Chase. All done up in bows and fluff, looking like a lady when she wasn't, putting on airs as though she owned the place. The type to lead a man on but kick up a fuss when he got close—she's the reason I'm stuck here."

"Her name." Not a question; a command.

"Lacey, though I doubt it was real." Kane looked ready to go off on another long-winded speech about the temptress.

"Surname, you fool. She should share it with her brother."

"Lyman."

Chase sucked in a sharp breath at the answer like a hound drawing in scent for the hunt. "The brother's name. Braden?"

Kane snapped his fingers. "Yep. That's it. Stuck in the doctor's bed."

"Why?" Chase had to be sure.

"Mine collapse, they said." Kane hadn't known any names going in, so whatever he came up with wouldn't be half-truths drawn from his own twisted conclusions.

Chase narrowed his eyes as he left the jailhouse. A rangy wolfhound abandoned its post in the shade to lope alongside him. There could be no doubt—Braden Lyman lived. This gave rise to a slew of new questions. Was the one man in Miracle Mining whom Chase had trusted involved in its collapse? Did the real Braden Lyman still own Hope Falls? And if both answers were yes—*why?*

Because despite what Kane told him, Chase knew one thing: *an attempt to conceal a sabotaged mine is still more likely than three good women advertising for husbands in the wilds of Colorado.*

Hope Falls, Colorado Territory, 1887

So this *is how it feels to be wrong.*

Lacey Lyman abandoned the laws of ladykind to gnaw on her nails. Of course she'd been wrong before—one didn't reach the advanced age of eighteen without a few token mistakes. But this wasn't always-talking-too-much wrong or even clashing-bonnet-and-dress wrong. She shuddered at the last one, but it still didn't come close to the current situation. No. *This* counted as nothing less than best-start-swooning wrong.

Creed, the man they trusted enough to make head of operations, had just dangled another logger by his suspenders in some sort of fit over a single coin then rushed out of the kitchen. Normally, that would be odd. Just now, it was ungentlemanly to abandon ladies in such alarming circumstances.

An all-out brawl was taking place beyond the swinging doors of the kitchen, where twenty or so loggers pummeled each other. Some defended the honor of whichever woman caught their eye, some tried to prove their masculinity, and a small cowardly number simply defended themselves. But there was no escaping the fact that, to a man, they clashed in competition over herself and the three friends she'd talked into coming West. The rain hadn't stopped in hours, so they didn't even take their fight outside the diner like somewhat civilized mountain men.

Even worse, it was *all her fault.*

"Oh, hush." Evie jabbed her with an elbow, although that might have been an accident. The newly built storeroom Lacey dragged them all into hadn't been made to house four women amid its shelves. "It's not *all* your fault, and you know it."

Lacey shot her friend a sharp look before realizing Evie

couldn't see it. In addition to space, the storeroom also lacked a lit lantern. Nor did it share the warmth of the stove, which had made the kitchen much more inviting until a pair of loggers came flying in from the fight and hadn't gone back.

"Then whose fault is it?" she demanded, stung by the way her friend emphasized *all* as though, indeed, Lacey bore the lion's share of guilt. *If Evie thinks I'm to blame, she could at least show the decency to be agreeable about it!*

A jumble of answers bounced around the tiny space all at once, but Lacey caught who'd said what in an instant. They'd been through too much not to know each other's voices and the thoughts of their hearts by now. Tangled together, they went: "Creed!" The loudest burst from Evie, who'd been fighting the rugged stranger for weeks—mostly because she was fighting an attraction to him. About an hour ago, Evie ran out into the rain, distressed over a callous comment made by one of the men. Creed followed, but obviously failed since Evie came back alone.

"Braden!" The most vehement came from Cora Thompson. Evie's sister and fiancée to Lacey's own brother, Cora had every right to blame Braden. He'd convinced them to invest in a Colorado mining town then destroyed everything by falling victim to its collapse. But when word of his miraculous survival surprised them in Charleston, Cora didn't think twice. They all moved to Hope Falls only to hear Braden denounce them as fools.

Lacey brightened at the fact that if it weren't for Braden, none of them would be here at all. Truly, it was all her brother's fault. The world made sense once more, and—

"All of us!" The longest and fairest answer came from Naomi Higgins. Her elder by nine years, Lacey's cousin observed, "We all invested in Hope Falls as a mining town, and nobody forced us to come here when things changed."

Three women shifted uncomfortably in tight quarters.

Whether Cora and Evie moved to ease a sense of shame, Lacey couldn't be sure. But she suspected they, like herself, found the quiet truth in Naomi's answer too compelling to ignore.

Except. . .a sort of needling sensation in her chest wouldn't let Lacey accept Naomi's answer. She wanted to. Oh how she wanted to, but Lacey had a gift most people never suspected. Not an astounding talent. She simply. . .remembered things. If she heard them or read them, Lacey could repeat them years later. Not precisely word for word, but with surprising accuracy.

Surprising because, when she most needed to, she couldn't pay attention. Life offered so much. Color and sound, textures and tales, sparkles and sensations forever calling her away from the moment. . . So people never imagined Lacey could *remember*.

But she did, and right now Lacey was remembering a conversation from when they'd still believed Braden dead. Mere weeks past, it seemed a lifetime ago.

TWO

*L*acey took a deep breath. "Hope Falls can be saved."

"Towns don't have souls, and even if they did, Hope Falls would be the exception." Cora all but spat the words. "There's no redeeming it. No eking anything worthwhile from it now."

"Without ore, nothing can sustain the town," Naomi agreed.

"That's not true. What Hope Falls now lacks in ore, it more than makes up for in another valuable resource." For once in her life, she didn't let everything rush out all at once.

This time Lacey needed them to ask. Investing time and thought would bring them a little closer to agreeing to her plans. She suspected she wouldn't be able to taste anything for a month, but kept her tongue between her teeth. Literally.

"What resource?" Evie spoke up for everyone.

"Trees!" She almost bounced in her enthusiasm. "The San Juan Mountains are absolutely covered in the lumber New England lacks. Even better, we have railroad access to meet the demand."

"You're proposing to turn a mining town into a sawmill?" Disbelief tinged Evie's tone, but interest sparked. "How?"

"We'd need to buy up the surrounding land, but if looking into selling our property has shown anything, it's that we can get it cheaply. Then it's a matter of labor." Lacey hesitated.

"Hire men, you mean." Naomi raised a brow. "Setting up a sawmill is an expensive venture. You'll need investors."

"Or husbands." Lacey winced at the way she blurted it out.

"Never!" Cora jumped to her feet. "We won't travel there and make our home without Braden. I won't have it!"

"If we let Hope Falls die"—Lacey tried to be gentle—"we've lost the last part of Braden we could have kept alive."

"But marrying another man—" Cora shook her head. "I can't."

"I anticipated that. But the rest of us can marry." Lacey's hopes faded at the shock painting Naomi's and Evie's features. "Husbands provide protection and legitimacy."

"Preposterous. Absolute lunacy." Evie stood beside Cora, shaking her head. "Finding investors, perhaps. But binding ourselves to complete strangers over a sawmill? Never!"

It took all of two moments for the scene, fluid with sights and sound, to unroll in her memory like a bolt of watered silk. Silken memories binding her to her own mistakes. . .

He'd overplayed his hand. Corbin Twyler knew it the moment he saw Creed with the square luck token he'd lifted off that body six months back. Seemed as though he'd been on the run since he shot Granger and claimed the self-righteous fool pulled his gun first.

Yes. Nothing but bad luck since then. That's why he'd put the token in the pot. After Kane's mischief made every man in Hope Falls suspect, Twyler had to get rid of any hint of bad luck or incriminating remembrances. They came through the Game, and the Game would help him pass them on to another player. Surely the time drew near for Twyler to win once more.

Why else would a man keep on playing? What use was the challenge of living if a competitor never moved ahead? The Game taught a man patience, how to read small tells and anticipate another player's next move, all for the sake of winning.

And while he'd overplayed, Twyler hadn't lost this hand yet. So he asked himself, how would Creed move next? How quickly? And how could Twyler get the goods—and the last laugh?

Funny thing about mistakes, Lacey reflected less than an hour later, *they travel in groups. Become familiar with one, and all of a sudden a girl finds herself besieged with a slew of them.*

The gun pressed to her temple brought the realization she might not have the opportunity to meet with any more mistakes. Of course, nothing less than a pistol at point-blank range would convince Lacey to let herself—or her blue worsted wool—be dragged through the muddy mountainside in a frigid downpour.

This, too, was *all her fault.*

And none of her friends were around to tell her otherwise. No, all the other women remained safe and dry in the kitchen, most likely unaware that Lacey should have returned with those peppermint sticks by now. How horrifying, the idea she might not even be missed while a crazed criminal kidnapped her.

She concentrated on breathing shallowly through her nose until he abruptly removed his grimy hand from her mouth.

"What do you want? Where are you taking me? Couldn't you have waited for better weather?" Lacey didn't waste her breath screaming—he'd obviously waited until they were beyond earshot of the town. Why bother howling when she could harangue?

"Money, you'll see, and no." The man had the effrontery to grunt, as though hauling her about required more strength than he'd anticipated. Honestly, what kidnapper expected a woman to go tromping to her doom? Sagging into deadweight slowed the man down at least. "Now shut your trap and start walking, woman."

"I'll pay you well to return me, I'll walk back to town, and I'll even be silent," Lacey offered. Guns made her generous. The mention of money made her more comfortable. A greedy man might negotiate where a man intending personal harm would not.

"You couldn't pay me to go back to town with Granger lurking about," the logger refused. "As for the others, you'll do as I say or live to regret it, missy." He jammed the pistol into her tender skin, bruising to underscore his meaning.

So long as I live. Lacey almost chirped the response, but sensed it would provoke her captor. So she stayed quiet for a moment while she thought—and shuffled her feet in a show of grudging obedience, falling back with her full weight on his shoulder with each "step" she took, as though walking backward up a muddy mountainside in sodden skirts might be difficult.

"We'll order anyone named Granger out of town, Mr.—"

"Twyler." He cut her off, coarse speech dissolving beneath a sneering mockery of cultured tones. "We haven't been properly introduced. You think me a logger, but I'm a gentleman."

"Of course. True gentlemen kidnap ladies and trudge them up mountainsides at gunpoint regularly." Lacey coughed as the arm wound beneath her ribs tightened mercilessly. "My mistake."

"I wouldn't do this at all if it weren't for Granger," the man hissed into her ear. "He's hunted me here, and now I don't have time to woo one of you women and win your fortune legally."

"That makes sense," Lacey allowed. "Fortune hunting has been an honored sport of gentlemen for generations. But I'll still pay you to release me—and we'll send this Granger from town. We don't need any new men anyway." Not so much as a twinge of conscience for all the lies she told. Twyler wouldn't get a cent, and she might not send Granger away at all because once the massive brawl in the diner ended, several loggers would be leaving Hope Falls in disgrace. But none of that mattered.

"You stupid twit." Twyler's arm moved from around her waist. Almost instantly, his hand fisted in her hair as he jerked her backward, quickening the pace. "Do you really think I'm the only man to give a false name? Ah, but I fooled him until today, just as he fooled me. The difference is my bluff wins because I fooled all of you longer. *Creed is Granger*."

Fear, ice-cold, slithered down Lacey's spine as Twyler went on about games and bluffs and Creed. *He's not sane.* She no longer pretended to drag her feet; dread made them heavy and plodding. All hopes of reasoning with her captor or waiting for the two dozen loggers to come searching for her unraveled in an instant. Her kidnapper's plan couldn't work—he headed away from the train—and when he realized it, the wildness in his voice would be vented upon his victim. *Me.* Lacey gulped in air.

"Now you're quiet, eh? Creed's not your hero anymore? Don't you worry, Miss Lyman. You'll be nice and safe right here." He patted a large tree stump slightly downhill of them.

"What?" Lacey gaped at the nondescript logger whose dull clothes and brown hair seemed so normal until one caught the maniacal glint in his eye. "You're leaving me here to wait?"

Hope fluttered once again. If he planned to tie her to a tree, she'd be found eventually. Or she might work herself free.

"Yep. When I get the money, I'll send them your location." Twyler rocked back on his heels. "So you just hop on in there."

Thoughts stuttered to a stop as he gestured again to the hollow trunk of a massive old tree. "Did. . .did you say. . .*in*?"

"I'll boost you up, and you can't get back out on your own. It'll be tight quarters, but a bitty thing like you should fit."

"No." Lacey looked at the jagged edges, brittle at the top, which she could see from her vantage point. Rain streamed into the narrow black opening, and she didn't want to think what creature hollowed it out in the first place. Or how many types of rodents and insects made their home within now. She didn't care whether or not she *might* be able to fit inside. "I won't."

"Don't test my patience."Twyler tightened his grip on the gun. "I said I'd tell them your location. I didn't promise you'd be alive. So you can climb on in and they can find you snug and spitting mad, or I can waste a slug and cram you down there so they find whatever the bugs leave behind."

"Because you're a gentleman," she muttered, debating.

"Yes." His eyes narrowed. "That hooped skirt isn't going to make it though. You'll have to shimmy out of it first."

"I beg your pardon?" Lacey stopped debating. Surely the man hadn't just instructed her to *disrobe* before descending into the dark bowels of a forest prison? As though she'd simply cast off her best worsted wool in the middle of the day. While it rained.

"You heard me. The cage thing and bustle have to go, at the very least." He brandished the gun again, making Lacey decide there really ought to be some sort of limit on how many outrageous demands a man could make per pistol. In all fairness, Mr. Twyler had to have used up all the good threats in that one.

Which really isn't fair, when I'm probably a better shot than he is. Lacey heaved a sigh over the pearl-handled pistol in her purse. Back in the kitchen in Hope Falls. *It only goes to show*, she decided, *that of all my recent mistakes, the absolute worst was neglecting the importance of my accessories.*

Evie gripped her purse, hoping she wouldn't need to use the pistol inside it. Lacey tried to teach her to shoot when she gave each one of them a matching firearm, but every woman knew that the safest thing in range was whatever Evie aimed at. It still rankled how Cora and Naomi learned to shoot so quickly.

Even worse, she knew Lacey wasn't carrying the weapon she'd ensured they all possessed. Her friend's purse, with the first of the pearl-handled pieces inside, remained on the baking table. She'd left it there when she ducked back in the storeroom in search of peppermint sticks to settle an uneasy stomach.

The women let her take an extra moment to compose herself—Lacey felt irrationally responsible for the men's poor behavior—but the man Evie now knew as Twyler announced he'd look at the mercantile for the peppermint sticks and left the room. Then Jake burst back into the kitchen, abandoning a false trail and desperate to find his brother's murderer. But they were too late. Time's slow crawl had sped, and the only sign left of Lacey were scuffs in the mud beyond the storeroom door.

Now Evie watched with her heart in her throat, following behind the man trying to save her friend and clear his brother's name. Jake Creed held more than his fair share of courage, and, she was afraid, about the same amount of her heart.

"Let her go, Twyler." Jake edged out from behind the uneven row of trees concealing him from view. "She's no good to you." The sight that greeted him wore his considerable store of patience very thin indeed. "You can't shove a full-grown woman into a hollow tree stump, Twyler. And there's no reason to anyway. Drop your gun, set her free, and we'll go back to town."

"Ah, ah." With that, Twyler hauled Lacey against him, pressing a sharp blade against her delicate throat. With his free hand, he pointed a pistol at Evie, as though threatening the women made him powerful. "I suggest you drop your weapon, Granger, if you want both—or either—of these ladies to see another sunrise. Your one shot might just as well hit Miss Lyman as myself, but I'm guaranteed success with at least one of my targets." Satisfaction oozed from his voice. "Let's get on with it, shall we? A stacked deck is a gamer's greatest ally."

"I wonder"—Evie pretended nonchalance, trying to look unthreatening—"whether that's not something like a woman with a well-packed purse." In an instant she pulled out her familiar dainty pistol with an inlaid mother-of-pearl handle.

She ignored the fact she couldn't shoot worth a burnt biscuit. Evie also overlooked Lacey's renewed struggles. Obviously her friend didn't want to be anywhere near the direction where Evie chose to fire. Not that Evie wanted to fire at all, but Twyler didn't need to know that.

"You've proven more perceptive than most, Miss Thompson." A gleam of appreciation lit Twyler's gaze. "But I find myself unimpressed by your toy. This is between Granger and me."

"Then let the women go." Creed jumped on the idea.

"We've come too far for that. Throw down your gun, Mr. Granger, and admit that the woman at your side wouldn't be able to hit a target if I drew one three feet from her nose."

"Oh, that's absolutely true, Mr. Twyler." Evie's smile widened. "It used to be that I couldn't hit the. . .what's the expression my mentor used? Oh yes, I couldn't hit the broadside of the bunkhouse. But it's such a cunning little piece."

"No." Twyler's self-satisfied ooze dried up in a hurry. "You want me dead. You want me to ignore that little pistol." He darted glances around himself, edging farther out of reach. "She changes the game. Changes the cards, different value. . ." He degenerated into strange rambling mutters.

"Why did you kill my brother, Edward?" Jake asked.

"He noticed me cheating and started to raise a fuss. Two men I'd fleeced a few nights prior sat just one table over, so I couldn't allow that. And I'd already marked him for carrying a large amount of cash." Twyler clicked his teeth together repeatedly. "So I fired first, paid off the other players, and pocketed the profit. Double the windfall when your old man started paying off people to not besmirch dear Edward's memory. And then you came after me, and I did more and more paying off of my own until I ran dry and needed a rich wife." Twyler's eyes narrowed. "But here you are again, forcing my hand. With two skilled shooters against only myself, I can't hope to make it out alive. So I can either take revenge on Granger here, before leaving this earth, or hope your misguided sense of feminine kindness precludes you shooting a man in the back."

With that, Twyler shoved Lacey so she fell downhill, and Jake had to catch her before running after his prey.

A shot echoed in the forest, followed by a terrible cry.

THREE

Al was silent. Evie huddled with Lacey as time grew heavy and wore her nerves thin.

"Please tell me you wouldn't have fired," Lacey said after the silence became unbearable—and Evie handed over the pistol.

"Have a little faith, Lace." Evie scanned the horizon, anxious for Jake to come back. It hadn't escaped her notice that Twyler hadn't dropped his gun before taking off.

"Does that mean you would've uttered a prayer and pulled the trigger, or that I should have faith you wouldn't do anything so foolish?" Lacey blanched at the idea.

"We can do all things through faith, Lacey Lyman." *Even wait when it's taking Jake forever and a day to mosey back.*

"In that case, I have faith that you'll never fire a gun unless faced with a man like Twyler, or whatever his name was, with absolutely no one else anywhere near the vicinity." Lacey rubbed her throat, where the knife had rested. "Thank you for following. I couldn't have gone into that stump."

It was then that they heard it, the snap of twigs beneath boots as someone heavy headed their way. They froze, Lacey's hand tightening on the gun until they made out Jake with a prone form slung over his shoulders.

"Oh, my leg," Twyler groaned. "Why couldn't you let me go, Granger? Or let the woman shoot me outright, at least?"

"Because I can't shoot the broadside of a bunkhouse. We told you that, Twyler." Evie couldn't smile at the sight of blood soaking the man's right leg, but he deserved far worse.

"You mean. . .it was true?" A wheeze of laughter escaped. "A double bluff, then. I was outdone by a double bluff from an amateur?" The gambler's wheeze stretched and thinned into a series of wispy cackles. "An amateur! I deserve my fate then. I held all the winning cards and threw them away."

Midmorning light shafted through trees, striping the ground in sun and shadow. Thirsty earth rested after a long drink of yesterday's rain, leaving puddles and slicks in every path.

Chase Dunstan strode through, keeping sure footing with a heavy step. Today, he didn't need to slide soundlessly through rock and brush and dirt. Today, he closed distance on quarry that couldn't move. Today, he traveled to Hope Falls.

What he expected to find, he couldn't catalog beyond Braden Lyman, risen from the ranks of those killed in the mine collapse months before to languish in a doctor's bed. Alternately, the bed-ridden "patient" could prove an impostor pretending to be Braden Lyman to usurp his claim to the land.

Either option brought questions regarding the collapse— reasons behind it, the way it was handled afterward, what current plans pushed "Braden" to stay in Hope Falls. And of course, what on earth any of it had to do with the incredible ad. Chase couldn't forget Kane's assurance that four women, supposedly attractive, attempted to run a town full of loggers.

All lumped together, it created the worst mess Chase came across in all his days. None of it made a lick of sense. *Which is why I steer clear of towns and keep to myself and the mountains. Bad enough men make messes. Women make woes.*

A mighty racket made mincemeat of his thoughts, spurring Chase toward the sounds of a town in trouble. He stopped a moment to take off his pack and tuck it into a small grove of Gambel oak. The low-lying, shrub-like trees made for a distinctive visual marker against the tall pine and spruce dominating the area. That taken care of, Chase broke into a jog, scarcely noting as the dog at his side did the same. He came up to the train in a matter of minutes and halted.

Decoy came to an abrupt stop at his heels, tilting his head in canine question. Chase held up a hand in the "wait" motion, allowing Decoy to sink to his haunches while Chase listened. Observation didn't always require a line of vision, and he never went into a situation without gathering any information at hand.

Angry voices tangled across the tracks, their owners made mysteries by the train. Men—no fewer than seven—yelled in a bid for respect. Shuffling steps and cracking knuckles told of glares and the advance-and-gain-ground precursor to every fight. The words themselves offered fragments of the excuse behind it.

A howl of "I'm not leaving!" vied with a plaintive, "Don't make me go, I'll miss the cookin' too much," which was almost lost beneath the bluster of "Ya cain't make us go—". All mixed together in a noisy din of men protesting being forced out of Hope Falls.

"Yes we can." A familiar voice broke through the others, comfortable in giving orders. "And we are. Get on the train as you stand, or be thrown on as we hog-tie you, but you'll go."

Granger? It took Chase a moment to identify the man he'd

worked with about three years back, working as a guide through prospective timberland higher in the Rockies. *With Granger here, the claim they're trying to build a sawmill gains credibility. Grangers know lumber like no other family in North America.* His jaw set as he realized Kane deliberately omitted the name.

"You can't hog-tie all of us, Creed," one of them argued.

"I'll have help." Granger's voice came back.

Granger is answering to the name of Creed? *Why?* Chase took a soundless step closer, plagued with more questions than ever.

"Aye, that he will." The burr told of an Irishman—the rumble could have come from nothing less than a deep well of a chest. A sort of Gaelic giant sprang to mind, matching the heavy stomp of massive boots as the speaker stepped forward.

"You don't insult the ladies and stay." A slight German accent, in an unremarkable voice made all the smaller compared to the giant's, agreed. "And no fighting was one of the rules."

"Though I'll pitch in if it comes to it." This last sounded so self-satisfied, Chase took the fellow into immediate dislike—particularly as he sounded farthest away from all the arguing.

"Four of you," sneered one of the rougher protesters, "against eight of us. Even with Bear Riordan there, you don't have the manpower to run us all out of town, Creed."

Chase heard enough. Rough customers who insulted ladies and brawled in streets, and a man he respected—albeit going by an alias—standing up to them against bad odds. He ambled around the train, taking his time to look over the men involved.

The loggers not wanting to leave looked much as he would've expected—large, unkempt, and, apparently since they'd been fighting, sporting an assortment of bruises and lumps. The four men shoving them on the train were a more unlikely assortment.

Granger, as Chase already knew, stood lead. A redheaded giant—the one called Bear, Chase assumed—flanked one side.

If they'd stopped there, things looked promising.

But a short man with ruddy cheeks and too-big boots glowered from Granger's other side, and a puffed-up logger with more mouth than muscle brought up the rear. Little wonder the outcasts thought to protest their send-off. If they fought the enforcement crew, they stood a considerable chance of winning.

"Five." He came shoulder to shoulder with Granger, not bothering to make eye contact with his old ally. "Six counting the wolfhound." Chase didn't bother to gesture at Decoy, knowing full well the dog stood almost four feet tall and six feet long.

Instead he eyed the rabble-rousers with casual interest. "Just fists?" He slid his hunting knife from its sheath with a predatory smile. The sun shone on its razor-sharp blade as he flipped it into the air, didn't watch the piece spin, and caught it by the handle again. "Or knives, too?"

"You only get one vote." Lacey matched Evie glower for glare.

"Jake deserves one, too," her friend protested. "And, since he's not here, I have to represent his best interests!"

"He does not deserve a vote." If a tone of voice could convey an eye roll, Naomi's did just that. "We all agreed that when we decided on our grooms, we'd put it to a vote among the four of us, and we needed a three-quarters majority before marriage. Your vote counts as one of four, which means you still need another two. And, no, the prospective groom doesn't count."

"Particularly when you're asking us to approve two men in one." Cora rubbed out a mark in her ledger and sighed. "Hypothetically, that would mean you'd ascribe him two votes."

"Don't be silly!" Evie rebuked her younger sister. "Just one man. . ." Her face took on a dreamy look. "Jake."

"But Jake Creed or Jake Granger?" Naomi's now-gentle tone

wrapped the query in concern but couldn't quite hide its edge.

Lacey recognized that edge. She'd walked it as a sharp line of doubt since she discovered her kidnapper's crazed splutters held truth. The four of them were deceived by two men wearing false names: one a criminal and one their protector. So which man could be trusted more? Such thoughts made her stomach lurch.

"He's both!"

"No." Cora refuted her sister, much to everyone's shock. "Either he's Creed, a man all four of us admire and rely upon, who's proven himself knowledgable and trustworthy, or else—"

"He's still all of that," Evie broke in. "We've simply learned he hid his name for the noble purpose of tracking down his brother's killer. If he whipped into town as Granger, Twyler would've hied off before Jake could see through his disguise!"

"There's purpose to his plan and his actions." Naomi's attempt to soothe Evie tore through the crooked stitches holding Lacey's layers of emotions in check, unearthing ragged edges.

"His purpose, and his plan," she choked. "Things your Jake, whoever he is, never bothered to tell us while he used Hope Falls to enact them. He deceived us as much as Twyler did."

"There's nobility in clearing his brother's name and catching his murderer." Naomi's judgment leveled things for a moment. "But Lacey's right; Mr. Granger knew who we are and what we want to accomplish. His failure to repay our trust is a betrayal."

"What would you have him do? Flaunt his real name at the cost of justice?" Evie flared. "Abandon his responsibility to the people Twyler would hurt if left to roam free?"

Cora laid a hand on her sister's shoulder. "Return our confidence. Perhaps not the first day or so, but at some point he should have revealed his identity and warned us."

"He warned us about being careful and not trusting the men from the moment I met him! Every step of the way, he watched over us to provide protection. Who helped enforce town rules? Kept order? Stopped those evil men from sneaking into our house with Mr. Kane that night? Jake, that's who. And you turn on him?"

"Creed did." Lacey tried to make her see. "Not Granger."

"All right, then who's out there right now, ridding the town of the brutes who began brawling yesterday? Eight burly men who won't leave quietly, and who's protecting us right now?"

"They think it's Creed, but it's not, is it?" Lacey pointed out. "If those men knew Creed wasn't real, he wouldn't hold any sway with them either. That's why you're having difficulty getting our approval. There's a reason we implemented the vote, Evie. Remember, you convinced me of its wisdom when I balked."

"But I never imagined there would be a problem with *my* choice of groom," Evie grumbled. "The three of you practically pushed me into Jake's arms, and now you won't give me your sanction for a wedding? Seems to me you three have changed."

"Don't go admonishing me about changing my mind, Evie." Cora held ground against her older sister. "If Jacob Creed existed, I'd still agree he'd make a fine groom. But he never did. This Jacob Granger stands little more than a stranger."

"His name doesn't matter—the man wearing it does!" Evie wrung her apron into a mass of wrinkles. "Jake hasn't changed."

"Then I'm even more worried. You're willing to bind yourself to a liar." The heat of anger eased some of the ache from constant tension, but Lacey didn't welcome it. "Bad enough, his words hid his identity. His silence hid a killer."

"A killer he saved you from, Lacey Lyman! A criminal he tracked down and exposed when Twyler would have gone free."

"I wouldn't have needed rescuing if I'd been warned." Stung, she snapped the words. *I came here to prove I don't need to be treated like a china doll, and I wound up being rescued?* But beneath the rage

30

simmered a lingering fear. "We all trusted him, Evie, but none of us will let you make the mistake again."

"We all make mistakes." Naomi's reminder held a private sorrow, and Lacey winced alongside her cousin. "Which is why I won't say nay to Mr. Granger. I feel I know enough about the man to see how he cares for Evie. He has the time it takes the rest of us to choose husbands to iron out the rest."

"We'll be watching to make sure you don't get burned." Cora's vow made her sister smile, though it died swiftly. "We'll start by finding some way to be sure the former Mr. Creed is the real Mr. Granger. Once that's certain, we can investigate more."

"Mama's old friends back in Charleston will help. There's no one like a society matron to sniff out a bachelor's background. Particularly if he's eligible, and Mr. *Granger* would fit that bill." Satisfaction starched her spine as Lacey found something to take charge of—a concrete way to safeguard her friends. *I should have done it before. Why didn't I stop to think?*

"Mr. Lawson and Mr. McCreedy vouch for his identity," Naomi pointed out. "Since he knew we approved of him as Creed, I doubt the man would trouble himself inventing a name at this point. I believe he truly is Granger, and now that he's caught Twyler, he's setting things straight. It's only good sense, after all."

Cora nodded, but added, "He brought Lawson and McCreedy, so we might do well to assume they'd support him regardless."

An exasperated sound escaped Evie, but she didn't remark.

"Stop huffing." Lacey resolved to telegraph Charleston that very day. "If there's one lesson we can take away from this entire debacle, it's that we can't trust anyone in Hope Falls. From now on, we take a hard look at every new hire."

For instance, Lacey didn't quite like the looks of the fellow conferring with Riordan, Clump, Williams, and Cree—Granger. She caught herself thinking of Evie's intended by his false name and stopped short. But thinking about fake names was the first step in a dance she'd rather sit out, so she studied the new man instead. She took in his broad shoulders. The confident stance. The sun-bronzed skin, and head of hair dark enough to drown doubts. Lacey Lyman gave a heartfelt sigh.

Of regret. After all, nothing good came dressed like *that*.

FOUR

"Y ou're going with the next train." With the biggest threat safely stuffed onto the train and on their way to who-knew-where, the rooster bringing up the rear of Granger's crew bobbed his head toward Chase. "Nice of you to step in, but you weren't needed then, and you sure as shooting aren't wanted now."

Two sentences, and the man cemented Chase's poor opinion. *Yep. More mouth than muscle, and more muscle than mind.* He shook his head. Once. That's all it took to acknowledge the man's insulting order to board the train and refuse it. It also served as a silent invitation for the rooster—which was always just a chicken with a strut—to try and enforce it.

Granger stayed clear, a silent show of respect from a man whose esteem he'd earned long ago. Bear, the big Irishman, gave a growl of disapproval but otherwise held his peace. The German, whose primary concern had been for the women, ignored those cues. The man either disregarded or didn't know the Rule.

There were few unspoken exceptions having to do with protecting women and children or preventing injustice, but otherwise male interaction could be boiled down to one rule: handle your own business; leave other men to handle theirs.

Most conflict in the world could be traced to some idiot ignoring the Rule. And here stomped the German, spluttering about how the other man lacked manners. Poor sap never even saw the blow coming, just doubled over with surprise in his eyes and no air left in his lungs, the wind knocked clean out of him.

Chase waited for the rooster to turn to him before letting fly with a right hook to the jaw. Stepping over the chicken now crumpled in the mud, he offered his hand to the fallen German and pulled him to his feet. "Leave it be, next time, yes?"

"*Ja.*" A shaky nod belied a hearty handshake. "I'm Klumpf. Friends and men who knock over Williams call me plain Clump."

"Dunstan." He pulled back his hand. The rooster—Williams, he now knew—didn't stir. Perhaps when he woke, he'd crow less.

"Riordan." Another handshake, this from the redheaded giant. "Most call me Bear, but I'll answer to either, ya ken."

"Ken?" The word caught him. "Not Irish?"

"Ah, a canny one." A broad smile split his face. "Scots-Irish I be, and you'll hear the lilt and the brogue and a whole hodgepodge of phrases from me. Most never notice."

"When Riordan gets riled, no one understands him." Granger clapped him on the shoulder. "Good to see you, Dunstan."

"Likewise. Hadn't heard you were back in Colorado." Chase raised a brow but held his tongue. Whatever his old friend's reasons for calling himself Creed, it wasn't his business.

Not yet.

Why now? Jake Granger eyed the newcomer warily, doubts warring with relief. *There couldn't be a better time for Dunstan to blow into town, but that's what's suspicious. Why does he show up now, when*

I have most use for him but didn't send word for him?

"You didn't hear I was back in Colorado for good reason." He addressed the question behind his old friend's statement, glad he'd taken Bear and Clump aside earlier that morning to fill them in on his real identity. The men leaving town hadn't known. Any hint that Jake wasn't whom they thought, and their pride over being lied to would rile them even more.

"No one knew. I've been going by Creed to keep it quiet."

Dunstan's short nod affirmed Jake's memory of the man. Observant, Dunstan noted the name change. Quick thinking, but methodical, he chose not to ask in front of others.

"The others still don't know." Clump nudged Williams's arm none too gently with one overly large boot. The man didn't stir.

"With the rabble-rousers gone, the rest won't prove problematic. Worst case, they won't believe I'm a Granger. He"— Jake jerked his head toward Dunstan—"can help there. I've worked with Dunstan before—three years back. He hires out as a guide, hunter, tracker, you name it, along this stretch of the Rockies. Some of the others will have heard of him. McCreedy and Lawson will vouch for me, and Lyman always knew."

"The name Granger holds clout." Bear nodded. "Once it's established that you've finished your family business to reclaim your name, things will go smooth again."

"Hold it, Bear." Clump stepped forward, thumbs threaded protectively through his suspenders. The other man clearly hadn't forgotten when Jake dangled him by those same suspenders and interrogated him. "Just what kind of business did Creed finish? He didn't get around to explaining that part, and I want to know why he lied and why he doesn't need to anymore."

"Granger." Dunstan's amused correction marked his first, and possibly only, contribution to the conversation at hand.

"Now, I'm going to level with you three." Jake cast a swift glance to ensure Williams was out cold. "The men in the bunkhouse will only hear what I've already said. Understood?"

"Ja." Clump nodded for good measure. "This has something to do with your strange questions yesterday about the square coin?"

"My brother Edward carried that coin. A cheating gambler shot him point-blank, robbed him, sullied his name, and got away with it." Jake paused. "Until now. That piece—it's really an old balance used to check coins for weight and prevent clipping or shaved edges—marked the murderer I've been tracking for months."

Dunstan rolled his shoulders, evincing an easy readiness. He'd obviously weighed Jake's earlier statement about finished family business and decided whatever was left wouldn't be urgent or difficult. That frame of mind told, as nothing else could, Dunstan was the only man who had yet to meet the women of Hope Falls.

Good. It meant he might be talked into staying while Jake hauled Twyler in. Dunstan didn't like towns, and the less he knew about this one, the more likely he'd be to hire on awhile.

Next to him, every muscle in Bear's arms and neck strained. From the way the Scots-Irishman's breath came out in great huffs, Jake judged him ready to thrash any murderers still lurking around. Then again, the big man might be straining to hold back his rage over not being informed about the problem.

Equally good. Big Bear had a protective streak a mile wide when it came to the women and the stature to make good on it. If he got worked up over having misjudged Twyler, he'd keep an even sharper eye on Evie and the rest until Jake got back.

Clump. . .brightened. A grin split his face in a smile wide enough to look painful. "So you held my suspenders to find out who stole your brother's coin and hunted him down for justice. With Earl and the others gone, now all is good in Hope Falls, and I can return to Miss Thompson and ask her to be mine."

Not good. Jake fisted a hand around those familiar suspenders before he even decided to do it. "Listen, Clump. You're a good man, but I'm only going to say this once. Evie's my fiancée now, so you aren't going to try to court her anymore."

An outraged growl sort of strangled from Clump as he jerked his suspenders free and backed up. "I called dibs on her!"

"And I refused." Jake grinned. *Evie was mine from the start.* "So admit you lost with good grace, and tell me you'll look after her and the others while I'm gone. Otherwise I'll have to ask you along when I haul Twyler back to Maine. Doc says he'll be able to travel day after tomorrow, and I'm not letting him postpone his meeting with justice a second later."

"Who?" Bear practically choked the question. "Who is this murderer in our town, who fooled us all? How did you catch him?"

Seeing the look on the other man's face, Jake thought it best to give the short version of Lacey's kidnapping. No sense working so hard to capture Twyler and override his own need for vengeance just to have Bear kill him before the law tried him.

"Ye best be takin' him soon, Granger." Riordan's voice darkened. "Afore I decide to teach the man a lesson about how to treat a dainty thing like Miss Lyman." He cast a sorrowing glance toward the women's house. "The poor, sweet lady."

"Vile, wretched beasts!" Lacey trudged along, swatting high-rising shrubs and low-lying branches out of her way. "Should all be strung up by their thumbs until they learn common decency."

Surprising how good it felt to go for a brisk walk, exertion and exasperation driving the breath from her lungs and venting the trouble from her thoughts. Each step felt lighter, each word rang louder, and the forest seemed to welcome her.

She hugged her shawl—a light kerseymere chosen more for its soothing softness and beguiling strawberries-and-cream stripes than for warmth—around her shoulders as she muttered, "Or at least manners, which everyone knows are the pretense of common decency. Men should at least learn *that* much before being allowed in any sort of town. No matter how isolated."

At first she'd rushed to get out of sight before anyone realized she'd slipped away from the house but hadn't joined Cora at the doctor's. Lacey didn't want to face Braden just now. She knew full well what her brother would say about yesterday's events— they'd all heard it well in advance. Memories tumbled through her thoughts like buttons shaken from a glass jar.

He'd been incensed when they first arrived in Hope Falls: *"You don't belong here. This is no place for women, and you need to pack up what I'm sure is too much stuff and head home!"* Of course, Lacey knew her brother was wrong.

Until that terrible night when Robert Kane led a few men to the house where they slept, intent on ruining more than their reputations. If it hadn't been for Granger—well, Lacey couldn't stand to think about that. Neither, she knew, could her brother. The almost-attack was Braden's worst fear sprung to life. How many times had he said it, trying to run them out of Hope Falls? *"Leave for your own good. It's not safe for you women here."*

But instead of leaving Hope Falls, she and the others simply had Mr. Lawson move in downstairs, where he could be close to his sister. Granger hired him to be their engineer, not knowing he'd tow a newly widowed, heavily pregnant sister along. But it worked out well for the purposes of protection.

Inside the house at least.

Outside, it didn't guard against Braden's judgment. *"No matter your intentions, no matter your plans, the outcome put you at risk."* Which meant Lacey couldn't walk far enough or fast enough to outrun the most earth-shattering realization yet: *my* brother *was right.*

It was enough to make any woman question her surroundings, her plans, and even her own good taste. *Well, perhaps not that last.* Lacey ran a loving hand along the cheery rose of her surprisingly soft woolen skirts. After such a dismal yesterday, she'd chosen a bright new dress to lift her spirits, her resolve, and her ability to face the consequences of her mistakes.

The bonnet, with its matching ribbons trailing in a jaunty wave as she marched along, seemed a sort of battle standard for a formidable and fashionable woman. Yes, she'd planned for a difficult day full of brotherly recriminations by dressing to impress. Then promptly turned an about-face and avoided it all.

"Because, truly, after a woman's been kidnapped at gunpoint, lost any hope of her beauty sleep, and awoken to a morning without one of Evie's delicious breakfasts the first time she really needs one, she deserves some peace and quiet." She announced this to the trees and sky at large, testing her argument. "Not that I'm typically the sort to enjoy quiet, but I've not had a moment alone in weeks. 'It's not safe'."

She mimicked her brother's censorious tones then sighed. This little excursion would only earn her more scolding from everyone—but with the worst of the loggers booted out of town and half the others still abed nursing wounds from yesterday's fray, it seemed the best possible time for a little private thinking.

"Not to mention that the odds of being manhandled by another crazed criminal the very next day must be incredibly low," she informed a squirrel, which had frozen midscamper. The small creature seemed transfixed by this logic, as it didn't so much as blink, so Lacey continued. "Besides, I remembered my purse and am keeping one hand on my pistol. But you wildlife seem quite hospitable thus far. I doubt any bears lurk near—"

A massive, shaggy beast lumbered out of the shrubbery before she finished the sentence, sending her tiny friend shimmying up its tree and leaving Lacey speechless. For one wild moment, she imagined her comment conjured a bear—if for no other reason than to continue her recent streak of mistakes—but the animal now picking its way across a few boulders wasn't a bear.

Its size could give anyone a fright, but once Lacey's heart stopped fluttering along with her bonnet ribbons, she recognized the creature. She'd seen that shaggy silver-gray coat standing beside the new man in town. *A tamed wolf, perhaps?*

Lacey remained still as it came to a halt a mere foot from her skirts, nose thrust forward in a curiously impertinent sniff. *Wolves aren't described as shaggy, nor this large.* She thought back over everything she'd read, looked over the creature now wagging its long, curved tail at her. She saw a dog's wide brown eyes, perked ears that nevertheless flopped back, and rounded cast to the muzzle. *Some sort of mix then.*

"Good wolf-doggy," she crooned, ever so slowly extending one hand for a more thorough, moist sniffing. "Where's your owner? Lets you roam free? Lucky puppy." A rough slurp of approval rasped her palm before Lacey gingerly scratched between his ears. Definitely a he. No female would be so unkempt.

Besides, males always like me. She grinned as his tail wagged harder, mouth falling open in an unmistakable grin at the attention she lavished upon him, falling into step alongside her when she continued. In fact, she sped up a bit, enjoying the warm breeze and easy acceptance of the animal at her side.

Until her new friend tensed, fur rising along his spine in a long, thin patch. His nose thrust forward as he breathed deep, swiftly turning his massive head eastward to locate the source of a new scent. Growls rumbled low in his throat, a warning Lacey wasn't foolish enough to ignore.

FIVE

She pulled the pearl-handled pistol from her purse, spinning around to scan the trees for whatever upset her new friend. The dog crouched back on its haunches as though ready to spring. A blur of tawny brown flashed from Lacey's right, descending straight toward her with an unearthly howling. She barely had time to shoot before a cacophony of sounds and sensations overwhelmed her.

Everything seemed distorted. The shot had an unexpected, too-loud echo. Lacey heard a woman's scream, but would have sworn she hadn't the breath to make a sound. The animal from the trees knocked her down, but another force barreled into it before the thing did more than swipe her bonnet loose.

The dog, she realized, pushing herself up on her elbows. "Here, puppy," Lacey gasped. *It must have sprung on the other one.* Suddenly her friend filled her vision, concern clearly written on his furry face as he tried to nose her shoulder.

"I'm all right, boy. What was it?" She peered around him. *There.* A few lengths away, a large tawny animal lay unmoving.

"Cougar." Without warning, a man spoke from behind her, hunkering down after appearing as though from nowhere.

Lacey shrieked and would have jumped if the dog weren't anchoring her skirts to the ground. Its wagging tail gave her an inkling of the man's identity before she really saw him.

"Decoy's made grown men run in fear." The deep voice held an intriguing rasp, almost as though it went largely unused. "A cougar jumps you; you get back up. But I merit a scream?" An amused black brow arched at her over bottomless brown eyes.

Now that she'd gotten her breath back, Lacey realized a blush traveled along with it. *And he's laughing at me.* Rising to her feet without taking the hand he offered, she snapped, "Absolutely. Between a wolf-dog, a cougar, and a man, every sane woman knows which animal is the most frustrating!"

When he first spotted her, Chase closed his eyes, hoping when he opened them the vision would disappear. He cracked one lid open. Nope. Everything looked the same. Blue sky, green trees, gray boulders...pink fluff. And this time there could be no doubt.

The pink fluff was on the move.

Which meant some foolish woman traveled alone in an area rife with wildlife, placing her in danger, and therefore under his protection. All because he couldn't pretend he hadn't seen that pink fluff ball bobbing down the mountainside.

No matter that it interfered with his plans. Chase had seen cougar tracks in the area. He started down toward her, giving Decoy the signal to go guard their target while he closed in.

Before he spotted her, Chase had two options. He could wait in the forest for Granger to take Twyler off, roaming about at will with pretty much just Bear and Clump knowing anything about him. Problem with that idea was limited access after the initial observation stage, plus the Williams fellow he'd clocked earlier would set to squawking if he somehow managed to spot him.

No, the smarter option, which Chase now had no choice but to accept, was to take Granger's offer. He'd hire on as the Hope Falls hunter/tracker, keep an eye out for large predators, and keep the cooks in as much fresh meat as possible until Granger returned. At least, in title. Granger expected him to look out for the ladies, too. One of whom roamed alone.

Which meant more time in town, more trouble, more questions from other people. But it also meant more opportunities to discover if the bedridden Braden was the true Braden Lyman, and if so—or even if not—what caused the mine collapse. Why did the Miracle Mining Company sell out so soon? What was going on with that incredible ad and this strange sawmill proposition?

Granger's presence threw him off—it meant that either a legitimate logging enterprise was going up, or they'd fooled a shrewd businessman whose sawmill expertise couldn't be beat.

Too many questions to ignore, and it all started with the man claiming to be Braden Lyman. But to get close, Chase would have to start by working for Hope Falls—and protecting the women. Starting now. He closed the distance, wanting to witness her reaction to Decoy. How people interacted with the wolfhound—and how the dog responded—told Chase more than ten conversations.

She didn't faint. The first realization brought him to a halt. He'd expected her to faint. *Or scream.* His unassailed ears approved. But when she didn't run off, Chase began to wonder about the woman. Did her lack of cowardice indicate idiocy?

Decoy butted his massive head against frothy fabric, but the woman in pink held still. By now Chase drew close enough to see she hadn't gone stiff with fright. She simply stayed put while Decoy sniffed her skirts—a literal version of what two dozen loggers must be trying with the pretty girl.

"Good wolf-doggy." Her sweet voice, with its clear, high-pitched inflection, echoed her feminine appearance.

Probably practiced.

Chase almost reached them, but she began walking again. With that bonnet blocking her vision, she wouldn't see him until the last moment, meaning he'd probably frighten her. *Not good.*

The wind shifted, Decoy tensed, and Chase spotted the cougar whose tracks he'd seen earlier. Yellow eyes fixed on wind-swirled pink ribbons. It pounced with an unearthly shriek. He fired, running toward the girl the moment after the recoil. In one of those strange mountain moments, the shot seemed to echo. The wounded cougar landed, swiping the bonnet as Decoy bounded into the cat, bowling it off the girl and to the grass.

Now seemed as good a time as any for introductions. Chase squatted over by the fallen cat, turning to face the woman when she let out a shriek and jump made futile by Decoy's weight.

"Decoy's made grown men run in fear. A cougar jumps you; you get back up. But I merit a scream?" Honestly, it amused him, but he figured it would embarrass the stuffing out of her.

A rosy blush crept across her cheeks before she answered. "Absolutely. Between a wolf-dog, a cougar, and a man, every sane woman knows which animal is the most frustrating!"

For a second Chase stared at her. Then the chuckles came, piling atop each other until they became guffaws. The woman looked like an angel, all rosy blushes, golden curls, and big blue eyes. But those big blue eyes held an unholy anger, and those petal-like lips spouted insults to make politicians proud.

Chase wanted to set her back down and take a closer look at her shoulder, where claws had caught, but knew better than to touch her. Her wariness gave way to peevishness at his teasing, which helped, but wasn't enough. Mad made a better mood than scared, but something shared would lower her guard more.

With no suave words to offer, Chase wielded humor in a return shot. "And between a she-wolf, cougar, and a woman, we both know which has the sharpest claws."

For a moment it seemed as though she'd take greater offense. Then her scowl shifted like a branch in the breeze, a reluctant smile tugging at the corners of her mouth. "I shouldn't have snapped at you like that. My nerves were worn of course, but you didn't deserve the shriek nor the snark."

"Snark?" Chase couldn't stop challenging the changeling.

"My friend Evie makes up the most marvelous words," the girl explained. "Snark is when someone is waspish."

"Ah." He leaned forward while she spoke, pressing a folded bandanna against her shoulder, where pink fabric gaped in three slim stripes. The jagged tears flashed glimpses of cream and crimson not unlike those decorating the scrap of fabric twisted alongside her. "Hold this here. You've been scratched." He frowned at a thin, darker line etched along her neck.

So this is supposed to be a dainty society darling, who suddenly places scandalous ads and heads West on a whim? The sort of woman who's kidnapped one day and wanders the woods alone the next, but knows the difference between a wolf and a behemoth gray dog and remains calm through a cougar attack. Lacey Lyman, intrepid pink fluff ball? He snorted.

"Oh, so that's why your dog was nosing my shoulder." She cautiously pressed the tips of her fingers to the edge of the bandanna in an obvious bid to avoid touching his hand. "What is his name, by the way? I'm greatly in his debt."

"Decoy." As much as it amused him to let her think the dog killed her cougar, honesty made him add, "But I shot the cat."

"Balderdash." Her finely drawn brows knit closer in a glower. "How dare you attempt to take the credit for that?"

"Check and see—the cat was shot. Decoy didn't kill him."

"I know full well the cat was shot since I shot it." She gave an indignant sniff before admitting, "Well, it only looked like a great streak of tawny brown coming at me, but I still shot it, and that's really the important thing."

Chase stared at the set line of her jaw and knew Miss Lyman truly believed she'd shot her cougar. A swift perusal of the ground turned up a small pearl-handled pistol. "With that?"

"Don't sound so disbelieving. It's a cunningly crafted piece of weaponry. Simply because something is lovely doesn't mean it isn't useful or even extraordinary, you know." The growing ferocity of her glower warned him she might apply that principle to more than ludicrously miniscule pistols.

"Explains the echo." He didn't say more, just checked the carcass. Most likely she'd fired her little toy and not hit anything. The large hole left by his shotgun would convince her, but Chase doubted he'd ask her to look. Bullet wounds were too much, even for this oddly adventurous female.

Except. . .the cougar took *two* bullets to the chest. One from his shotgun, and one considerably smaller, but no less deadly.

"I can see by the surprise on your face—which it hardly needs be said isn't flattering—that you've discovered I'm a good shot." Satisfaction laced her voice. "I thought *your* shot was the echo, so I'm glad that much is explained. But what about that awful scream? You yourself mentioned I didn't do it."

"Cougars do that unearthly shrieking howl. Even the males— though this one's young, about sixty pounds. Just over a year, I'd say." He looked it over. "Still a big kitten, too curious to resist the lure of your fluttering ribbons. Must've thought he could pounce, grab the 'wounded creature' you carried, and be off to play with his prize before Decoy moved."

"My bonnet?" For the first time, the girl went pale. "You think

46

I was attacked over my *bonnet*?"

"Yep." Of all the things for her to get upset about. Only a woman wouldn't mind the idea of a predator leaping for her throat until someone pointed out it endangered her headgear. Chase decided it was time to head back to Hope Falls.

"My bonnet in no way resembles a wounded animal!"

"This wouldn't have happened if you had someone with you." He ignored the issue of her hat. It didn't matter. "Even young cougars aren't foolish enough to attack something traveling in a pair or group. What were you doing out here alone?"

Becoming quite angry and trying not to show it of course.

Lacey didn't say so. Instead she stared at the stranger before her. Here stood a man daring to chide her as though she were an infant who'd wandered too far from her nurse. Why, the first words he'd spoken were a taunt over her shock at his sudden appearance. Who was this man to dictate her behavior?

Obviously, such rudeness deserved a proper dressing-down.

"What am I doing out here?" She repeated the impertinent question, raising her chin. "*I'm* enjoying a walk on *my* property. And just what, may I ask, do you think *you're* doing here?"

Aside from trying to take me to task, she silently added.

The grimmest grin she'd ever seen pulled her into his answer before she considered whether or not a grin could truly be grim. "*I'm* enjoying your walk, too."

"Of all the ridiculous—" Lacey caught herself and changed pattern. "In that case, I suggest you enjoy the walk heading that way, while I enjoy the vistas in this direction." She gestured widely to illustrate the opposite paths, but stopped abruptly at a swift stinging in her shoulder. *The scratch.*

"No." His grin disappeared, leaving only the tension stretching tightly around his surprisingly square jaw.

Surprising that Lacey could make it out through that much scruffy stubble, not surprising that the man would boast a square jawline. It seemed, somehow, the shape of stubbornness.

Rounded chins, she suddenly decided, implied better ability to compromise—both a strength and an art. That her own chin happened to be round, rather than square, simply proved it.

"Very well, I'll trade. You go that way, and I'll head back from whence I came." She made the offer with modified, less sweeping gestures to again illustrate opposite directions. But again, a sharp sting in her shoulder made her drop her left arm.

"No." Something she could only describe as fierce lightened the dark ash of his gaze. Now he stared at her through a rich burnt umber. "Let me look at your shoulder."

"No." Lacey belatedly realized she'd echoed him and hastened to add, "I'll just keep this bandanna pressed against it until the doctor can take a look, and everything will be fine."

While she finished refusing, he moved. Lacey didn't note any sway of his shoulders indicating a step, heard no scuff or shuffle of his boots. It looked as though the ground itself shifted to bring him forward because now he stood too close.

"What are you doing?" She shrilled the question, loud voice a ladylike assault designed to force him back a measure. Or two.

He didn't step back. Nor did he answer. In fact, he did nothing but take up far too much space for any single person. And even that seemed more a side effect than anything planned. No, this tall, dark stranger managed an almost unnatural stillness as he just. . .stood. Silently. Looking at her.

SIX

It gave her a case of the woollies. *Because this disconcerting, itchy sensation can't be my dress. Doesn't the man know long silences make people nervous?* Lacey tilted her head to the side, the pretext of shifting her now-askew bonnet allowing her to break eye contact. When its bow finally gave way and the entire creation slipped to the ground, she breathed a sigh of relief. Since she'd risen from the cougar's impact, those ribbons chafed against the scab Twyler—

Lacey froze as the offhand brush of memory set her prickling anew. *I'm alone in the forest with another strange man, and absolutely no one knows where I've gone or that I might need help. Every man in Hope Falls will already be accounted for.*

It wasn't as though she'd failed to notice he was a he and they were the only two people. But he didn't seem threatening.

After all, she thought wildly, *threatening men don't save women from cougars—or try to save them, because he truly didn't know I'd already shot it—or scold them for walking alone. Fathers did that. Big brothers did that. Gentlemen with good intentions and high self opinions order women about.*

Except. . .gentlemen didn't don dusty leather and go climbing mountainsides with shaggy wolfhounds. Nor would any gentleman stand overly close to a lady and demand to touch her—no matter the reasoning. Which brought Lacey right back to the woollies.

Because every instinct God granted and every lady lesson learned warned Lacey that the man before her was no gentleman.

"A gentleman would pick up my bonnet," Lacey pointed out, trying to prod the man. Any attempt to pick up the hat—or, better still, the shawl which might better conceal her torn bodice— meant releasing her grip on the bandanna pressed to her shoulder.

And, though Lacey wouldn't have believed it in a thousand years, that bandanna now ranked as the most important part of her ensemble. It didn't match—in fact, everyone knew red clashed with pink—but since coming West she'd found that clashing, faded articles of clothing seemed almost du jour in mountain wear.

Even more important, the blessed thing stopped the non-gentleman who owned it from inspecting her wound, a process she strongly suspected might involve him coming closer and touching her bare shoulder. No man had ever touched her bare shoulder. In fact, Lacey was hard pressed to recall a time before Hope Falls when a man touched so much as her ungloved hand. Obviously a mysterious stranger couldn't be permitted the liberty.

Besides, she tried not to make a fuss about it, but—

"It hurts." The gravelly voice shook her from her thoughts as the man inclined his head toward her wound. "Let me see."

She still needed to say no, but at least he sounded nicer and as though it mattered to him that the scratches burned. Lacey could be gracious since he'd been kind enough to ask.

"Thank you for asking, but—wait." Her eyes narrowed. "You didn't ask at all, did you? You ordered me in a nicer tone!"

"I've found questions usually are just that: orders phrased nicely to make the other person feel like they have a choice." He shrugged then reached for the bandanna as though she agreed.

"Oh no." Lacey skittered backward, not even ashamed at the retreat. "I do have a choice, and you didn't phrase your request nicely enough to acknowledge it. You best try again. . .buster."

I don't know his name. She held back a groan. *I'm trying to hold him to manners when I neglected basic introductions.*

"Dunstan. It wasn't a request—now stop moving." He shadowed her in a slow waltz around the felled cougar.

The man most likely didn't recognize the steps of the dance. Counting the beats took almost none of Lacey's concentration, and the movements both avoided crushing her bonnet and kept her from his reach. Unless he lunged, which she'd be prepared for once the pattern brought her beside her pistol.

"I'm Miss Lyman. That's the problem. . . ." Lacey's comment trailed off as she darted to the side, grabbing her pistol despite her now-throbbing shoulder. "And *now* I'll stop moving."

Honestly, I'm not certain I could keep going even if I wanted to, she admitted to herself as she raised her pistol. Lacey didn't aim it at the man—Dunstan—nor release the safety. She simply held it between them in readiness, a silent message she wouldn't be ordered around.

"Plan to shoot?" He showed the audacity to sound amused.

"Careful, Mr. Dunstan." She gritted the warning from behind clenched teeth. Keeping the pistol aloft cost her, but he needn't know it. "That sounded more like a real question."

This time the silence-and-shrug combination didn't fool her. Dunstan only kept quiet when he didn't have a good answer.

That means I'm winning!

"Have you lost your wits?" Braden Lyman yelled at her.

"No, though my hearing might be at risk." Cora Thompson

neatly snipped through a stitch of her embroidery and knotted it. "Do you realize, dear, that you yell more than you speak?"

"I do not," he roared. "And I'm not your 'dear.' "

"There. You did it again." She hid a smile behind the needle she threaded with another color. "Loud and loathsome."

"Then loathe me and leave me." His grumble made her smile.

Good to know my needling still has its uses. Cora avoided looking at the mess she'd made of her embroidery. Not that her crooked stitches mattered. The past few weeks taught several lessons, but the one Cora found most practical when visiting her reluctant fiancé was to bring something to occupy her hands.

Full hands helped keep her from strangling the man.

"No such luck, sweetheart." She beamed a sunny smile and jabbed the needle back through her hoop. "I'm here to stay."

"Then you'll be in a pine box before long. All of you will." He pushed against his pillows, sucking in a sharp breath. Whether Braden braced against pain from his dislocated shoulder, his broken knee, or both, Cora couldn't guess. He wouldn't want her to ask, even if he hadn't continued his lecture.

"You sit here as though yesterday doesn't change anything, pretending the danger still doesn't exist, when the proof snuck up and grabbed Lacey. My sister could have been killed!"

"The way you could have been killed in a mine collapse?" Cora's needle dipped and rose, gaining speed as she spoke. "You don't use danger as a determining factor in your decisions."

There. She'd stopped tiptoeing about his ordeal. *Long past time we stop pretending the cave-in didn't happen, as though not asking questions or acknowledging the horror of it will somehow help him battle through the lingering effects. The light of day will shrink it, no matter if it makes him feel smaller for a while.*

"No one can predict a cave-in." Her beloved no longer spoke. He snarled. "But any twit with half a mind and half a thought to rub alongside can spark a warning against gently bred women wandering out West. If you were honest, we all foresaw—"

"That one of our hired men happened to be a deviously disguised murderer whose sick need to fund high-stakes gambling would make him kidnap Lacey and try to stuff her into an old tree?" Cora stopped stitching to gape at the man sitting stock-still in his bed. "Of course you're right. That sort of thing happens far more often than a cave-in, so we women knowingly put ourselves in the most danger simply by staying in town."

"Stop trying to make it sound as though I'm being foolish."

"I'm not trying." She shook her embroidery hoop at him like a tambourine. "There's no need, foolish as it is already. If Evie were here, she'd say your argument is meringue."

A brief battle ensued. Braden stared her down, refusing to ask about meringue but obviously wanting to. Cora stared back, refusing to elaborate unless asked. The old Braden would ask.

A sudden tightening at the base of her throat made Cora put down the embroidery. *Foolish.* A warning hammered in her pulse, advising against empty hands and heated arguments. Last time she'd yanked the pillows from beneath Braden's head in retribution for his harsh words. She hadn't known about his dislocated shoulder yet, and the resulting jolt brought him low.

And now I know. I know about the shoulder, about the deeper wounds to his pride, and the truth about why I pulled that pillow. Cora swallowed against the crest of emotion. *It wasn't just the words; I tried to punish him for not being* my *Braden.*

But that Braden died in the mine collapse as surely as the sparkling, unstoppable Lacey would have died if she'd been trapped in a hollowed tree stump for days. For now, hope kept her believing time and love—along with healthy doses of ignoring him as needed—would bring back the Braden she knew and loved.

The old Braden—her Braden—would have asked about the meringue, a whipped-egg topping Evie put on lemon pies. Cora would have explained that Evie called arguments meringue when someone clucked themselves silly, so worried that they laid an egg. Then the only thing they could do was whip it up in hopes it would be impressive enough to top everything else. But mostly it owed its size to air. No substance.

Then Braden would smile, and they would have laughed. But today Braden shrugged his good shoulder and started lecturing her about safety again, leaving her to sigh over memories.

I miss the days when he had a sense of humor.

Chase just about hooted when the fluff ball came up with that plaything of a pistol, but pegged her for the type to lose her temper first and regret her reactions later. Which meant he didn't smile at her triumphant tone, much less laugh.

His amusement died a swift death when he caught her slight wince, prompting him to catalog other signs that Miss Lyman's show owed more to bravado than substance. The hand clutching his bandanna to her shoulder pressed harder, her knuckles now faint shadows beneath pale skin. Skin that went from pale to practically translucent around the fingertips of her other hand, where she gripped her pocket pistol. The revolver dipped then righted once more, evoking another hastily hidden wince.

Swiping the gun would damage her pride more than anything, but Chase didn't want to jar her arm and shoulder. He bore no doubts about whether or not she'd fight him; he'd never met a less biddable, more contrary woman. *Or a more amusing one.*

Despite her one good point, Miss Lyman still counted as a woman. Which meant he might *not* have to take her gun away. Whistling a slow tune to warn away any nearby scavengers who might have caught scent of the cougar's blood, Chase did what any man should when faced with an irrational woman. Ignored her.

Except for keeping her in the corner of his eye, he focused on the cougar instead. Chase angled toward the fallen cat as he slid his rucksack off his shoulder. He hid a smile at her disbelieving huff when he sank into a crouch, riffling through his essentials and withdrawing a coil of tightly braided rope. But as far as any onlooker could see, Chase ignored her.

And it worked. She lowered the gun, stopping the pull against those scratches. It didn't let him examine her shoulder, but he could already hear her breathing more easily. When people braced against pain, they tended to hold their breath, exhaling almost as an afterthought when the pressure became distracting.

Women are the only creatures known to avoid attention then become irritated when they succeed. And the pretty ones were worst. Right now Miss Lyman stood, stymied by his sudden lack of interest. Any minute now she'd start chattering at him to reestablish the familiar scenario of a man focusing on her.

Chase focused on the cougar. He took his time binding the cougar's paws, so it'd be easier to sling across his shoulders without sliding to the side or back during the walk to town. With her arm no longer raised and pulling at her shoulder, he had no reason to hurry. Particularly since Miss Lyman hadn't started blithering at him yet. Come to think of it, he couldn't hear her breathing any longer, which meant she might be in greater pain than he realized. He straightened, turning to see—

His pink fluff ball was on the move. Again.

Not again, Chase snorted. *Still.* Since the moment he spotted her, Miss Lyman refused to bow to convention, much less any expectation. He should have guessed he couldn't use typical female behavior to predict hers, could have seen this one would choose to be difficult and take the opposite position. *But no one would expect her to head the opposite* direction, *too.*

He hefted the cougar across his shoulders and headed after the woman. Despite her shoulder and a disgruntled Decoy trying to corral his stubborn charge back toward Chase, Miss Lyman managed impressive headway before he caught up to her. Usually he appreciated that sort of determination and efficiency.

This time it made him want to dump the cougar in the dirt, scoop up the girl, and head through Hope Falls until he hit the doctor's doorstep. But Chase wouldn't touch her unless she looked ready to collapse. Judging by the set of her jaw, Miss Lyman would march clear to Cape Horn and back before admitting she needed assistance or accepted his help. So she'd just have to accept his company until she reached town.

Unfortunately, that meant he had to accept hers. Preparing for verbal buckshot, Chase stepped within blathering range.

SEVEN

I can always shoot him, Lacey comforted herself as the disconcerting Mr. Dunstan gained on her. *If he makes one false move or a single threat, I'll fire without hesitation.* Never mind her hand shook at the very thought of harming him.

This mysterious stranger pounced into her life with the lithe grace of that fallen cougar, but showed the snarl to match. If push came to shove, Lacey didn't intend to test the man's ferocity. Too much kept her off balance lately.

Yet here I am. Still standing. Walking, with great vigor, despite multiple attacks by man and beast. I haven't gone down yet. She squared her shoulders with pride, only to wince at the burning sensation chasing trails from her neck downward.

Perhaps she *would* lie down for a while once she got back to town. Lacey slid a sideways glance toward her unwanted companion. *Not that he needs to know I took a rest. In fact, if I can somehow lose him, then sneak back into the house and change before anyone notices my state of disrepair. . .* She couldn't suppress a shudder at the thought of how she must appear.

One sleeve hung in tatters, no bonnet in sight, and the back of her skirts were most likely smeared with alternating streaks of grass green and muddy brown. Nature set rose pink amid those shades with admirable results, but Lacey doubted her rear wore the combination well. *So much for my Battling Braden outfit.*

Now her brother had this little incident, in addition to Twyler's kidnapping and her husband-hunting advertisement, to convince his doctor Lacey shouldn't be the executor of Lyman estates. He'd persuade the doctor to declare him more competent, citing his recovery compared to her repeated "poor judgment."

She halted so abruptly that Mr. Dunstan managed another few strides on sheer momentum before recognizing her pause and returning. Not that Lacey wanted him to return, much less wanted him to accompany her back to Hope Falls, but suddenly personal pique faded. She had an entirely more important reason not to want this man making his way to *her* town. If he regaled her brother—or the doctor—with tall tales of wandering women and deadly cougar attacks, Hope Falls wouldn't be her town anymore.

No matter Braden's experience in the collapsed mine turned him into a new, but definitely not better, man. No matter that if Braden had those rights, he'd legally force all the women from Hope Falls until he deemed it safe. No matter they were in the middle of saving the town with the new sawmill.

"Which was *my* idea!" Some of her indignation escaped in that small outburst, but it didn't make Lacey feel any better. Nor did it provide any way to rid her of Mr. Dunstan.

"What was?" He shrugged his shoulders, adjusting the damning evidence of her run-in with a wild predator for the second day in a row. Otherwise, Mr. Dunstan stood eerily still, gaze fixed on her shoulder as though trying to determine how much it pained her and whether or not she'd let him examine it.

Which of course she wouldn't. Nor did she want to answer

that question and explain to such an interfering male that she was trying to thwart yet another interfering and overbearing man. Mr. Dunstan would most likely take Braden's side, sight unseen, on the sheer principle that of course men knew better than women. *That sort of principle just proves men know* less!

"I have lots of ideas," she evaded. The less he knew, the more room Lacey had to design a plan. "And even more questions."

"Ask later." The dratted man started to turn away, as though he'd continue on to town without her, his dog following.

"Later will be too late!" It burst out before she could swallow the sound of her desperation. Lacey leveled her tone. "You won't get another chance once we get to town, Mr. Dunstan."

"For what?" He hadn't moved back toward her, just stopped leaving. It was as if her answer would determine his next move.

What does he want? Her mind raced. *Why did the stranger come to town? Men come for two things: a chance at marrying one of the women from the ad or a job with the sawmill. He's obviously not interested in marriage—the only smiles he flashes are at my expense—so work must be the lure to bring him here.*

She shoved aside a swirl of curiosity about this man who'd been unimpressed by her looks and unswayed by her stubbornness. "A chance for a position in Hope Falls. It's what you came for, and if you don't speak with me now, you won't have another opportunity to be hired on. That much I promise, Mr. Dunstan."

Just in case her winning combination of lure and threat didn't work, Lacey began formulating an alternate plan. *I'll have Granger send him from town posthaste before the damage can be done and dismiss his stories after he's gone.* Except the afternoon progressed past the point any trains would come through, saddling her with the problematic man until tomorrow.

Tomorrow is too late if he chooses to amuse the men with his version of today's events. Word of the cougar attack—and my impetuous wandering—will reach Braden in an instant. Which meant her only hope lay in Mr. Dunstan wanting a job.

He still didn't move as he uttered, "Already have one."

Drat. Lacey would have winced, but she knew he'd notice. Then she'd either have to fend him off from examining her shoulder—which stung quite strongly now, though she refused to dwell upon it—or leave the man thinking she'd been disappointed to hear he wouldn't be staying in town. *Which is ridiculous.*

"Already have one what?" The question may be inane, but it purchased invaluable time to think. *Only it's difficult to think with him looking down his nose like he disapproves of silly, time-consuming questions from women with injured shoulders.*

Even worse, he didn't bother answering. One quizzically raised brow absolutely didn't count as an acceptable response.

The churning sensation in her stomach warned the situation slipped further from her control. Lacey always felt sick to her stomach when it looked as though things wouldn't go her way—and she had a sneaking suspicion her stomach would never feel settled so long as Mr. Dunstan remained in the vicinity.

On the balance, I suppose I should feel rather glad he won't be staying long. Her attempt to look on the bright side met with failure as the churning intensified. *Such a pity I need to convince the man he wants to stay in town for a good while.* Somehow the acknowledgment Mr. Dunstan needed to stay—because once Lacey made a decision, she inevitably found a way to carry it through—calmed her innards. Except for one trifling detail.

How do I convince him to stay in Hope Falls when he has a position elsewhere? How does one bargain with empty hands?

The answer burst from her memory, setting Lacey's teeth on edge. *Ask for help.* She drew a deep breath to cleanse away the echo of Naomi's refrain whenever the two of them did charity work. *"Empty hands ask for help; full hearts fill the need."*

No! Every iota of pride shouted against the idea. *I did not sell my family home, buy Hope Falls, and keep control from Braden only to beg favors from a stranger!* She'd come too far, and still had too far to go, to give any power away. *Naomi, Cora, and even Evie are counting on me. I brought them here; I convinced them we could advertise for husbands and choose our own mates. If I ask Dunstan to stay, I'm giving him control—even a tiny measure is too much—over the lives we're building.*

If it came to that, Mr. Dunstan would simply have to leave. Unease curdled in her midsection at the realization, but she argued it away. *After all, even if I do ask for his help, how can I know whether this stranger has the heart to give it?*

He'd given her more than enough time to gather her thoughts. Judging by the expressions chasing across her fine features, those thoughts were as scattered as chicken seed in a barnyard—and maybe they should be left to lie where they fell.

Her stance progressed from skittish to still to tense, indicating she'd wrestled with the situation before settling on a decision he wouldn't like. People only set their jaws when prepared for a fight, and Miss Lyman's looked braced for war.

All because he didn't want to discuss his position in Hope Falls with her. *Just like a woman to want to discuss things that didn't need to be discussed. And at a bad time, too.*

"We don't need to waste any more time." Chase planned to plunk the stubborn woman in front of a doctor—let another man deal with the minx. He needed to track down Granger before his old friend left town—and Chase's growing questions—in the dust.

"You're absolutely right." Her too-agreeable response started a prickle of warning between his shoulder blades. Thus far this woman reveled in causing difficulties, and the glimmer of determination in her narrowed eyes tattled that, despite her agreement, Miss Lyman didn't intend to make things simple now.

Chase shifted the cougar across his back, letting the movement distract her while he gestured with his left hand and gave the command Decoy, at least, would follow. He held grave doubts about the lady showing such good sense. "Stay close."

"No need." Her immediate refusal didn't surprise him.

Nor did Decoy's prompt obedience. The wolfhound rose from his haunches, where he'd sat at Chase's side during the entire exchange, to take the single loping step, turn, and butt his massive head beneath Miss Lyman's injured arm. He leaned a bit of his considerable weight against her skirts until the woman compensated by resting her hand atop his head. Then he calmed, looked for Chase's nod of approval, and closed his eyes to enjoy the way Miss Lyman's fingers absentmindedly ran through his fur.

Wolfhounds were hunters, but most people didn't know they had a knack for herding as well. Decoy would help shepherd the woman safely back to town, and his massive height gave Miss Lyman a place to rest her arm so it didn't pull against her injured shoulder. Best of all, she wouldn't realize the dog was following Chase's orders—she'd just assume the mutt liked her.

With her arm seen to as best as he could arrange—suspicious woman still wouldn't let him close enough to tell whether the marks were skin scratches or deeper tears—Chase started walking. Turning allowed him to let loose a self-satisfied smile. *Miss Lyman might not want to stay close, but she'll follow my lead.*

"Wait just a moment, Mr. Dunstan." She elected to talk rather than walk, as no sounds of shoes on rocks or twigs accompanied her suddenly sweet voice. Her *overly* sweet voice.

The prickle between Chase's shoulder blades expanded, raising his hackles. All the way back to a time before Christ, the Greeks wrote legends to warn of women with too-sweet voices luring good men to their doom. An ounce of sense warned that sugary tones were a womanly wile to be avoided at all costs. Especially when wielded by so skillful a warrior as Lacey Lyman.

"Since you already have a position"—she continued speaking to his back, since Chase refused to answer her Siren's call and turn around—"there's no reason for you to visit Hope Falls."

"I disagree." His own words emerged as though fighting through a pit of gravel—rough and sharp. *Good. Let her see I'm more man than manners. No amount of chitchat will sway me.*

"Of course." She still sounded pleasant as she rattled on. "I rather thought you might prove difficult. It's my growing experience that most men do, you see. Prove difficult, I mean."

"*Men* prove difficult?" Disbelief blackened his echo. "I disagree again." Partly because women, with all their emotions and mandates, were always far more difficult to deal with than men. And partly, though he'd never admit it to the pink fluff ball, because he suspected she usually managed to manipulate his gender with great ease. Beautiful women had that advantage, and Miss Lyman was nothing if not beautiful. *All the better reason not to turn around. Just start on and keep going.*

"Disagreeable is merely a minor case of being difficult." Steel now underlay the sugary tones. "Which is precisely why we don't welcome men who don't wish to take part in building Hope Falls. They have no reason to follow the rules, you see, and that makes men with their own agendas far too troublesome to be allowed entry. Surely you can understand the logic?"

Something important lurked in that barrage of words, but it took Chase a moment to separate the bullet from the babble. When he did, he turned back to look at the small woman with big orders. "Are you, Miss Lyman"—he bit back his mirth—"by any chance telling me I'm not allowed to go back to Hope Falls?"

"As owner of the town, it's my responsibility to keep things orderly." A sanctimonious nod bobbed blond curls loose from a few of their pins. "So it would be best if you and your hound— who is agreeable enough *he* can stay, but I presume loyal to his master—to keep on toward that position you spoke of."

A simple admission that his position was in Hope Falls would clear this up, but first Chase wanted to punish her high-handedness. And see if he could uncover some information about just how she claimed ownership of her brother's town.

"I'll take up my position sooner than you imagine." Relief slumped her shoulders, almost making him feel guilty for continuing. "But I'll enjoy your town's hospitality tonight." Sure enough, that produced an immediate reaction—just not the anger or irritation he'd expected. That he could brush off.

Watching as her entire small frame tensed even more tightly, her eyes widening then closing in an expression of desperation. . . that, Chase couldn't brush off. *She's scared.*

EIGHT

O f what? What could scare a woman who doesn't mind walking through the woods alone, isn't fazed by a wolfhound the size of a small bear, and bounced back from a cougar attack?

The prickles of unease started up again. It looked more and more like Granger was right about these women needing protection. At the time, Chase assumed he meant that the women needed protection from the situation they put themselves in. Now it looked like maybe there was more to it. Something worse.

What was it Kane called Miss Lyman? *"A girl who didn't belong in the backwoods. . . . All done up in bows and fluff, putting on airs as though she owned the place."* And for once the oily good-for-nothing got it right. Miss Lacey Lyman belonged in high society. And Chase himself dubbed her a pink piece of fluff.

Now that's a new one. Thinking like Kane. He shook his head to dismiss the uncomfortable idea and focus on a more important one. She called herself the owner of Hope Falls, but Kane said it was her brother, and that made more sense. Braden Lyman—if it's really Braden at all—would have already owned a good portion of the land after the mine collapsed. So why was this girl, who may or may not be Braden's sister, claiming to own his town?

And why doesn't she want me going near it?

He'll ruin everything! Lacey closed her eyes and tried to think.

Strangely enough, her thoughts marched in more orderly fashion when not distracted by the sight of the unkempt man wearing a cougar carcass strung over his shoulders. Then again, that wasn't strange at all. It would have been far stranger if she could think properly with such a spectacle loping in her line of vision, heading toward Hope Falls to destroy her dreams.

If it weren't for the cougar, it wouldn't be so bad. Some part of her mind couldn't help but notice that, beneath the dust and displeasing lack of manners, Mr. Dunstan cut a fine figure. The icy depths behind his brown eyes alone gave her shivers.

No. Not shivers. Shudders. Lacey resolved to look over a few editions of *Harper's Bazaar* to remind her what a fine male figure actually was. The very notion that such a wild and woolly mountain man held any points of attraction at all just went to show how far Lacey had come from civilization—and how much she'd compromised her standards of an acceptable suitor.

Although obviously Mr. Dunstan isn't a suitor. A deep sigh let loose some remorse. *Not because I want him as a suitor—although I suppose I might be offended by his lack of interest, if I had the time or inclination for trivial pettiness—but because if he were a suitor, he'd be easier to manage.*

Because, truly, she could think of no way to manage the man. She couldn't very well threaten to shoot him if he walked into town—he'd most likely call her bluff. So she'd have to shoot him. *And of course I wouldn't, as no matter how disagreeable the man is, he doesn't deserve to be shot—or let him go into town with something even more ridiculous to add to his story of how I traipsed out alone and got mauled by a cat.*

She opened her eyes to find him still staring at her in that disconcerting manner and realized she'd been lost in her wandering thoughts far too long. Even worse, they hadn't brought her to any plan. Which meant, short of threatening him with her pistol, Lacey didn't have any recourse but to accept the fact Mr. Chase Dunstan fully intended to stroll into town, cougar slung across those broad shoulders, and show the world she'd gotten herself into more trouble than she could handle. Again.

Except it wasn't true. She'd killed the cat and come this far, after all. Therefore the cougar could be used as proof that she, Lacey Lyman, could look after herself. A smile pulled at the corners of her mouth. *And Mr. Dunstan will attest to it.*

Why, if one looked properly, this could be a godsend!

"Very well, Mr. Dunstan. Wait just a moment." She darted back toward the scene of the incident, stooping to retrieve her shawl. Lacey knew she'd need it to conceal her injuries—those would only distract from her triumphant portrayal as huntress.

Oh, well now. A wave of wooziness, punctuated with streaks of pain shooting from her shoulder, halted her when she straightened up. *I'll just take it more slowly then. No rush.* After all, she'd endured a difficult day—after yesterday, she really had been due for a pleasant one, but no matter—without the benefit of breakfast. Come to think of it, she'd been too overset to choke down any supper the night before either.

"What are you doing?" Dunstan's thunderous voice rumbled directly behind her. He'd followed when she left then.

"Fetching my shawl." Slowly, hoping he took her snail's pace for nonchalance, she folded it about her shoulders.

"You'd be plenty warm if you'd walked. By now you'd be snug in town in front of a fireplace with a doctor taking a look at that shoulder." The flurry of words seemed to exhaust his speaking abilities as he subsided into a fierce glower.

"Yes, let's go back. I'm certain the men will enjoy hearing your tale about how I shot and killed a rampaging wildcat."

He blinked at her smile, but for once Lacey doubted her beauty caused a man's bemusement. Her hair, straggling loose of its pins since her bonnet was knocked askew, tickled her neck. Smudges of dirt did little to enhance the once-cheery stripes of her shawl. By now Lacey knew her nose, too long exposed to sun and wind, matched the pink of her walking dress. Not her most attractive moment, to be certain. No, Mr. Dunstan's momentary confusion was caused by her sudden shift toward pleasantry.

All told, this day did little to bolster her womanly pride. *Luckily, I had womanly pride to spare,* Lacey soothed herself. *What I need is to maintain my position as acting owner of Hope Falls. And for that, I need the respect of men—not admiration.*

"I don't spin stories." His dismissal stung almost as much as her shoulder. Dunstan turned away again. "Now stay close."

He shifted the great cat as he spoke, making an awkward gesture with his arm as though to shoo his dog away. The dog obeyed.

Having been shooed away from his master, Decoy butted against her skirts once again, shoving his massive head beneath her arm. A gentle giant, the dog's motions didn't jostle her arm much to set it atop his skull—a convenient resting place.

If, of course, Lacey wanted to rest her arm atop the dog's head and follow his master at a docile pace. Which she did not.

"I'll thank you to put down my cougar first." She quelled a spurt of triumph as the man froze midstep with an odd sound.

"Your cougar?" Strangled, that's how the words sounded. As though squeezing through the tight vocal chords of an angry man.

"Yes." She brushed around him to stand directly in his path.

"*My* cougar. It attacked me, then I shot and killed it." Lacey made a show of tucking her gun into the hidden pocket in her skirts then holding out her arms. "Give it to me."

"What?" Chase wanted to give her a thorough shaking and a one-way ticket back to civilization, where men had patience to deal with beautiful wantwits like the woman standing in front of him.

Of course, the men in civilization hadn't stopped her from leaving their midst to wreak havoc amidst the mountains. For all Chase knew, they packed her trunks and toasted a job well done.

"Give me my cougar," she repeated, bobbing her arms as though to emphasize the empty space in which he should deposit the sixty-pound cat currently slung across his own shoulders. Imperious as she sounded, the movement made her wince. "Now."

"Enough foolishness." Chase stepped around her and headed toward town, determined not to stop this time. Whether or not she followed, he would be in Hope Falls for supper. And a talk with Granger. If necessary, he'd send someone after the minx.

So long as it was someone else, it'd work out just fine.

"It's not foolishness!" Her cry gained volume as she took to her heels and whipped around him, trying to stop him. Instead she wound up skittering beside him, unable to match the length of his stride. "It's my cougar, and I want it!"

Spoiled society darling. He curled his lip at the assessment. "Is that how you grew up?" Chase couldn't help but ask. "Getting anything you wanted just because you whined?"

Her outraged gasp let him get in a few more steps before she launched a renewed verbal assault. "You arrogant cretin!" Her spluttered insult made him grin—making her angrier.

Cretin? She's spitting mad and that's the best she has?

"I didn't get everything I wanted when I was growing up!"

Her swiftest denial revealed what hit closest to home. If he hadn't already known it, little Miss Lyman just gave away how much her family indulged her. Still, she kept right on chattering. "Although I admit I was somewhat privileged and enjoyed many fine things others did not, those were gifts freely given."

"Why?" Let her reveal more about herself as her words measured the steps back to town. Maybe she'd let something slip.

"Because my parents loved me!" Her exclamation slammed into him with the force of a fallen tree. "They wanted to protect me and encourage my many fine qualities, so I could make my way in the world. Didn't yours do the same for you, Mr. Dunstan?"

No. Dad drowned his worry over the farm in the nearest tankard of ale, and Ma was too busy keeping away from his fists. Neither one concerned themselves much with me or Laura. We looked after ourselves. Anything we got was earned twice over.

"So you give insults but no answers?" Her observation stung. He rarely insulted anyone, but she'd brought out the worst in him. "Well, I can assure you, Mr. Dunstan. I *never* whined."

No need to respond to that. He snorted and kept walking.

"For one thing, *I* never stole from anyone to make myself look better." She gave a pointed glance toward the cougar. "Nor do I try to take credit for another person's accomplishment."

"Woman, I'm not going to claim the kill." Goaded beyond forbearance, he growled at her. "Tell your people whatever you like, but I'm not going to let a slip of a woman with an injured shoulder carry a carcass down a mountainside. Understood?"

The blindingly beatific smile she bestowed upon him told Chase he'd said the wrong thing—exactly what she wanted.

"Understood."

"You want to run that by me again?" Jake Granger crossed his arms and rested one shoulder against the far back corner of the house. The telltale swish of skirts on the move and random cries of disbelief formed a background to feminine activity. What activity that may be, Jake couldn't say, but muffled thumps told of items pulled from shelves and deposited elsewhere.

Yep. They're upset all right. He eyed his longtime associate. Eyed the fallen cougar Dunstan started skinning. It didn't take a genius to figure out what had the women in a tizzy. What he needed to know was how much of it was his friend's fault—and if it meant the women wouldn't let him install Dunstan as acting authority in Hope Falls while he was gone.

The women got touchy about letting anyone take charge. If they took exception to the tracker squatting behind their house, methodically skinning a cougar, they'd kick up a mighty fuss. Jake needed to be prepared to soothe their ruffled feathers. But how to go about it depended on what Dunstan could tell him.

And Dunstan wasn't in a talking mood.

"Ask Miss Lyman," came the taciturn response to Jake's question of how the man came to be skinning a cougar.

Dunstan skinning a large predator wasn't something Jake would normally need to question—the man tracked and hunted better than anyone he'd ever met. But behind the women's house? Dressing any large animal counted as a messy, smelly process.

"I'm asking you." He didn't bother stating the obvious; only a madman would saunter into a house full of upset women.

"Granger,"—his friend's frustration seeped through the two syllables—"your two eyes can tell you I'm dressing a cougar. The rest is Miss Lyman's business. Take it up with her."

Dunstan met Lacey Lyman? Figured. Take the woman who'd have the most volatile reaction with his friend, and have them meet with no one to intervene. *It's a wonder only the cougar got shot.* Jake blinked and switched tactics. "How did you meet Lacey

Lyman? I thought you went for a thought-walk in the woods."

Dunstan snorted and wiped his bloody blade on a piece of hide he'd retrieved from his rucksack. "Thought-walk?"

"Enough." Jake levered himself away from the wall, circled the other man, and lowered to look him in the eye. "I meant to introduce you to the girls tonight, easy and proper, so they'd accept you as my temporary replacement. Instead I turn around to find the women all aflutter, you skinning a cougar, and somehow Miss Lyman had a part in it. Looks like a royal mess I'll have to clean up before I leave. So what happened?"

NINE

N othing happened I couldn't handle. Don't fret so." Lacey ignored the churning in her stomach and forced a smile.

Not one of the other three women offered one in return. Naomi sucked shallow breaths through drawn lips, apparently fighting horror over the idea her charge might be injured, and reached for the witch hazel. Evie's wide-eyed gaze flitted from Lacey's mussed hair to her rumpled skirts and blood-stained shawl in obvious disbelief before the kettle called her away.

"Don't you say a word until I get back, Lacey!" she shrieked as she bustled into the kitchen and began a series of thuds to indicate something delicious would soon emerge.

Cora tilted her head in silent question. Her mismatched eyes—one hazel, one blue—held the same concern and curiosity evinced by her companions. The suspicion glittering in those depths belonged only to Cora. When Lacey couldn't meet her gaze, Cora slid toward the window. She shifted curtains, peering out as though trying to see around to the back of the house.

The back of the house—where Lacey asked Mr. Dunstan to

take the cougar, thinking it would be out of sight of the workmen. Out of sight, away from prying questions she wasn't yet prepared to answer. Cora, her best friend and brother's fiancée—never mind what Braden said—knew her a little too well.

Luckily, she didn't have time to dwell on that before her cousin ushered her over to the nearest wingback chair. Naomi had Lacey's feet plumped upon a slightly rickety ottoman before she could protest. But when her cousin reached for her shawl, Lacey clamped a hand upon it and shook her head. *They can't see my shoulder. I don't even know how bad it is, but things always look worst before they're cleaned up. I don't want them alarmed.*

"If you don't let me see to it, the stains will set and you'll lose that shawl." Naomi's reminder would have done the trick any other time, but today Lacey shook her head again.

"It's of no importance." Lacey's response did little to assure them, most likely because they knew how very important the proper accessories were. Particularly soft, charming shawls woven of expensive kerseymere and dyed in one's favorite color.

Her cousin's eyes narrowed in suspicion—obviously caught from Cora, who'd come back over from the window to oversee things. "The last time you wore one of these shawls, a chipped teacup allowed the merest dribble of liquid to fall upon its corner. Then it was important enough for you to leap from the settee and disappear to your room for a quarter of an hour."

"You make it sound as though I ran off sulking," Lacey denied. "It needed to be tended immediately and done properly!"

She remembered the incident and had indeed taken the blue and primrose paisley printed shawl to her room for immediate treatment. A bit of blotting and a judicious sprinkling of talc— swiftly brushed away once it served its purpose—and the shawl looked good as new. A quarter of an hour was a small price to pay to save something of great beauty and artistry, after all.

"Precisely." Naomi reached for the shawl Lacey kept clutched about her shoulders. "And today is no different."

"Oh, but it is!" she cried, twisting slightly to avoid her cousin's grasp. The movement sent hot streaks licking from her shoulder down her arm. "Today we have urgent things to discuss!"

"You waited, didn't you?" Evie rushed in, bearing an overloaded tray. All Evie's trays came in loaded beyond good judgment. Nevertheless, they always left without so much as a crumb remaining. Just the sight of that tray set Lacey's stomach to rumbling, and she didn't even know what sat beneath the covers. But her friend kept talking as she set it down. "I want to hear absolutely everything about Mr. Dunstan and the cougar!"

"The cougar?" Naomi's echo came in a faint whisper.

"The *what*!" Cora's wasn't so much a question as a shriek loud enough to conceal the sounds of two men entering the house.

"Cougar." Mr. Dunstan's grunt confirmed Evie's statement and robbed Lacey of the chance to soften her story before getting to the parts that would make Naomi worry too much. The man obviously held a gift for intruding at the worst times.

"Oh Lacey." Her older cousin looked horror-struck.

"Now, Naomi." Lacey leaned forward, but fell back as her shoulder protested. "I'm here safe and sound. Don't fuss so."

"Who's this?" Cora's gaze darted from Lacey to Dunstan. "Where did he come from, and what part did he play in Lacey returning to the house more disheveled than we've ever seen?"

Lacey raised her good arm to check her hair, found things even worse than Cora let on, and went back to clutching her shawl. *I knew I looked a fright, but she need not have said so.*

"I don't know." Jake held up a hand in defense against Evie's raised brows. "I asked, but Dunstan said to ask Lacey."

Abruptly all five pairs of eyes turned to her. Four held unanswered questions. One held an unspoken accusation.

Obviously Dunstan realized she'd tricked him. Now he resented his promise to let her say whatever she wished about the dead cougar. She met his bad humor with a smirk. *Too late.*

"Oh, nothing much. A mountain lion with exceptional taste coveted my hat. The thing let loose an unearthly shriek and launched from the trees, but I shot him before he did any real damage." She gave a nonchalant shrug, ignoring any pain. A grimace would entirely undo her carefree facade. "Thankfully, my ensemble bore the brunt of the encounter. Mr. Dunstan happened by in time to hear the cat then helped me to my feet."

"Oh Lacey!" Her friends' exclamations held a gratifying mix of concern and admiration. None of them seemed frantic.

"Just yesterday you could have been killed out there! What were you doing alone in the forest?" The hard edge beneath Granger's question did little to endear him to her.

Oh, I'm glad I withheld my vote, and you don't yet have permission to wed Evie. If you hadn't lied about who you were and why you came here, yesterday wouldn't have happened! The gall of the man to imply that situation had been in any way her fault—or that she needed to be kept on some sort of tether!

"Walking." The distinctively low timbre of Dunstan's response pulled her from the quagmire of her musings. "That's what she told me when I asked. Miss Lyman was walking."

"I don't happen to enjoy running," she agreed. *Why did he interfere? And why did he have to let everyone know he interrogated me about why I was alone?* It seemed as though whatever she least wished to draw attention to, the men seemed equally determined to focus upon. "And after yesterday, which could not have been forseen by anyone in this room save one Mr. Creed-now-Granger, I felt the need to clear my thoughts."

Granger snorted the way a horse did before it bucked. "It's not safe for you to roam the mountainside alone. Any of you."

The other women shared glances. Naomi's considering look meant she leaned toward agreeing with the man. Cora's frown gave away little. Evie—well, Evie went ahead and spoke her mind.

"Seems to me Lacey did just fine this afternoon dealing with the *natural* predators of the area—though I sincerely hope none of us has need to repeat her success. Even if you're concerned, Jake, you don't have the right to tell Lacey whether she can or can't go for a stroll on her own property."

"Do you plan to publicly contradict me after we're wed?" Granger's scowl found a new target in his bride-to-be.

"Don't make this a choice between being a woman and a wife—I can't be one without the other." Doubt shadowed Evie's features. "I speak my mind, same as always. But this isn't public, Jake. This is you trying to issue orders to all the women in town and me saying that's neither fair nor appropriate. If I waited to tell you you're wrong in private, then it means everyone here would think I agreed with you."

"You should." Dunstan broke in for the second time.

Cora's question sounded more curious than outraged. "Because they'll be married, or because you think he's right?"

"Because Granger *is* right." The man excelled in short statements dropped into the conversation like blunt objects.

"He's wrong, and so are you." Lacey decided a reminder was in order. For both men. "You're new here and not staying long, but let me assure you, Mr. Dunstan, that the women of the town own—and run—Hope Falls. We make every decision, from whom we choose to marry all the way down to who's allowed to stay."

Silence reigned after her pronouncement. Granger didn't naysay her. Even if he wanted to, he couldn't. But the new man didn't respond either. After a too-long pause, he took action.

His jaw slid to the side before he emitted a whistle so high-pitched as to be almost inaudible. Instantly the enormous, shaggy frame of Decoy bounded through the entry hall. Which meant he leapt through the front door and sailed through the second door into the foyer in a single jump. He came to halt at his master's side and sat down.

His master, the far less tractable creature, flashed his own smile at Lacey. A challenge lurked behind that grin, and they both knew it had more to do with their interaction than with the moose-sized mutt now imitating a throw rug.

"What"—Cora goggled at Decoy—"is that supposed to be?"

"I think it's a dog," Naomi ventured. Her stiff posture indicated precisely what she thought about the presence of such a large, unkempt animal within the house. "A rather large one."

"Why is it inside the house?" Evie paused in the act of setting her heavy tray atop a side table. Decoy raised his head and gave a hopeful sniff in her direction, but didn't move.

"Miss Lyman assured me *he* is welcome in Hope Falls." Dunstan's emphasis of the word *he* reminded Lacey not only that she had, indeed, said this. It also told her he held a grudge. The man clearly hadn't appreciated her directive to leave Hope Falls and not look back. Now he'd found his revenge.

"Whatever was said, I'm certain you misunderstood. The. . . dog. . ."—Naomi's pause signaled doubts as to the animal's parentage—"may be welcome in town. But it is beyond expectation that he be allowed into the buildings. Surely you understand."

"Where I go, Decoy follows. Miss Lyman lauded Decoy for his loyalty before issuing his invitation to town." Dunstan didn't glance Naomi's way as he reached down to rub the dog's ears. "I don't believe honor is limited to men, but I believe only people who stand by their own word can expect the same of others."

He's threatening me! Lacey sucked in a breath. The man had some nerve. Unfortunately, he had enough brains to make it a problem. Dunstan backed her into a corner, and she'd have to capitulate. For now. *It won't be for long. I'll make sure he heads out for his new position before Granger leaves.*

"Unlike so many male creatures"—Lacey's grin was more a baring of her teeth, and she knew Dunstan recognized it—"Decoy is both useful and well behaved. The dog is most welcome."

"Lacey Lyman, what happened to you?" The question burst out before Evie could stop it, judging by her slightly sheepish expression. "You wouldn't get so much as a perfumed lapdog back in Charleston. Didn't you cite shedding as the reason animals—aside from cats proven to be good mousers—belonged outside only?"

"Now, Evie," Cora cautioned her sister, still eying Mr. Dunstan. "Every rule needs the exception to prove it."

"This man," Granger added, "manages to be the exception more often than not. You might not be thrilled about his dog, ladies, but I'm sure you'll welcome the newest addition to Hope Falls."

"Of course we welcome Mr. Dunstan. He already plans to enjoy our hospitality tonight before going on to start a new position." Lacey tried to smooth the conversation back on track. It looked as though Granger knew the man, but that curious coincidence needn't be explored now. When Granger was gone, so would be any pretext for Difficult Dunstan to remain.

"So you decided to sign on?" Granger clapped his friend on the back. "Glad to hear it, Dunstan. Ladies, you won't regret it. This man's the best hunter in the Rockies. He'll keep Evie's stewpan full and all four of you safe until I return."

TEN

W hat?" Miss Lyman rose from her chair as though getting to her feet for battle. "He plans to stay the night, but *only* tonight."

"In town. I don't much care for bunkhouses." Chase felt the slow grin spreading across his face. "Your kind welcome of Decoy is what finally convinced me to take Granger's offer."

She didn't like that one bit. Miss Lyman's nostrils flared as she struggled to maintain her composure. *She allowed Decoy in the house thinking to keep me quiet about how dangerous the cougar attack was. Now she'll be stuck with that decision.*

"What offer?" The woman Chase judged to be eldest—more for the wisdom she'd evinced rather than the distinctive streak of white tracking through her hair—spoke from beside Miss Lyman's now-empty seat. Her attempt to tug the younger girl back into her chair failed when Miss Lyman pulled away to remain standing.

Bad idea. An eggshell boasted more color than she did at the moment. The stubborn woman refused to see the doctor until she spoke with her "business partners," so that shoulder still pained her. Added to a heated conversation, it was enough to leave Miss Lyman unsteady on her feet. She needed to sit down.

Not that she'd appreciate the observation. Chase heard enough to figure this was one woman—Granger's little lady made another, with the other two still undecided—who absolutely refused to follow male orders. They didn't look past their own importance to see sense, and while Chase found this a common failing in men, women worsened it tenfold. Men could be left to their own devices, but often wound up hurting innocent women. Which was why females needed to be looked after. At least a little bit.

Chase reached over to rub Decoy's head and gave a soft snap behind the dog's ear. When he sat at attention, Chase rolled his shoulders toward Miss Lyman, moving his hand in the gesture for "push." These almost imperceptible signals stood him in good stead many times over the years, and now would be no different. Decoy stood, ambled over to Miss Lyman, and all but tromped atop her boots in an effort to get close. In the coup de grâce, he leaned, resting his weight against her knees.

Like so many before her, Miss Lyman couldn't withstand the weight of Decoy's show of affection. This time the target wasn't knocked over, but forced to abruptly sit down. At Chase's short nod of approval, Decoy's tongue lolled out in happy satisfaction. The dog shifted to rest his head atop his victim's lap—effectively holding her in place for a while.

"Decoy!" Miss Lyman spluttered, unable to gain her footing but surprisingly unwilling to shove the dog away. Ultimately she recognized the inevitable and patted the top of his head. "What poor manners you have. Someone should teach you better."

She left no doubt just whose manners she felt were lacking.

"Maybe he wanted you to sit down," the eldest—Chase began to wonder when he'd have names to put to the women—suggested.

"Someone did." The other one whose name he didn't know—the sister to Granger's woman—assessed him with one coolly logical blue eye and one amused hazel one. She looked just long enough to make him wonder whether she'd noted his signals to Decoy before turning her attention back to Miss Lyman. "You'd gone pale as a new moon, and—Lacey! What have you been hiding?"

Her gasp barely preceded a storm of movement as she descended upon her now-seated friend and whisked away the concealing shawl. Decoy's antics had nudged it askew, so it came away easily. "Why didn't you go directly to the doctor?"

Now here's a woman a man could get along with. Chase shifted to the side to get a better view of Miss Lyman's now-exposed shoulder. The converging womenfolk managed to oust Decoy, who came slinking back to Chase's side. He caught another glimpse of pink fabric gaping open in jagged rips along one side, revealing a creamy shoulder smeared with darkened blood. At this distance he couldn't tell how deep the scratches were, only that Miss Lyman lost what little color she had left when her oldest friend brandished a bottle of witch hazel.

"Make your choice, Lacey. Either we go upstairs and you submit to my ministrations,"—a threatening wave of the bottle punctuated this—"or you let me take you to the doctor."

"Later. First we need settle the issue of Mr. Dunstan." She bobbed her head to glower at him through the crowd of women.

"Thanks for the thought, but I'll see myself settled, miss." He really shouldn't enjoy poking fun at her this much.

"He'll get on just fine," Granger hastened to assure them.

"That's not what she meant." Granger's woman tossed the comment over her shoulder. "But we'll see to it after we see to Lacey's shoulder. It needs cleaning to prevent infection."

"All this over a scratch!" Miss Lyman twisted away, only to

gasp when the motion pulled her wound. She closed her eyes.

The one with the witch hazel admonished, "Stop trying to make it sound like nothing. That wasn't a little kitten, Lacey."

"It wasn't full grown." Her defiant mumble made Chase fight a chuckle. At least she'd listened to his assessment earlier. "I'll go see the doctor as soon as we finish this discussion."

"You'll have to trust us to finish it without you." Cora knew when her best friend had decided to dig in her heels. Worse, Lacey's pretty shoes left wicked marks behind any scuffle.

For whatever reason, Lacey decided she didn't like the enigmatic man quietly watching them. If Cora hadn't seen otherwise, she would have assumed it was the mammoth beast accompanying the fellow that put Lacey on guard. Instead her fastidious friend favored the beast and overlooked—no, openly set herself against—this most interesting male. *But why?*

She'd certainly never find the answer so long as Lacey stayed in the room, shooting daggers at the poor fellow. Besides, her friend had committed several sins against the agreement the four of them made before journeying to Hope Falls, and now she needed to pay the price. Lacey Lyman might own the bulk of the town, but that didn't mean she escaped its rules.

"It's not that I don't trust you, Cora!" Lacey sounded aggrieved. "But if I'm not present, it won't be a united decision, as all of our judgments are supposed to be."

"We already disagreed once today," Evie answered for them all, reminding Lacey that she'd voted against allowing Jake to be her husband. "In any case, you've already failed to uphold some of the decisions we all agreed to. Now you need medical attention, and you can't expect Hope Falls to grind to a halt."

"That's. . .that's not fair, Evie! You know I don't expect

everything in town to stop just because I see the doctor."

"But you did break agreements—first by not telling any of us where you were going, then again by not seeing the doctor straightaway." A familiar, helpless anger threatened to cut off her words, so Cora spoke more quickly. "Everyone gave me her word not to take any risks if one of us was sick or injured."

The single assurance I asked before I came here, the simplest way to safeguard us all, and Lacey didn't honor it. From the stricken expression on her friend's face, Lacey's knack for reliving conversations caught her now. *I followed Braden here after my fiancé broke his promise to me, instead going into the mines on a regular basis until they caved in atop his stubborn skull. Now his sister does the same sort of thing. It must end before another of us winds up bedridden and bitter.*

"Oh Cora." Lacey could see the tears Cora swiftly blinked back—her dearest friend always caught her distress before anyone else. Even her sister, Evie, couldn't match Lacey's perception when it came to these things. The vivid, guilty flush came in startling contrast to her previous pallor. "You're right, of course. I didn't think—I'll go see the doctor straightaway."

"Jake will see you safely there." Evie volunteered her fiancé, throwing him the don't-even-think-about-arguing glare for good measure. That glare never failed, so far as Cora knew. "Since he doesn't want any of us going anywhere alone, and it looks as though you could use the support of a strong arm."

None of the women missed the questioning look Jacob Granger aimed at the new man—Mr. Dunstan. Nor was there any mistaking the nature of the question behind it. Something along the lines of, *If I escort your main detractor to the doc, will you resent being abandoned to the mercy of the remaining three women?*

If she didn't find it amusing, Cora would think it insulting. Instead, she waited for Dunstan's response. If he indicated he wanted Granger to remain, the man didn't possess enough strength to stay in Hope Falls—much less look after it. Lacey seemed dead set against the idea, so he'd need considerable backbone to convince the rest of them otherwise.

Ah. There. Dunstan didn't nod or shake his head in overt answer to Granger's oh-so-obvious query. Nevertheless, Cora caught the slight angling of his jaw toward the door, a silent bid for Granger to take Lacey and take his leave.

The man didn't say much. It would be interesting to see how he fared in the ensuing conversation. *It'll take more than tilting his head and silently issuing orders to his dog before we decide Hope Falls needs him. Although,* she acknowledged, *a woman could glean a lot from the way he made Decoy nudge Lacey back into her seat. If his words speak half so well as his actions, I'll welcome him here. He'll do Lacey some good.*

These women were up to no good, but they weren't boring. Chase denied Granger's nonverbal offer to remain in his company. No offense to Granger, but it didn't look as though his friend were faring all that well for himself. Falling in love with the spunky cook probably had something to do with the veteran sawmill manager's sudden demotion to taking orders from women.

Chase would fare better without Granger trying to smooth his way. Rough edges kept a man sharp, and Chase learned early on to keep his instincts well honed. If that shaved off a few of the finer points, so be it. Best that the women understood from the start he wouldn't pander to their finer sensibilities.

"Thank you, Mr. Granger." The cook's sister turned her two-toned gaze toward the door as he escorted Miss Lyman outside. Whatever lay behind her reminder of the promise to safeguard one's health, it had proven effective in guilting her friend to the doctor. Guilt was one of those weapons women wielded well, and a man could do nothing but stand in awe of the results.

"After you see Lacey settled, I'm certain Mr. Dunstan would be pleased by your return." The woman spoke pleasantly, but anyone could hear the statement wasn't a request. "After the intensity of yesterday's events, I'd rather not see Braden overset again. We won't be delaying his recovery any further."

Granger frowned. "He'll not thank me for the omission, Miss Thompson. You know good and well the only thing to upset your fiancé more than a cougar attacking his sister is for him to be the last to know about it. Besides, he should meet Dunstan."

So Granger knows Lyman—at least, the man claiming to be Braden Lyman. Chase digested this, batting around the idea of allowing the meeting. *I'd find out if it's really Braden. If it isn't, I'll know what direction to take my investigation of the mine collapse.* That would save a great deal of time and wondering over the bedridden patient, as well as whether the pink fluff ball of the forest was Miss Lyman or an impostor.

But if the true Braden Lyman lies in the bed, he'll recognize me, and I'll be wedged into a too-tight corner. Because Chase had no way of knowing whether a Braden injured in the mine collapse could know of the shifty practices employed by his partners during his absence. If Braden were involved in skulduggery, the man would either protest Chase's presence outright or throw up obstacles to impede his search.

Too risky. I need more information. There might be a way to discover the identity of the man in that room before I face him. The only real decision to make was how to avoid the meeting without raising any suspicions, but he had an idea.

"No sense in meeting the man when I might not be staying." Chase shrugged and shot his friend a grin. "Looks like I still have to run the proverbial gauntlet before I'm found worthy."

"Hardly anything so barbaric as a gauntlet." The woman with the single white streak in her hair protested the comparison.

"Though we'll be sure to keep your suggestion in mind," Miss Lyman promised as Granger half escorted, half tugged her out the door. She knew she'd been temporarily outmaneuvered, but that last comment told Chase she wasn't declaring surrender.

ELEVEN

O ne skirmish at a time. He might not understand why women ran the town, but Chase understood he wouldn't be able to unearth the answers to his questions unless they tolerated his presence. Even with Miss Lyman out of the room, the remaining three women left him and Decoy seriously outnumbered.

The fistfight by the train offered better odds. He shook off the unwelcome thought and offered the ladies a rusty smile. He didn't interact much with ladies. The mountains provided the food, shelter, and living he needed. Decoy made a better companion than most men, unquestionably a more honest one.

Usually he let prospective employers approach him. Most boss types didn't like having to persuade a man to take a job; it took away too much control. But it worked well for Chase. He had no trouble walking away, and he liked folks to know it.

Not this time. If he was going to find answers for Laura, he'd be the one doing the convincing in this interview. Problem was, he didn't have the first idea how to reason with one woman, much less a pack of them. Particularly when they already had their hackles raised by Granger throwing his weight around.

"Ladies, looks like Granger neglected introductions." His opening gambit should appeal to their sense of propriety and make them think he shared it. "Chase Dunstan, at your service."

"Our service?" Granger's woman raised her brows. "Seems to me you and my fiancé hatched your own plans, Mr. Dunstan."

True. He held his peace on that one. Not only had he fallen into Granger's scheme, he held a few of his own, and none of those focused on serving these women. On the contrary, if he discovered any involvement with the cave-in or fraudulent claims filed under the Lyman name, the women wouldn't fare well at all.

"You'll have to excuse Evie, Mr. Dunstan," apologized the one Chase pegged as eldest. "A challenging day, preceded by several others, has put her in a somewhat adversarial mood."

An understatement. "If I understand correctly, she's agreed to wed Granger." Chase offered a plausible explanation for the woman's lapse. "That would be enough to throw anyone off."

"Under normal circumstances, my sister would follow the introductions *before* interrogation model of conversation. I'm Miss Cora Thompson, sister to Evelyn Thompson." The slightly built woman with mismatched eyes launched into a recitation. "The lady apologizing for my sister is Miss Naomi Higgins, cousin to Lacey Lyman. You've already made her acquaintance. Her brother, whose company you're spared, is Braden Lyman—my fiancé, nominal owner of Hope Falls and general curmudgeon."

The whirlwind recitation calmed long enough for her to take a breath. Chase couldn't have gotten a better setup if he asked, but he aimed for a casual tone. "Nominal owner of Hope Falls?"

"Until he recovers from the mine collapse, Lacey's been designated de facto executor of the Lyman estates." The one he now knew as Miss Higgins offered the implausible, but succinct, explanation with a wry smile. "The cause for the curmudgeonly behavior he's exhibited since we arrived in Hope Falls."

Not trusting himself to comment, Chase merely nodded. The entire situation was farcical, but so far every factor remained cohesive. From the ad, to Miss Lyman's remarks, to Granger's behavior, and even Kane's dubious report, every avenue available supported the women's claim that they ran Hope Falls.

Whether or not they had any right to do so remained in grave doubt until he resolved the matter of their Braden Lyman's true identity. But if this was a fraud, the women managed an unrivaled consistency and attention to detail.

"Let me make sure I have this all straight." He met Miss Higgins's gaze before beginning the recitation that would cement everyone's role in his mind. "Your cousin, Lacey, owns Hope Falls while her brother, your fiancé"—he gestured to Miss Cora Thompson—"recovers from a mining accident. Meanwhile, the four of you decided to turn the town into a sawmill and posted a highly unusual ad to make your plans a reality?"

At this point, he put his copy of the advertisement atop a centrally located tea table. The familiar bold print marched between him and the women in a brash request for God-fearing, single men with logging experience and a desire for marriage.

Here things got interesting. An unwilling smile played about the corners of the elder Miss Thompson's mouth. Miss Higgins issued a small, very regretful-sounding sigh. The younger Miss Thompson, supposed fiancée to Braden Lyman, didn't bother looking at the scrap of paper in the first place.

"Is this what brought you to Hope Falls, Mr. Dunstan?" Surprise crept in around the edges of her question.

The laugh escaped him before he could consider whether or not it might be considered insulting. "I'm no logger, ladies. You can rest easy on that. My business is to know the lay of the land." Here he reached out to tap the ad. "When this crossed my path, it seemed pretty clear you ladies aimed to change things."

"So you didn't follow the ad, and you didn't come here to find Jake?" Granger's woman—this business of two Miss Thompsons was just plain irritating—lost the vestiges of her smile.

"I didn't know Granger followed the ad here at all."

"He didn't." Her hands clenched into telltale fists. "His brother's murderer answered the ad. Jake came for Twyler."

Chase might not spend much time around women, but even he could see this struck a nerve. Hard to imagine he'd missed Jake trapping the killer and revealing his real identity—and purpose— by a mere day. He looked at it as a lot of fun missed, but obviously it hit a woman hard to hear her beau hadn't come to Hope Falls looking for love. He'd been looking for justice.

Easy to forget how much you have in common with a friend when you don't see the man in three years.

"Regardless, if we take you on, you won't be working for Mr. Granger." Miss Higgins didn't prance delicately around the issue. "How do you feel about answering to four women as your employers, carrying out their plans rather than those of your friend? We need to know your loyalty to Mr. Granger won't prove problematic should we enter into a good-faith arrangement."

Time to tread carefully. What sorts of plans does she anticipate Granger protesting? If they weren't what they appeared, they'd hidden a good deal from his friend. *And done so well Granger proposed to one of them.* Chase would have to walk a fine line between placating them and following his own plans.

"I answer to myself and don't take sides in matters between couples. Four women running a town deserve the respect of anyone within it, and employers have a right to expect the same. Seems only a fool would think otherwise." The women murmured favorably to this, so Chase cashed in on their approval before he lost it. He'd exchange that newfound goodwill for grudging tolerance, so long as it leveled the field. "But it's only fair to tell you I've never been one to report for orders."

"There's a difference between receiving orders and taking direction from one's employer, Mr. Dunstan." Braden's supposed fiancée pokered up in an instant. "By the same token, we can't accept a renegade who does as he pleases. We have rules in Hope Falls for a reason, and you'll not be exempt from them."

"Hold on now. I'm not going to be flouting the authority I'm here to uphold." He needed to nip that idea in the bud. "If you want a guard dog you can bring to heel, I can train you one. But if you want me making sure no one gets insolent while Granger's gone, I'll use your guidelines and my own methods."

"And if we dislike your methods?" Miss Thompson pressed.

"Like I said"—Chase shrugged to keep the tone nonchalant—"your guidelines. I'm happy to help ladies in need and put a friend's mind at ease, but I offer assistance. Not obedience."

"Obedience is required of children and expected of wives, Mr. Dunstan." Miss Higgins smoothed her skirts. "Biblical, wifely submission is far too often confused with obedience, but that is a conversation for another time. The pertinent matter is that all of us understand—and have rejected—the idea of owing obedience to a person with whom we wish to form a partnership."

Chase blinked. *What revolutionary ideas for gently bred females.* He drew a breath. *Of course, they may not be gently bred at all. Only time, and thorough investigation, will tell.*

"Then we understand each other. I'll maintain order in Hope Falls. Aside from that, I'll tackle your wildlife problem."

"Should you officially be hired, yes. There are other things we may yet require." The younger Miss Thompson still seemed hesitant. "To what wildlife problem do you refer? Lacey already killed the cougar that attacked her this afternoon."

"You're situated right on the water source hereabouts, so

the animals come to you." He wrestled with whether or not to add anything then decided to go ahead. "Same as you've already experienced on account of that ad—anything precious draws bad with the good. The volume of what you're dealing with should be cut down to something more manageable, just as a precaution."

Granger's woman gave a slow nod. "I won't argue against good sense, and we can certainly use the fresh meat in the kitchen. But, if you'd indulge my curiosity, Mr. Dunstan, I would ask how you came to know my husband-to-be?"

"Worked with him about three years ago, when his family started the RookRidge Mill. Granger put out word he wanted the best guide in the area to help scout his location." Chase shrugged. He'd never been one for false modesty. "Folks recommended he track me down and hire me on if he could."

A ghost of her former smile shadowed its way back. "Good way to catch his attention. Jake does like a challenge."

"If it's worth the reward." Granger ducked back in through the entry hall, making his way toward his woman and placing a propriety arm around her shoulders. "I like having the best."

"Is Mr. Dunstan really the best hunter and trapper you know? The best man to help keep Hope Falls under control until you can get back?" It looked like Miss Thompson planned to defer to Granger's judgment—maybe the compliment softened her up.

Miss Lyman, Chase couldn't help but notice, didn't follow him. *She must still be with the doctor.* Irritation lanced through him. *I should've made her stop as soon as we hit town.*

"Quit scowling, Dunstan." His friend read him too easily. "Miss Lyman got held up by Mrs. Nash asking whether or not she had a current Sears ordering catalog. She'll be fine once she stops being annoyed that she missed the entire conversation."

"That means she'll be back any moment." Miss Higgins straightened in her seat, sounding vaguely apologetic. "We'd best take a vote before she returns and wants to rehash everything we've discussed and argues against Mr. Dunstan. Surely you must have noticed she's taken you into dislike."

Some things didn't need a response. This was one of them.

"All right. I agree we hire on Mr. Dunstan. Although you should have discussed it with us before offering him the position, I could use the fresh meat for my kitchen. So long as he's also willing to teach us something of the animals on our land so we know how to trap them even after he's gone, I can see nothing but benefits to having a hunter around." Miss Thompson's yea earned her a grin and squeeze from Granger.

"Few ask how to identify and manage the wildlife on their land," Chase approved. "I'm happy to share my knowledge."

"I'll support her decision if you agree to keep a special eye on Lacey." Miss Higgins's brows slanted upward in obvious concern. "Evie and Cora are both spoken for, and I'm of an age to be more cautious, but Lacey is more vulnerable."

It took a deep, fortifying breath before Chase agreed.

"Without Lacey here, the decision must be unanimous—we decided early on there must be at least a strength of three." The younger Miss Thompson fixed her magnetic gaze on him. "But before I go against the wishes of my best friend and hire you on, Mr. Dunstan, I need your word not to meet with my fiancé."

Suspicion seized Chase. *The easiest way to conceal an impostor is to keep him isolated.* For now he avoided meeting with Lyman purely because he didn't know what to expect. As soon as he could anticipate the results of coming face-to-face with the man injured in the mine collapse, Chase wouldn't hesitate to confront him. *Any impostor will be ousted, but the real Braden Lyman would have much to answer for as well.*

If he'd survived the mine collapse to buy up the town, did Braden know how his former company treated the widows of its former employees? If not, would he have to be forced to make amends? Only a frank discussion would clear the issue, and Chase fully intended to have that conversation. Something of his reluctance must have shown on his face as the woman continued.

"Any little thing perceived as a threat to myself or his sister makes him so frustrated there's no dealing with him. I need your word that you'll focus on doing your job so Braden can focus on getting better. Any concerns will be brought to us, or Mr. Granger, before proceeding." She raised her chin, obviously determined to get her way or see him on his. "Are we agreed?"

TWELVE

N o, Mr. Lawson. I did not agree to the arrangement." Lacey
gritted her teeth at the reminder of what transpired the evening
before when her friends betrayed her trust and their own good
sense. By the time the doctor finished with her, the girls finished
making the monumental mistake of hiring Mr. Dunstan.

Looking back, Lacey clearly saw she'd been maneuvered
away so she couldn't make them see reason. While she smiled
sweetly over gritted teeth, allowing the doctor to bathe her tender
shoulder in a stinging solution and cluck at her over the dangers
of cougars, her friends were smiling at Mr. Dunstan.

Of course, Mr. Lawson held no share of the blame for any
of it. The well-meaning engineer looked faintly bemused by the
news they'd taken a mountain man into their employ. Of course,
Mr. Lawson looked faintly bemused since they day he arrived in
Hope Falls with his heavily *enceinte*, newly widowed sister in tow,
which made it difficult to discern his thoughts.

"I wondered. Mr. Dunstan hardly seems the sort you'd enjoy
having underfoot." Mr. Lawson took off his spectacles and gave

her a penetrating look, making Lacey wonder whether perhaps only the spectacles made him seem perpetually absentminded.

The highly polished thin bands of gold encircling those lenses caught the light oddly, and the perfectly round shape evoked a stunned owl rather than a practical engineer. *A more oval shape would do better justice to his features,* she decided. Certainly the man who'd gallantly taken up residence in what used to be the downstairs study deserved to look his best.

Even if he had brought Mrs. Nash to the wilds of the mountains mere weeks before her child was due, and as her brother was the only appropriate choice to move into the women's house. Again, it wasn't Mr. Lawson's fault that they needed a live-in defender against any dishonorable men who might descend upon the house. *That business with Mr. Kane and his rabble caused quite a fuss, though Mr. Creed, er, Granger prevented them from so much as stepping foot inside the house.*

"Miss Lyman?" Mr. Lawson sounded concerned, making her realize she'd slipped off into her own musings for far too long.

She fought to regain her place in the conversation. "I beg your pardon. Recent distractions don't excuse my woolgathering."

"I say they do." He spoke with surprising force. "While I'm not one to argue semantics, the past weeks have offered more difficulties, challenges, and ordeals than mere distractions."

Odd. He seems precisely the sort of man to argue semantics. Lacey shook the thought, and his vehemence, away. "While one undergoes an event, it is as you say. But once something becomes part of the past, thinking of it becomes a mere distraction."

Unless, of course, one can still do something to alter the course of decisions made the previous evening. In that case, the thinking isn't a distraction; it's practical planning.

"In any case, I didn't intend to dredge up unpleasant memories by inquiring after Mr. Dunstan." Mr. Lawson wiped the lens one last time and carefully placed the spectacles back atop his nose. Almost instantly he acquired the familiar, puzzled look Lacey associated with him. "I should have known it would bring to mind your unfortunate attack. I do apologize."

"My attack?" *Planning doesn't constitute an attack, precisely. And I won't feel guilty about waging a campaign to oust Mr. Dunstan.* She squared her shoulders, but found her motion hampered by the mounds of bandages padding her left side.

It must have been apparent, as Mr. Lawson gave her a look brimful of empathy. "You poor, brave woman. I referred to the cougar, but with Twyler's abduction and the previous attempt to storm the house, you've undergone three in the past week!"

"Oh, never say so!" Lacey cried out, wishing to stopper his observation before it could leak out and befoul the ears of others. Dunstan needn't hear it, and Braden absolutely couldn't.

"Your sweet, gentle nature dislikes to dwell upon it." He blinked, looking, if earnest, still more owlish than before. "And I'll not discomfit you further. Miss Lyman, I hope you know you can rest easy and come to me with any concerns. If this Mr. Dunstan upsets you at all, I'll set him straight."

Words eluded Lacey as she stared at this would-be knight in shining spectacles. *How very kind and thoughtful he is.* "I'm certain Mr. Dunstan intends no harm. But thank you, Mr. Lawson."

He puffed up in response. "Whether he intends harm matters little if he achieves it. Your fine nature and fragile feelings have withstood great assaults lately. I'll do whatever possible to ensure nothing more threatens or even offends you. With Mr. Granger planning this short trip, it falls to me to safeguard the few delicate blossoms of womanhood adorning Hope Falls."

If you dip our dainty feet in wax and arrange us carefully in a sealed bell jar, we'll keep perfectly for a twelve-month. Lacey smiled at the thought of Mr. Lawson attempting to preserve her, Naomi,

Cora, and Evie in the manner of true blossoms. Just as swiftly, the ridiculous idea robbed her of all amusement. *Why must men continue to look at us as such weak articles, easily susceptible to corruption and useful only for decoration?*

"I prefer to think we're more than adornments."

"You are." The very edges of his ears, sticking out from under sandy hair pushed down by the handles of his spectacles, became tinged with a brilliant pink. "Much more, Miss Lyman." Ears still pink, he slapped on his hat and hastily took his leave.

"What did you say to Mr. Lawson to turn his ears such a vibrant shade?" Cora came down the stairs looking blithely innocent—the same look she'd worn when she'd first kissed Braden and wanted to tell Lacey she'd fallen in love with her brother.

Cora looking innocent meant Cora felt guilty, though only her best friend—or perhaps Cora's sister, Evie—could discern the signs. But Evie wasn't here to notice her sister's distress, and last night's betrayal was too fresh for Lacey to overlook. *After all, they all banded together to make things difficult for me.*

Go easy, Cora reminded herself. *Lacey's been through a lot the past couple of days. She wasn't thinking when she wandered off alone, put herself in danger, and got herself in a mess big enough to set back Braden's recovery and lose her control of Hope Falls.* Trouble was, the more she tried to remind herself why she needed to be gentle and careful with her best friend, the more worried she became about both of the Lymans.

But the Lymans were a stubborn set, difficult to manage when together and impossible to look after when they veered apart. *Which is why I needed Mr. Dunstan to stay on. Lacey won't like it, but his promise to look after her comforts us.*

"I'm not sure." Her best friend glanced toward the door

where Mr. Lawson had taken his leave. "He gave quite a pretty speech about the trials I've endured recently and how my delicate nature should not be called upon to withstand such aggravation. Unfortunately, I couldn't reassure him, since Mr. Dunstan is sure to bring me still more unwanted aggravation and trials."

"No more aggravation than you'll bring him." Cora moved forward to pluck her cloak from the peg beside the door. "Hopefully, we can all refrain from progressing to trials."

Lacey gave a dismissive wave and fetched her own cloak. "Perhaps there will be no provocation. Mr. Lawson seemed particularly concerned over Mr. Dunstan's presence nearby."

In the midst of opening the door, Cora snapped it shut. "Lacey Lyman, tell me you did not go to Mr. Lawson and make Mr. Dunstan out to be some sort of threatening wild man!"

"How could you imagine I would do such a thing?" Lacey opened the door and held it wide. "There is something untamed about Mr. Dunstan, but I spoke no word against him. Mr. Lawson came to me with his intentions to better 'safeguard the few delicate blossoms of womanhood adorning Hope Falls.' "

"For pity's sake!" Cora slanted an incredulous glance at her friend and went through the door into the unusually cold summer morning. She and Lacey were far behind Evie and Naomi, naturally early risers who somehow threw off warm, snuggly covers in favor of predawn darkness and cold stoves.

After the recent turmoil, it seemed as though the other two women decided Lacey needed some extra rest. Either that or their courage balked at rousing an already irate Lacey first thing in the morning. Since they'd all agreed not to go anywhere alone or leave anyone behind, her sister generously allowed Cora to sleep the extra measure and remain Lacey's companion.

Had I been consulted, I might well have chosen not to sleep late. Cora waited for Lacey to follow her outside, letting the brisk mountain air invigorate her for what was sure to be a trying conversation. Most likely several trying conversations.

"For pity's sake?" Lacey echoed Cora's outburst. "You showed no pity or forethought when you hired the man."

"I didn't refer to Mr. Dunstan, who's shown impressive integrity and will prove an asset to Hope Falls." She ignored her friend's strangled sound of disbelief. "Mr. Lawson's poetic expression of his regard for you is a bit overblown."

"Less an expression of personal regard and more of a concern for the welfare of us women." Lacey paused as though thinking over Cora's interpretation. "Despite his ears."

"Don't discount them." She tried and failed to stifle a giggle. "Perhaps his ears are the windows to Mr. Lawson's soul."

"How ridiculous you are. Everyone knows it's the eyes." Giggles softened Lacey's denial. "Though I did decide earlier his spectacles make for a splendidly tragic disguise of them."

"Only you would use a phrase like 'splendidly tragic,'" Cora accused. "Though it works. No matter how Mr. Granger assures us of Lawson's ingenuity in the field of engineering, his round lenses make him look perpetually perplexed."

"I wonder whether the glass within the frames is equally ill suited," Lacey mused. "Certainly such a problem would cloud his vision and explain why he thinks us such delicate blossoms."

A sweeping gesture indicated Lacey's cheery primrose dress and matching bonnet. "Ah, but you look the part and always have. For as long as I've known you, you've divided your time equally between dressing yourself like a china doll and bemoaning the way every man you meet persists in treating you like one."

"My wardrobe proclaims me a lady." Lacey shot her an indignant glower, and Cora knew her friend added that assessment to a remembered list of recent betrayals of her trust. But her best friend chose not to comment on the notion that Cora should show more support and less sarcasm. Instead she busied herself. Anyone who didn't know her would think it mere preening, but Cora knew Lacey used the time to compose her reply. Lacey might tend to speak before she thought, but she'd confided long ago that tending her ensemble offered enough distraction to keep her thoughts from flying free willy-nilly.

So neither woman spoke as Lacey stopped walking to tuck a single errant hair back into her coiffure and fluff the lace frilling her high collar. Then she rested a hand over her injured shoulder to make a solemn declaration. "Yet one must look beyond mere design. Much of the merit of any piece lies in the strength of the fabric from which it is cut. I am made of stronger stuff than most assume; they should look more closely."

Cora reached out to grasp her friend's hand. "How you relate anything and everything to one's clothing constantly surprises me. You're absolutely right." She could agree with that much and knew Lacey was sore in need of hearing she was right about something. Anything. "But that's not the way things work. People—men in particular—will judge by sight and behave accordingly. Some will manipulate, others destroy, and a very few will attempt to protect and preserve your beauty."

Lacey's laugh startled her, but boded well. "Protect and preserve. . ." She snickered as they reached Evie's kitchen. "Do you know, as he spoke I fought the strangest image of Mr. Lawson dipping my feet in a vat of wax and trying to seal me within a bell jar? All the better to keep me safe, you know."

"Then to be placed atop a nice pedestal?" Cora caught the giggles, too. "Because you're a blossom adorning Hope Falls?"

"I told Mr. Lawson I'm more than an adornment. Despite what he and Mr. Dunstan seem to believe." Giggles gone, a dangerous glint entered Lacey's eyes. The same glint Cora remembered from when her best friend hatched a plot to humiliate a foolish man who'd dared insult Cora at a dinner party, succeeding so well Mr. Dinper left town to visit relatives the next day. The *same* glint Lacey sported when she suggested moving to Hope Falls. In short, the glint warning they were all in for a lot of trouble.

"What's more, I intend to prove it."

THIRTEEN

H ow do you want to do this?" Jake tracked Dunstan where his friend camped out in the woods near town. The previous evening the women ate apart from the men, leaving Jake to explain about the incident with Twyler while they avoided any potential fray.

Jake didn't blame them. Even with the worst of the rabble forced onto a train out of town, every man left in Hope Falls nursed bruised knuckles and egos from the town-wide brawl the day before. If they caught sight of a woman, each and every one would start yammering, either bragging how they bested another man or bawling for sympathy over an underserved assault.

And they'd be barking up the wrong tree. None of the Hope Falls women had any patience for fools who began brawls, exacerbated one, or opened his fat mouth in a way sure to make his defeated opponent demand a rematch. Only the men who sustained their injuries trying to end the brouhaha would be welcomed warmly by the women. But Clump, Lawson, and Riordan wouldn't ask for accolades, even when they could use the aid.

Not even Lawson, the mild-tempered engineer, nor Clump, nor the behemoth Scots-Irish bear of a logger escaped without a bruised rib or two. The only three men unmarked by the town-wide scuffle were a bedridden Braden Lyman, his doctor, and the squeamish Mr. Draxley. This last reportedly took to his heels at the first sign of trouble and hid out in the telegraph office.

These men, along with the women who brought out the worst in them, all became Dunstan's motley mess the moment Jake left. *No wonder he's glaring at me fit to tear a strip from my hide.*

Jake held up his hands to both apologize and ward off that glower. "Dumb question. You don't *want* to deal with any of this at all. But you're going to, so I'd like to know your plan."

Dunstan grunted, yanking tent pegs from the ground in orderly succession. "Seeing as how you didn't tell your men why I'm here, I'll have to start there. Clump and Riordan already spread the word about yesterday's clash by the train tracks, so the others will circle with caution before challenging me."

"I forgot your tendency to predict human behavior as though you were still dealing with wildlife." Jake chuckled. "Even worse, you're right. Clump and Riordan's praise establishes you as someone not to be messed with, but it's Williams's silence that cements your reputation. I can't tell you how impressed everyone is that you managed to shut his yap for a while."

"Didn't hit him hard enough to break his jaw. Why'd he stop wagging it?" Dunstan plunged the pegs in a small canvas sack, folded his one-man tent down, and nestled both in his pack.

"For all his faults, and he boasts a slew of those, Williams isn't a liar. If he can't find a way to make the truth look good, he keeps it to himself." Jake riffled Decoy's ears. "But him gritting his teeth tells the story even better than Clump's recitations. The few comments Riordan's thrown out about how you handle yourself finish off any lingering doubts."

"Then I won't expect much trouble from the men. Safe to say Williams will wait awhile before he risks being beaten again."

"Never thought the men would be the ones to give you trouble." Jake grinned, but wiped the smile from his face before Dunstan turned that glower on him again. "What about the women?"

"I'll deal with the women same as I've always dealt with women." Dunstan shouldered his pack and started walking. At the movement, Decoy abandoned Jake to follow. "Make sure they're safe and otherwise keep as far out of their way as possible."

"Keep away from him, Lace." Evie bustled back from the storeroom with an apron full of strawberries. "He'll be busy keeping an eye on the men or out hunting in the forest, so your paths won't cross much unless you're determined to make trouble."

"*Me* make trouble?" Lacey saw red, and it wasn't just the strawberries tumbling onto one of the kitchen tables. *How typical that I'd be blamed for causing difficulties when they're thrust upon me!* "You know our paths already crossed once."

Fuming, she wrapped a towel around her right hand, opened the oven door, and slid forward one of the piping-hot bread pans. The enveloping, yeasty scent of fresh-baked bread beckoned her with a temporary distraction. Reaching forward, she gently flicked the top with her left middle finger, testing for the slightly hollow thump that told of finished loaves. Satisfaction blossomed, lending her a measure of composure and allowing her to form a logical response rather than an all-out attack.

"In any case, *I'm* not the one who hired on new help when it wasn't my place. Granger overstepped his bounds, Dunstan followed, and you did the same by supporting your fiancé's schemes rather than your business partner's wishes."

"Lacey! Your mother taught you better than to lash out in

anger, much less deliver such low blows." Naomi's disappointment twinged her conscience. "Cora and I agreed to hire on Dunstan."

"*I* didn't imply anyone would cause trouble." Lacey sniffed as she carried her loaves to the large worktable set along the wall next to the outside door. Here, where she baked bread at least twice a week, Lacey claimed a corner of Evie's kitchen. "If you see facts as insults, I suggest you look to your own consciences. For my part, I feel I'm the one struck down. When I left the room and could no longer speak for myself, rather than looking out for my interests—*our* interests—and giving me a voice in the proceedings, you deliberately undermined me."

You wanted me out of the way, so you could do what you wanted. Same as Papa and Braden. She drew a shaky breath, focusing intently on her small corner of the kitchen and excluding the rest of the room the same way they'd excluded her the night before. Let them talk among themselves now; she wasn't ready to listen to any excuses. Not when Evie started out by throwing down the gauntlet and accusing Lacey of stirring up trouble. The other women could look to themselves.

Lacey would look to her loaves. Only here, a safe distance away from the flurry of activity and pots bubbling atop the stove, did she turn loaves from their pans, tap their bottoms, and pronounce another batch ready to cool atop the windowsill. For a loaf to slice well, without the bread squishing down into sad smooshes, it needed cooling for two or three hours.

Bread is easy that way, Lacey acknowledged. *My temper heats, and I haven't finished cooling down by the next day!* But tempers weren't loaves of bread popped in the oven and baked. *It takes repeated tries before someone manages to fire my temper.*

She placed the two loaves on the sill, took a crock of butter, and regreased the pans before setting the next two loaves— already neatly rolled with ends folded beneath—inside. With their seam-sides down and tops bathed in a generous brushing of melted butter, this next batch would take about three quarters of an hour to complete a second rising.

Lacey peeked beneath the towels covering two waiting pans, judged these loaves roughly doubled in size, and lightly pressed the tip of her finger near the edge to see if an indentation remained. It did. Those towels went to cover the latest batch. These were off to the oven, and Lacey returned to her station before any of the other women caught her in their conversation.

Mr. Dunstan managed to ignite my temper in such a short time, she marveled. *Did he intend to, or did he blunder into it?* Maybe he got on her bad side purely by behaving like every other man who'd told her she couldn't possibly take care of herself.

Huffing at the insulting notion, she pulled her largest bowl across the table, whisked away its cover, and pressed in two fingers to the depth of her first joint. The dough did not spring back, having risen sufficiently for the next phase. This, though Lacey was loath to admit it, was her favorite part of baking bread. In fact, watching cook punch the dough down, turn it out upon a floured tabletop, and begin kneading the mixture so fascinated her as a child she begged to learn.

There'd been no time before, nor since, when she'd seen a woman permitted to punch anything, much less push and pull and test her strength against it. The power of imposing one's will on something else and forcing it into the form of one's choosing, Lacey knew well, was a privilege enjoyed only by men.

Entirely unfair! She cried against this injustice as she rolled up her sleeve and punched the dough, feeling it billow about her fist before deflating far lower. *I'm capable!* She turned the dough atop her floured table, sprinkled it with still more flour, and folded the whole of it toward herself.

There's no reason I can't learn new things. She pushed down with the heels of her hands, feeling the cool mass obey her motions as she folded it again. *Find new interests.* Lacey spun the lump a quarter turn before pulling it back. *And master them!*

She rhythmically worked the mound for a couple of moments before reaching for her knife. A swift, decisive stroke severed it in two. A few swift motions, and two smooth balls sat beneath their towel for a brief rest. Next she'd use a pin to flatten each ball then tightly roll them into the desired loaves.

"Are you even listening?" A voice almost directly beside her ear made Lacey jump. Naomi reared back, as startled as she. But her cousin recovered more quickly, disapproval tightening her features. "That's what I thought. You spoke your piece and didn't bother listening to anyone else's. For shame, Lacey."

"I don't have time for remonstrances." Lacey knew from practice she'd have just enough time to mix another batch of dough, perform the initial long kneading, and leave it for first rising before the pans in the oven were ready to come out. So she truly didn't have time to listen to Naomi's chiding, even if she'd tucked some spare patience away to call forth. Nor did she feel inclined to deal with the hot slide of shame loosening the anger at the back of her throat. *If I start talking, I don't know what I'll say. Apologizing isn't right because I won't entirely mean it, and I'm sure I'll just make things worse by trying to make it all right again. Why can't they let me be?*

"That's a nice trick." Cora slid into her path, forcing Lacey to step around her. "But we're not going to let you get away with it. You can't just opt out of a conversation."

"Why not?" She dodged Cora and kept on moving.

The first time she'd tried to make a dozen loaves in one morning, she'd run about breathless for hours, always a step behind. The next time she treated the entire production as a painstaking ballet of baking, allowing significant lengths of time between the starts and stops of each stage so she wouldn't miss a step. It worked, but it took an entire day.

So the third time, Lacey choreographed more carefully. If she staggered loaves in different stages of preparation throughout the kitchen, moving fluidly from one space to the next to keep each post ready, she finished the fastest. Today the practice would serve her well. Nothing and no one would keep her in that kitchen an instant longer than necessary!

No matter the other three joint owners of Hope Falls disagreed with her plans and tried to block her way. If cooking demanded their hands, they lobbed comments she couldn't ignore.

"Why not?" Evie put down her wooden spoon, an almost unprecedented occurrence when she stood beside the stove. "If common manners aren't enough reason, then because a woman who won't listen to others is a woman who no one will listen to!"

Lacey gave a humorless chuckle. "Now there's a moot point since we've already established that no one listens to me."

"Save the self-pity," Cora snapped. "Braden shows no sign of letting loose his hold on that monopoly, and I'd hate to think such self-indulgence represents a Lyman family trait."

"Just as I'd hate to think—" Lacey stopped short of firing back an unforgivable insult. Never mind her best friend accused her of being self-pitying and lumped her in with her sulking brother. Braden's pity party cast a cloud over all Hope Falls, raining with particular force on his former fiancée.

When Lacey herself wasn't bearing the brunt of her brother's poor temper, Cora stepped in to shoulder the burden. And since Braden tried to cast her aside, Cora didn't have to anymore. *What I bear out of obligation, she bears in love.*

Shame began its familiar hot prickle at the thought.

Cora's jaw jutted forward, eyes filled with suspicion. "You'd hate to think what, Lacey? Come on. We're *listening*." It was the emphasis on the last word to tip Lacey back to anger.

"Now you choose to listen?" She reached behind her waist and tugged at her apron strings. "Then hear this much, ladies. If you can choose to listen only when you want to, but deny me the same right"—the knot gave way and she whipped the apron off triumphantly, balling it up and tossing it atop her table—"then I can at least choose whether or not I wish to speak."

With that she left the ladies and the loaves to their own devices. Because, while Lacey didn't have anything to say to the women, she found she had a lot to say to someone else.

All she had to do now was find him.

And when she did, she'd make good and sure he listened.

Chase could hear her coming from a mile away—and so could any animal he might have hoped to bring to the dinner table. Not that it mattered. Once he identified one of the women blundering around the mountainside without the benefit of an escort—or basic common sense—he knew he'd be cutting his hunting short.

There go my plans to reassure the women they made the right decision. Without any game to prove his skill, Chase still relied on Granger's word to prove his worth. It didn't sit well.

Grudgingly, he engaged the safety on his shotgun and slid it through the leather straps across his back. He palmed his pistol and retraced a few steps before veering off to look over the edge of a bluff. A wise man never traveled through the wilderness unaware of his surroundings. Or unarmed against them.

Decoy trotted after, poking his nose over the rock facing and peering toward their stalker with misplaced enthusiasm. His panting shifted into the louder, more huffing version Chase knew signaled a particularly happy dog. Eyes widened, tongue lolling out, and tail wagging, Decoy clearly approved of the view below.

Most men would, Chase admitted as he watched the trim figure weaving through the trees. Clad in green, she blended more easily with her surroundings than she'd managed yesterday, but Lacey Lyman's ruffled skirts and overblown headgear still stuck out like a peacock among pigeons.

FOURTEEN

Pretty. . .but loud.

The excess fabric of her skirts rustled with every move she made, the heels—and Chase had no doubt they were higher than strictly necessary—of her boots rang at random intervals whenever her steps struck stone. But more than that. . .the daft woman was talking to herself. Chase couldn't quite make it out, but furious mutterings made their way up the mountainside.

He strained to hear, but the wind carried the words away, and eventually he gave it up as a bad job. Now the question was whether to start down, head her off, and traipse her back to town. . .or wait for her to find him. The obvious answer would be the former, as he might be able to return to his plans for the day afterward. But surprising her in the woods yesterday earned him nothing but enmity. Chase got the impression Miss Lyman had too much experience having her every move tracked by men.

The more intriguing option was to let her turn the tables and see how long it would take the intrepid Miss Lyman to find him. Because, oddly enough, in spite of his typical caution not to alter the landscape as he passed through, Miss Lyman seemed eerily good at tracing his path. Was it luck? Instinct?

Certainly it was worth waiting awhile to find out. Besides, the hike could siphon some of the wind from her sails before she caught hold of him. Chase may not know what the mutters said, but a man would have to be a fool not to know they meant the same thing as a snake's rattle. *Beware and back away.*

In this case, he'd settle for not getting close. Mind made up, Chase eased back and brushed aside some rocks and rubble before settling in. Dipping into his side pack, he drew out one of the biscuits Granger brought him that morning. Chase had already eaten a hearty helping of his own flapjacks by then, but biscuits traveled well, so he'd brought them along for lunch.

Still. . .Chase rarely ate food he hadn't cooked himself or at least seen prepared. He'd seen too many men retch their guts out after a poorly made meal not to take precautions. He split the bread open, noting its light, flaky texture with approval before lifting it to his nose and giving a cautious sniff.

Butter. He'd bet these smelled even better fresh from an oven. Chase peeled off a layer and looked at Decoy, who sat stiffly at attention, eyes fixed on the biscuit. The drool pooling between his paws showed his assessment of the biscuit. Chase tossed the piece, watching the dog catch and swallow the treat by thrusting his massive head forward. He didn't move another muscle. Or chew. But then, Decoy never chewed. He just gulped down whatever food came his way before turning plaintive brown eyes toward Chase as though to ask, "Where did it go?"

He grinned, shook his head, and sank his teeth into the biscuit. *Good as it looks.* Chase chewed a moment then conceded. "Better." He dug around in his pack, unearthed some cheese, and made a nice snack for himself as the muttering drew nearer. By the time he finished, he could make out the words.

"So very bright out here today. Should've brought my parasol." A scuffle that sounded as though she almost lost her footing. "Really must order more sensible footwear. Naomi was right, though only about the boots. Not about *that man.*"

Chase held little doubt who "that man" might be, and his suspicions were confirmed when her short silence ended.

"And where *is* he?" Frustration made her huffy—or was it the climb? "Up ahead is all rock, and there'll be no boot prints."

Ah, she's worried. Chase put a hand on the ground, preparing to lever himself up. Now he knew how she followed him. There was no reason to wait longer and cause her distress. Who knew? Perhaps she'd even be glad to see him at this point.

"Wouldn't that be just like a man?" Her gripe froze him.

He'd gathered she didn't hold a high opinion of his gender, but that made no sense. *Wouldn't* what *be just like a man?*

"Lead you down the pretty path, show you just enough to get you interested and make you think you're really getting somewhere, and then cut you off with nothing to go on and no way to follow." Her footsteps halted on the other side of a large boulder, her voice taking on a deeper note as though mimicking someone from her past. "Oh no, Lacey, it's too dangerous. Run along back now, Lacey, you don't want to think for yourself or do anything interesting or try something new, do you?"

"Is that what you're doing?" Chase cut her off before she gained more steam with this speech. Interesting as it was, he knew she'd never forgive him if he heard more of the depth of what angered her about men. And since she stood a few steps away, he couldn't pretend not to hear, nor find a way to avoid her. The best he could do was break in before it got worse.

Though, from the expression on her face when she saw him turn the corner, he should have done a better job of it.

Things couldn't be worse! Lacey bit back a shriek of rage as Chase Dunstan loped around the boulder, clearly having heard her giving vent to her ire over being treated like a china doll.

There went all her plans to track him down unawares and explain to him, calmly and in a manner so utterly authoritative and superior he had no alternative but to accept her direction, the things she expected of him. Instead of looking impressed by his coolly collected employer, Chase Dunstan looked as though he was barely managing not to laugh at her foolish tirade.

Why must my mouth always ruin my best-laid plans? Lacey struggled not to turn around and march back down the mountainside, away from the site of her humiliation. Lymans didn't back down after all. *Oh yes. Because whenever I'm around people, I keep having to bite my tongue. So the moment I feel free to unleash my thoughts, they fly about and batter everything and everyone nearby.*

That's why I wait until I'm alone. But I'm never allowed to be alone anymore! Frustration mounting, Lacey eyed Chase Dunstan with growing dislike. *Not even when I think I'm by myself can I be safe with this man on the loose. Which is part of the reason I didn't want him here!*

And, most likely, part of the reason everyone else does. The sudden realization drained her. The anger, seething and swelling beneath her every step, carried her along this far. But sorrow made for a far weightier companion. Lacey acknowledged her friends might have a point in wanting to keep her more tempestuous side tucked away. It was safer for them. Maybe safer for her, too. *But it's boring. And constraining. How can Hope Falls become everything I came here to escape?*

She raised a hand to rub the bridge of her nose, hoping to ward off an impending headache. The resulting sting in her shoulder made her gasp, realizing she'd been far more active than the doctor authorized after her cougar run-in yesterday. Worse, her gasp made Dunstan's eyes narrow, bringing her an awareness that she hadn't responded to his question.

"What?" Lacey tried to sound unconcerned, but rather thought she might have sounded confused because Dunstan's expression softened slightly. There, in the way the lines of his jaw became less tense and his brows rose a fraction.

"I asked if that was what you were doing," he repeated, reaching for her elbow and leading her to sit upon the large boulder's smaller cousin nearby. "Trying something new, I mean. Most don't find solitary walks overly interesting, and it's obvious the women of Hope Falls already think for themselves."

"Oh?" Suspicion tinged the question, but his answering smile hid no barb. "Well. . ." She relaxed a bit but played for time as she answered. "If you were never allowed to do it, you might not think so little of going for a walk alone, you know."

"You mistake me." He answered after a lengthy pause, during which he seemed to be considering her limitations. He sank down, resting lightly upon his heels and drawing her arm forward to rest upon her knees, where it didn't pull against her bandages. "I spend a great deal of time walking alone. I enjoy it."

"Though I doubt I'll ever be allowed enough experience to form an opinion, I might share your affinity for the pastime. I envy you the freedom to explore it, Mr. Dunstan." She cocked her head to the side, stretching her neck. Honesty compelled her to add, "Though I doubt walking alone is what you meant earlier."

Again, the fleeting hint of a smile, gone before she could be sure. "I hoped talking to yourself ranked as a new activity."

"I'm afraid not," she confessed. "I find I'm good company for those times when I've something controversial or unpleasant to say and don't wish to burden others with the conversation. Or, conversely, they make it clear they don't wish to hear it."

"Airing your grievances, so to speak." He pushed back to his feet and offered her his hand, his expression inscrutable.

"Precisely." She took it, startled by the warmth of his strong grasp as he led her over the rocks and back to the earthen portion of the path she'd traversed on her way to him.

"If you've a grievance against me"—his grip tightened when she began to draw her hand back—"I would listen, Miss Lyman."

She'd tracked him down to give him a piece of her mind and demand his cooperation, but now that he asked for her thoughts, she found herself reluctant to share them. After all. . .

"It is not your fault you can enjoy more freedom in my town than I myself will be afforded. But it chafes, Mr. Dunstan. It rankles that you were hired—twice—without my approval and, indeed, once despite my express displeasure at the prospect."

She met his gaze unflinchingly, waiting for some response. He offered none, but did not break the eye contact. Nor did he release her hand from the reassuring warmth of his own. *We are stuck together, he and I,* she mused. *So long as he remains, and that is something I accept I have no say in, we must be allies. I don't know how much to trust him, but I know enough to be honest with the basics he must have surmised by now.*

So she plunged forward. "I do not know you, but you have seen me at my lowest point and that concerned me. My workers must not perceive me—nor any of us women—as weak. And recent events have greatly undermined us in that regard."

Here she stopped. She saw no need to share more about those recent events than he might already know. No doubt Granger shared whatever particulars he felt pertinent—and no doubt even that was more detail than Lacey cared for Mr. Dunstan to be told. For instance, he might already know about Twyler's abduction and her subsequent rescue, which was not something she wanted running through his mind whenever he looked at her.

It simply didn't put one in a flattering light. *Not,* she caught herself, *that I want Mr. Dunstan to flatter me.* But almost being crammed into the base of a dead tree hardly ranked as an identifier to inspire respect or establish her authority.

"I see." He gave a single nod and released her hand.

What he saw remained a mystery, but he looked far more businesslike. Never mind the sudden chill now that his hand didn't hold hers and he'd turned the intensity of his gaze away.

She pressed onward. "We're trying to accomplish something entirely new here. Not just the sawmill—there are other sawmills. But women as partners in business and managers of property, capable of more than adorning a man's life and home."

A long moment of silence stretched between them, pulling her nerves before he finally gave voice to his response.

"Capable is not the same thing as able. In business, there are allowances which must be made, and many will not be willing to concede them to women." He reached down to rub Decoy's ears. "It is both a surprise and mystery how women run a town at all."

"And no doubt it will be an even greater surprise and mystery to many when we turn it into the most successful sawmill in these parts, Mr. Dunstan." She squared her shoulders. "But make no mistake. We will succeed. Come what may, whatever price we must pay, Hope Falls will be the proof of what women can do."

He looked up so fast it seemed his neck might crack, and his eyes narrowed to dangerous slits. "With the help of men."

"Why not?" She barely kept herself from taking a step back, so intense had he become. "Women helped men for centuries."

"Be careful what deals you strike and where you find yourself compromising, Miss Lyman. Some decisions cost dear."

"I know, Mr. Dunstan." She drew a deep breath, pushing back thoughts of Braden's anger, of the unsuitable suitors swarming Hope Falls intending to court herself and Naomi, of the many mishaps they'd already encountered. *Surely things will improve?*

She steeled herself to finish. "No cost can be too great to gain one's dream and further one's freedom."

"Don't even think about moving," Braden ordered. "It's my turn."

Cora blinked at him. "No, you just moved your knight, and I've still not gone. It simply takes me longer to strategize."

"Strategize?" He gave a snort loud enough to make an ox proud. "Is that what they call cheating these days? If so, I don't know why I'm surprised to find you excel at it."

Refusing to rise to his bait, Cora moved her rook and took one of his pawns, carefully lining it with two others along the left side of the board as her fiancé continued his diatribe.

"Though you sell yourself short. You, along with our sisters, are swift enough in bilking a man out of his property." To punctuate the statement he reached over and flicked the pawn, sending it tipping into its fellows and toppling all three.

"That was unnecessary, Braden Lyman." Cora righted the pawns and corrected her errant betrothed in one gesture. "Besides, I believe you'll find 'your property' "—she curled her fingers in the air as she spoke the words—"better cared for and much improved for our brief tenure as landholders."

"Tenure?" Another snort made Cora idly upgrade Braden to an ox with a cold. "Usurpation, you mean. And you sound like my mother or a bitter schoolmarm, calling me 'Braden Lyman.' "

"Your mother would be appalled by your lack of manners, and we'd both agree you could use some schooling to regain them." Her anger, always at a slow simmer these days, became hot enough to burn the back of her throat with words best left unspoken.

"Careful, Cora," he cautioned as he snagged one of her bishops. "Schoolmarms are usually bitter old maids. It's starting to look as though you fit the bill nicely enough."

That stung. Tears needled behind her nose, pricked beneath her lids, but she blinked them back and sought refuge in prayer.

Every time I see him, he reminds me he's tried to throw me over. Lord, how am I to continue to love him when he's not the Braden I knew? How do I go on when the promise I gave is now at odds with the hurt of my heart? I wait on You to bring about a change in him and to give me peace until that day.

Seeking the Lord gave her the strength to respond.

"We both know better. I won't release you from our engagement, Braden, so you might as well stop acting like a petulant child picking a fight." She shifted her queen. "Check."

"I'm not picking a fight." He stared at the board, avoiding her gaze. "I'm trying to avoid a lifelong battle." He moved his piece away from her queen, much as he had been distancing himself from her since the moment she arrived in Hope Falls.

"Men live with the decisions they've made." She waited until he had no choice but to look at her. "I'm one of the best decisions you can lay claim to, and I'm not going away." Cora sprang her trap, moving her own rook. "Checkmate."

FIFTEEN

Y ou should stop playing with her, Lyman," Jake observed. He strode into the room after Cora flounced out, having waited while the two exchanged chess pieces and verbal spars with increasing ferocity. "We all know she's going to win."

"I'm usually better," his friend grumped as he started setting the board. "Why don't you get over here and try me?"

"Because I wasn't talking about chess." Jake dropped into the chair Cora so recently left, but only after he turned it around so he could straddle it and rest his arms along the back.

Braden froze in the act of setting down a pawn then slowly pulled his hand back. "Don't know what you mean, Granger."

"I'd tell you not to act dumb with me, but given the way you've been treating your fiancée, I can't be sure it's an act." Jake watched irritation flash across the other man's face, swiftly replaced by consternation before his shoulders slumped.

"Whatever it is, Granger, it's not working." Lyman gave a gusty-guts sigh. "Not even a little bit. Doesn't matter how mean I manage to be to her, how well I ignore the way she looks and how good she smells, how often I tell her I don't want to marry her, Cora won't have any of it. Says I'm stuck."

If the man before him didn't look so miserable, Jake would've gone ahead and laughed. As it was, he fought for a straight face and asked, "I'm assuming you don't let slip any of that stuff about how pretty she looks or how good she smells?"

Lyman's head shot up. "Hey now! You're not supposed to be noticing things like that about my Cora. I thought you were good and wound up over Evie, or I would've warned you that I'm not going to tolerate you sniffing around Cora for half an instant."

At this, Jake let loose a guffaw. Shaking his head, he hooted, "And you sit here wondering why you haven't managed to convince her you don't want to marry her anymore?"

"Here now, I haven't done a thing to show any interest or soft feeling toward her." He had the honesty to look abashed. "In her presence, at least. That much I manage to do for her."

"For her?" Jake's laughter died. "I figured this foolishness had some twisted notion of nobility behind it."

"It's not foolish when my legs are what's twisted," Lyman shot back. "If you want to call it noble for a man to keep his word instead of be selfish, then I'll abide by the description."

"How do you figure that going back on your proposal—the promise to take a woman to wife and be true to her alone for a lifetime—is anything but the exact opposite of keeping your word?" Jake couldn't wrap his head around it, but figured this was where the "twisted" part would come into Lyman's actions.

A muscle worked in Lyman's jaw, ticking a long moment before he answered. "I promised I'd make sure she was taken care of for the rest of her life, that she wouldn't have to worry about the day-to-day for so long as we were together."

"Well, there's a problem for you." Jake tilted forward until he balanced on only two chair legs, leaning close to the bed. "It's easy to see how you backed yourself into a corner."

"Yeah. It's hard to admit you can't take care of your woman. Harder to let her go." A ghost of a smile passed over his face. "And hardest of all when Cora's so stubborn about it!"

"Maybe you should stop focusing on pushing Cora out of the corner you created and work on tearing it down instead." Jake thought about it for a minute. "In fact, I bet she could help."

Lyman goggled at him. "You haven't been listening at all!"

"No, my friend. You haven't been thinking." Jake allowed all four legs of the chair to crash back to the ground. "Your problem isn't that you're oh-so-noble about keeping your word. If you think about it, you made promises that cancelled each other out—either she could be your wife, which means your helpmeet through good and bad, or she could expect you to take care of her for the rest of her life. You set that up for failure, and now you're choosing to uphold the wrong promise."

"How dare you!" Lyman leaned as far forward as he could, upsetting the chessboard in the process but scarcely noticing.

"How dare I?" Jake got to his feet and headed for the door. "How dare you promise to love a woman, but abandon the effort and refuse to accept her love the moment you make a mistake."

"I'm doing what's best for her! She deserves better than to be tied to a crippled man for the rest of her life. Cora's too great a prize for a failure and a shell of a man like me, and eventually she'll realize it." He was yelling so hard, the veins in his neck stood out in sharp relief. "I'm doing her the favor of not having to fight her own conscience once that happens!"

"You mean you're making sure you never see it happen." Jake shook his head in disgust. "Your problem isn't being too noble for your own good, Lyman. It's pride."

"No cost can be too great," she'd declared in a quiet tone, equal parts pride and determination, trying to skewer him with those blue eyes as though he alone stood between her and success.

For all Chase knew, maybe he did. It all came down to what she'd done so far to get her way and whether or not his newly widowed sister paid any of the price for Lacey Lyman's ruthless streak. If Laura's husband had counted as part of that cost she spoke of so matter-of-factly, it had been too high for Chase. And that would mean he'd make sure these Lymans, whether they be impostors or schemers, paid in equal measure.

If she took part in masterminding the cave-in, Lacey Lyman would yearn for the day she grumbled over the strictures of Hope Falls. She'd enjoy far fewer freedoms and fashions behind bars.

"Then what troubles brought you out to the forest today?" Chase kept his tone light, giving away no hint of the suspicions edging his thoughts. His unwanted companion had already given away more than she imagined—no sense frightening her off now.

"You," she blurted out, brows winging inward in a sudden scowl; it appeared Miss Lyman remembered her dislike of him. Just as suddenly, she remembered her manners. One hand clapped over her mouth a moment too late to hold back her implication.

The woman spoke before she thought, but did she think more than she let on? Had she really cottoned on to the fact Chase Dunstan might mean deep trouble for Hope Falls, or did words spill from her lips faster than she could catch them? Chase figured on the latter, but couldn't count out the possibility he was making the critical error common to any man confronted with a beautiful woman. *Don't underestimate this one.*

He let the silence sit between them, comfortable for him, not so comfortable for her. Only when she looked ready to give in and mutter her apologies did Chase offer, "If I'm the worst of your troubles, things are beginning to improve for you."

Even if he sent her behind bars—and particularly since *if* remained the key condition for just about everything having to do with Hope Falls—Chase wasn't lying. The way he figured it, an attacking cougar counted as a worse threat than he managed. At the least, the cat presented a more immediate, lethal danger.

Or it had until they both shot it. *Which goes to show she may be every bit as dangerous, despite the frills and dimples.*

And Chase, with his own theories about why God gave various creatures certain attributes, didn't have much positive to say about such purely feminine lures as dimples. An honest, hardworking woman of character wouldn't need something designed to beguile. Nor would she stoop to using hers against men.

He'd noticed Miss Thompson—Granger's intended, not the one claiming to be Braden Lyman's fiancée—had a dimple as well. It begged the question how a man like him wound up in a town where roughly half the feminine population showed the trait. But the chef didn't wield hers the way Miss Lyman did as she flashed a saucy smile, deliberately deepening her dimples.

"You're an optimist, Mr. Dunstan. It seems we share something in common after all." She flattered him in a blatant attempt to give a sense they were allies. "I believe Mr. Granger told you enough for you to guess that yesterday, despite the cougar, provided a dramatic improvement from the day before it?"

If the woman had a parasol, she'd be twirling it. Chase took in her newly demure stance, gentle smile, and vulnerable gaze, assessing the picture she manufactured so easily. He may not be much for feminine wiles, but a man would have to be both made of stone and around pretty ladies a good sight more often than Chase before he'd stop himself from appreciating one so fine as Lacey Lyman. So Chase stood and looked his fill.

He considered the wide blue eyes with their lush fringe of lashes. *Probably flutters those at every man she meets.* Beneath the fussy bows of her hat brim, worn to draw attention, glimpses of blond ringlets glinted in midmorning sunlight as though enjoying their match. *Curling tongs and coloring? Surely that effect isn't achieved without some sort of womanly deception.*

If they stood inside, he'd judge the sweet rosiness of her cheeks and lips to be the work of pinching or cosmetics—he'd seen his sister smuggle rose stain into her room in days long gone by and best left forgotten—but after Miss Lyman's mountain climb Chase thought she might be flushed from exertion.

Certainly the fullness of those lips owed nothing to artifice, and a man would have to be blind not to notice. Especially with those dimples drawing his eyes back with every smile. And should a man strive to avoid the temptation of staring at those lips and dwelling on what thoughts they inspired? He found himself in still greater danger.

Because once a man managed to look past Miss Lyman's face, he discovered an even more spectacular figure. How much of her remarkable shape she owed to a constricting corset and perhaps even some strategically placed padding, a man could only discover one way. And once that thought crossed Chase's mind...

He walked away.

He'll come back. Lacey wiggled her shoulders to ease their tightness and shift her bandaging so it stopped rubbing. Certainly Mr. Dunstan would return in a moment or so. He must have heard something in the bushes and didn't want to startle it before getting close enough to evaluate the situation.

Which explained why he didn't utter so much as a word before striding away. *Hmmm...he's gone past those bushes now. Beyond that stand of birch. I can't think where he's off to.* Still, no need to worry about their abruptly ended conversation.

Although things seemed to be taking a turn for the better, and Lacey would prefer to finish charming Mr. Dunstan as soon as possible. When a lady conceded to alter her plans, the gentleman should remain present to enjoy her magnanimity. Otherwise she might recall her urge to berate him for his high-handed behavior and again decide to browbeat him into a model employee.

Of course, it became increasingly apparent Mr. Dunstan would never be a model employee. His headstrong, independent ways, coupled with uncanny intelligence, threatened those "troubles" Lacey accused him of in her earlier slip. Only his response, acknowledging her concern without embarrassing her further, prompted this sudden change in tactics.

Optimism and a sense of humor were qualities to be prized and boded well for a reasonable conversation. *Besides, men are more easily persuaded than ordered. At least*—Lacey peered off into the distance, where no sign remained of her errant employee—*they are so long as they remain in the conversation!*

The slight twinge of doubt swelled, but Lacey had the means to reassure herself: *Obviously he means to come back; he left his massive bear of a dog sitting on the toe of my boot!*

A shrill whistle, issued in three staccato bursts, pierced through the trees. Lacey jumped, her surprised shriek almost matching the same note. She did, however, succeed in dislodging Decoy from his perch atop her boot. The dog gave her a reproachful glance before heading off after Dunstan, in the same direction from which the whistle came. The whistle, she rapidly realized, he'd trained the dog to recognize and follow to him.

"He's *not* coming back," Lacey marveled. For an instant the chill of disappointment held her in its grip. She shivered, even that slight motion making the tears in her shoulder prickle. The discomfort jarred her from her brief bemusement and into action.

She took off back down the mountainside, rushing to keep Decoy in her sights. Following Dunstan this far proved she could track back to town, but if the obstinate hunter went in another direction she might not be so fortunate. The dog, blessed with four feet and a long, loping stride, trotted—she hadn't even known dogs could trot, but this neither walk-nor-run quickstep seemed just that—at a far faster pace than Lacey managed to muster.

Encumbered as she was with corset and her full skirts, keeping her guide in sight claimed every drop of her energy and focus. She halted abruptly after rounding a particularly large pine tree and finding both dog and man. *Waiting*.

She itched to give him a telling off, but on the balance decided she wouldn't accomplish much by wheezing at the man. Instead Lacey borrowed a page from his book and waited. For her breath. To lay down the law. For the chance and ability to tell him in no uncertain terms what she thought of his conduct thus far and what she had a right to expect from every employee.

No, not expect. Require. Her eyes narrowed as she watched him, insolently rising to his feet from where he'd been sitting on the ground, with his back propped against the tree, while she raced through the forest, answering his whistle. *With his dog.*

She gulped in another breath, as deep as her stays allowed, while the oblivious lout glanced at her and shrugged. Lacey watched, open-mouthed and with no nod to grace as she continued to struggle for breath, as the man grabbed a low-lying branch, swung his foot up onto another to ascend farther, and easily brought down a large pack. He nonchalantly shouldered it while she remained gasping like a landed fish. For all his expression could have been carved from stone, some indefinable aspect of his bearing told of deep amusement at her predicament.

No, not what I require, Lacey seethed. *What. I. Demand.*

SIXTEEN

She looked like she'd almost gotten her wind back. Chase judged it time to ease up on the ropes before she set sail on her rant.

"Water?" He gave his canteen an inviting shake. Chase emptied it himself on the way down in a bid to cool off then tracked off a ways specifically to replenish the supply. Freshly filled, the water within sloshed in an irresistible offering.

She gave the canteen a look of such pure longing Chase found his own throat working as though taking a swallow. Miss Lyman's thoughts played out across the canvas of her face. Desperation replaced desire as she remembered who offered her the canteen and what ground she might lose by accepting it. Square-jawed determination trumped both to emerge victorious.

"You. . ." She paused to lick her lips in a motion even Chase knew owed nothing to seduction and everything to do with thirst. Looking as parched as before, she tried again. "You think. . ."

Chase thought his gambit failed. He started to withdraw the canteen, only to watch a finely boned hand snatch the thing from his grasp with the deadly precision of a rattler strike. No words spoken. At that point he realized she'd stopped talking without finishing her thought. *First time for everything.*

If he'd thought of anything to say, scraped up any reason for leaving her talking to nothing but the air and herself, here lay the opportunity to start spinning the explanation so it sounded enough like an apology to mollify the woman. Now, while she tilted the canteen and glugged back half its contents in one go.

He didn't. The water would have to wash the awkwardness away without any help. From the looks of it, it might work.

"Good?" Relief rode in his chest when she nodded, took a deeply satisfied breath, and screwed the top in place before passing it back to him. "All right then. Back to Hope Falls."

"Hold it right there!" Water worked wonders. Her voice regained volume and took on a shrill quality Chase recognized easily; most mammals used warning cries to presage danger.

Since his boots remained right where he'd stood for the past five minutes, he didn't take that as an order. He did, however, see it as foolishness and saw no reason to keep the opinion to himself. "Regained your dulcet tones, have you?"

"What. . .ooh!" Something akin to an outraged squawk sounded. "How do you have the nerve to criticize my tone when *you* can't manage to use words at all, but resort to whistling as though expecting anything and everyone to come running like a dog?"

Chase bit back a smile. The woman made it too easy. With a little luck and some quick thinking, he could make it so she would avoid him like the plague for the rest of his stay in Hope Falls. He shrugged. "Always works with Decoy. Until you, can't say I knew it'd work on women. It's something to bear in mind."

Astonishment and, judging by the fire in her gaze, pure rage held her silent before she gathered herself to attack. "Now you listen, Mr. Dunstan. I don't know what passes for manners or even basic communication for a mountain man, but I'm beginning to believe you're unable carry on a civil conversation." The lone feather atop her bonnet quivered in indignation as she finished.

Close to pushing her over the edge now. All he needed to do was squint awhile and say, "Yep."

His answer deflated her some. She visibly grappled with trying to find some way to answer that before throwing him a look filled with disbelief and a tinge of defeat. "Yep?"

"Yep." He crossed his arms and bobbed his head. "You got it right." *Or at least closer than most, even if you don't know it.* "I'm a mountain man because I'm no good at civil conversation."

No need to split hairs about the difference between not being good at civil conversation and not being good at pretending to be civil to people who routinely acted like idiots.

She stared at him a long moment before her eyes widened. "You're bamming me!" Disbelief vanished beneath fury. "And it almost worked! You think I don't see what you're up to, Mr. Dunstan? You think I can't deduce you're treating me with such obvious disdain and mockery simply because I'm a woman?"

"*Bamming* you?" He raised a brow at her. "Can't say I have." Chase never heard the expression before. While he figured it meant joking, the phrase itself sounded questionable at best, and he wasn't above teasing her to regain the upper hand.

It didn't work.

"Yes, Mr. Dunstan, you most certainly have." She rounded on him. "Call it what you will—putting me on, pulling one's leg, playing me for a fool—it all amounts to the same thing. Callous disregard and flagrant insubordination will not be tolerated."

He expected her to go on like a spitting cat for a good while, getting out all her anger and denigrating his character until she got it out of her system and went more docile. Instead the woman confounded him midstream. With one pause, she transitioned from affronted female on the attack to a more hopeless, quiet sort of anger. Her voice lowered, and Chase got the sense the following words weren't just for his benefit. Chase might have believed the words weren't for his ears at all.

"I feared this when the prospect of hiring you first arose, and you wasted no time making a difficult position even worse." With that dismal statement, she brushed past him, apparently heading back to Hope Falls without any further argument.

A sharp tug in his midsection, long unfamiliar but recently reintroduced to him in association with his brother-in-law's death, caught Chase off guard. *What do I have to feel guilty for?* But no man battled his gut and won, and Chase knew he'd acted the part of a jerk too well for a lady to understand or forgive. No matter what his suspicions, until he turned up something concrete, he needed to tread softly. That meant treating her like he would any other beautiful lady who happened to be his new boss.

If he'd ever worked for a woman before, that is. And if he didn't usually avoid beautiful ladies as a matter of good sense. Chase rubbed the bridge of his nose and prayed for wisdom.

Lord, I have need of wisdom. Proverbs warns, "It is better to dwell in the wilderness, than with a contentious and an angry woman." And well You know my preference in the matter. But here am I, with a purpose and a need for patience. Guide me through this new wilderness of women, Father. It is strange. Amen.

Somewhat restored, but not without a sense of foreboding, he jogged after Miss Lyman, determined to keep her from Hope Falls until the two of them could reach some sort of understanding.

"You misunderstood me." His deep voice sounded right at her heels, the only warning of his presence before Mr. Dunstan fell into step at her side. The man moved with the sleek, silent grace of a hunter even when not tracking anything down.

Foolish, Lacey. He's tracking you *at the moment.* The realization shivered through her. Even with her gun, Lacey knew on the deepest level, with no argument, that nothing she did could match this man nor evade him. She sped up anyway.

After all, she'd spent most of her life recognizing her own limits then fighting against them anyway. *Hopeless doesn't mean helpless, and helpless doesn't mean hopeless,* she recited. Which quality she possessed changed by situation, but Lacey took comfort in knowing she always had one. She'd allow nothing less.

This morning the betrayal of her friends and the unchangeable fact she'd be stuck with Mr. Dunstan left her somewhat hopeless. Her refusal to be helpless spurred her to seek him out in an attempt to hash through their positions.

Now, given his behavior, it could not be clearer to Lacey she remained helpless to change him or his treatment of her. Worse, she'd be helpless to alter his impact on the other men if he remained. But now, armed with solid examples in his treatment of her, as well as his own admission of incivility, she had high hopes of convincing the other women to dismiss him.

No matter those fleeting moments in the woods, when she'd almost liked his humor. Priorities must be maintained. Examples must be set. Standards should never be lowered. And besides, "I understand you quite well, Mr. Dunstan."

Lacey refused to look at him, instead keeping her chin high and gaze fixed firmly forward as she plunged ahead. "You disdain to afford me the essential respect and courtesy due an employer then make light of it by claiming to be incapable of civil interaction."

"You're right that I didn't give you proper respect." The words came haltingly, grudgingly. Still, he said them. "But I wasn't making light about my lack of social graces, Miss Lyman."

Lacey fell over at that confession. More accurately, she'd hooked her boot in a protruding tree root and gone sprawling to the ground. *Which might be what one deserves, going about with one's nose in the air when a man makes an attempt to apologize.*

Nevertheless, it hardly made for a dignified position in which to accept that apology. If Lacey were inclined to accept the apology at all, when it sounded suspiciously more like an explanation than an apology. *Not an apology at all,* she decided as she rolled over. She sat for a moment and took stock as Dunstan hunkered down. Besides embarrassment at her clumsiness and the pain in her shoulder, mainly she felt...damp.

So she held out her hand in a silent request for his assistance to her feet, only to find it ignored. Rather than help her up, Dunstan wrapped his hand around her boot. She fancied she could feel the warmth of it clear through leather and stocking, a sensation so foreign she lost her breath.

Though, again, that might have been the fall. Whatever the cause for her lack of breath, she didn't immediately order him to remove that hand from her person. He gave a gentle squeeze. Lacey gasped and tried to yank her foot away, under the safety of her skirts, but he tightened his grip and made it impossible.

Unbelievably, he shot her a disgruntled glance from beneath lowered brows and issued the terse order that she, "Hold still."

"I will not!" She tugged her leg back, attempting to dislodge his clamp-like hold on her boot. For a long, ridiculous moment, she pedaled the air. Lacey pulled her foot back; he tugged it forward with surprising gentleness. "Unhand me!"

And then everything changed at once. The contrary man gave a deep, booming chuckle and did the last thing she expected. He complied with her request, letting go at the same moment she gave a final tug and effectively hurled herself flat on her back. Sharp pains shot up from her shoulder, stunning her.

She lay still for a moment to let the pain to both shoulder and pride subside, ignoring the damp seeping steadily into the green cambric of her dress. After all, a few more moments of indignity could do no more harm to the fabric. She'd tend it later with a solution of tepid water, glycerin, and vinegar to stave off general discoloration. Any persistent stains she'd treat with still more vinegar or, at worst, pure alcohol.

At least this dress stands a better chance than yesterday's pink, she consoled herself as Decoy sniffed about her bonnet in a show of canine concern. Green blended better with forest mishaps. *All to the good, as I seem doomed to plummet toward the ground whenever I'm in Mr. Dunstan's company.* Once might be an error, but twice bore the unmistakable markings of a pattern—a pattern Lacey was loath to sacrifice any more fabric toward.

"Miss?" His hesitant query made her aware she'd not spoken since her ignominious return to the ground. Also, he'd stopped chuckling and moved from her feet to the vicinity of her head.

Now that she gave the matter some attention, Lacey rather thought he'd stopped laughing the moment she'd winged backward. Dunstan even sounded. . .concerned. *As well he should be, dumping a lady on the ground after scandalously groping her ankle.*

Lacey gave an indignant sniff, but it didn't sound at all impressive from her current position. So she tried again, making her second attempt louder. *There. That's more impressive.*

"Don't cry." Dunstan certainly sounded impressed, if for the wrong reason. A bit aghast, too, as though crying females rarely crossed his path and he didn't know what to do with one.

Lacey gave another great sniff to cover up the urge to smile and again held out her hand in silent request to be helped up. This time he responded by helping her sit up.

Then she felt a rough square of fabric thrust into her hand. She rubbed the bandanna between her fingertips, testing its texture. Roughly woven for sturdy construction, made for long wear. Time and use softened the surprisingly clean blue square.

A mountain man's handkerchief. The gesture touched her more than she expected. Lacey slid it between her fingertips for a moment, considering why he'd decided to be kind. Wondering what changed since he'd laughed at her moments before. *He stopped laughing when I fell backward,* she thought again.

"Why were you laughing?" Lacey kept her gaze fixed on the soft blue square, bunching and unbunching it in her hands. She didn't know why, but that bandanna seemed the equivalent of a peace flag if she could just understand this one other thing.

"What?" Astonishment wrapped the word. "You're about to go weepy, not because you're hurt but because I laughed at you?"

His answer, or rather lack of it, made it clear she'd never understand him. *Foolish to think I might. Maybe he doesn't want me to?* Lacey folded the square and proffered it back to Dunstan. "Thank you. I almost never cry, so you keep it."

"It's clean." His lips compressed into a tight line.

"I know." Surprise made her add, "It was a very civilized thing to do, offer a lady in distress your handkerchief."

He looked at her a long moment before tucking the cloth into one of his pockets. "It's a bandanna. And I already told you, Miss Lyman. I'm many things, but I'm not civilized."

"Of course you aren't." It seemed Miss Lyman, in another of her quicksilver changes, decided to be agreeable. "The question then becomes, Mr. Dunstan, what are you? More specifically, why are you in Hope Falls? And why, if you cannot behave in civilized fashion yourself, have we hired you on to oversee the behavior of a town full of unruly lumbermen?"

For his part, Chase far preferred her when he caught her off guard and she was all flailing and ridiculous protestations. He hadn't admitted to it, but it was her melodramatic demand that he unhand her to give him one of the best laughs he'd enjoyed in several years. There'd been no artifice or scheming behind the overblown order—just female foolishness at its most endearing. Right until she fell over.

Then she'd hurt her shoulder. He felt guilt over mishandling his attempt to ensure she hadn't broken one of those tantalizingly trim ankles. Overtaxed, she looked ready to cry, and he handled that even worse and provoked her back to poking after his reasons and qualifications for coming to Hope Falls.

Having said her piece, she sat in the middle of dirt and dappled sunshine, blinking up at him as though she hadn't just tossed a series of shrewd questions designed to undo him. When angry, she'd been dangerous. When logical, she became deadly.

Her first question was easiest and most convenient to answer and gave him time to consider the other two. "I'm a hunter, guide, and best left on my own without interference."

A cursory examination told him he'd be a fool to tackle the second, so he moved on to the third. "Bullets know no manners. Brawls aren't stopped by polite requests. Lumbermen find their work an escape from the limitations of civilization. That goes without saying for most folks, but you're new to the sawmill business, so I'm laying it out as plain as possible." While he spoke he held out his hand and helped her back to her feet.

From the way she'd wriggled and kicked earlier, he figured she hadn't sprained or broken one of her delicate ankles. Despite a burgeoning tendency to lose her balance, Miss Lyman proved far sturdier than she looked. *More intelligent, too.*

Watching her, a man could be fooled into thinking her pretty little head held nothing but concern for her rumpled dress. Chase waited while she shook her skirts, smoothed them, then set about picking off bits of grass and pine needles. His amusement gave way to impatience when she began methodically removing her hatpins and tucking them into an unseen pocket before she took off her bonnet and looked about for a place on which to set it.

Finding none, she tied its ribbons and looped it about her arm before she set about tidying those lustrous golden curls. Patting her coiffure, she apparently considered the job satisfactory because she returned her attention to the bonnet. This time she cradled it in the crook of one arm and began fussing with the bows along its brim as though this were the most important thing in the world. The woman was *humming*.

SEVENTEEN

So practical to accomplish two things at once, Lacey marveled.
First: her ensemble sorely needed tending before she ventured
back to town, else others would notice her uncharacteristically
shabby state and ask uncomfortable, nosy questions.

Second: as she'd once confided to Cora, tending to the tiny
details of her appearance was one of the few ways she could avoid
speaking too soon and allow time to gather her thoughts. Why
this worked, Lacey didn't know. It wasn't, as Braden suggested, a
by-product of vanity. So long as something kept her hands busy,
be it making bread or learning to shoot or any old thing at all, she
found it much easier to concentrate.

Thus, when Lacey stood up after hearing Mr. Dunstan's
answers, she found both outfit and thoughts quite disordered. So
she shook out her skirts and reordered her concerns; brushed off
bits of grass and picked out some key issues; straightened her
seams and realized she was ready to give her opinion.

But she rather fancied the idea of making him wait to hear it.
Lacey hadn't forgotten the way Mr. Dunstan abruptly abandoned

her atop the hillside. Nor, as she set her dress and mind to rights, had it escaped her notice that he'd yet to give any reason or even an apology for his behavior. Lacking manners might explain poor conversation; it didn't explain walking away from one entirely. *Turnabout,* she decided, *is fair play.*

She didn't walk away, as returning to Hope Falls just yet wouldn't suit her purposes. *It's time Mr. Dunstan learns that a woman doesn't need to leave to make a man follow her wishes.*

She relished every moment he stood there, waiting on her every tiny move the way Decoy waited on his. The biggest challenge, Lacey found, was keeping her smile from showing through. To prevent that from ruining her little lesson, she fussed more than necessary with her bonnet so she could keep more of her face hidden. Finally, just when it seemed as though he'd never break the silence and declare her the victor, he spoke.

"Miss Lyman?" The man sounded hesitant, but also curious. "Are you, by chance, trying to teach me better manners?"

Smile or no smile, the fleeting rigidity in her shoulders as she stifled a laugh probably gave her away. Still, Lacey played it out. "Why, Mr. Dunstan. Whatever gives you that idea?"

"Something in the way you withdrew midconversation and abandoned the topic at hand in favor of primping." The words came out flat, as though he'd stepped on them before speaking.

"If I *happened*"—she lingered on the word overlong before continuing—"to lose track of the conversation in such a way as to convey disinterest or even disregard, that would have been unforgivably *rude.* Particularly were the conversation a matter of business. In such a case, my partner would immediately deem me flighty and unworthy of continued association, don't you think?" She ended the lecture—which she'd planned so precisely—with a challenge so he couldn't wriggle out of responding.

"Maybe." The one-word answer wasn't the apologetic

revelation she hoped for. Worse, he'd gone steely-gazed again. "Maybe the person you're talking to would think your high opinion of yourself is undeserved, and you shouldn't try giving out lessons in manners until you've learned some virtue."

SMACK! The sound of her palm striking his cheek ripped through the forest before Lacey even decided to slap him. Iron bands closed around her wrist in an unbreakable grip, their pressure forcing her to turn or let her wrist be snapped in two.

"Down!" It sounded more like a bark than a word, given alongside a sinister growl, but Lacey rebelled at the order.

"No!" She flailed, jabbing back with her elbow and almost connecting with something. No. It was his hand, releasing her wrist but catching her elbow and pushing her away in a spin.

"Not you." His terse dismissal registered after she came to a stop and got her bearings. Dunstan crouched over Decoy, one hand behind the dog's neck, now murmuring low, soothing sounds.

When Lacey moved forward, Decoy tensed. So did Dunstan, changing his hold and saying, "No." Lacey froze at the scene, trying to fit the pieces together. A vague suspicion began to take form, solidifying when Dunstan extended a hand back to her.

"Come forward. Slowly now." He guided her to his right, away from Decoy's head. The dog's eyes followed her, but he didn't move as Lacey lowered to her knees. Dunstan kept his hand over hers, reaching forward to stroke the coarse but somehow soft brindled fur, still making those soothing sounds.

In time, Dunstan removed his hand from Decoy's neck, and slowly his tail began to wag. When he rolled onto his stomach, sphinx-like, Dunstan took his hand from hers and backed slightly away. He kept close, very close, as Lacey made friends again with the dog whose master she'd attacked and who'd tried to defend him in turn. Only after the fact did Lacey understand how Dunstan protected her from the loyalty of this massive beast.

Her shoulder ached more than it had when the doctor prodded it, but Lacey thought her heart bore the deeper bruise. *I don't want to be in his debt*, she protested. *Twice over!* But it went deeper than pride or who came out stronger from this interlude.

This even went deeper than worrying about what Chase Dunstan meant for Hope Falls. Deeper than not understanding why he walked away from talking to her or why a man who disliked her saved her from his dog. The thing that hurt was stranger, less important, and somehow more important than all of that.

How can he know me for less than two days, yet already see how far I fall short of being the woman my friends are?

"It'll take a better man than me to get Twyler to justice in one piece," Jake admitted. Then added, "Aside from his leg, I mean."

"You shot him in the leg rather than shoot him in the back as he ran like a coward," Evie soothed. "We both know the choice not to kill him already makes you the better man, Cree—Jake."

Regret over how they'd met—that he'd needed to give her a false name, that the woman he loved still sometimes thought of him as Jake Creed rather than Jake Granger—stabbed him. He shoved it aside by taking her in his arms and stealing a kiss. Sure, kissing Evie didn't take away the mistakes from his past. But somehow bad memories didn't stand a chance against an armful of warm, soft woman with a warmer heart and the sweet smell of something delicious always lingering around her hair.

"Mmm... Jake...," she breathed, all thoughts of proper last names good and forgotten as they held each other. "Maybe it's not such a bad thing the doctor said he couldn't be moved for a while. This way you didn't have to leave right away." A satisfied smile played around the corners of her mouth, prompting him to kiss her once more.

"You know I'd like to stay," he agreed, ignoring the fact he'd been hunting Twyler to bring him home for half a year. Once an all-consuming quest for vengeance, now that he'd caught his brother's killer, it had transformed into a more tedious chore of tying up loose ends. "When this is over, I'll hurry back."

"I know, but I'm still not sorry you were delayed. If anyone deserves an infected gunshot wound, it's Twyler." Her vindictive announcement so beguiled him, he laughed.

"It's not the complication of his leg—worse comes to worse, Doc will amputate so Twyler can't escape clearing my brother's name and facing his own sentence." He peered at her in the dark of the storeroom cupboard, where they'd gone to sneak a few private moments. The others wouldn't oblige them much longer. "I'm anxious to finish it, put the old away and begin anew."

Light flooded the small room, ending their private conversation in an instant as Naomi Higgins peered around the doorway and cleared her throat. The oldest of the four marriageable women of Hope Falls, Jake got the impression Miss Higgins appointed herself something of the group's chaperone.

A thankless position, but one Jake appreciated. When it came to the other women. As far as he and Evie were concerned, they were engaged adults, and Miss Higgins's interruptions failed to amuse and succeeded in spoiling a fine interlude. He scowled.

"Don't you glower at me." She planted her hands on her hips, only to have the door start to swing shut. At that, she abandoned the schoolmarm pose in favor of propping the door. "Up until you two decided you liked cuddling more than arguing, nothing got Evie out of her kitchen before suppertime!"

"We're engaged, Naomi." Evie's exasperated remonstrance held more fondness than real irritation, but that was just one more thing to love about Evie. His woman loved other people.

"So are Cora and Braden, but back in Charleston we didn't let them traipse off alone for more than a quarter of an hour." Miss Lyman joined her cousin, effectively blocking the doorway.

"Of course, once Braden recovers his health and enough of his brains, we could change that policy. Your sister might well—"

Even before she finished, Jake knew Lacey Lyman won the war. The slightest mention of her little sister and the mother hen in Evie came out clucking. To be fair, he didn't like the idea of a healthier Braden spending unsupervised time with Cora either. The man might need another whack in the head first.

"Oh no!" Evie slipped from his arms and pushed through the chaperone barricade at the door. "As soon as Braden is able to get out of that bed unassisted, those two won't be left alone."

"Those two deal with different circumstances." Just because Cora shouldn't be alone with Braden didn't mean Jake would give up any and every opportunity to hold Evie. He was a red-blooded man, after all. And she was. . . He looked over at her. *Mine.*

"Only so long as Braden's incapacitated." Cora Thompson shrugged, seeming vaguely apologetic without giving an inch. How women managed that sort of thing, Jake would never know.

"If you envy his privileges"—Lacey Lyman gave him an appraising look that chilled him—"something could be arranged."

"Hush, Lacey." Evie didn't shout, but might as well have.

"It's all right, ladies." Jake walked across the kitchen and lowered himself to straddle one of the work stools. From this position, he made it clear he didn't intend to leave before supper, but he also lowered himself so he didn't tower over anyone. That was important for what he needed to say next.

Apologies weren't easy, but at certain important points in a man's life, they were inescapable. Much like chaperones.

Mrs. Nash was resting before the meal, and Mrs. McCreedy—always a discreet soul—had ventured off to go check on her and help her back to the diner. That left the four women of Hope

Falls—three who'd written the infamous ad to bring Twyler here, and one woman resolutely staying by the side of her querulous and now reluctant fiancé. In short, the four trusting women whose welfare he'd placed below his own personal vendetta.

"I owe all of you an apology." This statement had the instant effect of silencing the room; no mean feat even when one of the women was distant and huffy toward the others. It surprised him that, out of all the women, it was frilly little Lacey Lyman who seemed most furious and least inclined to forgive Jake's deception. *Then again, the victim of Twyler's final crime probably* should *be most difficult to placate.*

Hopefully, what Jake had to say would smooth the way for all of them—especially Dunstan, whom Jake suspected bore the brunt of Lacey's anger over how he'd mishandled things so far. Only later, when they seemed so put out, did he realize he shouldn't have hired Dunstan without consulting the women. He didn't regret the decision, but he didn't want them to either.

"There's a verse in Proverbs that keeps running through my mind." He started in full steam, intending to blast through this apology at top speed. " 'Bread of deceit is sweet to a man; but afterwards his mouth shall be filled with gravel.' "

"Since this is going to be an apology," Miss Lyman broke in, a reluctant smile twitching the corners of her mouth, "I'll just ignore the fact you've singled out the one item I bake."

Everyone else smiled wholeheartedly, whether amused by her comment or simply relieved at the indication she had a mind to listen. A little humor went far, as Jake had hoped when he chose the whimsically appropriate verse, though he hadn't known the particulars about who baked the bread. *I assumed Evie made it.*

"I arrived under false pretenses, using a made-up name and letting everyone believe I wanted to work in Hope Falls." His admission sobered everyone in a hurry. "I came here looking for my brother's killer and found myself a bride along the way. That's how I found the truth behind that verse—revenge seemed so sweet while I chased it, but the aftermath is bitter indeed.

"I tried to protect you, but chose to hide it. It leaves me sour to know my silence put you in danger." Here, he looked to Lacey. "Small deceptions have big consequences, no matter the intentions behind them. Please forgive my mistake and know I'll work hard to earn back the trust I failed to deserve."

Having spoken a lot longer than he'd thought he'd need to cover everything, Jake fell silent. And became distinctly uncomfortable as no one said anything. Four women, united by circumstance, but divided by emotion, stared back at him.

EIGHTEEN

Cora stopped gaping at her sister's fiancé before anyone else managed it. Naomi hadn't blinked in so long, she looked as though she'd forgotten how. Lacey seemed thunderstruck, unsure what to make of this and not certain she wanted to examine it.

If Cora knew her best friend, Lacey wanted to stay mad for a while longer, and Granger's humility pulled the rug from under her. Would Lacey forgive him or resent him even more for pressing her already overstressed emotions? Cora couldn't guess. Too much had gone wrong with her friend's grand plans, with no way for Lacey to express her frustration, for anyone to predict her reactions as of late. She was too hair-trigger.

Evie, predictably, looked at Granger as though he'd hung the moon, which seemed an almost equitable feat to what he'd just done. Silencing a room full of women wasn't easy, but, then again, men so rarely apologized for anything. . .and he'd *meant* it!

But how to acknowledge the extraordinary nature of what he'd done, when it was no less than he should have? No wonder they all sat there, dumbfounded and pleased, as things threatened to grow awkward. What could one say to the man?

Maybe I don't need to say anything to him! Instead of addressing Granger directly, she directed her comment to Evie.

"Do you think he might be able to teach Braden to do that?" She glanced at her sister's fiancé, offering a broad smile. "Because if he can show Braden how to admit when he's wrong. . ." Cora felt her own smile fade as the request freed her strictly pent-up thoughts about the Braden she'd found in Hope Falls.

Everything sprang forth, tumbling over each other in an unstoppable tide. Snatches of conversation, hurtful words Cora tried so hard to ignore, threatened to overwhelm her. To the fore rose the memory of the first time she saw Braden since mourning his death, discovering his survival, and leaving everything she knew to rush to his side. The first time in more than a year they'd laid eyes on each other, and her beloved shouted. . .

"Get out!" More and more agitated as she tried to console him, reassure him of her love and dedication, he ordered: "Just leave. . . . I don't want you here."

Things worsened until the only man she'd ever loved, who'd sworn he loved her, too, refused to even look at her. And suddenly it didn't matter so much that Braden survived the mine collapse after all. Cora was losing him all over again.

"She's not my fiancée."

"Some things can be shown, but not taught." Granger's voice pulled her from the bog of her thoughts, his gaze sad and kind. "A man has to admit to himself that he's wrong before he can do anything else about it. It takes time, patience, and prayer."

"I'm giving it all three." Cora sighed. Then, because everyone seemed to understand how much she'd been holding inside, she murmured, "But as time goes, so does my patience!"

If Cora's patience wore thin, Lacey imagined hers reached the breaking point last night. When everyone hired Dunstan against her wishes, she'd lost the last support shoring up her meager supply. Whatever patience Lacey possessed, it had been strained by cougars, kidnappings, and curmudgeonly brothers insisting she couldn't run Hope Falls.

It didn't help matters that the cougars and kidnappings made Braden's doubts seem somewhat realistic. Nor did an apology from the man responsible for provoking the criminal who kidnapped her do much good. All Granger's speech managed was to take away her righteous indignation, leaving behind all the worry and fear to churn her stomach into a mighty mess.

Worry and fear made short work of patience, after all. *Maybe that's why Mr. Dunstan claimed I lacked virtues? Then again, there are plenty of other virtues I lack. What did he mean?* Slapping him for his insult hadn't made her feel better. If anything, it added guilt to the unpleasant mix of her emotions since he'd protected her from Decoy's defense attempt.

So here she stood, plenty of guilt and worry and supposedly no virtues to soak any of it up. Lacey sighed at the hopelessness of it. Then she got to work on not being helpless against it. After all, just because Mr. Dunstan thought her incapable of loftier traits, that didn't make him right!

"Thank you, Mr. Granger." She tried to summon a smile, failed, and settled for a nod. "I, for one, appreciate how difficult it is to apologize for something. Especially"—now a rueful smile touched her lips—"when you were doing what you believed best. Intentions, we all hope, count for something."

I hope they do. She tucked a hand into her pocket and began worrying the fabric between her fingertips. *No matter how often*

I hear about God's great mercy, I don't manage to convince myself it really outweighs His sense of justice. If we "reap as we sow," then that advertisement for husbands will see myself and Naomi saddled with unacceptable mates for the rest of our lives...and it would be my fault! My only hope is that God takes my good intentions into account when He decides our futures.

"Gracious of you, Miss Lyman." If he sounded surprised, Lacey didn't blame him. Jacob Granger, intelligent enough to see the error of his decisions, knew how much they'd cost her.

"Thank you, Lacey!" Evie enveloped her in a warm hug that said what she couldn't in front of Granger. By accepting Evie's fiancé's apology, Lacey began making amends for her outbursts.

In turn, her friend was willing to put aside the argument from this morning. The breach between them began mending, and the hug said it all. The tumult in Lacey's stomach calmed, their unspoken reconciliation giving her some much-needed peace.

"We had good intentions when we agreed to hire Mr. Dunstan," Naomi ventured then seemed to hold her breath.

"As had I when I didn't wish to." Lacey thought it would be safe to speak her mind now. She'd had enough time to think and let the hurt ebb so she wouldn't make things worse. "It wasn't just the decision or even Mr. Dunstan himself that had me so overset. If we don't stand strong together, Braden will have the ammunition he needs to take back control of Hope Falls."

"We know. It shouldn't have happened that way." Cora shared glances with the others. "But you were hurt and angry, and it looked as though you and Mr. Dunstan got off on the wrong foot."

Naomi laid a reassuring hand on her shoulder. "Forgive us for thinking that, after the past few days, your snap judgment might not be the best basis for such an important decision."

"Dunstan doesn't spend much time around other people, much less around women." Granger's observation reinforced what his friend had told her. "Since I'll be taking Twyler back East, I jumped at the chance to have someone I trust watch over you. He's short on conversation, but long on loyalty and ability."

He's right about the short on conversation part. As for any abilities, I've only seen Dunstan display a knack for insults. Maybe he'll improve on further acquaintance. Or maybe I'll improve at avoiding the opportunity to further our acquaintance?

"What's done is done." Lacey didn't want to be angry anymore. Her temper wouldn't change their minds or make Dunstan leave. From here on out, she was stuck with their decision. . .and his presence. "I'll find a way to make it work." *Somehow.*

Chase couldn't believe it worked, but could only be grateful his hunch to visit that particular stretch of the river paid off.

Thank You, Lord! You provided me the means to prove my skill and at the same time a way to pacify whatever lumbermen go against the idea of me filling in for Granger. You are good!

Even when he was undeserving. Chase paused in the act of dressing his kills. Since Lacey Lyman thanked him for keeping Decoy in line, she'd not uttered a single word. Not while he walked her back to town. Not when he turned and went back into the forest to continue the hunting she'd interrupted.

Silence didn't sit well on her. Or maybe her silence after she slapped him—deservedly—didn't sit well with him. If he knew more about women, he'd be able to tell whether his actions with Decoy equaled an apology or some sort of truce. But he didn't. As far as he knew, she'd bypassed insulted and become wrathful.

The tricky thing, he mused as he tied his day's catch, *is that she didn't look angry. More. . .thoughtful. But what was she thinking about to make her abandon her plans to tell me off?* That's what made him uncomfortable. He'd set out to anger her, alienate her to the point she avoided him. *Did I succeed?*

He lifted his prize off the ground and headed back to town in evening's waning light. The closer Chase drew toward Hope Falls, the more restless he grew. Towns always made him restless, but this time felt different. And it was *her* fault.

Why couldn't she stalk off with her nose in the air again? That sort of thing a man could read clear as day. No questions, no qualms about whether or not he'd angered her properly. Instead the confounded woman turned around and *thanked* him for stopping his dog from mauling her when she had every right to defend her honor. Then she walked back to town with an air of...

Of what? The puzzle pricked his curiosity and his conscience until Chase finally admitted what Miss Lyman's mien reminded him of. She'd walked away with the dejection of an old moose, used to coming out on top, who'd finally lost the match to a younger bull. *She's just more...feminine about it.*

Which explained his unsettled gut. He'd meant to drive the woman away, not drive her into the ground. Chase groaned. Now that he knew what he'd done, he'd have to undo it. *Somehow.*

He didn't have time to figure out how before the forest's calm shattered. Chase kept walking, slowing his pace as he watched the Hope Falls workers. These were the men he'd been hired to keep in line. These were the men he'd need to impress tonight to build on his reputation as a force not to be crossed.

Everyone trickled toward town, sunset signaling suppertime for the lumbermen. Most boasted the woodsman's build: tall and muscular, their movements abrupt. By and large, axmen took their steps the same way they swung their axes, powerful and controlled. This helped balance out their top-heavy frames when going over uneven terrain. Chase could tell a lot about a man by the way he moved, and this sort of gait came from experience. Their jobs kept them in areas littered with debris, where a warning gave mere seconds to spring out of danger's path.

Lumberjacks couldn't afford long steps. But what their strides reserved in distance, they expended in sheer noise. The men descending on Hope Falls, with their heavy-bottomed boots and thudding steps, sounded like a herd of mountain goats. Or they would, if they stopped babbling for longer than a minute.

"Wonder what's for dinner tonight?" someone boomed.

"Doesn't matter," another grunted back. "It'll be good."

If the biscuits Chase sampled earlier were any indication, he agreed. When Granger promised him the best meals he'd ever eaten, Chase wrote it off as exaggeration. Now he started to allow a little anticipation. Lumber camps weren't known for their good company, comfortable beds, or easy lifestyle. What kept a man coming back was good pay and better food. When it came to his meals, an axman had high expectations and low tolerance for anything less than good food and lots of it.

All in all, Chase was glad to hear their appetites and their thoughts centered around supper. Their love for a special dish, particular to woodsmen, was key to his plan tonight.

"If the food didn't taste like it dropped from heaven's tables, I wouldn't stay on with no pay," someone muttered.

No pay? Chase angled closer to make out the rest of the conversation. The two hulking men paid no attention to him.

"It's always food with you," his friend dismissed. "Me? I'm working for a wife. There's only two left, so I have to choose which woman to cozy up to. Miss Lyman or Miss Higgins?"

At that point Chase drifted away. He'd already gotten everything of interest out of that conversation. And very interesting it was, too. Granger hadn't mentioned anything about the workings of the camp. Then again, there'd been no need. As far as everyone in Hope Falls was concerned, Chase didn't need to know that these three—four when one counted Braden Lyman's fiancée—women had hoodwinked these men into working for them in exchange for nothing more than their food and a fool's promise.

The whole thing reeked of fraud. Any idiot could see that these women wouldn't lower themselves to marry common lumbermen. Granger's fiancée, the only woman engaged thus far, nabbed herself a successful businessman with a fortune of his own. Bile burned the back of Chase's throat at the idea his friend was taken in, but he couldn't interfere there. *Granger's problem.*

Chase's responsibilities lay with his sister and the brother-in-law sent to his death by Lyman's Miracle Mining Company. As he walked up to the diner ahead of the rest of the throng, he knew he'd come one step closer to the truth behind this sawmill scheme. More would follow as he watched, waited, and went to the mine site for clues. He just had to win the men over first.

NINETEEN

Chase stepped inside, walked to the far wall, and stopped just short of the swinging doors to the kitchen. *Any minute now.*

"Hey!" An excited shout sounded. "Are those beaver?"

"Lemme see!" Someone farther away stirred the anticipation.

"Might be." Chase moved to face the men, effectively turning his prize to the wall. Out of sight or grabbing hands.

"Did you see them?" someone demanded of a companion.

"I saw summat brown and furry, but dunno what it were."

"Beaver." Reverence filled Clump's tone, and he stomped forward. "When you moved, I saw the tails swinging past." A roar of approval swallowed up the end of the German's pronouncement. It didn't matter. Everyone heard what Chase needed them to.

Now that their appetites had been whetted, he swung forward his day's work as mute testament to Clump's assertion. Things couldn't have played out any better. Chase had them right where he wanted them, pining for their beloved beaver-tail soup.

"What's going on out here?" Granger burst through the swinging doors, brows lowered in a stern expression. With all the ruckus, no way could he have missed Chase's victory. Swinging doors did little to block sound. No. Granger knew exactly what was going on and played into it like a master.

"New guy caught a coupla beaver!" A grubby thumb indicated Chase and punctuated the statement. "Good hunter after all!"

"Mighty hard hunting beaver these days," someone called from the back. "Not many left around these parts anymore."

"He's the best hunter, trapper, and guide I've ever met." Granger gave him a solemn look then swept a considering glance across the crowd. "Question is why any of you doubted it."

"We don't doubt it no more." The reassurance made Chase bite back a smile. When it came to men, stomachs held sway.

"Handy with his fists, too." Clump puffed up his chest. "Helped me, Riordan, and Granger get that bunch of galoots on the train yesterday morning. Ask Williams to tell you about it!"

Some laughs, some furious jabs as friends gave each other meaningful elbows between the ribs, and several smirks thrown Williams's way comprised the room's response. Whatever else Williams was, the man hadn't made himself popular.

"Fists, knife, guns. . .Dunstan here's master of them all." Granger clapped him on the shoulder. "That's why I asked him to keep an eye on things here while I take a trip to Maine."

Slowly the signs of jocularity vanished. General unease grew as Chase waited. Now was the critical moment. Either his claim to authority would go unchallenged or else—

Craig Williams lurched forward, face reddened with fury. His eyes narrowed to slits. "We don't need babysittin', Granger. None of us is going to start taking orders from a newcomer."

Lacey glared at the women blocking her way. Had it been mere moments ago that she and Evie hugged, allies once more? Her excellent memory must, for once, be wrong. No friend who was so recently regained would set herself against Lacey. *Again!*

But what other explanation was left for the sight before her? Cora and Evie planted themselves in front of the swinging doors, blocking her from following Granger into the hullabaloo beyond. Lacey attempted to push through, only to be rebuffed.

"What are you thinking?" she hissed, loath to miss anything going on in the next room. "We need to go out there!"

Granger's voice demanded an explanation for the noise, but Lacey lost the response as Naomi sidled up and began arguing. "Going out there is the very worst thing we could do right now. Somehow Granger has to make it clear that Mr. Dunstan is going to be taking his place. The other men will know that means he'll be taking charge of some things, and they won't like it."

"Who would?" Lacey shot back. "But it's *our* town. We're still the ones in charge, and we need to make our wishes known!"

"The men know Jake speaks for us." Evie seemed to realize she'd said the wrong thing as she hastily reprised, "That is to say, they know we speak through Jake. They respect that system."

"But he's telling them he won't be here," Lacey pointed out. "Him announcing that Mr. Dunstan will step in isn't the same as the four of us declaring that we wish it so."

"Exactly." Cora folded her arms. "Granger won the men's respect on his own. Otherwise he couldn't have kept order. Now Mr. Dunstan will have to do the same thing, or it won't work."

She makes sense, a small voice admitted. But Lacey was tired of hearing about how wrong she was about anything to do with Mr. Dunstan. The man hadn't bothered to earn *her* respect.

"We're the employers," she insisted. "We march into that dining room, explain that Mr. Dunstan will temporarily be filling in for Granger, and everyone else will fall in line."

"Right after you see mice turning cartwheels across my

kitchen," Evie added. "Face it, Lacey. You want to be seen as an employer, but we aren't paying them anything but their meals and the slim chance that you or Naomi will choose to marry them. They have their own sense of pride and will only take so much."

"So do I!" Lacey began pacing the kitchen, mind working furiously. Evie was right. The men weren't paid; they couldn't simply fire anyone insubordinate. If, en masse, they refused to accept Dunstan, the best she and the women could do was evict them from town. Which kept Lacey in the same place she'd been since Mr. Dunstan picked up that cougar. *Stuck on the sidelines.*

No longer arguing, they could all hear what was being said on the other side of the doors. It didn't sound promising.

"We don't need babysittin', Granger." A strident voice, familiar but not enough for Lacey to place him, broke through. "None of us is going to start taking orders from a newcomer."

The women shared worried looks, but none of them made a sound. Lacey couldn't speak for the others, but she held her breath to be sure she heard even the tiniest sound beyond. It didn't help. After a swell of agitated murmurs, no one spoke.

At least they aren't fighting. She tried to be optimistic. *Isn't that a good sign that Dunstan can take over peacefully?*

His voice, low and resonant, reached through the doors. "Granger didn't say I'd be giving orders." A pause as more low murmurs filled the room. The men sounded less agitated, but still undecided. At least that was the impression Lacey got.

"He didn't say you wouldn't," the belligerent man kept on. At that, the murmurs swelled to mutterings—a bad sign.

"Fact is, I shouldn't have to." This time Lacey realized a key difference between how Dunstan spoke compared to his detractor. The other man shouted to be heard; Dunstan spoke low and made the others work to listen. It made for a sort of effortless authority, forcing people to hang on his words.

I'm going to use that sometime, Lacey decided. *Against him!*

"I'm no mill worker or lumberjack to be telling anyone how to go on." Now the murmurs sounded approving, if louder.

The angry voice, which Lacey now suspected was Craig Williams, turned jeering. "If you know that, you know there's no reason to stay in Hope Falls. You're not needed or wanted."

"I want some beaver-tail soup!" Clump's distinctive, choppy pronunciation clued her in to the speaker's identity. From the round of swiftly stifled cheers, he'd also given them a hint as to what made the men so excited when they walked into the diner.

"Beaver-tail soup?" she mouthed, questioning whether she'd heard correctly. *Why would the men cheer for something like that? I'd be busy finding a way to politely avoid eating any!*

Cora and Naomi looked every bit as puzzled—and slightly repulsed—as she felt. Only Evie, with overemphatic nods and wide eyes, seemed to understand the sensational nature of beaver-tail soup. Her friend mouthed something back, but Lacey couldn't make it out. Neither did Naomi, nor Cora.

Finally, Evie leaned forward and hissed, "It's-a-delicacy!" making all the words run together in a single breath.

That, Lacey understood. Duck liver was a delicacy. Fish eggs were a delicacy. Some people considered *brains* to be a delicacy. As far as she was concerned, many a "delicacy" should never grace a plate. At least beaver-tail soup sounded edible. More than edible, if one went by the men's comments.

"We can all agree there's nothing finer than a bowl of beaver-tail soup after a long day," someone rhapsodized.

"Been pining for a taste for two years," another mourned.

Pining? Lacey stifled a giggle. She'd heard of pining for lost love, but she'd never imagined such a thing as a burly lumberjack pining for beaver-tail soup. But it sounded like several men agreed with that one—lots of yeahs all around.

Williams attempted to regain ground. "Wanting some soup isn't the same as needing the man butting into our business."

"He said he doesna plan to give orders, Williams." Riordan's brogue confirmed the identity of the rabble-rouser. "Don't mistake your personal grudge for business concerns."

An expectant hush fell over the room. Lacey could well imagine Williams's face just now. Red with humiliation, vein in his forehead pulsing with rage, teeth clenched as he fought for control of himself and the men he so badly wanted to lead.

At length he fired back his last, desperate shot. "If the bloody beaver are already dead, and he admits he's no lumberman with no plans to issue orders, what do we need him for?"

"My cougar." Lacey Lyman sailed through the swinging doors the same way Chase imagined she would enter a grand ballroom.

Effective, he had to admit. Chase didn't doubt that she, along with her fellow females, waited behind those doors during the entire episode. How else could they know what was going on and precisely when to make their grand entrance?

Chase might have taken exception to the proof they doubted his ability to handle the situation. Instead, he acknowledged they listened and waited until only Williams remained squawking. With one birdbrain determined to ruffle feathers, Chase didn't mind letting the women swan in. After all, this was *their* town. Their show. He hoped it'd be an entertaining one.

"What?" Bemused by her beauty and confused by the cougar she mentioned, the men stood around like a bunch of imbeciles.

"My cougar." She stopped at his side, but her smile was for the crowd. "One showed the poor judgment to leap at me from a tree yesterday, so of course I had to shoot the poor thing."

Pandemonium. The woman's innocent comment elicited about

the same reaction as a skunk dropped in the middle of the room. No one wanted to go near the thing, but everyone wanted to talk about it. Questions flew from every corner, blanketing the room. And instead of looking mortified at the melodrama she'd caused, Lacey Lyman positively beamed. *Chaos must be her natural state.*

Abruptly, Chase wondered how any of the men got anything done with her around to distract them. Then it clicked in place. *She did it on purpose, all right. . .and made them forget Williams.* Sure enough, the rabble-rouser stood off to the side, now reduced to fuming in silence. No one paid him the slightest attention.

All that went to Miss Lyman, as she briefly and oh-so-bravely recounted the tale of her cougar attack. "And, to my surprise, there was Mr. Dunstan to help me to my feet!" She directed that dazzling bedimpled smile at him. "He made sure the kill was clean and kindly carried it back for me."

No mention that he, too, shot the cougar. No mention that she'd sustained wounds to her shoulder. Not so much as a word about her abandoned hat! If a man went by this version of the story, Lacey Lyman spotted the leaping predator, smoothly shot the beast, and nearly sidestepped the entire thing.

But I agreed to back her up when asked. Chase gritted his teeth at the realization he'd been drawn into one of her deceptions. *Worse, she uses the thing to validate my presence in Hope Falls, so even if I were the sort of man to go back on my word, I wouldn't be able to. She's devious.* He avoided the impact of her smile as she aimed it at him again. *And brilliant.*

"Isn't that so, Mr. Dunstan?" She, along with everyone in the diner—which was basically everyone in Hope Falls—waited.

Chase fought for the right balance between corroborating her account and maintaining his honesty. "All I can say, gentlemen, is that I'd watch myself around this woman. The little pistol she carries in her purse is more than decoration!"

A chorus of appreciative guffaws told him he'd hit the right note, though none of the men took his warning seriously. *Their mistake.* Chase hadn't come here to keep grown men from making fools of themselves. He'd come for answers. Tonight, however, all he'd get were questions. Of the stupid kind.

"How big was it? I mean from snout to tail, not tall...."

"Didya get a yeller one, or was it one a them pumas?"

"Which one screamed louder, the cat or the girl?"

At this last, Miss Lyman stiffened. Some of her glow dimmed, and she fixed the unfortunate lack-brains with a haughty stare. "What, Mr. Gripley, makes you assume that I'd scream?"

"Because"—Mr. Gripley swallowed hard—"that's what women do, isn't it? Not all the time, but when they're attacked?"

"Miss Lyman didn't." Chase stepped in to save the man. "But she's an unusual woman, just as Hope Falls is an unusual town."

"See? Unusual can be good." Williams, not one to learn from past failures, shouldered his way forward again. "We like things the way they are, Dunstan. We don't need you changing things."

TWENTY

"Life brings change whether we wish it or not." Cora joined the conversation from where she hung back with Evie and Naomi. Lacey and Mr. Dunstan managed well so far, but who knew when that tentative truce might fail? "If the growing needs of Hope Falls conflict with your own, Mr. Williams, you have choices."

"Fewer now that Miss Thompson's off the market." His snarl inspired several men to start muttering. "And you were taken before anyone so much as stepped foot in this place. Seems the choices around here are getting pretty thin on the ground."

"Don't be sayin' things to upset the ladies!" Clump trundled forward, bullish expression on his face. "Yeah, Granger got Miss Thompson's hand—but it's a fool who talks like Miss Lyman and Miss Higgins are anything less than treasures."

"Thank you, Mr. Klumpf." Naomi's voice held more warmth than Cora had heard in days as she spoke to the short German.

"We came into this eyes open." Bear Riordan, so huge he didn't need to move forward to gain attention, joined in. "All o' us knew there were three ladies to be won, and no more."

"Williams is just sore that the cook picked Granger," someone yelled from the back. Chuckles rippled through the room.

"That's right." A high climber by the name of Bobsley, memorable for his slighter frame and crooked smile, wasn't smiling anymore. "Nothin' round here's changed 'cept you didn't win your woman. You made it awful clear which lady you wanted, Williams. Now you cain't have her, you plan to make trouble?"

"We don't allow rabble-rousers." Shorter than everyone but Clump, Lacey nevertheless managed to look down her nose at the entire room, ending with Williams. "From the moment you came to town, you aired suspicions that our ad was a hoax. We overlooked your poor manners and groundless accusations once, Mr. Williams. Don't imagine we'll be so tolerant now that you know better."

"Ah, and when I expressed those justifiable concerns, what did your men do?" Williams spoke more calmly. "I recall them throwing around words like *old, spotted, hideous,* and the like. But here I stand, bemoaning the fact one of the three ladies is taken, and I'm taken to task for being insulting?"

"It weren't so much what you said as the way it sounded." Clump flushed at the reminder of their unsuccessful attempt to keep Williams from staying in town, but didn't give up now.

"Combined with the things he's said before." Lacey rubbed her forehead with her right hand—the signal they'd agreed meant "wait and listen." She'd never used it before, which made the possibility of what she might say next slightly unnerving for Cora. Nevertheless, she and the other women dutifully waited.

Williams shifted. "Things said before can be taken different ways now. It's best to go by my meaning here and now since no one can remember the exact words on a later date."

And now Cora saw where Lacey had led him. No one she'd ever met, man or woman, had anywhere near the ability to recall conversations the way Lacey did. *She remembers things I said more than a decade ago. Williams goes back mere weeks in comparison.*

"I remember, Mr. Williams." Lacey's triumph made her glow.

"Whatever you think you remember," he hedged, "it's best to leave as bygones. Like you said, I've learned better now."

"Now, sir." Tall and balding beneath his ever-present top hat, the veteran known as Gent began what he did best. Namely, admonishing the younger hotheads for their behavior. "You took it upon yourself to throw our ill-judged phrases into the conversation. Don't cry 'bygones' when faced with your own!"

Guffaws and agreement sprinkled the crowd. If embarrassment over hasty words was universal, so was the desire to see Williams get his comeuppance.

" 'Some men know right away which women they're willing to court and which they won't' " Lacey recited. " 'I'm one of those kinds of men who knows his own mind and doesn't change it.' "

Surprise held the men in its spell. Several looked astonished, some stared at Lacey in awe of this new ability. Granger, who'd taken a dislike to Williams from the start, grinned. Williams, of course, looked poleaxed.

But the most interesting reaction, from Cora's point of view, came from Mr. Dunstan. When Lacey first claimed to be able to remember Williams's words, the men were expectant. They'd been in Hope Falls that day and had a rough idea what sort of comments Lacey might dredge up. Dunstan looked mildly amused.

His amusement faded as soon as he realized Lacey was, in fact, quoting a conversation from several weeks ago. Instead of astonishment, speculation glinted in his dark eyes as he watched her put Williams in his place. Mr. Dunstan didn't give Lacey the admiring gazes the other men did, but he stood transfixed anyway. For the first time, Cora found herself wondering what had gone on between the two of them when they met in the forest.

"The lassie remembers it true." Riordan clearly approved. "And we all ken which woman you chose to court, Williams."

Williams kept his jaw shut, but a muscle worked as someone jeered, "Doesn't that mean you should be moving on?"

"Or have you changed your mind after all?" Lacey didn't challenge him. Maybe she should have, but instead she asked the question that gave Williams the opportunity to stay on.

"As Miss Thompson said, life brought that change. I'm willing to adapt to it." A wolfish smile spread across his bearded face. "Seems to me, a woman who pays close attention to what I say is the woman I should have courted from the start!"

Chase tensed. *Williams shouldn't be allowed anywhere near her.* It didn't have anything to do with their differences in background either. Miss Lyman had bested the bully, but Williams wouldn't leave with his tail tucked between his legs.

No. The man wanted to win, he wanted a wife, and he wanted to make her pay for it. His predatory hunger as he eyed Miss Lyman was tinged with malice. *Like a cat tracking a mouse.*

Some of the other men seemed to pick up on the same thing. A low rumble of dissent grew to more audible grumbles. But, as Granger had filled him in, Williams was a bull-of-the-woods. Leader of at least one work crew with an established temper, he carried enough weight to quell any outright challenge.

Sheep. Dunstan shook his head, disgusted with the lot of them. *A man determined to win her wouldn't leave it to Miss Lyman to refuse Williams. He'd stake his claim now by objecting.*

Yet here stood more than a dozen burly men, doing nothing.

The problem didn't lie with Miss Lyman. These fools couldn't know whether she schemed her way into Hope Falls. All they saw was a wealthy, beautiful woman willing to work alongside them to make a go of this sawmill. They wanted her—Chase could all but sniff it in the air. But they were cowards.

Riordan stepped directly in front of Williams and shook his head. At about the same time, a fellow with round glasses pushed forward from way in the back. No lumberjack here. Everything from his slight build to his neatly pressed suit to the words he spoke set him apart from the men surrounding him.

"Now listen here, Williams. Miss Lyman ought to be a man's first choice." He cast a nervous glance toward Granger and swallowed. Hard. "If he's to enjoy courting her, I mean to say. Thinking she would accept the attentions of a man who pursues her only after he fails with another is preposterous."

This one wouldn't last a minute if Williams started swinging, but Williams didn't look inclined to hit him. And Chase knew it wasn't just because the smitten engineer ranked higher. It was because Williams plain out didn't need to bother.

The engineer's words didn't put the upstart in place; they sent a ripple of unease through the room. With Miss Thompson no longer available, every man who'd declared an interest in her found himself looking at the remaining women instead. They knew good and well that if Williams went, they could be next.

"Are you planning to kick Clump out along with me then?" Williams played on their discomfort. "For that matter, how many more of you will be gone when the next bride's off the table?"

"Don't be silly." Miss Lyman's laugh tinkled through the throng. If Chase hadn't been standing close enough to see how tense she'd become, he'd have believed her little act. The other men perked up for her decision. "We foresaw this little issue. That's why we asked you all to name two of us early on."

The crowd relaxed at her reminder. They were safe.

"Williams didn't." Granger spoke for the first time since he'd announced Chase's position. "Only man here who didn't."

Williams looked like he'd been kicked in the teeth, but recovered quickly. "That's because a man should only focus on one woman at a time—then, once she's won, for a lifetime."

Clever comeback. Chase appraised the manipulation and found another reason why the lumbermen might not have spoken up. Brawls would earn them the boot, but he doubted any of these men could match Williams for verbal sparring. *What a shame.*

"That's that then." Miss Higgins, her low voice carrying well enough for everyone to hear, put an end to the disagreements. "No one's leaving but Granger. Until his return, Mr. Dunstan will help keep the peace and fill the stewpan."

"Thanks to him, tomorrow night we'll serve beaver-tail soup." Miss Thompson—the cook—gestured to the tables lining the room, already outfitted with plates and the like. "Now, if you'll get seated, we'll start bringing out your supper."

"If I may ask before you leave?" The supercilious, reedy voice belonged to a thin man Chase hadn't seen before. Stooped as though trying to escape notice and far too pale to be a worker, he stuck out anyway. With sparse blond hair tufted around his forehead and glasses, slipping down his nose toward a twitching mustache, he gave off an air of a nervous rabbit.

"Yes, Mr. Draxley?" Miss Lyman didn't like the man.

Chase read it in the way her shoulders stiffened and her chin rose. She looked down at him with the appearance of polite interest, but Chase could tell she wasn't inclined to waste much time on Mr. Draxley. *How did he get on her bad side?*

"We're all wondering…" He went ahead and asked the question on everyone's minds. "What is on the menu this evening?"

In his interest over the answer, Chase stopped wondering what Draxley had done wrong. During the entire time they'd been preoccupied with Williams, delicious smells had filled the air.

"Fried chicken, baked potatoes, coleslaw, and buns."

"Fried chicken!" Men scrambled for seats as the women whisked into the kitchen. At Granger's nudge, Chase followed.

The second he hit those swinging doors, the smell made his mouth water. Things looked even better. Platters heaped high with golden-fried chicken waited on a table next to baskets overflowing with plump buns. Bowls held the potatoes and massive quantities of coleslaw, none of which would be wasted.

"Now that it's official." Granger took the beaver to the largest pantry Chase ever saw. "Welcome to Hope Falls."

"Haven't you left yet?" Braden's truculent greeting warmed Lacey's heart the next morning. "With you not showing your face in three days, I'd started to hope you had a change of heart."

"In a short time, we've managed to hire on a crew of workers, chosen a mill site, and are pulling up the stumps to finish clearing it. By now I hoped you'd want this sawmill enough to stop asking us to leave." Lacey pulled up a seat beside the bed, refusing to let him disconcert her.

He harrumphed. "Between Evie's cooking for motivation and Granger's know-how to get things moving, you've gotten farther than I expected. I'd say you're lucky, but we both know better."

Not even five minutes, and he's angling to bring up that incident with Twyler. She gritted her teeth. Some small part of her had hoped her older brother, whom she used to look up to, would be supportive after her ordeal. Failing that, she'd try to avoid the worst of the conversation by skirting tricky topics. *I'd best pretend I don't know where he's heading with that.*

"It takes more than luck to start up a business. What you refer to is actually the result of research and planning." *My research into how to save Hope Falls from becoming a ghost town. My plan to advertise for husbands with sawmill experience.* Lacey wavered for a moment. *All right. That didn't go according to plan, exactly, but having the men reply to our ad in person brought us the workers we needed. If they'd responded by telegraph, as instructed, we'd have needed to hire some on.*

"You stole my property and dragged Cora and the others up here on the vague hope you could break into the lumber market." Braden no longer looked petulant. He was spitting mad. "Any success isn't yours. It's my land and Granger's effort!"

"The site for the mill and most of the lumber surrounding it are not your land!" Lacey burst out. "When word came of the collapse, we found our investment in Hope Falls next to worthless. I wondered about the lumber, did a great deal of reading, and asked some of Papa's contacts for their advice—same as you when you started to think about buying into the mine."

Braden opened his mouth, ready to refute what she said when he had no idea what things were like after news of his death. Lacey didn't let him get a word in; she kept going.

"Only when I was convinced of the project's potential did I move forward. I made the arrangements to purchase the other half of Miracle Mining and the surrounding land. Now when I've begun to prove my decision worthwhile, you call it luck? This took painstaking effort, thorough research, and personal investment."

And I did it all alone, thinking you were dead. Lacey felt a stinging in the back of her nose, the earliest warning of tears. She wiggled her nose and pushed the sentiment away.

"Ah, but that's just it." Braden leaned forward, eyes snapping. "It wasn't a personal investment at all. You used *my* inheritance to fund this project. And when you discovered you had no right, you contrived a way to keep control of *my* money."

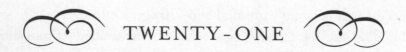 TWENTY-ONE

There. He finally came out and said it. Lacey drew a shuddering breath. Oh, Braden had been griping about her use of the family funds since he learned she'd sold Lyman Place. Even worse, he'd been caterwauling about taking back control of their finances since the second he heard Lacey held the reigns.

But until now he hadn't tried to claim all of Hope Falls.

Lacey started smoothing her skirts and rearranging the way its folds draped around her chair. *It wasn't pessimistic to take those legal measures.* But that didn't make her feel any better about needing to implement safeguards against her own brother.

"You're wrong." She fought to keep her voice level. Whether she fought not to yell or not to cry, even Lacey couldn't say. "I used *our* inheritance. I know I invested the bulk of mine in the mercantile and its goods, but you sank your funds into your half of the mines." She held up a hand to keep him silent. "But aside from those, our father left us each certain assets. You were given the house, and I was given a dowry. That dowry became accessible four months ago. When I reached my eighteenth birthday, you no

172

longer held it in trust." *Not your money. Mine.*

Braden started, obviously unprepared for that reminder. Or perhaps he'd not realized she'd reached her majority in his absence. Either way, the news didn't sit well with him at all.

"You sold Lyman Place." The pain of that loss sat on his face for a fleeting moment, almost making her regret it. Then his jaw thrust forward. "As you said, that was mine and mine alone. Whatever the sale price, I'll expect every cent of it."

"I never touched it." Hurt beyond what she expected, Lacey stared at him. "Lyman Place was sold because we couldn't transport you there, and we thought you needed care." *We thought you needed us.* "Also, when the mines failed, your investors and creditors came crawling out of the woodwork. There weren't funds enough to maintain the house indefinitely."

"But somehow you scraped together the sum to buy land here." His sneer, Lacey knew, covered his shame and anger that his own grand venture failed. "I guess I should be grateful you took what was left and reinvested in Hope Falls. Seems I'll be a wealthy man when the doctor clears me and the attorneys give control of Lyman assets back to me. And they will, you know."

"In a manner of speaking." The moment she'd dreaded had finally come. "They'll return control of Braden Lyman's assets to you. These include the money earned from the sale of Lyman Place, one-half of the land formerly owned by Miracle Mining, and one-third of the property sustaining the new sawmill."

"Not so fast, little sister." Braden slapped the bed. "You're forgetting something. Since you're an unmarried woman, you can't own anything. I'll control all of your share. And since Evie and Naomi invested in my name, I'll control theirs, too. That means it all belongs to me after all."

Lacey sighed. "We were afraid you'd try something like that. It's why I consulted Mr. Rountree about this very topic." She saw her brother pale, as though he suspected. "My house, my mercantile, my half of the mines, and my third of the sawmill lands have been placed in a new trust in the guardianship of Mr. Rountree himself. Not you. My approval is required for any transactions until the time of my marriage, when management is transferred to my husband. The same has been done for Naomi and Evie's houses, Evie's diner, and their shares of the mill."

He was silent for a long time, wrestling with the news she'd given him. And, more importantly, wrestling with the question she'd left unanswered.

Finally, he lost the battle. His shoulders hunched forward, and Braden looked every bit as tired as Lacey felt. The lines around his eyes and the grooves bracketing his mouth deepened, and she decided to ask the doctor to give him something for pain when she left. He'd been overly agitated, moved around too much, and his shoulder and legs must be paining him even more than usual.

But it seemed something bothered him more because the brother she'd always admired finally asked a question Lacey wanted him to. "You didn't mention Cora. What about her?"

"My sister refused Lacey's generous offer." Evie stormed into Braden's room.

Jake watched her go and silently debated following her for a moment. Overhearing what sounded like the end of Lacey explaining how she'd divided her property from her brother's made for poor timing. He'd missed too much to know the particulars of the conversation. The main thing he'd caught was how badly Braden needed another man in the room, now that Evie'd joined in. *Actually, he needs to shelve his pride and come to his senses.* Barring that, the conversation promised to pit Braden's pride against Evie's protective instincts for her little sister.

With news of how much Twyler's leg had improved during the past two days and the doctor's estimation that he could be moved tomorrow, Jake didn't want anything to upset Evie. He wouldn't have much time with her before leaving, and Jake fully intended to enjoy every minute of it. *Right after this conversation.*

"What do you mean, she turned it down?" Braden's roar didn't ask a question so much as demand an answer. Immediately.

"Sounds pretty self-explanatory to me." Jake shot the other man a warning glance. They may be business associates and even friends, but he wouldn't allow Braden Lyman to shout at Evie.

"I offered Cora her pick of the houses in town and the same type of trust to protect it and her share of the sawmill." Miss Lyman's answer didn't soothe anyone's ruffled feathers.

In fact, it was the one time Jake had seen Evie and Braden in complete agreement. Well, *almost* complete agreement.

Braden blamed the women. "Why did you let her turn you down? Contact Mr. Rountree and have him draw it up immediately."

"Why did you put her in a position where Lacey even needed to make the offer?" Evie shot back. "Don't you yell at your sister for trying to soften the blows *you've* dealt mine!"

This comment struck home. Jake could see the muscles at Braden's temples throbbing when he shook his head. How much longer would it take for Braden to stop making his own injuries more important than the woman he loved? If he wanted to jilt Cora and really didn't want her anymore, the man wouldn't feel so guilty.

"It's not my place to make Cora's decisions for her," Lacey pointed out. "As a friend, I can offer my assistance. As the sister of the man who's trying so hard to jilt her, I can't offer much comfort. She sees accepting the trust as a betrayal."

Braden's misery was palpable. "A betrayal of what?"

"Of her faith that you'll recover, you dunderhead." Evie raked her fingers through her hair, unleashing a few glorious mahogany curls. "Cora believes you'll remember how much you love each other and start acting like an honorable man instead of a thwarted child." She left off talking and settled for glaring.

"You know how loyal she is," Lacey put in. She paused, her voice softening as though sharing a secret. "I think she refuses it because Cora equates that trust with giving up on you."

"She should!" Braden and Evie exclaimed in tandem then looked at each other in surprise. For a moment neither spoke.

"No she shouldn't." Jake decided he'd found the time to step into the argument—and hopefully settle it. "If she stops looking at it as a good-faith gesture, she'll let Lacey do it."

"I meant she should give up." Evie colored at how stark the words sounded, but quickly rallied. "She should know by now that he's not going to be the man who won her heart. Never again."

Jake winced at the way she'd said it. He, Evie, and Lacey knew she referred to Braden's surly demands and blunt treatment of Cora. But Jake knew Braden would think otherwise. Although his broken legs were mending, he'd never be the same carefree, able-bodied man who'd once joined his workers in the mines. As far as Braden's narrow vision could see, the best way to protect and provide for Cora was to make her free to marry someone else.

For his part, Jake had an inkling of why Braden thought that way. It wasn't exactly easy to fall in love with a woman as fiercely loving, loyal, and godly as the Thompson sisters. *Evie deserves better than me, too.* He looked at where she sat, hair tantalizingly mussed, frustration stamped on her beautiful, expressive face. *Difference between me and Braden is that I'll become that better man before I even think of letting her go.*

"Step back and tell me how it looks," Miss Lyman directed the bespectacled engineer. Perched atop a ladder, holding a sign advertising FRESH-GROUND COFFEE, she couldn't see that her eager helper was looking all right. But not at the sign.

"I'm not sure." Mr. Lawson hedged a series of instructions, watching her movements with unconcealed interest. "Try moving it a bit to the right. No, down a smidge. And to the left."

Chase strode through the wide-open door, silently making his way to the engineer's side. "Like what you see, Lawson?" He'd spoken low to make sure Miss Lyman didn't hear his warning.

"Oh!" The other man jumped a bit then began spluttering. His ears began to turn red. "Helping Miss Lyman get the sign straight, don't you know. She asked me for my expert opinion."

"I know exactly what you were doing," Chase told him. "Don't let me catch you doing anything like it again."

"What?" Up on the ladder, all trim ankles and round curves, Miss Lyman remained oblivious. Or maybe she didn't. A gently bred woman would know better than to shimmy up a ladder and show off her petticoats. "I didn't quite make that out, Mr. Lawson."

Maybe she wanted to catch Lawson's eye. The thought had merit. Out of all the men in town, the engineer boasted the most education, income, and fine manners. *Could she be that scheming?*

She leaned farther over and nudged up one corner, giving an improved view of her backside as she did so. "Good enough?"

"Excellent." Doubts driven away by the show she put on, Chase answered for the mortified engineer. "Come on down now."

She whipped around when he spoke, looking down at him in surprise. "Mr. Dunstan? I didn't know you'd joined us." She hurried down the ladder, bustled over, and looked upward.

For the first time since he'd walked into the tableau, Chase evaluated the sign. After Lawson's haphazard directions, the thing hung catawampus, as though tacked up by a drunk giant.

"That'll never do." Puzzlement colored her features as she

turned to face them. She noticed the engineer's impressively red ears. "Don't worry, Mr. Lawson. We'll get it right next time."

While she consoled her embarrassed admirer, Chase mounted the ladder, untacked the drooping corner of the sign, and straightened the thing. Done in an instant, he hopped down.

"Much better!" She gave Chase a considering look. "But why did you pronounce its earlier placement as excellent?"

"Ladies shouldn't be climbing ladders." His reply made her smile vanish, and suddenly Chase remembered part of what he'd heard her muttering about in the forest. All that stuff about how limited women were and that she was capable of doing things men thought she couldn't. His words wouldn't be taken well.

"I assure you, Mr. Dunstan, I am fully able to climb my own ladder. You might take a page from Mr. Lawson, who encouraged me to ascend so he could gauge the angles of the sign from below. *He*"—her voice got very sniffy—"obviously thinks me capable."

He wanted an eyeful, and you gave it to him. But Lawson's guilty look confirmed Miss Lyman's explanation of how she came to be atop the ladder. She hadn't plotted the scenario after all—simply been naive enough to undertake it. Relief cooled his temper enough that he offered no argument, only a warning.

"Can and should are two different things, ma'am." He shot a dark look at Lawson, whom he'd have to watch more closely in the future. "Some dangers have nothing to do with your abilities."

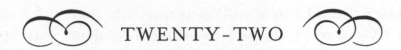# TWENTY-TWO

But I should have concerned myself more for your welfare than for pleasing you by getting the sign precisely aligned." Mr. Lawson resolutely ignored Chase's incredulity and addressed himself solely to Miss Lyman. "Ladders are perilous for ladies. Skirts, while fetching, aren't constructed for climbing." His voice grew fainter as he finished, most likely because he realized he'd said exactly the wrong thing to win Miss Lyman.

"Your concern is duly noted, Mr. Lawson." She smoothed the front of those very skirts as she spoke. As she did so, Chase realized the motion was becoming familiar. It didn't bode well for the engineer. "Though I am dismayed to realize I gave you far too much credit by believing you recognized my ability to perform the task at hand. My portion of which, I believe, I accomplished handily." She left unspoken the accusation that Mr. Lawson's direction as to the placement of the sign left something to be desired. Miss Lyman didn't need to say it.

"I say." Lawson's ears brightened as he began to try to dig his way out of the hole he'd jumped in. "Your work ethic is much to be admired, Miss Lyman. I merely meant that anyone would be hampered by this sort of attire." He made a flourishing gesture meant to indicate her well-tailored suit.

It made Chase take a harder look. Cut closer to the body without the fullness caused by bustles, these skirts looked less cumbersome than what she'd worn to go tromping through the forest. To be fair, the more billowy style would have made climbing a ladder difficult. But the lack of extra fabric made this outfit follow the lines of her body more closely.

"My attire is always appropriate." Everything about her bristled as she defended her clothing, of all things. "This walking suit, in particular, is designed to allow ease and economy of motion without the burden of excess fabric. It's a sensible choice for working in the store today with so much to be done!"

Chase frowned. *They're more sensible, but more revealing.* Little wonder Lawson grew fascinated with watching her bend and sway to shift the sign. Truth be told, Chase would have taken a moment to enjoy the view if Lawson hadn't ogled her first.

A woman shouldn't wear something so different as to make a man look at her all over again. Clothes were made for covering the body and protecting it from the elements, not attracting attention. But the fact was, Chase had been here for three days and not seen her wear the same thing twice. Three dresses, each in pretty colors with flounces or bows or lace to draw the eye.

Hadn't Granger mentioned something about her being more put out by her ruined dress than by the way her kidnapper marched her off at gunpoint and held a knife to her throat?

"You have a lot of dresses." The statement escaped before he thought it over. *At least I didn't come right out and say she had too many.* Chase waited for her to turn that glower on him.

"Precisely!" An enchanting smile lit the daft woman's face. "Something for every occasion and activity so I won't be 'hampered,' as Mr. Lawson so gracelessly described it."

"I meant no insult! Skirts allow less motion by their very design, requiring grace and discretion." The engineer protested vehemently, as though he held strong opinions on a topic requiring very little opinion or discussion. "You epitomize that grace, and each style you choose reflects your feminine beauty."

Chase looked around the jumbled mess of the store, wondering whether anything might serve as a gag before the man said anything else florid and foolish. *It's dung-brains like this that give women starched-up opinions of themselves.*

Spotting nothing offhand, he glanced at Miss Lyman. She'd yet to respond to Lawson's overblown compliments, so Chase figured she'd been stunned into silence. But those raised brows looked more disbelieving than flattered. *Good for her.*

"Thank you for coming to my aid, Mr. Lawson." It was unmistakably a dismissal, and the engineer took it as such.

"Call on me anytime, Miss Lyman. Particularly if you encounter any. . ."—he slid a sideways glance toward Chase, making the pause meaningful before he finished—"difficulty."

If I encounter any difficulty? Lacey bit the inside of her cheek to keep from laughing at Mr. Lawson's earnest offer. *I'm surrounded by men! They create difficulties on a daily basis.*

Not the least of which was their affinity for interrupting her ability to carry out her own business. Then, of course, they proceeded to dictate how and what she should be doing instead. Today was a perfect example. When Mr. Lawson wandered into the store, she'd seen fit to enlist his aid hanging the coffee sign.

Instead of climbing up the ladder and hoisting the heavy thing himself, as any gentleman would, he enthusiastically directed her to hold it aloft, so he could better judge its baseline. In the normal way of things, Lacey wouldn't mind a reason to climb a ladder. As a petite woman, she enjoyed the sense of height.

But after the past few days, her shoulder ached. Worse, Mr. Lawson turned out to be the most horrid sort of perfectionist. Why, she'd shifted and nudged and angled that sign six ways from Sunday trying to satisfy his sense of aesthetic. And in the end, she'd gratefully descended to find the thing slanted.

It did little to bolster her faith in the man's skills as an engineer. If he didn't come so highly recommended, with Granger having worked with him before to judge the results firsthand, Lacey would seriously consider looking elsewhere. For now she'd settle for seeing him leave the store—and her—in peace. Things lay hodgepodge in heaps and piles everywhere, and with the caliber of his assistance, the mess would double!

"I'll keep your offer in mind, Mr. Lawson." She tilted her head. Toward the door. Hopefully he'd take the hint.

"Anytime," he repeated before finally taking his leave.

Lacey started to breathe a sigh of relief when she noticed another interloper. This one stood amid a jumble of goods, intently sniffing a tin pail of None-Such Peanut Butter. She watched, thunderstruck, as Decoy decided he liked it enough to nose the thing over and start *licking the bottom of the bucket.*

"What," she gritted out, "is that dog doing in my store?"

"Where I go, he goes." Mr. Dunstan snapped his fingers, and the dog abandoned its exploration and trotted to his side. The man had the sheer nerve to look surprised at the question. "We already agreed. You called him well-behaved and welcome."

Before he started licking the canned goods. Lacey closed her eyes and fought for calm. "In the house, Mr. Dunstan. Your dog is welcome in the *house.* I've noticed you do not attempt to bring Decoy into the diner." *Evie would've thrown a conniption.*

The man looked supremely unconcerned. "He waits outside

for me. Decoy's well trained, but even I can't expect him to just drool when platters of fried chicken go by. I'm not cruel."

"Not cruel, but nigh unto impossible!" She pointed toward the upended tin of peanut butter. "I can't have him slobbering all over the foodstuffs every time you step through the door!"

He glanced at the peanut butter then took a long, considering look around the place. "Ordinarily, I'd tell you he won't. I trained him not to touch anything on shelves. Things on the ground or in junk piles constitute fair game."

"So it's *my* fault you can't control your horse of a dog, but choose to bring him into the store regardless?"

"Didn't say so." The dratted man looked like he was swallowing a smile. "I didn't expect someone so meticulous in other aspects would own a store that looks like someone picked it up, flipped it upside down, and gave it a good shaking."

Lacey decided to ignore the accuracy of his description. Agreeing would only encourage him, after all. What she needed was to get him out of the way and get things in order. Then the next time he brought Decoy on the premises and the dog so much as sniffed something he shouldn't, she'd throw them both out!

"For your information," she declared in tones that brooked no argument, "I've not yet opened for business. Today I opened the doors solely to capture some fresh air while I worked."

All the goods and displays she'd so carefully ordered should have been neatly stacked and sorted as per her explicit instructions. When she'd first arrived in Hope Falls and opened her mercantile, Lacey couldn't believe her eyes. Not only were none of the shelves up, but the main counters sat shoved against the walls. Reaching them required climbing over minor mountains of goods that had been removed from their packing boxes and crates only to be dumped unceremoniously across the floor.

No rhyme nor reason dictated the location of anything, dust

covered half of it, and the entire thing posed a Sisyphean task Lacey hadn't been able to make much time for. Too much happened all at once when they arrived in an abandoned town suddenly full of eager bachelors and a brother she no longer recognized.

"I can't believe you unpacked everything this way." Something akin to compassion softened his features, and once again Lacey was struck by how handsome Mr. Dunstan was. Or would be, if he trimmed his hair, became better acquainted with a razor, and stopped firing her temper every time they spoke.

"It doesn't matter," she sighed. "We take what's given and either triumph over it or let it defeat us. I don't intend to be defeated by something I can change, Mr. Dunstan."

He lapsed into that silent-but-looking-too-closely-for-comfort habit she'd noticed before. Rather than let his taciturn lack of response make her fidget, Lacey reached for the apron she'd removed before tackling the ladder. Its overlong ties could well have tripped her if they'd come undone.

As she tied it around her waist once more, she tried to stop herself from wondering what he was thinking. To distract herself, Lacey looked at the dog now lying placidly on a bare patch of floor. His brindled coat made it less obvious, but when she made a closer study, she could see areas of matted fur and the occasional burr clinging on. She wrinkled her nose. *He needs a bath. Maybe once the store is organized and Decoy's been properly cleaned, it won't be such a problem to let him inside.*

"Somehow"—Dunstan's voice snapped her attention back to the man—"I get the idea not much could defeat you."

But I will, if need be. Chase kept the last part to himself, curious to hear Miss Lyman's response to his statement.

She gave him a long, measured look. "Likewise."

No simpering, no effusive thanks, no coy denials for Miss Lyman. Her simple acceptance of the compliment, and matter-of-fact return of it, pleased him. He nodded in acknowledgment.

Then he rolled up his sleeves. Originally Chase wandered in hoping to find Granger and somehow work Braden Lyman into the conversation. Now he found himself reluctant to leave. Something in the way she'd declared her intention to triumph over the bad circumstances thrust upon her resonated with him. This sort of determination he not only understood, he approved.

She shouldn't be doing this alone. There were too many heavy items to be moved. Too many ways she could hurt herself, if she hadn't already overstressed that shoulder she kept ignoring. The place had too much. . .everything. And none of it where it belonged. As far as Chase could see, the wisest course of action would be to move everything out of the way, set up the shelves and displays, and sort all the goods onto them later.

"Essentially," she began hesitantly, as though unsure whether or not he intended to pitch in, "I planned to shift everything toward the front then set up the racks and counter."

"Smart thinking." Without another word, they set to work. Whatever sat in their path, they either scooted or carried out of it. Pails of Partridge's Pure Lard stacked alongside Velvetina Talcum Powder. Bottles of Liquid Doom insecticide loomed threateningly over Sawyer's Animal Crackers. Carter's Indelible Ink smugly sat atop Hansdown Hand Cleaner.

Irony earned a few smiles, but Chase took particular pleasure in tucking Shaker's Choice Garden Seed packets next to cans of Birdseye Sorghum. The Birdseye, a new product, came labeled with a single eye flanked by two swooping birds.

"Looks like they're going to peck it out." He expected the comment to elicit some sort of horrified reaction. Dainty ladies didn't think about such things. Nor were they acceptable topics for the sort of civil conversation she sounded so fond of.

Instead she laughed. "Do you know, the same thought crossed my mind! And somehow the eye follows you no matter where you move. It looks like it's watching everything."

"Let's test it." Chase climbed over mounds of rope, coffee, and tubes of Cow Clean to perch one of the Birdseye tins atop a tall shelf. After returning to the cleared area, he looked at the thing. It stared back from beneath a single, arched eyebrow.

"Eerie, isn't it?" Miss Lyman slid to the far left of the bare area. "I'd swear it's still looking at me even over here."

"Can't be." Chase went to the far right to test it. "It's watching this way. Only one eye, so it can only stare one way."

"Oh?" She scoffed. "Trade me then, and see for yourself."

He obliged, only to discover she'd been right.

"I like to think it has a blind spot somewhere." She sounded downright cheerful. "And when this whole place is cleaned up, I'll be able to walk far enough away to find it!"

"It's got the advantage." Chase went back to work.

"What advantage?" Miss Lyman tarried over by some canvas.

"It doesn't blink."

"I'll beat it anyway." She laughed as she said it. "You don't know me yet, Mr. Dunstan. But when you do, you'll learn there's no obstacle big enough when I set my mind on something."

Chase felt the day's lightheartedness drop right out from under him. *No obstacle big enough. . . . What, exactly, did Miss Lacey Lyman set her mind to? What if Miracle Mining was an obstacle standing in the way of this grand sawmill idea of hers?*

He didn't have any answers. But he wouldn't let her charm him into forgetting that he'd come to Hope Falls for a reason.

I can't afford to let her become a blind spot.

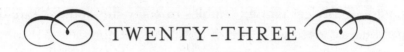

TWENTY-THREE

Lacey took particular care preparing for dinner that night. The walking suit she'd worn earlier held more dust than fabric after hours spent shuffling items in the store. She'd taken it outside, flapping the skirts to release much of the debris, but henceforth the outfit would be worn strictly for work.

Tonight we're having a party! Lacey wore the anticipation around her like a bubble bearing her toward happiness. How long had it been since she went to a celebration of any kind? She couldn't even remember with any certainty except that it was before news of the mine collapse. When she'd been told her brother died alongside the majority of his best workers.

At first, mourning protected her from having to attend social gatherings and smile through the staggering loss. But even when they received news of her brother's miraculous survival, she'd not taken the time to celebrate properly. Her brother waited, alone and unable to move, thousands of miles away. Festivities would have to wait until after she'd seen to the seemingly endless preparations necessary to join him.

And of course, once they arrived in Hope Falls, the onslaught of suitors turned everything on its ear once more. Besides, no one felt like celebrating Braden's survival once they realized the Braden they knew had been replaced by this belligerent, selfish dictator. *We mourned his death, but who would rejoice about the hash he's making over his life now?*

Tonight they'd give Granger a cheery send-off and best wishes for his journey tomorrow. Lacey didn't envy the man—she'd heard enough of Twyler's ranting rambles to know she wouldn't care to spend days cooped up in a train car alongside him.

Beaver-tail soup took pride of place on the menu. Lacey had watched in the early hours of the morning, before daylight strengthened its hold on the town, as Evie began preparations. Those prized tails, thick flaps covered with protective cross-hatching, had begun to exude a sort of oil. This, Evie explained, made for part of its distinctively gamy flavor.

It didn't sound appetizing. It didn't look appetizing either. Not even after Evie plopped the things in her soup pots to eke out the most flavor. When she fished them back out to remove the underlying meat and bone, at least they weren't so slippery. *Ugh.* Lacey grimaced at the memory. *How that is supposed to make some mythically delicious meal is beyond me.*

For her part, she looked forward to a slice of one of the layered lemon cakes Evie spent most of the day baking. If she did say so herself, Lacey thought she'd done a superior job icing the treats with sweet-cream frosting. The dessert, if not the much-prized soup, would be both delicious and beautiful.

She tugged free another golden ringlet to better frame her face and decided she was ready. The maroon-striped sateen evening dress, though laughably simple when compared to ball gowns she wore back in Charleston, was ostentatious by Hope Falls standards. Lacey thought tonight deserved her fanciest dress.

Only her wedding garments, carefully tucked away, topped it.

The world seems brighter when one is well dressed. The thought, long familiar, seemed especially true tonight. How else to explain why her stomach finally ceased its anxious roiling? The constant worries accompanying her faded in the expectancy of a merry evening. *And Mr. Lawson will see that Mr. Dunstan is correct; I do have a dress appropriate for every occasion!*

Leaving her room, she went to check on Naomi. Her cousin and longtime companion had dressed for the occasion as well. "You look smashing! Blue always becomes you so well, Naomi."

Her cousin eyed Lacey's dress. "You quite put me in the shade, my dear." Naomi's smile made the compliment sincere.

"Stop putting yourself down," Lacey chided. Her cousin, while lovely with her single streak of shocking white cresting her midnight locks, never seemed to accept a compliment.

"I didn't." Naomi looked uncomfortable, as though uncertain how to say what she wished. "I've not seen you look so well since back in Charleston, Lacey. You must be very relieved to know that Granger removes Twyler from Hope Falls tomorrow."

"I'm certain we all will be glad to see the last of him." Her fingers skimmed over the healing cut at the base of her throat as she tried to change the topic. "It's always nice to find a reason to celebrate. Would you like to borrow my pearl hairpin? It matches your broach and would look wonderful, I'm sure."

"Not tonight." Her cousin rose from her dressing table to join Lacey at the door. "Evie and Cora are already decked out and waiting for us back in the kitchen." The women had changed in shifts, so as not to leave the food unattended.

The men of Hope Falls, while not thieves, would make short work of anything edible left unwatched and unlocked. With the promise of their beloved soup—no matter that Lacey couldn't understand the appeal—the temptation to sneak a sample would prove too great. And having to exclude anyone over poor behavior tonight would put a damper on the festivities for everybody.

They fetched Mrs. Nash, whose unborn child had grown so greatly in the past few weeks she'd taken to napping most of the day. The extra sleep appeared to be doing her some good since she looked bright-eyed and rested as they headed to the kitchen.

When they drew close, they spotted a herd of hungry lumberjacks milling outside the kitchen. Since the front door to the diner remained locked until Evie declared things ready, they crowded around the back door like a jumble of eager puppies.

"Can't I have a taste?" Bobsley wheedled loudly.

"Of course you can!" Lacey swept past them through the door. "You and everyone else—as soon as it's set on the table."

Some groans, but no one contested the rules. Riordan, who'd pushed back the group so the women could get through, pulled off his hat. "You ladies look a sight for sore eyes, I'm thinkin'."

Belatedly, a few others whipped their hats off and began a chorus of accolades. Lacey ignored the rest to smile at the powerfully built Scots-Irishman. "Thank you, Mr. Riordan."

Chase saw the smile she aimed at Riordan and decided the man's sheer size kept him on his feet. That smile aimed to single him out, but even more to exclude the other men in the crowd.

First she finds Lawson and invites him to help her in the store, then she turns her attention to Riordan. Either the woman was fickle or playing a very deep game. If she didn't intend to marry any of them, the easiest way to avoid it was to play them against each other. Then, if a man became territorial about the others sniffing around her, he'd be out of the running for good.

If he didn't need to find Granger, Chase would've turned back and waited for the beckon of the dinner bell. As things stood, his friend planned to leave in the morning—this time with the doctor's approval—and it would be Chase's last chance to slide some pointed questions his way. Granger knew more about this town and its strange occupants than he'd let on.

It didn't take much thinking to deduce that Granger sat in the kitchen, soaking in the smiles of his fiancée and the smells of her good cooking. Chase wouldn't mind stepping into that kitchen himself. Home-cooked meals and homey warmth eluded his campsite fires. Getting by on his own food for so long gave a man a healthy appreciation for Miss Thompson's domain.

What he did mind were all the people who felt the same way. The rough-edged passel of lumbermen pressing their noses to the door wouldn't take kindly to watching Chase walk on through. The front door stayed locked tight—he'd already tried coaxing it open, but the stubborn thing remained as obdurate as anyone connected to the Miracle Mining Company when asked a question.

Time ran out as he walked around the building in search of another entry point. Once dinner got underway, there'd be no getting Granger alone. No open windows allowed access, but he found a third door in the back of the place. *Maybe...*

Yep. This knob turned. He pushed it open and slid inside, closing it quietly behind him. It took a moment for him to be sure none of the other men had followed, but that allowed his eyes to adjust to the darkness of what seemed a very small room.

The pantry. He figured they'd put in the door for ease of loading goods after they arrived on the train. Not only did it make for a smart design, it turned out to be very useful. Reaching forward to keep from smacking into anything, Chase made his way to the second door and groped for the handle. *There.*

" 'Scuse me," he said to anyone and everyone in the bustling work space. No sense frightening them with his sudden appearance.

After the dark of the storeroom, the cheery brightness of the kitchen made him narrow his eyes so he could get his bearings.

"Mr. Dunstan?" An older woman Chase recognized by sight but not introduction tilted her head curiously. Not one of the four from the ad, Granger had said she came with her husband when he called McCreedy to round out his number of team bosses.

"Mrs. McCreedy," he acknowledged. Scanning around the room, he spotted an unfamiliar face. A heavily pregnant woman balanced herself on a stool near the swinging doors. Something about her seemed familiar, but it wasn't until her ears turned red under his scrutiny that he made the connection to the engineer.

"Mr. Dunstan." Miss Higgins glided over to perform introductions. "This is Mrs. Nash. Mr. Lawson's widowed sister."

No need to wonder why she added the part about her being a widow. These women already faced enough danger from men assuming they were less than ladies since they placed that ad. An unmarried mother-to-be in town would reflect poorly on them.

"A pleasure." He doffed his hat and offered a quick nod. Come to think of it, one of the women had mentioned that Mr. Lawson shared their house. Chase had just forgotten that the smitten engineer lived below stairs to better watch over his sister. Supposedly the arrangement helped protect the ladies.

But what of the man's obvious interest in Miss Lyman? It wouldn't be difficult to abuse his position in the household and take advantage of a sleeping woman. It hadn't happened yet, as evidenced by Miss Lyman requesting Lawson's help earlier, but it still could. *Are they all blind to how he looks at her?*

Abruptly he realized he'd missed Mrs. Nash's response. The woman looked at him expectantly. "Er—" He floundered a moment before coming up with, "It's good to see you up and about."

It worked. Women all around smiled at his thoughtful

comment. Granger looked amused but held his tongue.

"Granger, I wondered if you'd give me a hand with Miss Lyman's cougar?" Filled in with sawdust and framed over the cat's own bleached skull, the cougar's head was ready to be hung. Chase could easily carry it alone, but hanging the thing made a good pretext to draw Granger aside for some questions.

"It's ready?" Miss Lyman plunked down a crock of butter and came scurrying over. "When you left the store to work on it, I hadn't imagined you'd finish everything so quickly!"

"Wanted it out of the way before Granger left." He shrugged. *She better not decide she wants to come with us.*

Her eyes sparkled. "I'll come along for the first peek!"

Chase bit back a groan. Didn't she have something better to do than ruin his final opportunity to question Granger? One look at her excited face told him the answer: *No such luck.*

"We'll be back in a moment," she called to the others.

"Everyone wait a minute." Miss Thompson looked suspicious. "If it's finished, where are you planning to hang that thing?"

"On the wall beside your 'Hats off to the Chef' sign." Miss Lyman's voice shrank to something almost apologetic.

"No." Done with the conversation, Miss Thompson returned her attention to the bubbling soup pots atop her stove.

The beginnings of a smile made Chase look down at his own hat. Suddenly he was glad he'd removed it before being told.

"Now, Evie, you know all the men are going to want to see it." Her sister's entreaty fell on deaf ears until she continued, "With proof of her shooting staring them in the face, maybe the men will think twice before crossing the line!"

They don't know I shot it, too. Chase held his peace. He'd bothered to dry the hide, scrape it clean, oil it to keep it supple, and mount it. What was the use if no one ever saw it? Besides, the other Miss Thompson made a good point. Lawson sure looked like a man to take a woman's skill with a gun seriously.

"Cora." The cook wavered but held her ground. "It's not as though they'll never see it if Lacey hangs the thing elsewhere."

"Out of sight, out of mind," Chase cautioned.

"Dunstan's right. Besides"—Granger looked fondly at his woman—"none of us wants every man in town trooping through your house. The diner and the bunkhouse are the only places the men spend any amount of time in. This will make the best impact."

"You know I can't hang my cougar in the *bunkhouse*." Miss Lyman sounded scandalized at the prospect. "Please, Evie?"

Miss Thompson's deep, put-upon sigh admitted defeat.

It was only later, as he carried the trophy back to the diner, that Chase realized what he'd witnessed. *The obstacles hadn't mattered a bit—Miss Lyman got her own way. Again.*

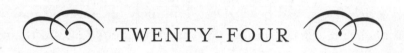

TWENTY-FOUR

Time plodded on for Cora. After the unveiling of the cougar and farewell dinner for Granger, the entire week might just as well have been one long, drawn-out day. The routine didn't vary: cooking for the workmen with perfunctory periods of supportively ignoring her own fiancé in awkward visits. Everything else went smoothly, so she counted her blessings. *I think we all expected some sort of trouble once Granger left.*

Oh, there'd been a dicey moment or two when he and Mr. Dunstan shepherded Twyler onto the train. Riordan and Williams flanked them, creating a sort of guard for the criminal on crutches. Clump scurried behind, but somehow Cora doubted the good-natured German would be much use if a fight broke out.

Several of the men had lined up, shouting threats and begging Granger to leave Twyler with them for a few minutes. Lacey's abduction was still a sore spot for both her admirers and the other men who'd missed a chance to prove their bravery to Naomi. Now they wanted an outlet for their frustration.

Granger and Dunstan didn't give it to them. Even in the days since the departure, no fights broke out among the men. As far as Cora could see, Dunstan managed most of it through eye contact. His icy stare quelled conflict, as though the men knew his vigilant watch was a warning. It impressed them all.

Except Braden, whose more subdued behavior lately couldn't be credited to a man he'd never met. *Lacey went to visit him, and he hasn't been the same since. I wonder if something she said got through to him? Or if he's just waiting for Granger?*

Evie's fiancé had been giving him daily updates and reports on their progress. Granger answered Braden's questions and ostensibly incorporated some of his ideas into the work routine. Cora didn't really know what all went on with the sawmill—but it occurred to her Braden would want to. Without Granger, he lost his information supply and link to the men. He grew listless.

"Do you think he's starting to come around?" She posed the question to Lacey as they headed for the kitchen one morning. "I mean, he's stopped bellowing all the time, and either I'm becoming accustomed to them, or he isn't putting his heart into his snarky comments." *Always assuming he still has a heart.*

"Well," Lacey's hesitation didn't exactly inspire confidence. "I believe he's giving up his plans to force us all from Hope Falls. You know he doesn't like to admit when he's wrong and turns sulky. If you want to call that coming around. . ."

"No, I don't." Cora rubbed the back of her neck where the tension built up. "I want him to be realizing how terribly he's repaid our concern for his well-being and hard work to make a success of this town. Sulking isn't the same as remorse."

"They both make people quiet," Lacey observed. "We don't have much choice but to give it time. He's already changing plans. Once he admits he's wrong, maybe the regret will come."

"I hope so." Cora's fervency startled Lacey, whose eyes widened. "Oh, it sounds awful to wish someone flooded with so much remorse he can't withstand it. But something has to break through this wall he's built around himself, and I think regret might be the only way. He hurts, you know." The tears welled up.

"Braden refuses the laudanum." Her friend frowned. "It seems to me the only sleep he gets is when we sneak the medicine so he can't turn it down. Then he's always so furious with us. Why? This stubbornness does him no favors. I keep trying to find the reason for his decisions, but I can't make sense of him."

Cora dabbed her eyes with a hankie. "More than anything, he needs rest. Otherwise, how can he heal? And if he's in pain all the time but never getting any sleep, is it any wonder his thoughts are so full of himself?" She'd puzzled over this so many times, trying to understand why he changed so drastically.

"Do you think that if he slept, he'd start thinking normally again?" Lacey paused with her hand on the handle of the kitchen door. "Would it improve his condition if we began administering more regular doses of the laudanum, do you think?"

"I don't know." Cora tucked her hankie away. "Let's not consider whether it will make him angry. He's angry no matter what we do, regardless. But if it might bring *my* Braden back, I'm willing to do just about anything to get the job done."

"Done!" Lacey nudged the last tin can in place and stood back to admire her sparkling, orderly shop. It had taken days of sorting, stacking, and scrubbing—and that was after she'd conscripted a few of the men to move the shelving one night—but the results made all the effort worth it. *It's what I pictured.*

The wooden counter ran along the far wall, its heavy iron coffee grinder easily visible the moment someone walked through the door. Underneath, it held bins filled with rice, flour, sugar, and cornmeal—all shown through little glass panels along the front.

Matching shelves stretched behind it from floor to ceiling, stacked with bolts of fabric and ordering catalogs down one half. The other held delicacies to tempt her customers. A wheel of cheese, a vat of the biggest pickles Lacey had ever seen, and clear jars containing taffy pulls and peppermint sticks beckoned the hungry. Here, too, were laid a massive quantity of paper bags in varied sizes, intended to contain the measured dry goods. A small door in the right corner led to the storeroom.

More shelves abutted the two longer walls, evenly spaced between the freshly washed windows. These held a variety of goods Lacey placed according to value and category—most expensive items resting at eye level. Everything from cleaning supplies to chewing tobacco waited for buyers to find them.

The larger items took more ingenuity to house, but Lacey thought she'd risen to the task. Saws and axes hung to the left of the door. Folded overalls, long underwear, bandannas, and balled socks nestled in wooden crates below the display of tools.

Along the right, she'd placed bins of apples and potatoes. Above these hung a selection of smoked ham and wrapped sides of bacon. A long, low shelf ran down the center of the store, creating two long aisles out of the single room. Here sat the pails of peanut butter, buckets of apple butter, and cans of condensed milk and honey. The Birdseye Sorghum looked up as though wary of anyone wanting baking soda or cream of tartar.

The potbellied stove sat at the midline of the room, back toward the counter. Off to its side, in the warmest spot, she'd set the enormous cracker barrel. A checkerboard leaned against it, ready to be laid down for a game any minute. Two chairs bracketed the barrel, inviting players to while away an hour.

Enough room remained to widen her selection of products once the mill was up and running. Lacey looked around the place and gave a sigh of satisfaction. *Someday families will live in Hope*

Falls. Our workers will bring their wives and children into my shop for aprons and pennywhistles. Someday. . .

The bell above the door clanged a welcome as Mr. Dunstan strolled in. Lacey's smile faltered when she caught sight of Decoy—fur looking decidedly grubbier than it had a week ago. Still, his stubborn owner might be her first real customer.

"What can I do for you, Mr. Dunstan?" Her smile returned as she saw the approval on his face as he surveyed the store.

"Nice." His comment, when it finally came, left something to be desired. The man looked every bit as impressed as he should be, considering how he'd seen the place at its worst.

Couldn't he say something about what an amazing difference she'd made? Or tell her how clean and organized everything was? Lacey would even settle for a simple heartfelt congratulations on her accomplishment. But no. The man came up with "nice."

Well, that doesn't make me *feel very nice.* There wasn't much to say, though Lacey wouldn't thank him for dredging up a single syllable to describe days of difficult, meticulous work.

"Mm." She made her acknowledgment shorter than his.

He didn't notice.

Dunstan stayed absorbed in perusing her shop. He circled the entire place and picked up and put down items from almost every shelf, all without saying another word. Finally, he lowered himself onto one of the checker chairs and placed his order.

"One pickle." He'd kept her waiting while he touched almost everything she sold, only to buy one lousy pickle?

Lacey yanked the glass lid from the huge vat, grabbed the long tongs lying beside it, and plunged them in to nab a pickle. Pickle chosen, she reached behind her counter and picked up the pail of None-Such Peanut Butter Decoy had desecrated on his earlier visit. Tongs held out far in front, far enough to keep brine away from her skirts, she marched to meet him.

"I'll put it on your tab," she sweetly told him. "Along with this!" She plunked the pail of peanut butter atop the other chair. Lacey intended to whisk back behind the counter and ignore him, but the man didn't take the pickle she offered.

So she stood there, uncertain, while he gave her one of those long, penetrating looks he used to keep the men in line. She turned, ready to go back behind the counter, return the pickle to its jar, and order Mr. Dunstan out of her store.

He reached up and snatched the pickle. Biting into it, his eyes closed in appreciation. After he swallowed, he mentioned, "I haven't had one of these in months. It's been too long."

Dunstan proceeded to finish it off before speaking again. "Pickles are tart and salty on their own, Miss Lyman. You don't need to go around with a sour look on your face to spice it up."

Shock held her speechless for a moment. "Out." She pointed toward the door, reduced to simply repeating, "Get out."

"I brought in an elk." He rose to his feet. "It needs dressing and butchering before it'll fit in the smokehouse." Apparently he expected praise for this because he paused.

If Lacey hadn't been so riled, she would've grunted, "Nice." But as things stood, she felt he didn't deserve even that much.

One hand reached down to rub the dog's ears. "Decoy here has a special fondness for elk. It would be helpful if someone watched him while I took care of things. He'll find a way out of the barn if I leave him alone with the smell of elk in the air."

"You aren't saying you want to leave him here!" Lacey was so aghast she forgot her anger. "In my nice, clean shop?"

"Told you before, Decoy's trained not to bother anything on shelves." A thoughtful look crossed Dunstan's face. "Or bins either. If he gets restless, you might have a care for those hams you have hanging in the window. They're low enough he wouldn't have any trouble reaching them if he wanted to."

"But," Lacey spoke in desperation, trying to avoid what Dunstan, at least, seemed to consider inevitable. "It's all put away perfectly. Didn't you notice how clean everything looks?"

"Yep." He headed for the door. "You got this place in order just in the nick of time. I'll be by later to pick him up."

"What am I supposed to do with him while you're gone?"

"He likes you." The door opened, its bell clanging an alarm. "You can manage him—you're a resourceful woman." With that, he abandoned Lacey to his dog, and the dog to Lacey.

Decoy sauntered over to his pail of peanut butter and gave a great, happy sniff. It fell to the floor and rolled away, the massive dog lumbering after it as though playing a new game.

"I suppose chairs weren't included with shelves and bins in your training." Lacey rubbed her forehead. By the end of the day, the smell coming off Decoy would fill the place. *Unless. . .*

She made a beeline for the hygiene shelf and pulled out a box of Snow Boy Washing Powder. A large tub sat in the back of the storeroom, waiting for the time when someone would need it. Well, that day came sooner than she expected. If Chase Dunstan thought he could leave a smelly moose of a mutt on her hands and ruin her store, he'd learn just how resourceful she could be!

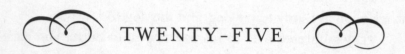

TWENTY-FIVE

Miss Lyman?" Chase peered into the store an hour later. If he'd had any doubts, he wouldn't have left Decoy, but his trust lay more in the dog than the woman. So he'd come to check in.

She didn't call back an answer. Decoy didn't come bounding up as was his habit whenever they separated and Chase returned. Nothing stirred in the shop—except a few sudden misgivings.

He walked toward the back counter, thinking to check the storeroom. Along the way he surveyed the store for any damage. No signs of trouble. Not a single thing stood out of place in the newly pristine mercantile—Chase knew because he'd made a thorough study earlier. He rounded the potbellied stove and bypassed the cracker-barrel chairs. By now Decoy would have sensed him and come running, even from the back room.

A dull clang sounded as his boot hit something solid and metal. Decoy's peanut butter pail rolled a few forlorn inches. Chase doubled his pace to the storeroom door and yanked it open. Even in here, things were eerily tidy. No Miss Lyman. No Decoy.

Where did they go? Irritated, he turned on his heel and headed outside. Chase paused, unsure where to go. *Not to the diner. Miss Thompson wouldn't allow a dog within ten feet of her kitchen. But maybe she'll have an idea where Miss Lyman went?*

Too many tracks muddled the ground outside the door, imprints from people going in and out as they helped her get the store in order. Chase held slim hope of tracking them, so he headed for the diner. *She'd better not have gone out walking in the woods again*, he stewed. *I asked her to keep an eye on him in the store. What has that stubborn woman gotten into this time?*

"Hello?" He stuck his head through the kitchen door. Since the night Granger told everyone why he was here, Chase made the kitchen his base for Hope Falls. It harbored everything a man needed to keep tabs on: most of the women and all of the food.

"Hello!" The high, girlish greeting came from Mrs. Nash. She sat on a bench, shelling peas and trying to look past him. "Are they finished yet? I mean, did you see your surprise?"

"What surprise?" Those faint misgivings from back in the store grew to dread. "Surprise" was the name for unpleasant things people snuck up on you, suspecting you would object if asked about it beforehand. *Not good. Not good at all.*

"Well, if you have to be asking us, they haven't shown you yet." Mrs. McCreedy shook her head. "It's not for us to spoil."

"Oh, go on, Martha." Mrs. Nash finished shelling her peas. "He came back too soon, and he'll go poking around looking for who knows how long before he finds them or they find him. I'd say we might as well tell him he should go by the house first."

"Thank you." Chase started in that direction, only to duck back into the kitchen. "Do you know where they put Decoy?" The dog got underfoot in just about anything, his sheer size making it difficult to work around him. If they weren't careful, they'd trip over him or find their dainty toes bruised by his mammoth paws. Decoy hid a fondness for tromping on people's feet.

Whatever the women were up to, they'd most likely needed to shut the dog away from the action. And Decoy didn't like being cooped up for long. Disaster loomed large if they'd left him—

"Find the ladies." Mrs. McCreedy beat Mrs. Nash to the punch. "And you'll find your dog. We won't say anything more."

He looked to Mrs. Nash, but she smiled and pressed a hand over her lips, indicating they were sealed. Chase would get no information to prepare him for his "surprise." That left him with no choice but to head down to the ladies' house.

As he drew closer, snatches of laughter and muffled shrieks reached his ears. *Sounds like they're having fun.* Their merriment went a long way toward easing his tension. Such carefree sounds couldn't accompany anything too awful.

His knock on the door found no answer, but the noise was all coming from around back. Chase left the porch and crept around the house, the better to take stock of the situation.

No one would be catching *him* unawares. He'd turned the tables.

"I think we used too much." Someone sounded worried.

"It'll all wash out." Miss Lyman's giggles floated by. If a man could catch a sound and keep it for sad times, that would be it. She sounded positively gleeful. "Pass me the bucket?"

The sound of sloshing water as the bucket was emptied—not poured—made Chase thirsty. He took a sip from his canteen and wondered what they could be doing. He crept closer to find out.

"We're going to need a lot more than that!" This huskier voice belonged to Miss Higgins. Though she spoke least out of the four women, her throaty tones were easily identifiable.

A great deal of splashing drowned out anything else for a while. Then came a bark. It was the short, low blast of sound Decoy made when he played. The spasmodic thump of his tail sounded against something metal, underscoring more laughter.

Chase froze. Decoy loved the water. Any water. Whether it was a stream to wade through, a puddle to pounce on, or a deep pool for diving into, his dog enjoyed water to the fullest. Combine that knowledge to the sounds and comments bubbling behind the house, it added up to one mounting suspicion.

He poked his head around the corner of the house and confirmed it. *Those daft women are giving him a bath!*

"What do you think you're doing?" he demanded as he advanced on the tableau. Things were worse than he imagined.

Buckets of water trailed back toward the water pump, where Granger's cook stopped in the act of filling yet another. Miss Higgins clutched the end of a long rope knotted into a makeshift leash. The other Miss Thompson dropped the now-empty bucket she'd just poured over Decoy in an attempt to rinse him clean.

A failed attempt. There, behind the house, Miss Lyman crouched beside a tin hip bath, froth gloving her hands all the way up to her elbows. Cramped inside the bathtub sat a very happy, very wet, and very foamy dog. At least, it *used* to be a dog. Now it was a white, sudsy mess wriggling with delight.

"Giving Decoy a much-needed bath." Miss Lyman managed to sound nonchalant as she gestured to the frothy mountain rocking the tub from side to side. "What else would we be doing?"

"Anything!" Chase raked his hands through his own shaggy hair. "Cooking, puttering about your shop, wading through the calf-eyed glances of your moony men. Anything at all," he repeated, "except turn my dog into a walking mop!"

At this outburst, the women slowly began returning to their respective tasks. Miss Thompson fetched another full bucket from her sister at the pump, upending it over Decoy's back while Miss Lyman tried to work out the suds. She succeeded in raising more bubbles than had been washed away in the first place.

"He's not a mop, but I would've taken one to him if it would've helped clean him up." She sounded muffled as she scrubbed at the dog's fur. "He was absolutely filthy, you know."

Another bucket of water and more scrubbing unleashed another crop of bubbles. At this rate, they'd never get it finished.

"He's a *hunting dog*." Chase scowled at them all and picked up a bucket. "Or he used to be until you four decided to turn him into an overgrown, soap-strewn parody of a poodle."

Miss Lyman gave a half-strangled snort of laughter, so Chase figured he could be forgiven if half a bucket's water *accidentally* slopped over the tub and onto her skirts. Decoy wagged his tail even harder, delighted that Chase joined in.

"I've never seen a dog"—Miss Higgins shifted to the side to give him more room—"who looked less like a poodle."

With his silver-gray brindled coat further darkened from the water, even the soap continuously springing up couldn't hide his coloring. And nothing could cover his size. Still, whatever soap they'd used made a spectacular effort.

"Just how much soap did you pour in?" Chase asked after his fifth bucket of water made little headway against the froth.

The women darted sideways glances at each other, but no one saw fit to answer. Nor did they immediately respond to his query about what sort of substance they'd seen fit to use. As far as Chase knew, and after relocating most of the contents of Miss Lyman's store the other day, he had a fair notion no company manufactured dog wash. *Which should have tipped them off.*

It didn't smell like lye, which was harsh enough to irritate Decoy's skin after the bath ended. He would have asked again, to be sure, but found he didn't need to. He spotted Miss Lyman nudging something around the tub with the toe of her boot.

Chase grabbed it. He read the box then looked at the ground for the rest of its contents. With growing exasperation, he realized why he didn't see any granules or flakes—he didn't know which form Snow Boy came in—scattered across the grass.

"You used the whole box?" He shook the box in disbelief, confronting them with the evidence. "An entire *box* of soap?"

"He's large enough we thought it best to be sure." Miss Lyman carried on trying to rub the stuff from his fur. "With his thick coat to get through, we thought we'd need every bit."

Miss Higgins looked a bit embarrassed as she confessed to the obvious. "It seems we overestimated. Significantly."

He saw no need to comment on that bit of hindsight. Setting himself not to let his temper get the best of him, Chase kept bringing buckets. *I can't very well yell at all four of them.*

It took more buckets of water than Chase bothered to count, and far too much time, before they won the battle of the bubbles. Added with his attempts to hunt down his own dog, he'd lost half an hour or more of time he couldn't afford to see wasted.

He'd not managed to trap Granger in a productive conversation. In the week following his friend's departure, Chase set himself to poking around the unused parts of town. Hope Falls bristled with abandoned buildings. Most looked thrown together to meet the needs of a mining town rapidly outgrowing itself, some of such poor workmanship they needed leveling.

If he didn't need to bring back fresh meat on a regular basis, Chase would've gotten a lot further. Periodically doubling back to check on the women severely hampered his hunting, which in turn curtailed his nosing-around time.

The smallest structures most likely to hold tools and equipment he'd already searched. These were the places Chase figured a man in a hurry might hide unused blasting papers, fuse line, or anything else incriminating. They were common enough mining materials to be overlooked by the new residents.

But Chase knew for a fact that Braden Lyman refused to store explosives or any of their paraphernalia on site. Once they'd blasted the main tunnels into the side of the mountain, he'd shipped any remaining items back to the dealer. Lyman considered it an elementary safety precaution against blast-happy miners who might accidentally get people killed.

His common-sense approach was one of the reasons Chase agreed to work with Braden Lyman in the first place. Usually he steered clear of mining outfits. Whatever land they didn't strip bare, they blew up to get to the coal or silver ore. Miners were bad for the land and bad for business. Miracle Mining had been the best of the bunch. Their plans to build a town and capitalize on the railroad route offered assurance that they wouldn't carelessly destroy the surrounding countryside.

For this reason, Chase signed on to walk them over their land, explain its basic features and the way one area connected to the other, and suggest the best site for Hope Falls itself. They'd needed help determining a spot close enough to be productive, but far enough away so the town wouldn't be affected if and when they needed to blast their way farther in.

And Lyman's point-blank refusal to overuse blasting powder or even keep it on hand had been typical of the outfit. His partner protested, but Lyman maintained he could always order more if need be—their train access made short work of waiting.

Which was why Chase found it so hard to believe the story he'd heard about a blasting accident bringing down the mountain. Lyman hired surveyors to gauge the rock and engineers to design custom supports at intervals along every tunnel they made.

The man did everything right—so it shouldn't have gone wrong. If Miracle Mining had been a two-bit operation with shaky methods, Chase wouldn't have recommended Laura's husband for a job. He'd put his faith in Braden Lyman's company and lost his family. Now Chase needed to prove he hadn't misjudged the outfit. Then he could find justice for the men who'd died.

But instead of investigating, he had to deal with the daft woman who'd decided to give *his dog a bath*. His anger over her presumption, and the difficulty it would cause, paled in comparison to his rage over the time her foolishness cost him.

Chase controlled his temper by not talking. The rest of today and tomorrow morning would be given to butchering the elk, but its size bought him a day without needing to make a kill.

Tomorrow I hunt the real prey of Hope Falls. The thought calmed him. *But today I take Miss Lyman down a peg.*

TWENTY-SIX

*O*ops. Lacey didn't quite know how to regain control of the situation. Bathing Decoy had been a wonderful idea—thankfully, his enthusiasm for playing in the water kept him in place through the prolonged ordeal. *If only Dunstan didn't come looking for us.* Lacey caught the thought and sternly stopped it. The only things "if only" ever applied to were things that hadn't happened and most likely never would. *Useless things.*

But the man's timing proved *most* unfortunate. Lacey would not have chosen for him to ruin the surprise and certainly would rather have kept the mistake with the soap between just her and the girls. Mr. Dunstan looked as though he'd taken it well enough. He stood there, somehow taller than he'd seemed indoors, casting dark looks when the others didn't notice.

Dark looks, Lacey could handle. *Particularly when they're dark good looks.* This time she didn't even try to catch the wayward thought. She kept busy sneaking her own looks his way.

Since coming to Hope Falls, Lacey accepted that proprieties couldn't always be observed. She accepted minor lapses not only for the sake of necessity, but also because it gave the women a bit more leeway than they could enjoy in an established town.

If she hadn't quite become accustomed to seeing men in their shirtsleeves, at least the experience wasn't new. Some of the workmen would either forgo or forget their waistcoats when they showed up for the midday meal. On long, hot days Lacey understood this to be common practice, and thus, unremarkable.

But there was nothing common about Chase Dunstan. Framed by the sunlight, he sported no jacket and no waistcoat—although Lacey had never seen him wear one. The tan trousers of hard-wearing canvas and his worn boots were familiar, if drenched.

The cambric shirt, striped by his suspenders, wasn't familiar in the least. He'd rolled up his sleeves. The futile attempt to remain dry exposed strong forearms sprinkled with dark hair. Decoy's exuberant splashing soaked into the once-white fabric up to Dunstan's shoulders. The fabric molded to those remarkably broad shoulders and an extremely solid chest. He'd left the top button undone, leaving his collar to gape open. Lacey was transfixed to discover a smattering of the same dark hair peeking just above the next button.

Who knew men had fur? And as far as she could see, he looked to be the same sun-kissed gold as his forearms. She tried to look away but found her thoughts running rampant. *Does Dunstan go without his shirt during those long walks in the woods?*

"You know better." His rumbling chastisement jerked her attention back to his face. Dunstan did not look amused.

Did he catch me ogling? The possibility mortified her. Lacey felt the telltale heat in her cheeks. *No! I can't blush! He'll see it as a sign of guilt.* Which, of course, it was.

"I'm sure I don't know what you mean." *I hope I don't.*

His scowl deepened, and he crossed his arms over his chest, mercifully blocking the distracting view. "Don't play games, Miss

Lyman. You had no right to try to change my dog."

"Excuse me?" It sounded like he was talking about the way she took initiative to clean his dog. Not. . .anything else.

"You shouldn't have taken him from the store at all." Dunstan rolled his shoulders, the movement shifting the collar of his shirt. A second button slipped its mooring, she noticed.

Lacey blinked. Now was not the time to notice such things. She blinked again. A lady *never* noticed such things! *Although, a small, utterly inappropriate voice mused, perhaps that's because ladies are never confronted with them in the first place?*

"I asked you to watch him in the store." Her lack of response drove him to expound, "You should have stayed there."

"It is not your place to tell me where I should or shouldn't go or when I might leave my own shop, Mr. Dunstan." Lacey refused to be distracted any longer by his state of dishabille. "You overstep your position to think otherwise."

A muscle worked in his jaw while he chewed that over. Clearly still angry, Dunstan couldn't refute plain facts.

"Furthermore"—she found her own temper fueled by his unreasonable one—"I very clearly protested you leaving Decoy in my barely finished, newly scrubbed store. You didn't listen."

He relaxed his stance a fraction. "When you asked what you should do with him, I took it you were accepting the task."

"You told me I would think of something," she riposted. "So I took the challenge and came up with a *resourceful* solution."

"Dumping an entire box of soap onto a dog doesn't qualify as being resourceful!" Clearly he remembered using the word, and Lacey's gibe hit its mark. "The kindest word is foolish."

"Mr. Dunstan!" Naomi's rebuke reminded Lacey that she and Dunstan weren't alone. Her cousin, Cora, and Evie stood around the yard, watching their every move and listening intently.

"The truth isn't always pleasant," he grumbled, looking

uncomfortable for the first time since Lacey met him.

"Everyone makes mistakes." Cora, who used the same sort of kind understanding in her continued visiting of Braden, came to Lacey's defense. "Besides, it turned out all right in the end."

Their championship of her acted like a balm to the still-remaining sore spot from when they'd hired Dunstan. Until that moment Lacey hadn't realized that she'd seen it as her friends taking his side, choosing him over her. *He's right—I am foolish.*

"It's not all right," he thundered. "Look at Decoy!"

At the sound of his name, the dog perked his ears. He left the tub, which he'd been sniffing as though curious where the water had gone, and gamboled to Dunstan's side. Just before he got there, the dog hunched lower to the ground and gave a massive shake that started at his shoulders and shivered down to his rump. Water flew everywhere. Then he plopped down at his master's side, panting happily as though pleased with his work.

Lacey looked at the dog, obviously none the worse for washing, then looked at Dunstan. She raised a quizzical brow.

"Useless!" the hunter declared. If he hadn't reached down to scratch behind Decoy's ears as he said it, Lacey would've felt sorry for the dog. "He can't go in the forest like this."

"What?" Evie scoffed at the ludicrous statement before anyone else could. "We didn't hurt him, Mr. Dunstan. It was your insistence that Decoy be allowed to follow you indoors that made this necessary. As you say, the truth isn't always pleasant." She paused as though trying to find a way around that then shrugged. "The dog stank. He's shedding from the heat. Something had to be done to make his presence indoors more acceptable."

Lacey could've cheered, but refrained. *Go Evie!*

Their opponent looked as though he'd dearly like to kick something. "He's a *working* dog. I don't bring him inside often."

"But when you did, you abandoned him to run loose in my

nice clean store." Lacey crossed her arms, mirroring his stance.

"You don't get it." He passed a hand over his face, rubbing his forehead. "When he smelled like a dog, it didn't alarm the animals. Now anything we track will bolt if it's downwind from us. Snow Boy Washing Powder might as well have been a warning cry."

"Then I suggest you attempt to remain upwind for the next few days." Lacey wouldn't give an inch. "It'll wear off."

He shook his head. "It doesn't work that way. Deer and mountain goats don't kindly turn around when the wind shifts. You just don't understand anything about hunting."

"And you don't understand anything about running a shop!"

"If this is what it takes, I wouldn't want to learn." Arms now resting at his sides, Dunstan revealed his drying shirt. Even the wet spots speckling its expanse no longer clung to him. "Cleaning a room is far easier than tracking an animal."

His dismissal of her hard work rankled. When he wasn't looking ruggedly handsome, Dunstan became irksome. He needed someone to push him off his high horse—and Lacey needed a project now that the store was ready but had no customers.

"We'll see about that, Mr. Dunstan." She gestured toward Decoy. "Having deprived you of your hunting companion, I'll join you tomorrow. Then you can show me just how difficult it is."

"No." He didn't waste any words refusing her company.

She'd suspected as much. What Lacey hadn't expected was how much she'd want to go tracking once the idea came to her.

"Hunting is your job. Knowing the ins and outs of Hope Falls is mine." She didn't come out and say she was the boss, but Lacey knew he caught the implication. "This is the perfect opportunity for me to learn more about my land."

"No." His return to monosyllabic responses goaded her.

"You agreed to teach us how to trap the wildlife hereabouts." Naomi's words made Dunstan go still.

"What?" Lacey slanted a curious glance toward her friends.

"It was one of the conditions of his employment," Evie filled her in. "He told us he'd be happy to teach us."

Oh, this is too perfect. Lacey beamed at this new development and made a mental note to ask Cora what other conditions Dunstan had agreed to in their meeting.

"Well, that settles it." She read the resignation on his features clear as day. "You'll start teaching me tomorrow."

And tomorrow would be a glorious day.

The next day dawned with one of those suddenly soggy quirks of mountain weather. Chase woke to the sound of rain beating on his tent. For a moment he lay there. With Decoy's shaggy—and admittedly better smelling—bulk warming the tent, he wasn't in any hurry to leave his bedroll and face the cold outside.

And that was before he remembered his plans for the day. Chase groaned at the thought of getting saddled with Miss Lyman on the day he'd earmarked for riffling through Hope Falls. *Of all days, it had to be this one.* Leading a pampered princess through overgrown brush already ranked as unappealing. Throw in a deluge of rain and the prospect went downright bleak.

Unless. . . *She won't want to go traipsing through mud and rain, getting cold and ruining one of those pretty dresses she's so fond of.* A smile crept across his face as Chase plotted.

All he had to do was show up ready to take her hunting. She'd refuse, and he'd be off the hook for good. Not even Miss Lyman could complain that he didn't fulfill his part of the bargain if she backed out. If she didn't follow through with their first set of plans, he wasn't obligated to make more.

And if she's stubborn enough to set out, I'll make Miss Lyman so miserable she'll head home early and not ask to go again. It wouldn't be difficult. Chase knew where the worst terrain lay, which low-lying areas turned to boggy muck from rainfall, where the river swelled to make crossing difficult. He made it a point to know and avoid those spots. If necessary, he'd direct the spoiled lady through every one of them.

It might even be fun. Starting to look forward to a day either free of Miss Lyman's interference or devoted to making her less demanding, Chase didn't mind leaving the warm tent. He got dressed, packed up, then booted a less-than-ecstatic Decoy out of the tent so he could take it down. Trying to keep a cook fire going in the midst of this weather was the act of a fool or a desperate man. And Chase had already learned that the breakfasts in Hope Falls were worth getting up for.

Dropping Decoy off at the cow barn, where the dog promptly curled up on a bed of warm, fragrant hay, posed no problems. He'd stay there until Chase came to fetch him, glad to be out of the rain. For a dog who loved water, Decoy sure didn't like rain. A shame, really, since Chase planned to bring him out in it for a spell. Some rain would help wash away the lingering detergent-like smell still clinging to the dog's fur.

Chase hit the door of the diner whistling. He stepped into the kitchen, found his prey, and gave a wolfish grin.

"Well, Miss Lyman, are you ready to start tracking?"

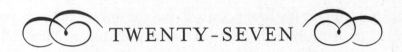

TWENTY-SEVEN

The man had to be joking. Lacey eyed him, wary of a trap. Dunstan knew full well that she—and he—couldn't leave the others alone with a group of lumbermen stuck inside all day. Not to mention that no one with an ounce of sense would go merrily marching through the wild in the midst of a downpour. *Did I actually hear him whistling before he opened the door?*

Something was wrong here, and it went beyond her usual suspicion of anyone who managed to be cheerful early in the morning. Dunstan didn't seem nearly so pleased with the prospect of taking her hunting yesterday. *So why is he raring to go now?*

There he stood, one eyebrow raised as in challenge, waiting for her to grab her cloak. Before breakfast. To go out in the rain. Surely he knew the weather would postpone their outing? Chase Dunstan was many things—aggravating, resourceful, blunt, and so on—but no one could confuse him for a fool. And only a fool would forgo one of Evie's breakfasts. What man chose to get drenched and sludge through mud over eating a good meal?

None. Not a single blessed one I've ever met, including Mr.

Dunstan. He's only inviting me because he's sure I'll refuse! Lacey's eyes narrowed as she tried to think of a way to refuse without falling into his snare. She'd trapped him into taking her. Now he was trapping her into letting him go.

And she had no intention of releasing him from his deal.

"Well?" He propped his hip against one of the kitchen stools, smirking at her. "Daylight, such as it is, is wasting."

"You cannot be serious, Mr. Dunstan." Naomi seemed to realize he meant it. "Your plans will have to wait; neither of you can go trudging through the forest on a day like today." Mercifully, she didn't mention the glaringly obvious fact that Lacey didn't *want* to go trudging through the forest.

A grin snuck across his face as though he'd expected their response. Even hoped for it, maybe. "Why not? Mud washes off."

But responsibilities don't. Lacey began to worry that she'd have to cancel after all. She held no doubts that Dunstan wouldn't allow her to reschedule either. *But I can't abandon them. How on earth can he even consider that I would?*

The answer stared her straight in the face. Lacey shook her head in disbelief that it'd taken so long to find the solution. She, after all, wasn't the only one with responsibilities!

"I take it that's a no?" He'd seen the motion and wrongly judged it as a sign of defeat. Victory showed in his smug smile.

"It's raining." She really shouldn't toy with answering, but he'd set her up to take a fall. Now she'd return the favor.

"I know. Why else would I tell you to bring your cloak?" He stretched out his long legs, making himself more comfortable. "It'll buy some time before you get too drenched. If you're worried about your dress, the cloak will catch the worst dirt."

Normally Lacey wouldn't take it askance that a man recognized her care in dressing. Even better if he avoided situations guaranteed to ruin whatever garments she wore. But Mr. Dunstan didn't say this out of courtesy or appreciation. Somehow, he made practical clothing concerns sound trite!

"Unless, of course, you take a tumble." Laughter crept around the edges of his nonchalance. "You do seem to make a habit of falling whenever you roam the mountainside."

"That is none of your concern!" Lacey couldn't contain her outrage. "And, for your information, a cougar knocking one off one's feet hardly constitutes a normal fall." Nor did jerking away from a man determined to examine her ankle, but she didn't want to mention it. The girls didn't know about that incident.

Nor did he apparently. He didn't pursue it further. Instead he again settled for trying to goad her into mucking around the mountainside. "It's my concern if you stumble while we're on a hunt. It might make us lose track of our prey."

At least he didn't pretend the protest stemmed from any genuine worry over her well-being. Lacey tried to bank her outrage. She failed. "Your devotion to your work is touching." She couldn't even try to make it sound like a compliment.

"Lacey. . ." Cora's call was a warning and a plea to control herself. Her best friend knew her temper too well.

"I do my best." At last Dunstan's grin disappeared.

"You'd do better to concentrate on the more important part of your post," Lacey informed him. "The rain means far more than mud. Slippery conditions keep the men from their work."

Recognition dawned on his features, but Lacey's righteous anger continued. "Do you consider it safe to leave Evie, Naomi, and Cora cooped up with a slew of bored men? Never forgetting the town-wide brawl that broke out during our last rainy day—"

"Enough!" The barked order interrupted her mid-tirade.

"It is not enough." She rounded on him. "The only reason you waltzed in here whistling is because, as you made so painfully clear, you expected me to forgo the excursion. And you didn't expect me to decline because I wouldn't dream of leaving my friends to entertain the men alone—you made it quite clear you believe my choices revolve around my own comfort."

"I did expect you to cry off in face of the weather," he conceded then fell silent. No apology followed the admission.

"We expected you to remain in town." Evie sounded disturbed to find this in doubt. "It seems our expectations of you are a good deal higher than your estimation of Lacey's priorities."

"I meant no insult." The statement bordered on apologetic.

"Yet you gave one. We all understood the implications of your plan." Only Naomi could make the remonstrance without making it an accusation. "I trust that will not be repeated."

"No, ma'am." He had the grace to look abashed before his gaze sought Lacey's. Speculation underscored his promise. "You can be sure I won't underestimate her in the future."

I probably won't have to. In his experience, people who overestimated their own worth made mistakes accordingly. And Lacey Lyman, so indignant over an implied insult, showed that pride was her Achilles' heel. The whole scene would've amused Chase if that pesky twinge of guilt would go away.

It didn't.

Whether he wanted to admit it or not, he'd let his own ambitions and grudges block his better judgment. Chase could've kicked himself for overlooking the obvious need to stay in town. If he'd thought beyond his own irritation at being stuck with the woman, he'd have already been in the diner with the men. It was his job to make sure the men didn't get restless and stupid.

Instead, restlessness brought out his own stupidity. *I got so caught up in wanting to get the better of her that I gave in to the worst of myself.* It shouldn't take the likes of Lacey Lyman to remind him of his responsibilities. That rankled almost as much as overlooking them in the first place. Chase wasn't used to being wrong and found he didn't much like the feeling.

Nor did he like the increasing number of ways the woman defied his expectations. She penned the ludicrous ad responsible for bringing overeager, difficult bachelors swarming down on her and her friends. Then she turned around and tried to protect them from those very bachelors. Her clothes declared her shallow, fussy, and dainty. But she didn't turn a hair over shooting a pouncing cougar, taking on a mess to stagger stalwart men, or taking on the task of bathing his Irish wolfhound. A mass of contradictions, the only thing she kept consistent was her temper, and it, like the rest of her, was spectacular.

It'll be her undoing, Chase told himself as he left the kitchen to join the men in the diner. What remained to be seen was whether or not he wanted to hasten it along. For all his time in Hope Falls, he wasn't any closer to discovering the truth behind the collapse of Miracle Mining. Until he did, Chase needed to do a better job of getting on her good side.

He hadn't missed the undertones behind what Miss Higgins and Miss Thompson said in the kitchen: the women he'd won over were starting to wonder if they'd made the right decision in hiring him. Chase would have to walk a fine line from here on.

The boisterous din of more than a dozen men drowned out any chance of thinking. Chase surveyed them, watching for any sign of trouble, but they seemed in good spirits. Mrs. McCreedy circled the room with a fresh pot of coffee, refilling mugs. Mrs. Nash claimed the end of a bench near her brother, looking faintly green around the gills. Chase decided to join them.

At best, he might learn something from the two people who shared a house with the women running the town. At worst, he'd be in position to keep an eye on Lawson. After the stunt he'd pulled a week ago in the store, Chase made a point of watching the man. Lechery lurked beneath those fine manners, making Lawson next to Williams as most likely to cause trouble.

"Morning," he greeted Mrs. Nash and plunked down on the bench facing her and her brother. Lawson, he noted, didn't look pleased to see him. Chase's mood improved a notch. *Good.*

"Good morning." Mrs. Nash made a brave attempt at a smile. From the way she looked and what Chase gathered about females in the family way, her stomach troubled her. She sounded upbeat though. "Looks like we're all rained in today, doesn't it?"

"Looks like it," he agreed and ran out of conversation.

"Shame to lose a workday." Lawson filled the gap. "Though perhaps we'll think of something to make the day interesting." He faltered at Chase's scrutiny, evidently remembering the last time he'd been caught finding something "interesting."

"I offered to teach you how to knit," his sister teased.

Lawson understandably chose not to recognize the remark. Instead he turned his attention to the diner door, which swung open to admit a thin man along with a blast of cold air. The newcomer paused at the threshold, scanning the room before making his way over to their table. Lawson supplied the name Chase couldn't quite recall. "Good morning, Mr. Draxley."

"Morning, Lawson. Mrs. Nash." The blond-haired man gave her a nod and folded himself onto the bench, looking like he attempted to fold himself away from attention. Only then did he mutter, "Mr. Dunstan. Didn't know whether we'd see you today."

After the debacle in the kitchen, this rubbed a raw nerve. Chase shrugged rather than ask why the man thought he wouldn't show up on a day the women needed protection. More likely than not, the man referred to Chase's habit of bypassing the bunkhouse in favor of his tent, but assumptions were dangerous.

"I knew you'd be here," Mrs. Nash assured him. She lowered her voice and leaned forward to add, "After what happened the last time we were all rained in together, you'd need to be."

"I should hope you didn't find yourself in the middle of that brawl," Chase said to her, but looked at the brother who should have been doing a much better job of protecting her.

"Oh no," she hastily corrected. "I heard of it later. Just before it all broke out, I came down with the most dreadful headache. My brother had taken me back to the house to rest."

"Good." He turned to the men. "If either of you saw it firsthand, I'd be interested in hearing your account." *And learning whether Granger really got rid of the rabble-rousers.*

"Like Arla said, I'd escorted her back to the house." Lawson acted as though that explained everything. "I wouldn't leave her unattended and undefended with the men milling about."

So you left Miss Lyman and the others to fend for themselves? Chase swallowed the accusation and looked to Draxley for his answer instead. He doubted the skittish fellow could offer much insight; Draxley looked the sort to hop away at the first sign of trouble. In fact, he looked terrified to realize Chase was even asking for his recollections of the brawl.

"Can't say," he mumbled. His glasses slid down his nose, only to be pushed up again and repeat their descent. "Went back to the telegraph office after lunch finished, didn't I?"

"Telegraph office?" Chase's interest sharpened. Was it possible Draxley had been hired on as part of Miracle Mining's operation and stayed on? "How long have you manned the post?"

"Since they put the lines in," he confirmed. Inspired by his work, he went on. "Before that I headed an office in Richmond, you know. Different sort of setup, much more advanced, but the code coming in always stays the same."

"What prompted you to make the move?" Chase directed

the conversation back to Hope Falls. "Thirst for adventure?" It took some doing, but he got the question out without laughing. If anyone would steer far clear of adventure, it was this man.

"Favor to a friend. Lost him in the collapse, you know." He sighed, mustache twitching at a rapid pace as though attempting to brush away the unpleasant memory. "Everyone had such high hopes for the mines, but you see how that turned out. My old office already hired a replacement, so I couldn't go back to Richmond when things went south. Terrible tragedy. . ."

The way he put it made it sound as though the loss of his old post was the great tragedy, but Chase figured the man meant well. Poor fellow was one bundle of nerves. Obviously he regretted his choice to move to the Colorado Territory.

But Chase didn't regret it at all. He'd just found the only person in town who'd been there when the mine collapsed. "Sorry to hear that. What was it like when it went down? I wonder if the town felt the vibrations or if it's set too far back."

"Morbid thing to wonder." Lawson looked at him askance.

"No, no." Draxley waved Lawson's protest aside. "Curiosity is natural, after all. And when one survives something like that, it's good to get it out in the open." The man made it sound as though he'd been inside the mines and clawed his way out rather than tucked safely away in his telegraph office.

"You must have been terrified." Mrs. Nash played into Draxley's dramatics and gave a delicate shudder. "Did everything shake? Could you hear anything? I wouldn't sleep for days."

"I very nearly didn't." His chest puffed at her appreciation of his ordeal. Draxley leaned forward to confide, "The shaking wasn't the worst of it. The sound when it came down. . ." He trailed off as though unable to describe it. "BOOM!" He slapped his hands against the table to underscore the volume.

Mrs. Nash gave a small shriek of surprise, but quieted when

everyone in the room started to stare at their table. She gave a nervous laugh. "You certainly managed to give a sense of what it was like, Mr. Draxley. Just the rendition frightened me!"

Chase, unnerved for an entirely different reason, settled into his own thoughts. An avalanche would have gained noise as it gathered speed. A series of tunnels giving way would issue a rumbling sort of roar. What Draxley described more closely fit the sound of a large explosion—the sort of thing that had to be carefully planned out and set up in advance. If Braden Lyman and his partner decided to expand the mines, no workers would've been allowed in the tunnels until the dust cleared and the engineers shored up the passages with reinforced timbers.

Chase finally had more than vague suspicions to go on.

The collapse of Miracle Mining was no accident after all.

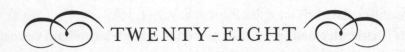

TWENTY-EIGHT

Cora watched as Chase Dunstan sat with his back to a corner, coolly surveying everything in the room. More often than not, his gaze returned to Lacey. *Something's going on there.*

But for the life of her, Cora couldn't figure out what it was. One day the two of them seemed to tolerate each other fairly well—Dunstan going so far as to help Lacey clear out the shop for reorganizing. The next, he became disproportionately angered over something like giving Decoy a bath—which had been an excellent idea, even if the execution of it had a few hiccups.

The way they bickered gave away their heightened sensitivity over the other's words. Sparks flew between the two, but they didn't ignite anything but arguments. This morning, for the first time, Cora wondered if a sort of instinctual wisdom made Lacey protest hiring the man. *Maybe it was a mistake.*

Then again, who knew the hunter's favorite target would be Lacey's temper? Besides, the man unquestionably succeeded in keeping the peace amid their shrinking population.

She'd looked around the dining room after they'd finished a

breakfast of Cornish cheese bread and bacon noting with some surprise how swiftly their numbers had dwindled. Originally two-dozen strong, only about fourteen men still remained.

Smooth-talking Robert Kane and the three men he'd led in a failed nighttime raid on the women's house took out four workers with one stroke. The town brawl prompted Granger, Riordan, Clump, and Williams to force another four overly temperamental failures onto the train. With Granger escorting Twyler back to Maine to face justice, they'd lost a solid ten fellows.

If she didn't let herself get worked up over all the unpleasantness preceding their departures, Cora could appreciate how much calmer things were around town. In startling contrast to a few weeks prior, this rainy-day diner congregation showed little inclination to cause a ruckus. They did, however, look bored—and when bored men tried to find a way to pass the time, Cora noticed they usually found trouble instead.

They needed some form of entertainment before they drove someone to distraction—or worse, brawling. And the only thing Cora could think of was the same thing that failed so spectacularly the last time around. Would this time be any better? *Do I dare suggest we attempt a cribbage tournament?*

After all, they had more than enough boards to play, and Lacey had gone through numerous trunks and boxes to unearth the pegs she'd packed. . .just in case. Between the four of them, Cora had no doubt that she, her sister, Naomi, or Lacey managed to haul almost everything along with them to Hope Falls.

Why let it all go to waste? It had been ages since she'd played any card games, save the whist Braden sullenly cheated at. Besides, Cora knew Mrs. Nash, for one, could use a break in the monotony of days spent resting for the sake of the baby.

"I have a proposition," she announced to the room at large. "Why don't the men go back to the bunkhouse and fetch their cribbage boards? It seems a good day to get around to that tournament." *At least, enough time's gone by to try again.*

"Cribbage never did appeal to me," Draxley declined. Then again, the telegraph operator hadn't taken the initiative to get involved in anything since the women arrived in Hope Falls. Why should they expect a game or two of cribbage to be any different?

"Those who don't wish to play can watch those who do," Naomi declared. "For more fun, we'll set it up in the style of a tournament. A little competition adds spice to the game."

"What does the winner get?" Williams, as always, made the question into a demand. His gaze slid to Lacey. "I can't think of a better reward than a walk with the lady of our choice."

"I'll play for a prize like that!" Chester Fillmore, a faded-looking fellow who blended in with the background whenever he wasn't working, sent a shy grin Naomi's direction.

"Four ladies. That means there should be four winners, ja?" stated Clump.

"Two winners," Evie corrected. "It would disrespect our fiancés if Cora or I agreed to go strolling with another man."

"I propose a change to the reward." Lacey, Cora noticed immediately, was looking at everyone except Mr. Dunstan. "Let there be four winners, and let all of us go for a little picnic on the next Sunday when the weather is fine. Mr. Dunstan will arrange the location and hunt for a suitable main dish."

Mr. Dunstan looked anything but pleased with the suggestion, but held his tongue. Maybe the man knew better than to argue after the debacle earlier this morning. Maybe he realized that keeping an eye on the four of them when they weren't in town, and possibly exposed to greater danger that way, counted as part of his position. And maybe. . .just maybe. . .he felt a twinge of compunction over the way he'd treated Lacey earlier.

Cora couldn't be sure of his reason for keeping quiet, but she knew Lacey volunteered his help as a form of revenge. Her best friend was as hurt as she was angry by Dunstan's low opinion, and that sort of thing always made Lacey lash out.

It must be a Lyman trait, she decided. Braden did the same. *I wonder whether he'll be unhappy letting another man accompany me on a picnic?* Jealousy, although not ideal, meant a man cared. Trust could follow love, if the feelings remained.

A sigh escaped her. *How low I've sunk if I'm hoping he's jealous!* There had been a time once when Braden wouldn't leave her side long enough to become jealous. Before Hope Falls.

"Sounds like a splendid idea," Cora seconded Lacey's plan. Whether or not the ploy worked would be telling. If Braden rose to the bait, it would be a good indication that he merely hid the feelings she kept hoping to rekindle with her visits to him. Otherwise, he no longer cared. His reaction would tell her if she should continue hoping. . .or if all hope was lost.

Lacey hoped her burst of inspiration would unsettle Chase Dunstan—and remind him of his place. *Not out of snobbery,* she reassured herself. *But because he deserves to feel as unsettled as he makes me. The man may not follow convention, but that doesn't mean he can do as he pleases and insult whomever he wishes!*

The cribbage reward clipped his wings, since usually Dunstan came and went as he pleased. But the contrary man gave no outward sign of displeasure at the imposition. He fought dirty to find a way out of taking her along on a hunt, but maintained total equanimity when faced with shepherding eight people on a picnic. A chill spread through Lacey's midsection.

He didn't protest because I curtailed his freedom, she suddenly realized. *The picnic doesn't bother him. Most likely, he wouldn't have* argued if Cora or Naomi wanted to learn how to track animals. *No. He's doesn't want to be saddled with* me.

An odd numbness gripped Lacey as the men around her enthusiastically agreed to the competition, rising to their feet to go fetch the cribbage boards they'd made weeks before.

Draxley, the avowed cribbage critic, looked like he was weighing whether or not to throw his hat in the ring. Strangely enough, his question wasn't about food—the only thing he'd showed interest in for the entire time Lacey knew him. "Where is this picnic going to be? Any sort of spot in mind, Dunstan?"

"Doesn't matter where we go, so long as the women are with us." Williams already took for granted that he'd win a place.

"What sort of food will there be?" Clump worried. "Will there still be lunch for those of us who don't get a spot?"

"No one misses a meal!" Evie sounded scandalized. To her, the very idea she'd let someone go hungry was deeply offensive. "I believe Lacey meant that Mr. Dunstan would be going out of his way to catch a special treat for the picnic goers."

"Already have something in mind. As for the place"—he wore an odd look of determination as he decided—"toward the south, just past the mines, there's plenty of spaces already cleared. It'll be far enough away from town so the party stays private."

"Braden won't like that." Cora's mutter didn't sound like a protest. In fact, her best friend looked pleased at the idea of irritating her fiancé. "He won't like that one little bit."

"Here, now!" Draxley's high, reedy voice reached the breaking point. "Those mines aren't safe! Even if there wasn't any danger, it'd be a dismal place to try and enjoy yourself. It reeks of morbidity to picnic in the shadow of such a tragedy."

"I think it speaks of honoring life," Cora argued. "The lives that were lost and the way life should move along for those who remain. Laughter leaches away sorrow, and we've allowed the sorrow to take hold for long enough, Mr. Draxley."

Lacey could only guess what that speech cost her friend, but Cora's face absolutely shone with the power of what she'd said. *She's ready to move past the tragedy,* Lacey realized. *Braden's the only one determined to wallow in it—and he drags Cora down along with him. Little wonder she's eager to tell my brother that we aren't making the mountainside a macabre memorial!*

"Mr. Dunstan has greater understanding of the land and how it lays than any of us," she chimed in. "Whether you agree with his choice or not, I have every confidence we'll be safe. It's not as though he plans to take us on a tour of the ruins."

Surprise and speculation stamped Dunstan's face before he schooled his expression into impassivity. Lacey abruptly became aware that she'd never complimented his abilities before. Declaring her faith in his judgment made a considerable leap from arguing with him over his faulty ideas about her character.

Well, Mr. Dunstan. There are some things we can agree on and others you'll have to learn. Perhaps I shouldn't hope to aggravate you—I should hope you'll get to know us well enough to become more agreeable! She smiled as the men brought their games and cards to the tables, their chatter humming through the room.

"Think he can rustle up some more beaver tails?" Someone spawned an avalanche of fond remembrances over the soup.

"Naw. They's too rare nowadays." Regret coated every word as the man slapped his cribbage board down atop the table.

"Do you suppose we get to choose which woman we want to take there?" Bobsley shot an assessing glance Naomi's way.

"Dunno, since two of 'em aren't up for grabs anyway." One of the buckers from Williams's crew gave an unconcerned shrug. "So long as you get to go along, you've got a chance to cozy up to whichever one you like." Bobsley's sharp elbows jabbed the man into realizing Lacey could hear every word. He quieted.

Lacey drew her packet of cribbage pegs from the pocket of her apron—she'd tucked them inside on the way to the kitchen that morning when the skies made it clear they'd be spending the day indoors. It never hurt to be prepared—or to save herself from getting soaked to the skin in a dash back to the house.

"All right. Now, everyone who doesn't wish to play can take a seat at that table." She pointed toward the front of the room, away from the kitchen. "Then head to the left if you know how to play, or go to the right if you need a demonstration first."

Thankfully, more men headed to the left. Lacey didn't have the patience of a good teacher, but she would've stepped in if more competitors didn't know the complex game. Her cousin, with unshakable composure and a fondness for giving lessons, made an excellent teacher. Lacey gladly left the beginner table and all the explanations of values, rules, and terms to Naomi.

Among the rest, she was surprised to see Mr. Draxley. "I was under the impression you didn't enjoy cribbage," she couldn't resist remarking. After all, the man made his opinion known to all of them, and to top it off he'd criticized the picnic site. *What made him decide to join the competition?*

"I'm curious to see what our new hunter brings to the table." He didn't look particularly excited. "Besides, I rarely take a day away from my desk. It'll break the monotony a bit."

Lacey didn't question him further, instead divvying up the remaining men into pairs. "We'll do this properly. Each pair will draw to see who deals, and the cards will be dealt and pegs in place for every table before anyone starts playing." Hopefully that would regulate the timing of the games and give Dunstan the opportunity to make sure no one tried to cheat.

With the exception of Naomi's table of learners, who'd already gotten underway in a team-style match, they readied themselves swiftly. When Lacey judged everyone prepared, she nodded to

Evie, who stood beside the dinner bell. Her friend rang it with an impressively loud, resounding *clang*.

On cue, Lacey called out, "Let the games begin!"

TWENTY-NINE

I'm being watched. Chase felt her eyes on him, sensed the impatience with which she waited for him to finish his outstanding breakfast of eggs in overcoats. He'd never seen the like of the dish and refused to rush through it.

Miss Lyman could cool her heels while he enjoyed this admirable creation. After the stunt she'd pulled last week, foisting a picnic on him with the cribbage winners, Chase didn't feel particularly inclined to accommodate her.

Maybe if Williams hadn't managed to snag a spot, he wouldn't mind so much. But the man had joined Riordan, Clump, and—surprisingly—Draxley in victory. Clump and Riordan were good sorts to have around. Draxley might prove useful if Chase could pump him for more information about Hope Falls when it was owned by Miracle Mining.

Williams ruined what could have been an enjoyable afternoon. Now, instead of questioning Draxley or even relaxing, Chase would have to keep a hawk eye on the rabble-rouser. The man made no bones about the fact he was angling for Miss Lyman, and he'd already started making noise about wanting to go for a little walk after the meal ended. *Not going to happen.*

Today they'd be hunting partridge for the special main dish Miss Lyman recklessly promised. Food was a form of art Chase really appreciated, and he intended to savor this example. Besides, he deserved to linger over breakfast before facing the next few days. Chase picked up another one of the eggs in overcoats and surveyed it closely before sinking his teeth in.

As near as he could figure, they'd baked potatoes, cut off the tops, and scooped out the insides. They mashed the potatoes real nice and creamy and added bits of ham to the mix. That alone would've made for good eating, but the estimable Miss Thompson didn't stop there. She'd gotten *creative* and plunked a boiled egg between layers of the ham mash and baked cheese.

Chase had no idea the egg lurked inside until he bit into the thing. Then the name made sense. *Eggs in overcoats, indeed.* He put away four of them before so much as reaching for the coffee. Since then, he'd polished off three slices of buttered toast and was now reaching for his fifth overcoated egg. Miss Lyman, he'd been instantly aware, started watching him while he enjoyed the third egg-and-potato surprise. Now the heat of her impatience could've kept a cabin warm on a winter day.

"If you're quite finished, Mr. Dunstan?" Apparently reaching her breaking point, she stood before him. Her graceful fingers played with a small watch dangling from a thin chain.

Actually, he had been. While she kept silent, he figured he'd kept her waiting long enough to get the message across. But she'd shot herself in the foot by coming over here. *Now I have to show her we're on my timetable—not hers. When we hit the forest, it's my way of doing things, and she either learns to live with that and follow my directions or gets left behind.*

Chase reached for a sixth egg in an overcoat, his gaze never leaving hers as he bit into it. *Too good. . .but too much.* He put down the food and reached for more coffee, slugging back an entire mug before he bothered to answer. "Ready when you are."

Her scowl got the better of her before she calmed. "I'll just fetch my cloak." She slowly picked it up from where she'd laid it on the bench, a silent testament to her long wait. They were the only two people left in the dining room now.

Chase pushed away from the table, walked over to the peg by the door holding his hat, and grabbed it. Hat in hand, he gave her a long, assessing look. Two things struck him about the dress she'd chosen. First, it was green, so the woman had some sense that they'd need to sneak up on their prey. Second, it was the *same* green dress she'd worn the last time she followed him into the forest. *Must be her stalking dress.*

"What do you plan to go after today?" She sounded eager.

"Partridge. Since you volunteered me to provide something out of the ordinary for the picnic, we have two days to take down nine birds." One for every member of the party.

"Eleven," Miss Lyman corrected. "Mrs. Nash decided she'd like to attend if at all possible. Her brother will be coming along to offer his arm and support, so she doesn't fall."

Despite his low expectations, Chase knew the picnic just got worse. Lawson wrangled his way in, even though he lost his first round at the cribbage tournament. *Selfish fool probably talked his sister into feeling like she was missing out.*

"Mrs. Nash shouldn't be trekking around the forest with the doctor back in town." The woman looked ready to go into labor at any moment, and Chase didn't want the risk of it on his watch.

"Do you think we should invite him as well?" Miss Lyman fastened her cloak. "That's a splendid idea. Not only for Mrs. Nash, but for his own sake. The poor man stays cooped up in that house with Braden all the time. Clump even takes him his meals.

Of course, he'll bring the number up to an even dozen."

"Ambitious, but not impossible." Chase reeled at how much the woman talked—and what she'd revealed. Why did she feel sorry because a man spent so much time with her brother? Did they arrange for the doctor to remain inside so he wouldn't talk to anyone? He'd bring down another bird for the chance to find out.

"Gun?" He didn't see a purse dangling from her wrist, and her cloak didn't have pockets. Remembering the day they'd met, Chase didn't think for an instant that she'd left it behind.

"Here." She reached into a pocket cleverly tucked into the billow of her skirts and presented the mother-of-pearl inlaid pistol. Someone taught her elemental gun safety. It rested on her palm, barrel facing away from her, away from him, and away from the kitchen where her friends were still chattering.

No more than five inches long, it nevertheless boasted six cylinders. Impressive, but not nearly enough for hunting.

"You're going to need more bullets." Chase knew he couldn't predict the day's events, but he planned on bagging several birds. In spite of her luck with the cougar, he didn't hold much confidence in her marksmanship abilities with that tiny thing.

"Check." She checked the safety before sliding the gun into her right pocket then drew an entire box of bullets from her left. "If you're satisfied, I'll just get my bag and we'll go."

Nothing snobby about that. She wasn't challenging whether or not her equipment met his criteria, but genuinely asking. For the first time since he'd known he'd be stuck with her for an entire day, Chase found hope it wouldn't be unbearable.

"Bag?" A quick look around the diner turned up nothing.

"I left it in the kitchen, since I noticed you didn't mention our expedition to the other men." She hesitated, and Chase knew she was pushing back the thought that she was going alone into the forest, entirely unchaperoned, with an unmarried man. "It might've raised some uncomfortable questions."

I have a few myself. Chase nodded and waited as she slipped through the swinging doors and disappeared into the kitchen. *Like why she's not more concerned about propriety. Or why she's so determined to go hunting if it's not out of spite?*

Because his first idea was that her decision to tag along had been simply to aggravate him. She'd accomplished that well enough last week, when she'd handed him his head over how little he knew what motivated her. But the woman had a point.

What do I really know about the woman claiming to be Lacey Lyman? Once you got past her distractingly good looks, something more complex peeked through. *Brave*—she conquered the cougar without any hysterics. *Loyal*—she stayed in town to protect her friends. *Fiery*—not many could hold their own against her. *Ruthless*—no price too great, no obstacle she wouldn't overcome to get what she wanted. *The last one's the kicker.*

It would be dangerous to get in the way of anyone with that sort of relentless determination—even worse to cross her. Because in spite of the intriguing traits, Miss Lyman didn't seem nearly as concerned with moral questions as she was with getting her own way. Chase didn't know if she was a believer or if she only put her faith in herself. In a lot of ways, she carried herself like a Christian, but the underlying motivation always seemed to come back to her plans for Hope Falls.

Did she hatch those plans back when the town housed a mine?

"Ready!" Excitement flushed her cheeks, as though she really looked forward to the grueling day ahead. Slung over her right shoulder, strap crossing her body, a leather game bag bumped against her hip. A *very full* leather game bag—which couldn't possibly be holding any game *before* the hunt.

"What all did you squirrel away in that thing?" Chase eyed it dubiously. They were in for a long trek, and she shouldn't be carrying any more weight than was necessary. Besides, she already packed her pistol and her bullets in her skirt pockets. What more did a fine lady think she'd need to go tracking?

"My canteen—I don't want too many things swinging around while I'm walking, so I put it inside." She started ticking things off. "My pocket-knife, for field dressing. Some good strong twine to use for carrying small game, a few handkerchiefs because it's going to be dirty work. . ." The woman sounded like she'd swallowed a manual for beginners. Otherwise, how would a fine lady like Lacey Lyman know anything about field dressing?

She'd trailed off as though she couldn't remember everything she'd crammed into the pack. This was proven when she sidled close to a table and plopped the bag atop it. Then the intrepid and overly prepared Miss Lyman began rummaging through, continuing her list as she rediscovered her necessities.

"A fan to use when I'm overexerted." She shot a quelling glance his way when he snorted at that find. "A fresh jar of feverfew infusion, so I can reapply it if the insects become troublesome later in the day. Oh, and lunch of course!"

For a moment Chase sat on the proverbial fence, trying to decide whether to laugh at her long laundry list or ask what she'd packed for their midday meal. It seemed a safe bet that anything from Miss Thompson's kitchen would prove better fare than the jerky and biscuits he kept handy while working.

It was a toss-up, but Chase figured he'd find out about the food later in the day. "Put your knife in the pocket with your bullets, put your canteen around your neck, and give the bag here. Anything you carry gets heavier as the day wears on; you can't tote that much." But he could see his way clear to toting lunch around, once he'd gotten rid of everything else. Except the twine—that might come in handy but would tangle in a pocket.

"Why, thank you, Mr. Dunstan." She slid the strap over her

head and held it out. "That's very kind and thoughtful—what, precisely, do you think you're doing!" She ended on a squawk.

"Lightening the load." He tilted the bag to one side, so things shifted. Chase reached in, pulled out an ivory fan, and tossed it on a nearby table. A garden of embroidered handkerchiefs bloomed in the emptied space. He chucked those, too. *What sort of nonsense is this?* A glass jar held some slightly cloudy liquid. Chase held it up for her inspection.

"The feverfew infusion," she informed him, her arms crossed over her chest as though to hold back a flood of angry words.

"Don't need that either." He placed it next to the hankies. "We'll stop by your shop and grab you a few bandannas, and that'll do. Everything else can stay here till we get back."

"Very well, Mr. Dunstan." She sounded as tightly wound as she looked. "If you insist on leaving the handkerchiefs and my fan, I'll not quibble. But the feverfew comes with me."

"Won't do a lick of good." He slipped her bag over his head.

"Oh, it most absolutely does!" Lacey fought the urge to pick up her fan and throw it at his obstinate skull. Her temper hadn't won her any favors, so she decided to appeal to his sense of competition. "In fact, I can prove it. Let me bring the infusion and use it, and as the day progresses we'll see who suffers more bites and stings. If I'm correct, I can bring whatever I like on our next outing together. If you win, I'll bring only what you approve on our future excursions."

"Future excursions?" Genuine surprise colored the question.

"Of course." She held out the jar. "I'm a quick learner, Mr. Dunstan, but I don't think either of us believes I'll catch on to more than the rudiments the first time around."

He looked at the jar as though it might bite him. Then

he looked at her, and Lacey knew with absolute certainty that Chase Dunstan never considered she might want more than one lesson. By taking the jar, whether he won or lost the game, he'd be agreeing to continue her education with additional trips.

"Or you could simply admit you're wrong, and we'll leave it at that." Lacey knew she was goading him, but the stakes now went beyond keeping her insect repellent. It was about safeguarding her only opportunity to get outside the shop or the diner and actually learn something about all this land.

"I'm not wrong." He swiped the jar from her hand, looking repulsed at both the idea she'd be right and the knowledge that he'd just agreed to take her on future lessons. "Let's go."

When he turned to lead the way, Lacey grinned. No matter what Chase Dunstan thought, she knew this was going to be fun.

THIRTY

Four hours later, Lacey was ready to admit that she might have been mistaken. While time seemed to trudge by more slowly than they did—Dunstan set a grueling pace and expected her to maintain it—an entire morning with nothing to show for it could put a damper on anyone's spirits. *Especially when the man who's supposed to be teaching you about the forest and how to track animals only opens his mouth to tell you to be quiet.*

Well, Lacey had stayed quiet long enough! "Mr. Dunstan?"

"Sssh," he hissed, not even looking over his shoulder. The man kept walking as though he knew exactly where he was going. Maybe he did, but he hadn't bothered to tell Lacey about it.

She put the tips of her fingers in her mouth and produced a gratifyingly shrill whistle. For the first time in hours, her guide stopped to look at her. Decoy came bounding back to sit atop her foot, and Lacey remembered the last time she'd been in the woods with his master. Then it had been Dunstan to whistle.

"What do you think you're doing?" He spoke so low it became a rumble of words more than actual speech. "I told you—"

"To be quiet," Lacey whispered back. "Yes, I know. It's the only thing you've said all morning! After following nothing but you and your dog around for the past four hours, it's safe to say I've learned nothing at all about how to track an animal!"

"You should have." He approached her. "Learning to be quiet is the first lesson, and it's one you're far from mastering."

"I haven't spoken a word in over two hours!" she protested. Forest scenery may be beautiful, but it didn't exactly hold her attention when there wasn't anything in particular to see. A little conversation—even instructions on the sort of thing she should be noticing—would've made things a lot more interesting.

"Talking"—he returned to a more normal tone of voice—"is the most obvious part of silence. The way you walk comes next. Every move should make as little noise as possible." Dunstan's glance swept down her skirts toward her boots. "First off, you need sensible heels to minimize the sound of your steps."

"I'll order some," she told him. "There's nothing I can do about my footwear for today. I hoped to learn something more..." *Interesting!* She paused and finished, "Immediately applicable."

"Fine," he ground out. "The most important tool a hunter uses is patience. Move slowly and surely, take time to notice the signs around you. Know that you might fail to best the beast you track, but don't abandon your task unless necessary. The largest portion of hunting lies in waiting, Miss Lyman."

I waited a couple hours to hear you tell me that? Lacey kept the thought to herself. Provoking him wouldn't make Mr. Dunstan become a better teacher. Maybe questions would.

"Is there a way to muffle my footsteps? Wrap my heels with cotton or some such?" She tried to think of a way and failed.

Dunstan looked at her a long time, as though measuring whether or not she truly wanted to learn. Heartbeats passed before he decided to speak. "Don't assume the problem lies with the shoes, though in your case they need to be changed. Start with controlling the way you walk. Step on soft ground wherever possible—not mud, but solid earth. Do a better job of avoiding rocks and twigs, which do nothing but broadcast your presence. If you need to push aside a low-lying branch, don't shove it back to rebound and smack against the tree. Dry grasses rustle when your skirts brush by; the same for low bushes."

That makes sense—but it's a lot to remember when I typically set one foot in front of the other without thinking. I'd try going on tiptoe, but we're walking too fast and far!

"All right. You said we're hunting partridge. What signs have we been following for so long?" She peered at the ground, already knowing she wouldn't spot any tracks. Not surprising, since birds flew more often than hopped up a mountain. What did Chase Dunstan know that he hadn't bothered to share with her?

"We aren't. I know a spot where they've roosted for years."

"You've been shushing me all day for *nothing?*" Lacey sucked in a sharp breath as disappointment stabbed her. *Are there any lengths he won't go to in order to avoid talking with me?*

He shrugged at her outrage. "You still needed to practice being quiet, and there won't be time once things get underway."

"I can hold my tongue!" *When I have to. If I bite it, at least.* For now, Lacey didn't feel inclined to prove it.

"No way of knowing that." He arched a brow. "Last time I saw you walking in the forest, you didn't stop talking even when you thought there'd be no one around to join the conversation."

She felt the blush coming but couldn't stop it. "This is an entirely different situation!" *I know you can hear me, so I'd be more careful with what I said, for one thing.* "You're supposed to be teaching me, showing me things I didn't know."

"Told you to get different shoes and stop tromping around without looking where you're stepping." Somehow his summary of the advice sounded far worse than when he'd first mentioned it.

"You could've done that much sooner," she argued. "If you mentioned the finer points earlier, I might've been practicing something *useful* all the way up here! Now I have a late start."

"Do your best. This is poor terrain for stealth. Your shoes will ring against the rocks." As he mentioned it, Lacey realized they stood at the mouth of a canyon. Rocky outcrops shadowed patches of the healthy stream winding its way down the mountain.

"I thought birds liked trees." Lacey eyed the beautiful landscape and realized they'd be leaving the forest behind.

He smiled, and it transformed his face. No longer stern, disapproving, or smug as he'd looked in turn throughout the morning, it gave Lacey a sense that he'd been a mischievous boy. "Partridges aren't good fliers unless they're heading downhill."

"Heading downhill?" Lacey pictured a bird hopping atop the rock faces, only to trip on a rock and drop down into the stream because it didn't fly well. "You mean falling?" *Do birds fall?*

"Nah." Dunstan looked like he was thinking of a way to explain it better. "More the equivalent of a running start. They run pell-mell up a cliff or mountain or what have you—and these birds run faster than you or I could ever manage—then jump over the edge. Quick way to hit the air and drop out of range. They land just fine when they get to the bottom. You'll see."

The birds in her imagination began to look like plump chickens trundling as fast as their legs could carry them. Trouble was, chickens didn't move very quickly. Lacey tilted her head and looked at Dunstan. *Was he trying to trick her?*

"I'm going to be outrun by a bird who can't fly well but hurtles itself over mountainsides?" She wanted to be sure.

"Don't be silly." He took a swig from his canteen. "You're not going to chase them. It's better strategy to have Decoy flush 'em out. Easier to shoot them when they hit the air."

"What do they look like?" They couldn't be small like sparrows or huge like turkeys if one could feed a man.

"Bit longer than a foot. Brown and white with black markings. Red legs longer than a chicken's but shorter than a snipe. Close to quail-sized but look more like pheasants."

This amalgam of comparisons made Lacey envision a long-legged chicken with the head of a pheasant. Either Dunstan's descriptions needed work, or her imagination was rusty. *We'll see when we get there. . .but I think it's the description.*

"This partridge sounds like a very strange bird."

"It is. Harder to hunt than most, so it'll be enough of a treat for your picnic." He swirled the top back on his canteen.

Lacey's stomach grumbled at his mention of the picnic. She'd been too excited to eat much that morning, and all the exertion left her famished. The sun shone straight overhead, and she didn't need her watch to tell her they'd hit midday. "Should we enjoy our lunch before heading farther?" The rocks ahead wouldn't provide shade, and a short rest sounded heavenly.

"There's a little pool a few hundred yards ahead." Dunstan started walking again, but Lacey took his words to mean they'd be stopping soon. Men didn't usually argue against lunch.

She followed after him, noting they were still moving upward. It seemed to Lacey they'd gone uphill all morning, and her legs protested the hard work. When she slowed, Dunstan moved out of sight around a thick copse of trees. The soft gurgle of gently running water enticed her to follow a bit farther.

When she turned the trees, Lacey smiled in delight. An exclamation tickled her lips, but she remembered to whisper.

"How beautiful!"

"Beautiful" didn't do the view justice. Chase brought her as a reward—he hadn't expected her not to say anything for more than two hours, but she'd surprised him again. She deserved a short rest in one of his favorite shady spots. It'd been a while since he'd come here, and Miss Lyman's wonder made him look anew.

Half forest, half grotto, the forest came right up against the back of the rock face overlooking the river. A small overrun, too small to count as a waterfall, trickled down the rock into a small pool beneath. By late August the offshoot would dry up, but for now the gentle burbling of water over rock played like soft music. Trees, long sustained by the pool's spring-and-summer appearance, dappled the sunshine with cool shade.

Its beauty gladdened the eye, and Miss Lyman made a fitting addition to its charms. She sank to the ground without another word, obviously enchanted with the place. After a few moments of silence, she scooted forward to dip her hand in the water.

"Ooh!" A breath of an exclamation told Dunstan the water remained every bit as cold as he remembered. She hastily drew her hand back and shook free several drops of sparkling water.

Decoy showed no such compunction. Hunkering on the bank, he bent his head and began lapping water with great enthusiasm and much slopping of water on his paws. When he quenched his thirst, the dog moseyed on over beside Chase and collapsed with all the grace of a train car. After bolting down the eight strips of jerky Chase laid out for him, the dog stretched into a nice nap.

For his part, Chase wouldn't have minded doing the same. This little nook, tucked into a rocky crag, made good cover. Nothing—and no one—could creep up from behind or either side. Unfortunately, his pretty little concomitant precluded napping.

Not because Miss Lyman wouldn't appreciate the rest—Chase read fatigue in the way she didn't just lean against the rock behind her. The woman practically sank into the boulder, letting it prop her up while her eyes drifted shut for a moment then snapped back open. Ladies didn't routinely go for half-day treks up mountains, so it didn't surprise him if she looked tuckered.

What did still surprise him was how good she looked, even when worn to the bone. Lacey Lyman might be tired, but restless energy still coated her from head to toe. She looked happy. *The woman,* Chase decided, *is a bona fide, beribboned adventuress.*

"Would you be so kind as to pass me a clanger?"

"A what?" Chase searched his memory and couldn't remember her mentioning anything by that name when detailing the contents of her pack. Which, by default, meant she referred to lunch.

"Have you never tried one?" Her blue eyes grew brilliant. "Then you're in for a treat. Evie made a small batch before we left Charleston, and we tried them on the train. She's always trying new recipes and thought this one would sell well in her diner. It's portable enough for passengers to pick up when the train begins to bring more people through Hope Falls." All those words, and she still didn't manage to answer his question.

Chase opened the bag and drew out something wrapped in a clean kitchen towel. He tossed her the first one and kept the second for himself. When he unwrapped his bundle to find two apples and a nice wedge of cheese, disappointment descended.

Did she really say this *is one of her favorite meals?*

"Why would you call this a clanger?" Chase tried not to sound accusing. It sounded so promising before he saw it.

"Bedfordshire clangers," she supplied. "I think part of the reason I like them so much—besides the delicious way they taste and how there's dessert included—is because the story goes that milliners invented them. They made an easy, hearty lunch to leave for their husbands before they went off to work. It shows how women can be good wives and still do something more."

"You call apples and cheese a hearty lunch?" *She must count the apples as the "dessert."* He stopped polishing the first apple with his shirttail to cast her a doubtful look. Then he froze.

"Apples and cheese?" She paused in the act of raising a large golden-brown, delicious-looking pastry to her lips.

"What is that?" Chase's mouth watered, and he began to hope. "Is *that* a clanger?" He didn't wait for her answer, but dove into the bag for the last towel-wrapped bundle loitering in its depths. Pulling aside the fabric, he uncovered a second pastry.

"I didn't realize Evie added anything else." Miss Lyman shrugged and took a dainty bite of her own clanger. "Mmmm...."

Mmmm was right. Chase chomped in, savoring the combination of crust with pork-and-peas filling. *That's more like it!*

"Oops, that's dessert." As he watched, Miss Lyman turned her pastry around before taking a second, much larger bite.

Now curious, Chase upended his clanger. Careful to keep his hand over the hole he'd made in the first side, he tried the second. Same buttery crust with sweet spiced apples this time.

Suddenly, he knew why Miss Lyman called it one of her favorites. The combination of sweet and savory made for a rib-sticking meal to satisfy any preference. And all in one easy-to-carry package.

"This is genius," he informed her between mouthfuls.

"Isn't it?" She beamed at him. "There's a sort of dividing wall of more pastry in between the two fillings. That way you can eat the meat side in one sitting and come back for the sweet side later. If you want to, I mean." Her eyebrows rose as he finished making short work of his succulent lunch.

Cool shade, good food, and a pretty woman to share it with. Chase leaned back, replete. He couldn't ask for anything more.

For now.

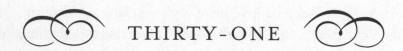

THIRTY-ONE

Since they'd stopped in the gorgeous hidden haven, Dunstan's mood improved. After lunch he became downright talkative. "See that?" Dunstan pointed to the edge of the small pool. "Funny little bird's called a dipper. Watch him and you'll see why."

Lacey squinted and didn't see anything at first. Then something moved on the rocks dotting the bank. "Oh, I see!" A little bird—small enough to rest in her cupped hands, perched atop a rock not much bigger. Beneath a head of brown feathers, it looked as though it wore a white cravat tucked beneath a red waistcoat. She didn't know much about birds, but his legs looked surprisingly long and spindly to support the rest of him.

As they watched, the bird stepped from its dry rock onto one partially covered with gently running water. Then it waded to an entirely submerged perch, hiding its legs and looking like a tiny, narrow-billed duck floating atop the water. Wading forward, it dipped its head into the pool and kept walking.

"Can he breathe?" she whispered. Lacey didn't really know why she was whispering, since she and Dunstan had been talking normally all through lunch. The little bird with its head beneath the water certainly wouldn't hear her and be spooked.

"They can hold their breath for a surprisingly long time," he told her as their feathered friend came up for air. "It's the only bird I know of who truly swims—flies underwater, really."

"Penguins do," Lacey recalled from her wildlife reading. "They don't really have feathers the same way others do though. But it's not really fair to say it swims better than a duck."

"Wait." With that enigmatic reply, Dunstan said no more. Then again, he didn't have to. Almost immediately the dipper dove underwater. His entire body plunged beneath the surface.

Transfixed, Lacey stared at the place where he'd disappeared. *Birds can't swim. He'll bob back up in an instant.* Only it seemed to be taking him rather a long time. Far longer than he should be able to remain underwater. *Maybe he drowned.* Sadness crept upon her at the idea they'd lost the brave fellow.

"There." Dunstan's voice called her to attention.

Lacey peered at the spot, anxious to still not see him. Her gaze scanned the bank, but still she found no sign of the bird. "I think you must have wished you saw him," she mourned.

"No." Dunstan leaned forward and tugged on her bonnet ribbons, turning her head to the far side of the pool. *"There."*

The little dipper splashed his way to the opposite bank—not such a great distance to Lacey, but impossibly far for him to have traversed below the surface. He held something triumphantly aloft in his beak. Happiness flooded her to see his victory.

"He made it!" Wonder filled her. "Dippers really do swim!"

"Yep." Dunstan rose to his feet and plunked his hat back on his head. "They go to the bottom, hunting for insects. Diving is more what they do than dipping. I'd have named it fisherbird."

"Because he fishes for his food," Lacey agreed. "Fisherbird makes a far better name. It describes how special his is."

"If you didn't pay close attention, you'd miss it." Dunstan's words somehow seemed to hold more meaning than the conversation warranted, but Lacey couldn't grasp why. "It's your next lesson. Don't look around for what you expect to see, or things pass you by. Always look to see what's really there."

Lacey couldn't answer at first, so electric was the force of his gaze. She'd had many men stare at her, but this was the first time one looked at her as though trying to plumb the depths of who she was. It was tempting to write it off as him trying to impress the lesson on her, but the fine hairs on the back of her neck prickled. He didn't force that intensity.

As quickly as the moment came, it ended. He turned to pick up the now almost-empty leather bag. Which reminded her. . .

"Wait a moment while I use some of the feverfew infusion," she half-asked, half-told him. When she took the jar from his outstretched hand, their fingers brushed. She pulled away, but chills traveled down her spine at even the brief contact.

She studiously ignored him as she set the jar atop the boulder where she'd been resting and began to untie her bonnet and roll up her sleeves. After unsealing the jar, she poured some of the cloudy liquid into her cupped palm. Lacey couldn't have looked at him now, even if she wanted to. The simple act of rubbing the solution onto her skin now seemed terribly intimate.

To avoid more discomfort, she turned her back and made swift work of the job. Only after she retied the bonnet ribbons beneath her chin, rolled down her sleeves, and smoothed the fabric, did Lacey feel composed enough to face Dunstan again.

He looked at her, expression now inscrutable, and held out his hand in an unspoken demand for the almost-empty jar. Once she'd passed it to him—careful not to touch him—he thrust it back into the bag. Without a word, he started walking.

But he didn't head toward the mouth of the canyon, as she'd

expected. Instead he skirted around the pool and began ascending a low incline up to the rocky overhang. Decoy followed him closer than a shadow, but Lacey found herself hesitating.

Walking or even hiking through the forest was one thing; scrambling up a series of large rocks was entirely different. *My feet hurt. My legs ache. I'll snag my skirts on those jagged edges. . . .* The litany ran through her mind. But swiftly on its heels came thoughts about how Dunstan didn't have to share the beautiful oasis with her—he could have kept walking. He didn't have to be congenial over lunch. In fact, Lacey expected him to remain taciturn. Instead he spoke pleasantly and decided to tell her about the dipper so she could watch it dive and rise.

Without making the decision to, Lacey began picking her way up the rocky slope, following the trail left by Dunstan and Decoy. *After all,* she reasoned, *who knows what I might miss if I look for what I expect? I expect the climb to be difficult, but what will I see when we reach the top? What more will I see of Chase Dunstan if I stop assuming he'll always behave rudely?*

She didn't know, but she'd never forgive herself if she quit trying to find out. Lacey kept her eyes on her feet and her focus on Dunstan as the incline sharpened, loath to look down. Who knew? The climb might take her farther than she expected.

She'd come a lot farther than he expected, Chase grudgingly recognized. Maybe she and the other women had been right in saying he underestimated her. *Dangerous habit, Dunstan.*

Yesterday he'd gotten to thinking Lacey Lyman might be every bit as innocent—and intriguingly intrepid—as she appeared. A woman who couldn't hold her tongue couldn't have much guile, after all. But today she'd destroyed that theory by keeping quiet for hours on end—though she hadn't been happy about it.

Well, I'm not too happy about it myself. Chase slowed his pace slightly, so he didn't get too much of a lead. He'd teased her before about her proclivity for tripping, but the smaller rocks this way shifted underfoot and made the going slippery.

Her shoulder healed well enough. Now that she'd gotten back into fighting shape, Chase didn't plan on watching her hobble about with a sprained ankle. *Predators go after the injured.* The rule of the wild applied all too well to men on the prowl. And Miss Lyman already had far too many men prowling after her.

Besides, he added, *I don't want to have to carry her back!* If he'd gone alone, Chase would've reached the summit of the rocky overhang hours ago. Then again, if he'd gone alone, he wouldn't have gotten to eat one of those tasty clangers. On the balance, having her shadow him almost seemed worthwhile.

"All right?" He waited for her to catch up a little ways from the top. When she nodded, Chase didn't know if she was determined to stay quiet or if she'd become too out of breath. He gestured to her canteen then took a drink from his own.

"Here's the way it'll work." He kept his tone low more from habit than necessity. "The roosts are farther to the west, tucked in a niche a couple yards beneath the overhang."

"Underneath the—" Those blue eyes widened. "From what I saw, it's a steep drop after that overhang. You don't mean we're going to try to weasel our way into some crevices down there?" Despite her anxiety, she managed to keep her voice fairly quiet.

"Not in the plans," he assured her. "When we get close, I'll signal like this." Chase made a fist and moved it sideways, as though pulling rope in a game of one-handed tug-of-war. "Then you'll know it's time to be absolutely silent. If the partridge hear us coming, they'll panic and flush before we're ready."

"How will we flush them?" Her brow wrinkled in confusion.

"Decoy. Those dinner-plate paws of his give him sure footing, and he's better able to navigate the decline than we are. He'll nose down there then look up and wait for my signal once he's beneath the roost. Decoy coming at them will make the entire covey rush right out into the air. That's our chance."

"Does he bring them back afterward?" She cast an admiring glance at the dog and reached over to scratch behind his ears.

"When they fall on parts of the decline he can reach. Often the birds flush and get heights of about fifty feet. If we're lucky, we'll drop a few right up here." With that settled, he started moving again. At the rate she traveled, they'd need a good bit of time to make it back to town. Longer than it took to get here, even. They'd be tired and hopefully weighted down with all the partridge they'd bagged. Chase snorted.

All right, all the partridge *he'd* bag. The little pearly pistol she packed wouldn't hit anything, but Chase didn't have time to teach her how to use a shotgun before they set out. He might've if it weren't for the picnic looming the day after tomorrow. *Maybe I'll show her the next time we go.*

The idea crept into his thoughts and hit him unawares. Before they'd headed out, Chase would've laid odds that Lacey Lyman would find hunting a miserable pastime and never ask for another lesson. Since then, she'd proven surprisingly adaptable. It looked more and more likely that she'd want to learn more.

Then the time for thinking was over. They crested the ridge and crept several hundred yards westward before Decoy began wriggling his back end and sniffing toward the edge of the cliff. Birding behavior, as far as Chase ever heard, was only ever ascribed to retrievers or pointers. But hounds were good hunters, and few people ever came across an Irish wolfhound. Decoy might well be the only one trained in bird hunting.

Chase made the gesture, moved toward the edge of the overhang, and lowered himself onto his stomach. Peering down, he spotted piles of droppings and an occasional feather. *Promising.* He started to slide back so he could gesture to Miss Lyman, but found her already at his side, shimmying down to lie on her own stomach and peek over the side for herself. *Good enough.*

He made the motion for Decoy to scent and hold the birds, and off the dog loped, picking his way carefully down the steep decline. Time stretched while he lay beside Miss Lyman, waiting, but snapped into high gear the moment he saw Decoy stiffen, locked up and staring fixedly at a point Chase couldn't see. After holding still for a moment, he tilted his head back, searching for Chase's signal. Chase got to his knees, still looking over the edge, and gave the silent command for Decoy to flush them.

In a heartbeat about thirty startled partridges burst from the shelf in the rock. Some sprang high, most dropped low in effective, gravity-assisted escapes. Chase focused on the ones to go up and started shooting, dimly aware that Miss Lyman had risen to her feet and was doing the same with her handgun.

After the long walk, difficult climb, and restless wait, the whole thing finished in five minutes. One bird lay at their feet. Chase immediately spotted two more on nearby outcroppings as Decoy made his way back with a fourth between his jaws. He dropped it at Chase's feet. Tail wagging and tongue lolling out to the side, he enjoyed some well-deserved praise and scratching behind his ear. On Chase's signal, he headed back down for more.

Only then did Chase turn his attention to Miss Lyman. There she stood, silhouetted in the afternoon sunlight, a smile on her face and a partridge dangling from her right hand. There was a fierceness in her victory, and it made her even more beautiful.

"My first bird!" She thrust it toward him, and it dangled close enough to hit him if he didn't take it. "Look at it!"

Chase looked. Sure enough, the bird Decoy had brought up bore a wound too small for his shotgun to inflict. *Well, I'll be. . . She hit something after all. And it's the right thing.*

He gave a solemn nod of acknowledgment and handed the bird back. Decoy maneuvered between the two of them to drop another kill at his feet. More praise, and he sent the dog off again. Belatedly, he realized he'd given the dog more encouragement than the woman.

"Most men I know don't bag a partridge like this one the first time they try." Any man would be proud at the compliment

Miss Lyman's brow furrowed. "So. . .you didn't think I'd be able to do it? Then why did you bother bringing me along?"

Chase knew he'd been run to ground, and he couldn't think of a way to escape telling her the truth. There wasn't even a way to make it sound better, so he told her plain and simple: "You didn't leave me any choice."

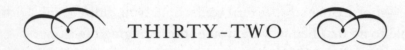 THIRTY-TWO

Ask a foolish question. . . . Lacey berated herself for forgetting, even for a moment, that Chase Dunstan didn't want to be saddled with her. Whether he went hunting or stayed closer to Hope Falls, the man couldn't be more eager to see the back of her.

"Turns out you're better company than I expected," he offered. Dunstan didn't give false compliments. In fact, he didn't give compliments at all, so she could trust he meant it.

Silly though it was, his words gave her something to grab hold of and pull herself from the sadness threatening to swamp her.

"It's easier to exceed expectations when they're set low." She sent him a small smile to show she wasn't haranguing him. Then she went about picking up another one of the partridges and stuffing it into her now-empty game bag. Lacey let him carry their lunch on the way up; she didn't plan to make him carry the fixings for the picnic all the way back without help.

"Up here it's easier to remember God has higher expectations for all of us." Dunstan adjusted his hat brim to better take in the vast panorama laid before them. "The lower you go, the less you expect to see people trying to match them."

"But the more chances you have to meet someone who's living that way," Lacey encouraged. "It's incredibly beautiful up here, but I'd imagine it becomes lonely with no one to talk with."

"Not all of us are as fond of talking as you." His murmur held no rancor as he made the observation. "Sometimes words can't do justice to what's displayed all around us in nature."

Curiosity battled with Lacey's newfound ability to keep silent. The curiosity won. "What do you see, Mr. Dunstan?"

"Power and majesty. A humbling, constant reminder of the verse in Deuteronomy." Dunstan left off appreciating the view to stare at her with unnerving directness. He quoted, " 'He is the Rock, his work is perfect: for all his ways are judgment: a God of truth and without iniquity, just and right is he.' "

It felt to Lacey as though the air itself grew thinner. The breaths she drew did little to fill her lungs as she contemplated the meaning behind the verse. *"All his ways are judgment."* The phrase seemed to resound, caught in the rock around her and hammering into her heart. *And how far will I fall short of His perfect judgment on the day I stand before Him? Will He look at my selfishness? My thirst to prove myself? The way I led my closest friends to an abandoned town, only to fill it with unscrupulous men posing as suitors? Or will He go straight to the worst of it? So many ways I've failed. . . .*

"Striking, isn't it?" His eyes hadn't left her face.

"Unsettling," she admitted. "Since my mother's death I've devoted less and less time to the study of scripture." *Since Braden's death, I avoid it altogether.* But she couldn't very well admit that to a man who'd recited a verse from memory.

"I've always liked to read how God is my Rock. His constancy is a comfort when the world and people around us change." His intensity grew. "He's the one thing that will never fail."

Lacey was eager to end this conversation. "Somehow, I find little solace in the constancy of His judgment when I'm one of those who fails far too frequently." *There. I admitted it. Let that be one less black mark against my character.*

Dunstan looked flabbergasted. "We all fail. It doesn't say our work is blameless; we celebrate the perfection in His."

"And He judges us for falling short," Lacey finished. As far as she was concerned, this conversation had finished, too. She turned to start walking back down the rocky incline they'd climbed up. If Dunstan planned to sermonize, she wouldn't wait for his help going back home. Lacey longed for solid ground and trees— staying up here in the wide open left her feeling exposed.

"He's merciful if we confess our faults." Dunstan's words made her freeze, as though stuck to the stone beneath her. "Just where did you fall so far short you're afraid to trust Him?"

He can't know. Panic clawed its way up her throat as Lacey started walking again. Faster. "That is none of your concern."

It concerns me very much. A woman so afraid of righteous judgment is guilty of something. Chase broke into long strides, determined to begin his descent before the foolish woman started down ahead of him. If she took a fall, he'd be there to break it.

"I can respect that." *Until I find more information.* For now he'd change the subject and try to sneak back around to the things he needed to know. "A woman who bags a partridge first time out deserves that much consideration. I don't know of a man who could bring one down with anything less than a shotgun."

"Men get more opportunities to practice," she retorted. "It doesn't mean they possess greater skill, Mr. Dunstan."

"True." *Occasionally.* "Even with practice and skill, there are times when no amount of preparation changes the outcome."

"If the bird gets away, you try again." She didn't acknowledge any deeper meaning behind his statement, and Chase wondered whether it was because she didn't notice or was avoiding it. "I find success is often measured in steps. Today, for instance, we bagged five birds. This success will lead to more when tomorrow we collect another seven for an even dozen."

We? Chase had no intention of taking her with him tomorrow. Nothing could be left to chance when one day remained. *This isn't the time to mention it,* he decided. *Besides, she'll awake in the morning with more aches than she anticipates.* He'd had full-grown, burly men who'd opted out of a second day of trekking with him after the first tested their strength. Granted, he'd not led her through terribly difficult terrain, but the vast majority had been uphill. That was unavoidable.

Instead of acknowledging her intent to join him the next day, Chase focused on the numbers she listed. "Seven at least."

"At least?" The swift patter of sliding rocks tattled that she'd halted. "They're large enough that we won't need more than one per person. Evie will be bringing some accompaniments, too."

Chase didn't stop walking and was gratified to hear her footsteps resume. It was time to spring his trap. "It occurred to me that since we can't bring Mr. Lyman to the picnic, we could at least bring a part of the picnic to your brother."

A faster skittering of rocks, a heavy footfall told him Miss Lyman slipped a bit at the mere mention of her brother. Turning to face her, he saw her arms extended in the act of adjusting her balance. She hastily put her arms at her sides, but her mouth held a pinched look telling of her displeasure.

"We're not all going to picnic in Braden's sickroom." This wasn't a protest with room to negotiate. It was a flat denial. She still didn't want Chase to meet her brother—perhaps didn't want anyone to meet him. Her reticence raised his suspicions.

"Of course not." His agreement immediately relaxed her, some of the tension leaving her shoulders. "I highly doubt we'd all fit, and that many people would be tiring. My idea was more that we could bring him a partridge after we returned to town."

"How thoughtful." Her lips pursed in that pinched look again. "I'm certain Cora would be delighted to do that."

Did he imagine the slight emphasis on her friend's name? Perhaps. . .but Chase knew he'd pricked a nerve at the thought he might want to venture into her brother's presence. *Good. When people are flustered, they're more likely to make mistakes.*

"You wouldn't want to take it to him yourself?" he pushed. "I've noticed that his fiancée spends far more time with your brother than you typically manage, since you have the store."

"To be frank"—she started walking, leaving him the choice to either get moving or collide with her—"you're not in town for the greater part of the day, Mr. Dunstan, and you are not privy to what I do with my time, nor whom I visit."

Chase resumed walking rather than let her run him down, but was aggrieved that he could no longer read her expressions. "My mistake. I'd simply thought you kept so busy you might welcome the chance to brighten your brother's day. The picnic is something everyone involved is looking forward to, and it might soften the sting if he takes exception to our chosen location."

"How very diplomatic of you." She sounded as though she gritted her teeth. "I'm surprised by how talkative you are, Mr. Dunstan. It makes for quite a contrast to earlier in the day."

Irritating, isn't it, when someone utterly ignores the fact that you might not be enjoying their company and conversation? Chase kept the jab to himself—provoking her further wouldn't get him any new information. He'd already discovered what he needed to know. *She's determined to hide her brother. But why do I get the sense Miss Lyman herself would rather avoid him?*

Put together with her earlier comments about falling short and facing judgment, Chase could easily believe Lacey Lyman's strong sense of guilt stemmed from something to do with her supposed brother. *Maybe Braden wasn't supposed to be in the mines that day.* His mind raced at the implications of that. Unmarried, she'd need a man to maintain ownership of the land for any considerable length of time. *Maybe her Braden did die, as was first reported, but she needed him as the figurehead.*

It all came back to his suspicion that the hidden invalid in Hope Falls wasn't the real Braden Lyman. *She might have found a survivor and cooped him up in a room to pose as her brother.* It wouldn't work for long though. Eventually the man would either recover or pass away, and she'd be in the same position.

Unless she found a husband. It felt as though all the air in the mountains had suddenly been sucked away. Chase couldn't seem to breathe properly. In the past few weeks, he'd decided the woman had no real intention of marrying any of the men. But what if he'd read the situation wrong? Her friend Miss Thompson snagged Granger right off the bat—maybe they were serious.

> *Wanted:*
> *3 men, ages 24–35.*
> *Must be God-fearing, healthy, hardworking single men*
> *with minimum of 3 years logging experience.*
> *Object: Marriage and joint ownership of sawmill.*

The words swam in his memory, the outrageous ad that sparked his suspicions to the point he'd sent Kane to Hope Falls. Back then Chase disregarded the post as a distraction to cover up the sabotaged mine. He still thought the whole plot interwove somehow with the destroyed mine, but now Chase wondered if the ad wasn't genuine. Miss Lyman couldn't hold the land indefinitely. She needed a man to keep her claim legal—and a husband with sawmill experience would be doubly useful.

What was it she'd said when they first discussed her plans for Hope Falls? *"No cost can be too great to gain one's dream."* Back then he'd suspected it referred to the lives lost in the cave-in. But maybe Miss Lyman referred to the price *she'd* pay to keep her goals aloft. The notion wasn't reassuring. If the woman was ruthless enough to marry for money—and force her closest friends to do the same—she'd be unscrupulous in other ways.

The picture became clear. *Too bad I don't like what I see.*

THIRTY-THREE

W hat are you looking at?" Cora walked into the parlor to find Lacey tightly curled into a wingback chair, catalog balanced on her knees and pen in hand as she perused the page.

Her friend looked up, nibbling on her lower lip. "Shoes." The single word explained her intense focus.

"Are you finally going to purchase some sensible boots?" Naomi came in from the opposite entrance and settled herself on the settee. "You won't be sorry once you feel the difference."

"After today, I can no longer ignore the fact that my Louis XV turned heels simply aren't practical for long-distance walks in the woods." Lacey wiggled the toes peeking out under the edge of her skirts. "I don't believe I've ever ached more than I do now," she confessed as she pulled her foot back to hide her shocking dishabille. Mr. Lawson had gone to the McCreedys' house to confer with the senior bull-of-the-woods over beginning the flume, but they couldn't be sure when he'd return to the house.

"You seemed so excited earlier." Cora remembered it well because when she'd seen Lacey burst into the kitchen, flushed with victory over her successful partridge hunt, she'd had to tamp down a spurt of jealousy. *She'd* spent the day with Braden.

"Excitement wears away more quickly than soreness." Naomi angled behind Lacey's chair to get a better look at the page. "Bloomingdales, then? Montgomery Ward has some good options."

"I already looked in that one." Lacey gestured to a stack of catalogs on a nearby table. "To make a good comparison, you know. But I've always felt Bloomingdales carries the best footwear options when one can't have her boots custom-made."

Although perfectly pleased with her own boots, Cora moved to stand at Lacey's other side and get a better look at the catalog. "Have you seen any that will suit your needs?"

"Those look practical." Naomi pointed to a picture of a low-heeled lace-up model with short ankle rises. "Comfortable."

Cora didn't understand how Naomi could think Lacey would ever wear low-fashion, sturdy lace-ups. She smiled at her friend's stricken glance as Lacey tried to come up with a way to refuse the dowdy boots without offending Naomi. Their friend, of course, wore sensible, low-heeled, long-wearing lace-ups.

"I simply can't see Lacey in Old Ladies' Shoes." Cora came to her rescue by reading the name above the picture itself.

"How can you call them that?" Naomi bristled visibly.

"She didn't." Lacey ran a fingertip beneath the print. "They're actually listed that way in the catalog itself!"

"They're shown under the Ladies Common Sense Boots column." Naomi squinted at the print atop the page—print referring to the picture just below it, rather than the next image of her favored Old Ladies' Shoes. "You see?" She ran her finger down and hitched on the protested title. "Oh dear."

Lacey giggled as Naomi snatched her hand back as if burned. "It's an easy mistake to make," she consoled her cousin.

"Those Common Sense Boots are much better," Cora commented. This model showed a modest blocked heel and side-fasten buttons.

"Oh, those aren't bad at all, Lacey!" Naomi transferred her attention immediately. "And the name promises what you need."

"It's between those or the ones pictured here." Lacey pointed to the bottom of the page. "Look at the name: Waukenphast. When you say it, it sounds like 'walking fast.'"

Cora evaluated this other pair of side-buttoned boots. Another stacked heel, but this one straighter than that of the Common Sense version. "Oh, look at the description! 'The most comfortable shoes manufactured.'" She read it aloud for Naomi.

"Yes." Lacey sounded decisive. "These are the ones for me. I'm also going to try one of these." Her voice lowered, and she darted glances about to make sure Mr. Lawson hadn't returned.

"What are you three up to?" Evie strolled over. Heeding Cora's warning of a finger over her lips, Evie didn't say a word. She simply watched as Lacey flipped through the pages and came to rest in the section entitled Corset Department.

Lacey pointed to the Pivot Corset and began to read in a very hushed voice. "'Has an expanding hip and bust, yielding to every movement of the wearer, constantly making an easy and elegant fit. . .which preserves the perfect contour of the figure.'"

No wonder her friend first looked about to make sure no man burst into the room! Evie looked at the picture, which didn't seem much different from any of the other corsets on the page. "What a find! It would be so much easier to walk and sit and cook and do just about anything if we weren't encased like sausages, unable to bend. I believe I'll place an order, too."

In fact, all four of them did. Lacey, who boasted the neatest penmanship, wrote up the order but left room along the bottom. "Thumb through and make sure there's nothing more you'd like.

By now we've hit the maximum for freight charges anyway."

Maybe I'll find something to shake Braden from his doldrums. As they each sat down with a different catalog, Cora took the Bloomingdale's Brothers when Lacey finished with it. Turning pages, she came across a sketch of a woman lying in a hammock strung between two shady trees. *He might be able to use a hammock soon. Once we're able to move him from the bed, it would be good to go outside. The fresh air might work wonders for his disposition.* She turned down the corner of the page.

Nothing more caught her eye until she turned to the section of advertisements taking up the last several pages. Everything from electric curlers to pocket watches to dumbwaiters and dress shields jumbled together with no rhyme nor reason. Cora began reading, stopping when she spotted a box with no pictures.

SCIENCE OF A NEW LIFE TO ALL WHO ARE MARRIED, proclaimed the ad in bold capitals. Slightly smaller beneath it added OR ARE CONTEMPLATING MARRIAGE and went on to declare the book recommended by both medical and religious critics and worth its weight in gold. In miniscule print, they ran the table of contents along the bottom, just above its ordering information. Cora pulled the page close to her nose. Some of the print smudged, and she could only make out some of the chapter headings.

Chapter I—Marriage and Its Advantages
Chapter II—Age at Which to Marry
Chapter IV—Love Analyzed

Several of the middling titles were hopelessly obscured, prompting Cora to give up and skip ahead to the last two.

Chapter XXVII—Subjects of Which More Might Be Said
Chapter XXVIII—A Happy Married Life—How Secured

Sorely tempted by the final chapter, Cora considered whether or not the book itself, containing more than four hundred pages and one hundred illustrations, would be worth three whole dollars.

Then she caught sight of the offer running just beneath the title.

Any person desiring to know more about the book before purchasing it may send to us for our sixteen-page descriptive circular, giving full and complete table of contents. It will be sent free to any address. J. S. Ogilvie & Co. Publishers.

Thoughtfully, Cora took up Lacey's abandoned pen and began jotting down the address. If the description pleased her, she'd buy the book and read the first and final chapters. A mischievous smile spread across her face as she decided. *After I'm finished, I'll make it a special gift to my fiancé.*

The woman had a gift for giving him trouble. Chase could think of no other way to describe it when Lacey Lyman insisted on coming to the picnic site to help prepare the main course.

"The entire thing was my idea, and I'm responsible for making sure things go as smoothly as possible," she argued.

She'd been put out by his refusal to bring her along to finish hunting partridges. He'd cited her shoes—and noted her wince as though reminded of aching feet—to justify his decision. All in all, she'd acquiesced easily. So easily, Chase suspected more than her feet ached. But a lady wouldn't tell him what men would admit to—no mentioning of anything half so scandalous as sore limbs—so it remained pure speculation on his part.

At least, it had been pure speculation until she'd insisted on carrying the cleaned, beheaded, and stuffed partridges to the site with him. Then Chase could trust his observations on the subject. He kept a close eye on her as they walked to the mines.

The mines where he'd hoped to explore a bit while the partridge cooked. The mines he'd come to Hope Falls to examine, but been unable to due to inclement weather and interfering females. The mines he wouldn't be able to examine even today.

No changing it though. So he contented himself with watching Lacey Lyman slowly make her way toward the picnic area. She'd never be anything but graceful—so long as she wasn't falling, at least—but there was a stiffness about her movements that hadn't been there two days before. *Headstrong woman.*

"Watch your step." They'd reached an area still raw from the collapse, with some spots of earth strangely pitted and others unexpectedly pushing up. Chase had seen this sort of upheaval in areas where there'd been large quakes, but while disturbing, at least those sights had been natural. This wasn't.

The sadness of the place seemed to catch hold of her, too. She didn't speak again until they'd gone through the trees and into the meadow he'd earmarked as their location. *Is her silence out of respect, guilt, or both?* Chase couldn't very well ask.

"You already laid the fire?" She looked at the place where he'd readied six smaller pit fires the evening before. From this angle, it wasn't surprising she'd thought it one large setup.

"Yep." Chase had, in fact, lit fires there the night before to help fill the pits with ash. The trenches, now partially filled with ash and debris, he'd topped with small tinder and again overlaid with larger branches. They need only be lit. He set down the two bags of prepared partridges he carried and set to it. The fires needed to burn long enough and hot enough for the ashes to cook the birds once they were made ready.

"What's that?" Miss Lyman set down her own bag, looking intently at the small silver box he pulled from his pocket.

"Man who gave it to me called it a 'chucknuck'." Chase held it up for her inspection then thumbed the steel band running around the box to open it. Inside lay a small store of dried moss to be used as punk and a trusty, battered piece of flint.

"I've never seen one of these before," she marveled.

"Never seen another one," he agreed. Removing some moss and placing a bit on the tinder of each prepared fire pit, he circled back. Chase knew she watched every move as he hunkered down and struck his flint against the steel to light the moss. The tinder around and beneath it smoked almost instantly.

"You don't like matches?" She sounded curious, not mocking.

"Get 'em wet and they're ruined," Chase told her. "Makes them pretty useless when you live in the open and need a fire whether it rains, snows, or sleets. This serves me better."

"How do you light a fire in the rain? Won't it extinguish?"

"If a fire's well-laid and started, it pretty well takes a torrential downpour to put it out." He finished lighting the final fire and stood next to her. "Take a good piece of bark and lay it down so your logs aren't resting on the wet ground. Split your wood to get to the dry middle, and keep it dry under a blanket until you're ready to lay and light the fire. Once it's lit, keep it covered from whichever direction the rain's driving until the flames leap and the logs are ablaze."

She watched as he grabbed one of the buckets of clay he'd hauled over yesterday. "I'd like to try it sometime, I think."

"It's not fun when it's necessary," he warned. Chase fell silent as he dumped out the contents of the first bucket and pressed it down to make a semi-flat surface on the ground. Then he took another bucket, emptied it atop the first, and grabbed his canteen. He sprinkled the riverbed clay with water until it became soft and pliable then added more until it gained the consistency of mud. *Now we'll see how delicate she really is.*

THIRTY-FOUR

It looks like he's making mud pies. Lacey watched, fascinated, as his strong hands kneaded the reddish-brown clay. She could have been suspicious about what he planned to do with that clay, since he'd been so reluctant to let her come along and help.

Instead, after his explanation of the chucknuck and concise directions on how to lay a fire in the rain, she adopted a wait-and-see approach. *Come to think of it, it's almost the same thing he advised after he showed me the dipper bird.*

"Bring out two of the birds." His blunt instruction sent her diving into a bag as he dumped more mud next to the lump he'd worked water through. "Keep one and give me the other."

Lacey sat, cross-legged, holding a stuffed bird. "Are we plucking the feathers now?" She still couldn't reconcile the fact that they'd cleaned, beheaded, and stuffed the partridge with their feathers still attached. How would they cook?

"We aren't plucking them, exactly." Dunstan grabbed a lump of runny clay and held it over his bird. Then he started *spreading the muddy mixture on top of its feathers!*

272

"What"—she struggled to mask her horror—"are you doing?"

"Prepping the partridge." He made it sound like the most natural thing in the world. "You're falling behind, Miss Lyman."

Suddenly she realized that he intended for her to do the same thing to the bird in her hands. Lacey eyed the sludge with revulsion. "You want me to slop mud on this bird, too?"

"All of them." He plopped another handful down and smoothed it over the feathers like a plaster. "And it's clay, not mud."

"But. . .why?" Lacey had to know. "What's the difference?"

"Mud dries, crumbles, and leaves dirt everywhere." By now he'd coated his entire partridge with enough of the clay to turn the bird brown. "Clay dries, hardens, and cracks when broken. By coating the feathers with moist clay and covering that again with a firmer, drier layer, it forms a sort of individual oven."

Even as he told her this, he grabbed a handful of the clay he hadn't put water into. This he molded and patted on top of the entire thing until the bird resembled a misshapen mud ball. Dunstan held it up for her to see. "When the fire pits are filled, I'll stir the new ash with the old to make sure it's hot even from the bottom. We put the birds inside and cover them."

"I can see how that might work with cooking them." Lacey tried and failed to find a diplomatic way of voicing her doubts. "But then we're left with hard balls of clay over befeathered birds. How is that going to make an easy-to-eat picnic?"

"After they cook for an hour or so, you fish them out and hit 'em with a thick branch." He set the prepared bird aside and reached for another. "When the clay comes off, the feathers come with it, so you're left with a ready-to-eat partridge."

"Well." Lacey blinked at the bird in her hands and thought of all the time she'd spent plucking chickens for Evie to fry for a dozen lumberjacks' dinner. "Isn't that convenient?"

She set the bird aside, pushed up her sleeves, and retrieved it.

Steeling herself, Lacey plunged her hand into the sticky clay and slapped it over partridge feathers, smoothing it over the same way she'd seen Dunstan do it. By the time she moved on to the more dry substance, she caught him staring.

"Is it wrong?" The bird looked properly muddy to her.

"Nope." He shrugged and grabbed another partridge. "I wasn't sure you'd believe me enough to get your hands dirty."

"Mud and clay wash off." Lacey proudly added her first partridge to his growing pile. "By now you've earned my trust." She selected another one and looked up to see him staring again. Surprise shone in his gaze, and she wondered why he would be so shocked to hear that she trusted him. Lacey stared back at him.

"Is your trust usually earned so easily?" He sat unnaturally still. "Do you change your mind that quickly?"

Regret pulled at her. "You know I didn't want to hire you on, and I won't pretend otherwise. And I resented your implication that I was self-centered and weak-willed on the day of the cribbage tournament." She sighed and kept going when it looked like he might speak. "But you weren't trying to insult me, and I can't fault you for an honest opinion. Even a wrong one."

"There's a vast difference between not holding an opinion against me and deciding I'm trustworthy." He sounded curious. "I've been here for three weeks. What changed your mind in that time?"

"Your temper is as quick to fire as mine." Lacey studiously avoided his gaze and kept working, finding she enjoyed the feeling of the cool clay squelching through her fingertips. "But there's an honesty in that. And although we've angered each other, you've tried to protect me from cougars and the men. You even became a really good teacher once we got past the silence."

He'd fallen silent again, and now he was the one focusing too intently on the partridge. It was the first time she'd seen him uncomfortable like this. *It's good to know he can be thrown off balance like anyone else. I'd been starting to wonder.*

"Besides"—she strove to lighten the mood—"you've told me other improbable things, like the dipper bird who swims and the partridge who falls more than flies, and they turned out to be true. I can't imagine, after all the trouble we went through to get these birds for the picnic, you'd be wrong about this."

"I'm not wrong about the clay." *But am I wrong about you?* Chase withdrew from the conversation by getting up and stirring the fire-pit ashes with a long branch he'd saved for that purpose. There she sat, blithely believing his word over her own experience, telling him he'd earned her trust with his *honesty.*

I've been careful not to lie to any of them, he acknowledged. *But holding back the true reason I came to Hope Falls means I've not been honest.* Not that he had a choice. A twinge of regret hit him as he surveyed a gleefully clay-smeared Lacey Lyman, who seemed to be enjoying herself now that she'd overcome her doubts. Tempting to trust her in return, but the woman boasted too much charm and hid far too many secrets.

Every bit of information he'd uncovered pointed to Lacey Lyman as the mastermind behind the mine collapse. But that didn't mean Chase couldn't hope his suspicions were wrong.

That he even entertained the thought proved she was dangerous.

And intuitive enough not to engage him in conversation while his well-founded suspicions raged against his foolish hopes. They didn't speak even as he pushed the ashes aside and allowed her to drop two clay-covered partridges into each pit. In silence he prodded ashes over the birds to cook all through.

"Hello!" The rest of their party, toting an assortment of

canteens, boxes, and baskets cleared the woods and moved into the meadow. They obviously had no trouble following the rope markers he looped around easily spotted branches along the way.

Immediately Williams broke away from the pack and hastened to Miss Lyman's side. He glared at Chase in accusation even as he hovered at her side. "Are you hurt? Did you fall on the way?"

"What makes you—oh!" She looked down at her hands, streaked with red-brown clay. "No, I'm fine. It's from our cooking."

"Here." He offered her a bandanna and his canteen to wash up. If anything, he looked disappointed at the news that she hadn't fallen. Or maybe Williams took exception to her use of "our," allying herself with Chase. Either way, the man's hackles rose high enough he could've jousted with porcupine quills.

For some reason this cheered Chase considerably. Instead of examining it too closely though, he turned to the rest. Lawson, the only man not carrying a parcel, supported his ungainly sister and trailed behind the rest. The glower he aimed at Williams should've left a hole in the back of his shirt.

It was the first time Chase would've sided with Williams in a fight. Williams might be a bully, but he'd won his way to the picnic fair and square. Lawson egged his sister into a clearly ill-advised trip just to sneak his way in. He not only lacked the honor to play by the rules and accept his defeat, but he also was willing to put Mrs. Nash's health in danger to get near Lacey.

Miss Lyman. Chase shook his head to clear the unwanted familiarity. Obviously, keeping company around riffraff like this made it easier to forget his own boundaries with her.

Aside from Williams stalking after Lacey Lyman's every move and Lawson resentfully tracking his rival's progress, everyone seemed in high spirits. When they began unpacking Miss Thompson's additions to the celebration, Chase understood why.

One box cradled plates, mugs, and cutlery. Out of another came jars of water and cool, sweetened tea. An entire basket overflowed with dozens of cornbread squares. Another basket boasted crocks of butter and jars of jam. Two dutch ovens, immediately tucked in the fire pits to stay warm, held fried parsnip balls. And the last basket, well bundled and tucked in the coolest shade well away from the fires, guarded a custard.

"It all looks wonderful!" Mrs. Nash exclaimed from where she'd been seated in the thick of things by her brother. The brother, of course, joined Williams in hovering by Miss Lyman.

"Quite a sight," agreed Draxley as he sank down next to her. His mustache twitched even more speedily than usual as he tried to situate himself atop the log without falling back.

"An unparalleled view." Lawson offered her a slight bow.

The sycophant bows to her in the middle of the mountains. At a picnic. While she wears a smudge of clay on one cheek.

Actually, Chase liked that smudge. She looked even better slightly mussed. But the bowing... Chase held back a snort.

Williams showed no such compunction. He lumbered forward, inserting himself between the other two. "Don't grovel, Lawson."

"Back up a wee bit and let Miss Lyman breathe, Williams." Riordan sauntered over. His sheer size, along with his status in town, worked in his favor. The massive Irishman loomed over the shorter, balding man for mere minutes before Williams conceded.

"Where's your food, Dunstan?" Clump peered around as though expecting it to magically appear on the ground before him.

"Almost ready." Chase crouched between the first two fire pits, using a well-curved branch to push the clay pods out of the heat. "I'll pass it out when everything else is served."

Grumbles of disbelief and curiosity followed him as he freed the partridges and corralled them in one area. Soon that spot was littered with thirteen clay pods—but Chase counted only eleven people present at the picnic. They were one short.

One of the birds was earmarked for the supposed Braden Lyman, but where was his doctor? Chase wouldn't be able to gather any information from a man who didn't bother to show up. "Where's the doctor?" he asked of Miss Thompson while she finished dotting butter and dishing up the fried parsnip balls.

"He doesn't enjoy the outdoors," the younger Miss Thompson answered. "We asked him to come, but he chose to stay behind."

No checking the mines, no interrogating the doctor. . . The afternoon was swiftly looking to be a great waste of time. The only man who might make the day worthwhile sat next to Mrs. Nash, looking supremely uncomfortable and unforthcoming.

"A shame. I'd think that a doctor would be more in favor of exercise." Inspiration struck. "Maybe we can all go for a walk after lunch, explore the area closer to the mines. It makes for interesting hiking, now that the ground has settled again."

"Absolutely not!" The forceful protest came from Draxley, who looked as surprised at himself as everyone else was. Mustache twitching and glasses slipping, he stuttered, "I mean, that is to say, it's dangerous that way. Dips and ridges and who knows what all. Mrs. Nash shouldn't take such risks." He gave her a look both anxious and adoring. "We must stay safe."

"Makes no never mind to me." Clump sat down like a bag of bricks between Miss Thompson and Miss Higgins. "We can walk around it, over it, or in the other direction. So long as we talk about it after we eat all this good-smelling food!"

And that quickly, Chase lost the chance to do any investigating. He couldn't slip away and leave Miss Lyman the veritable prize in a tug-of-war between Lawson and Williams. But why didn't she protest poking around the collapsed mines? Did she simply not get a chance when Draxley voiced his anxiety?

Now that the partridges had cooled, Chase vented his

frustration on the first one. He brought the heavy branch down with precise force, watching with satisfaction as the clay cracked open to reveal a feather-lined cook pod. The tasty white meat of the bird lay pristine and steaming atop its broken bed.

He pulled away the top half and handed the first bird, still dished in the other half of the pod, to Miss Thompson. Usually she cooked and served everyone else, so Chase thought it a fitting tribute to the chef of eggs in overcoats and clangers.

"I've never seen the like!" she exclaimed then promptly began firing a barrage of questions at him about how he did it.

"Ask Miss Lyman—she helped hunt the birds and then cook them." Chase gave her the opportunity to extract herself from the competitive conversation of the men bracketing her, and Miss Lyman hopped up in an instant to join her friend.

She cast him a grateful look, which Chase couldn't stop thinking about. *If I'm right and she wants a husband so desperately, why would she jump at the chance to avoid suitors?*

It made no sense. *But then again. . .* Chase eyed the woman as she pointedly ignored the men trying to win her attention. *Nothing about her makes much sense.*

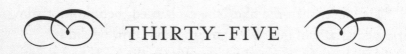 THIRTY-FIVE

It's almost over. After three weeks of travel and an expedited hearing, Jake couldn't wait to go back to Hope Falls.

He stood beside his mother and father, watching as the officials took Twyler back to the jail. After everything it had taken to get to this point, Jake expected to feel more of a sense of triumph. His brother's murderer didn't escape justice. Edward would no longer be remembered as a gambling cheat, and his parents had begun to openly mourn for their firstborn.

"Justice is finally served." His father sounded satisfied.

Finally? It still angered Jake to think that they'd ignored the notice of Edward's death, refusing to announce his passing so long as the story reflected poorly on the family. They'd gone on as though he'd never died—as though he'd never lived. *There should be some sort of punishment for parents who view their children as extensions of their reputation and nothing more.*

But the Grangers did everything in their power to suppress any mention of scandalous events, trying to hide Edward's "dishonorable death" after being told he'd pulled a gun over a card game. Jake's father went so far as to pay Twyler hush money in an attempt to keep the story from spreading.

I could have tracked him down sooner if he'd not had the money and head start to run. Jake still hadn't spoken to his father about this, too conflicted to broach the subject. If he'd found Twyler early on, he wouldn't have found his Evie. Besides, his father finally put good use to his riches by greasing the wheels and pushing the trial through the system. It landed before the judge far sooner than Jake ever would have expected.

"He won't hurt anyone again," Jake agreed. In fact, after hearing about the murder and the kidnapping afterward, the judge— whom Jake made sure his father didn't go anywhere near—didn't hesitate in his ruling. Twyler's established history of continuing crime made him an ongoing threat, and placing him in a prison wouldn't provide adequate protection to society.

When the prison wagon drove out of sight, Jake turned to his parents. "It's finished now. Everyone knows Edward was a good man." *Instead of thinking he'd run off with some of Father's money to fund a new life out West, as you let them believe.* He didn't speak the accusation—the time for blame had ended. The way his parents handled things would always spark some anger, but forgiveness wasn't a feeling. *It's a choice.*

"I don't know if I can watch," his mother fretted as they headed back home. "There's no time to consider it either."

"We're going." His newly vengeful father didn't share her reservations. "The wretch killed our Edward. We'll see this through until Twyler no longer twitches on the end of his rope."

"But to go into the prison. . ." His mother grew pale. "Even staying in the portion with no prisoners. . .it's so tawdry!"

"They don't do public hangings anymore," Jake reminded her. "It's a good thing. The sight of them didn't instill fear, it drove people into a frenzy and inspired even more violence."

"Hanging in the prison yard sends a message to the criminals held there without exposing the sight to more delicate sensibilities." His father opened the door. "I know it will be difficult tomorrow morning, my dear, but we must go."

"I'm going tonight." Jake made the decision that moment.

"It's not until the morning." They looked confused.

"I mean I'm going back to Hope Falls," he clarified. He'd hunted Twyler down—literally shot the man to bring him back. "There's nothing left for me to stay for now that it's over."

"You'd dishonor your brother's memory by not attending?" His father drew himself to his full height. "Unthinkable!"

"I honored Edward by believing him to be the brother I'd always known and tracking down the man who murdered him." Jake kept his voice level, stating facts rather than throwing the comparison in his parents' faces. "My part is complete."

"What do you mean, you're going?" His mother clutched the door frame, eyes darting down the streets as though gauging how much the neighbors might hear. "With this finished, you'll be able to step in and help your father with Granger Mills."

"No, Mom." He'd told her before. "I'm going back to Hope Falls to build a sawmill—with the woman I'm going to marry."

"Whether you like it or not, you have an obligation to this family." His father wasn't asking him to stay out of affection or gratitude—in his mind it was about the family name. "I founded Granger Mills, and a Granger will run it after me."

"My obligations are to God and my wife, and I've kept her waiting long enough. If you're set on keeping the company name for another generation, I suggest you track down cousin Billy." Jake started down the porch steps. "I've got other plans."

"You planned that picnic," Braden accused. It might have fazed

Lacey if he hadn't been caterwauling about the same thing for the past two weeks. "But you sit there and act like it's fine?"

"Absolutely." She cocked her head to the side and surveyed the color in her brother's cheeks. He looked angry, yes, but on the balance he was more animated and healthy-looking in these past weeks since the picnic than he had been since they arrived. Even better, the picnic didn't stick in his craw purely because of the location. He objected to Cora going—and Lacey had a fantastic, sneaking suspicion it had something to do with her being surrounded by the eager bachelors of Hope Falls.

He still loves her. Until relief overwhelmed her, Lacey hadn't realized that she'd begun to doubt Braden's affection for her best friend. *Why does he keep pushing her away? Why does he keep pushing all of us away? And how can I get him to remember the brother he used to be? The man I saw him grow into?*

"Now you have the nerve to look upset?" He snorted.

"You'll find I have every bit as much nerve as I did when I was six and you dared me to climb the Wilson's oak tree." The memory of her doting brother from back then made her smile.

"And every bit as gullible and foolhardy," he grumbled. "If you'll recall, you fell out of that tree, sprained your arm, and got me stuck polishing all the silver in the house."

"Backing down from a challenge isn't the Lyman way," she reminded. "You knew that when you decided to test my courage. Now that we're older, you try my patience instead."

"You beat my patience into the ground the day you dragged Cora to Hope Falls," he snarled. "Then I thought things couldn't be worse, but somehow you keep proving me wrong. Advertising for husbands, scurrilous mongrels trying to sneak into the house in the middle of the night, murderers carrying you off into the forest, cougar attacks. . .every time I think you've outdone yourself, you demonstrate an even more heinous lapse in judgment than the one before. It's nothing less than a miracle Cora and the others have survived your scrapes so far."

Now that's simply unfair. Lacey brushed his list away. *The only thing in that whole litany that can be attributed to my poor judgment is the ad itself. Everything else would have happened in spite of me, or to spite me. But maybe it means something good that he worries so much. I worry, too.*

"Our survival isn't the miraculous one, Braden." Her voice softened as she looked at the familiar face, once filled with confidence and happiness, now etched with misery. "It seems you overlook the fact *you've* been given another chance in your haste to make sure no one else makes good use of theirs."

"It's not the chances you're given which disturb me. It's the chances you take." He turned it back on her. "Of all the opportunities and places in the world, you bring yourself and the others squarely in the middle of danger and death."

Lacey thought for a moment, but was unable to be sure of his meaning. There was nothing for it but to ask. "Do you mean Hope Falls itself, or are you referring to the picnic again?"

"Both! But most recently it is your cheery visit to the site of my ruination which grates against my thoughts." His brows drew together, compounding his scowl into something epic.

"Pishposh. The land remains. We remain, and most of all we remain thankful that you were brought out of those tunnels alive. Even now your body heals." *But your thoughts and mind remain in the dark, and we don't know how to pull you out.*

She stared at her brother, willing him to hear the truth behind the words she now whispered. "The cave-in didn't defeat you then; don't let it defeat you months later."

"You don't know what you're talking about." His throat worked, telling her that her brother wasn't just angry. For as long as she could remember, he'd done that. She privately thought he was trying to swallow away anything upsetting.

She'd tried it once. It didn't work. *Maybe that's what's wrong. He can't move past the bad things by wishing them away.*

"Then tell me." Lacey laid her hand over his.

He looked at her hand, looked up, and looked right past her. Braden yanked away from her grasp. He turned to face the window. "Leave, Lacey." His voice sounded hoarse. "Just. . .leave."

"Come on." Cora spoke from the doorway, and Lacey suddenly understood why Braden pulled away instead of answering her.

She wanted to reach out and grab the moment again, but knew it wasn't possible. Lacey stood, reluctant to leave but knowing she wouldn't be able to get anything more from her brother. Drained of his anger, there seemed to be nothing holding him up.

Maybe this will let him think clearly and come to his senses. I should have reached out to him sooner and not let his snapping keep me away. Regret swam in her stomach as she followed Cora out of Braden's room and out of the doctor's house. Lacey tucked her hands in her pockets and rubbed the fabric between her fingertips, but the gesture didn't soothe.

"All I've done since I got here is argue with him," she told Cora. "We fight about everything and anything, but I haven't asked him to tell me about the collapse until now."

"It's not your fault." Cora sat down on the bench running along the front of Lacey's store and dabbed her eyes with a handkerchief. "None of us expected to find him this way."

"But I haven't done anything to help." Lacey sank down beside her. "Spending all my time and focus on preparing for the sawmill doesn't do my brother any good. If anything, the progress we've made seems to aggravate Braden even more."

"Everything aggravates him, and nothing pleases him." Tears slid down her best friend's face. "I kept thinking we'd see an improvement, but time goes by and he stays the same. Lacey, he says he doesn't want me anymore. . . . You've heard it, you've seen the way he acts. I'm starting to believe he's lost our love."

Dread overtook Lacey's feelings of regret. Cora had been so strong, always standing by Braden and refusing to give up. Her friend's constancy was Braden's last hope. *But no one can go on being rejected forever. Cora needs assurance, too.*

"Don't think that." Lacey wrapped one arm around Cora's shoulders. "He slipped today that he was angry you went to the picnic. When we talked about money, he asked about what I'd done to see you settled. Whatever he tells us, Braden always comes back to what's most important to him—and that's you."

"You're wrong, Lacey." Cora drew a deep breath. "He pouts about the picnic, yes. But when he asked about provisions for me it's because he hopes I'll no longer hold him to our engagement. He doesn't love. All this Braden cares about is himself. As soon as he's able, he'll leave Hope Falls, and us, far behind."

THIRTY-SIX

Chase's search remained at a standstill. Despite his well-laid plans, he'd made no progress in the two weeks following the picnic. *And it's all Lacey Lyman's fault.* He'd been avoiding the woman and the confusion she caused, but she still threw a spoke in the works. At least, her overeager suitors managed it on her behalf.

It started at dinner, the same night as the picnic. Lawson's round glasses looked nowhere but Miss Lyman, Williams, and then Chase. After the incident with the ladder and the way Miss Lyman's attention was monopolized by the burly lumberjack during the picnic, Lawson's courtship of Miss Lyman hadn't been progressing nearly as well as the man so obviously hoped.

The light reflecting off the engineer's owlish lenses made it impossible to tell what the man was thinking, but Chase suspected Lawson was calculating his chances with Miss Lyman. No surprise if he considered both Williams and Chase a threat.

But Chase couldn't prepare for the way Lawson went about minimizing that threat. When the man left his sister to join their table, he'd not suspected a scheme. The conversation turned to the progress being made on the sawmill. With the site cleared, first by cutting down the trees then by removing their stumps, the men could move on to the next important project.

"We need to map the route of the flume before we go about deciding the orientation of the sawmill itself," the slighter man mused. "I need input from one of the team leads as to the feasibility of the proposed route. If the trees or the landscape present too much trouble, I'll need to adjust the schematics."

It didn't mean much to Chase until the engineer turned to Williams and requested his assistance. His apparent eagerness to work alongside his rival set off alarm bells—but too late. The moment Williams agreed, Lawson roped Chase into the project by claiming he could make use of a guide's "geologic understanding of the region and familiarity with the landscape hereabouts." The women bought the twaddle hook, line, and sinker.

It couldn't have been clearer that he'd planned to make sure Williams and Chase didn't have the opportunity to get near Miss Lyman while he wasn't in town. And within five minutes, he succeeded in trapping both of them. Chase played peacekeeper for tense, tedious days as Williams gave orders and thinly veiled threats and Lawson made detailed riverbank sketches.

This afternoon marked the first opportunity he'd found to head out to the mines and poke around—but first he had to circle back and check on the women. Since the picnic, Williams doubled his efforts, edging out any other man who got near Miss Lyman.

Williams hadn't forgotten the evening he'd been humiliated by Miss Lyman's ability to recall his empty boasts. That the entire thing centered around his failure to win the cook provided a further blow to his ego—something bullies didn't take well. As time went by and he made no progress with his attempts to woo Miss Lyman—who'd given him no encouragement that Chase could discern—Williams might well try to take matters in another direction and force her to accept his proposal.

It wouldn't be difficult. Chase disliked admitting it, but Williams had the kind of sly cunning to recognize the way to make Miss Lyman bend to his demands. *If he threatens one of the others, she'll sacrifice her own happiness to protect them.* But the wily lumberjack would know he couldn't accomplish that while the ladies were surrounded by his fellow workers. He wasn't the type to push ahead when he knew he'd be outnumbered.

There was no telling whether Williams had hatched the plan Chase feared, but he'd seen the man studying a train schedule last night outside the bunkhouse. Which made it look like Williams planned to take a page from Twyler's manual and kidnap her while the other men were busy. If Williams timed it right, he could whisk the woman out of her shop, onto the train, and be halfway to Durango before anyone was the wiser. Once the two of them were wed, he'd return to Hope Falls to show off his new trophy.

Not going to happen. As this was the first day he hadn't been able to keep an eye on Williams while they worked, Chase made it a point to coincide his trips back to Hope Falls with the incoming train schedule. Just as a precaution.

So Chase doubled back to town, four braces of rabbits slung over his shoulder—enough for him to give to Miss Thompson and end the men's grumbling that they wanted fresh meat. Enough, he thought, to earn him a free afternoon. *If I don't find evidence very soon, I'll have to face the so-called Braden Lyman without it. The man might break down when faced with an accusation.*

Chase tucked the rabbits into one of the two smokehouses to bring out later when he returned to town that night. No one needed to know he'd finished his hunt in the morning, and this way he wouldn't get roped into helping with something else.

He checked the kitchen first, seeing most of the women inside.

"I'm becoming accustomed to you checking in on us, Mr. Dunstan." Miss Higgins slid a plate of cookies toward him. "It makes me glad to know you're diligent in seeing to our safety."

"So long as there's not trouble, I'm satisfied." Chase crunched into a crisp oatmeal cookie. "And I enjoy the perks."

They laughed at his appreciation for their culinary skills.

"Are Miss Lyman and Miss Thompson at the store?" It wasn't uncommon for her to be in the shop. Situated right between the diner and the doctor's house, they seemed to think she'd be safe working there alone so long as she kept the doors wide open. That way they could all see and hear if anything went wrong.

"Oh, Lacey went to visit her brother a good while ago." Mrs. Nash poured herself a tall glass of milk. "Cora followed after her, but she hasn't been gone very long yet."

So she's visiting her brother today.... Interesting. Chase wondered whether she'd made a practice of dropping by more regularly after their little talk. *Is she going to keep up appearances, or is she conferring with a coconspirator?*

He didn't know what to make of the fact the younger Miss Thompson visited the invalid often. In the long month since he'd met these four women, Chase had come to believe they were exactly who they said they were. Why not? Their identities didn't make them innocent. Miss Lyman could have schemed to take over Hope Falls more easily than a stranger, in any case.

But he leaned toward thinking she hadn't meant for her brother to be involved in the mine collapse. It was even possible she'd planned for the mine to be empty, but something went awry. *Despicable, but far more understandable.*

What he didn't understand was how the other women got roped into it. Chase might believe they had no idea the collapse was a crime, not a tragedy, and that they needed to marry to keep the town together. But this wasn't the case with the younger Miss

Thompson. As Braden's fiancée, she'd know instantly that the man in Hope Falls was an impostor. The others might be fooled by keeping the invalid in isolation, but Miss Thompson visited him.

Which made her just as involved as Lacey Lyman.

They were both at the doctor's house, visiting the supposed Braden, right now. Chase thanked the ladies and headed toward the general store. If he snuck around it and kept low, he might be able to go undetected until he reached the doctor's house.

But as he edged around the back of the store, he heard voices. Annoyance flooded him as he realized he'd missed the chance to eavesdrop on their visit with the impostor. Chase stood, fighting his frustration, until he heard snatches of the ladies' conversation. They were talking about Braden Lyman.

"All this Braden cares about is himself. As soon as he's able, he'll leave Hope Falls. . . . " Miss Thompson warned.

This *Braden? So he is an impostor!* Pulse pounding, Chase edged around the back of the building. He crept along the side, ducking windows, until he stood as close as possible without alerting them to his presence. Then he waited. And listened.

"You're wrong." Lacey couldn't temper the vehemence of the denial. "Deep down, he's glad we've done so much to save Hope Falls. Besides, you know Braden would never abandon us."

"The Braden I *used* to know would never abandon us. But he wouldn't have been so hateful either." Cora choked back a sob. "When I first saw him, I knew it would take time to adjust, but time won't be enough for either of us. He's too different."

Lacey fought to restore Cora's hope. "His temper will cool as he heals and accepts his new role in Hope Falls."

"Even if he accepts his place, I don't know if my place is at his side. He's still ordering us to leave his room!" All the pent-up hurt of the past few months came out. "How can I marry this hate-filled stranger who's taken the place of *my* Braden?"

"Cora, you don't have to marry any man you don't want to. Remember, that was one of the most important things we said when we wrote the ad, and it doesn't change for you." Lacey's heart sank, but she had to look after Cora. Her friend had gone through so much; it was amazing how long she'd persevered before the pressure and the loss went too deep. "I know you never expected anything like this. When we heard of Braden's death—"

"You decided to cover it up." Dunstan rounded the building, anger in the line of his jaw and the tone of his voice. "Did your brother mean so little to you, Miss Lyman, that you deemed him replaceable? I doubt he'd agree, 'cause I sure don't."

Lacey blinked, thrown off by his sudden appearance and senseless accusations. She glanced over, but Cora looked every bit as confused as she felt. "What are you talking about?" *And why are you so angry?* "Braden wasn't—isn't—replaceable at all."

If he were, we would've done it the same week we arrived, rather than be stuck with a foul-tempered fool who's abused Cora.

"Don't play the innocent with me, Miss Lyman. I heard everything you two said about your brother. I know what you've done, and now I want you to know you won't get away with it."

"Get away with what?" Cora couldn't make sense of it either, which relieved Lacey in some small measure.

At least I'm not the only one with no idea what he means. Why would the man even care that she'd told Cora no one would want her to marry Braden if she couldn't reconcile herself to it? None of them would be forced into marrying the wrong man.

"There you sit, talking about your brother's death in broad daylight," he thundered, "while the impostor you found is trapped at the doctor's, waiting for the day he can escape. Have you no shame for what you've done? No regret whatsoever?"

"Impostor?" An inkling began to dawn as Lacey realized Dunstan had heard them talking about the "different" Braden. "You've misunderstood, Mr. Dunstan. Braden is much altered after his ordeal in the mines, but that doesn't make him an impostor!" Though the word seemed to sum up how Lacey felt about the angry man who stared at her through her brother's eyes.

He took all three of the stairs leading to the porch in one stride. "The game is up, Miss Lyman. Stop this pretense."

"This is no game!" Anger began to simmer beneath her confusion as he loomed over them, rebuking her for something she hadn't done. "My brother survived the mine collapse, but even if he hadn't, why on earth would we bother creating a fake Braden?"

"To keep your claim on Hope Falls until the three of you could rustle up husbands to do it for you." He growled more than spoke. "That's what the ad was all about, wasn't it?"

She gaped at him. "We need husbands to guard our property—particularly because our country doesn't permit unmarried women to own any themselves—but that has little to do with Braden."

"It has everything to do with your brother. His name is on the deeds, isn't it? So you call him the 'nominal owner.' "

Lacey felt all the blood leave her face as she realized the full extent of what Chase Dunstan accused. "You believe that because my brother is the only one of us able to legally own or hold property, I covered up his death and am imprisoning an impostor until such a time as our husbands secure the claims?"

"Finally, you admit it." Grim satisfaction etched deep lines on either side of his mouth. "I didn't want to believe it, but you're so ruthless you believe 'no cost is too great.' "

"You've got it all wrong." Cora found her tongue. "How you can believe such terrible things? Why you would even bother to invent such a convoluted plot in your own mind is beyond me."

Lacey looked at Chase Dunstan, sorrow burrowing into her heart. "You use my words, but everyone understands some things cost too dear." *Like putting your trust in the wrong man.*

"Yes." Rage burned in his dark eyes. "Some things do. I'm sure your brother would tell you that if he were still alive."

"He is still alive!" Exasperation grew to fury. *How dare he think such things about me after the time we've spent together?* "How dare you accuse me of such vile schemes! Cora, my friends, and the doctor himself will all attest to Braden's survival."

"All with a vested interest in Hope Falls, needing to perpetrate fraud and deception." He waved away her witnesses. "I don't know whether you've threatened the doctor or paid him off, but it's obvious the man is under your thumb as well."

"Then you've made horrible, baseless accusations and left no way to prove how wrong you are." Cora stood beside Lacey. "You've cast aspersions on us all with no cause and no proof."

"The proof sits in the doctor's house, trapped by his health and your plots." Dunstan shook his head. "Who do you think acted as your brother's guide through these mountains, Miss Lyman? The Braden Lyman I knew was a good man and deserves to have his memory honored by the women he loved in life."

"The Braden Lyman you—" Lacey became speechless for a moment as she realized what he meant. "You knew my brother?"

"Oh yes." He curled his hand beneath her elbow and tugged her toward the stairs. "I knew the real Braden Lyman. Now it's time for you to take me to meet the man you've kept hidden."

"Oh," Lacey seethed, jerking her elbow away from him. "We'd be glad to take you to him. This way, Mr. Dunstan."

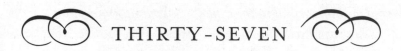 THIRTY-SEVEN

Chase stared. Braden Lyman—the real Braden Lyman—stared back.

How can this be? All his certainties came crashing down.

"Dunstan?" The pale man on the bed asked. "I didn't know you'd come back." His head fell back against his pillow, his eyes rimmed with dark circles. "Don't know why you'd want to."

This last was said in a resentful mutter that sounded nothing like the Braden Lyman Chase once knew and respected. Still, Chase couldn't answer. The shock of seeing Braden sent his mind reeling. The man before him obviously wasn't faking any injuries to deflect suspicion that he'd been involved in the collapse. *He didn't know what would happen. Maybe he still doesn't know what happened.* This gave him pause. *I still don't know what happened. What am I supposed to say to the man?*

"Well?" Lacey Lyman stood on the opposite side of the bed, arms crossed and glaring daggers at him. Suddenly Chase wasn't concerned so much with what he'd say to Braden.

What am I going to say to Lacey? Guilt and shame flooded him for his incorrect conclusions about her brother. *But someone still sabotaged the mines. I can't discount her as a suspect.*

"No one should see me like this!" Suddenly irate, Braden sat back up. Obviously the man took Chase's silence as shock over Braden's appearance. "Why did you bring him here?"

It began to dawn on Chase why Lacey and Miss Thompson spoke of this different man as replacing the Braden they knew. What had Lacey said when he began accusing her? *Braden is much altered after his ordeal in the mines. . . . You misunderstand. . . .*

"We brought him here to prove that you're you," Lacey informed her brother. "Your friend decided I'd gone to extreme lengths to conceal your death, and you were an impostor."

"I was wrong." The admission sounded hoarse even to Chase. Still, he couldn't bring himself to apologize around his thoughts. *Something is still wrong here. Too much doesn't fit.*

"I'll say." Miss Thompson's glower seared through him.

"What?" Braden tried to push himself into a more upright position. "What's all this about an impostor, Dunstan?"

"We knew you wouldn't want visitors." His fiancée referred to his anger mere moments before. "So we didn't bring Mr. Dunstan to meet you when Granger recommended we hire him."

"But I know him!" Braden looked incredulous. "Why didn't you tell them we'd worked together and ask to see me?"

"Because he'd already decided we'd hidden a fake Braden," Lacey hazarded a guess. "He wanted proof of our perfidy before he deigned to accuse us openly and come confront you."

"Where did you get such a fool notion?" Braden demanded.

"The ad." Chase could tell them that much before he finished putting all the pieces together. "The women were too desperate to find husbands. There had to be a reason."

"The reason is they don't have the sense God gave a gnat."

"Braden." His fiancée's tone was both warning and censure.

"Not from what I've seen." Chase couldn't let the insult pass when he'd provided the instigation. "These women keep tight control over the town and are more capable than most men." The women looked startled by his sudden defense, but it was true.

"Are you comparing their sawmill to my mine?" Braden started on a low whisper, but got louder with every word. "Are you saying that, because the sawmill looks to be viable, these women are more capable than I was at running Hope Falls?"

"Stop seeing insults where there are none," his sister snapped at him. "We're too busy with ones that actually exist!"

"Is that why you wanted us gone?" His fiancée moved closer to the bed. "Not because you were afraid we'd be in danger, but because our sawmill might succeed where your mine failed?"

"The mine didn't fail!" He slumped and whispered, "I did."

"No you didn't." All three of them spoke the words at once, trying to wipe away the defeat lining Braden's face. A second of surprise, and then everyone looked at Chase.

"What do you mean, Dunstan?" Braden looked so tired. "I lost three-quarters of my men in that collapse and didn't even manage to die with them. I failed on every possible level."

The women gaped at him, apparently horrified by the revelation that Braden held himself responsible for the cave-in. Dunstan wasn't surprised to hear it at all. Every good leader took on responsibility for both his men and their mission.

"Isn't that why you've come here? For restitution?"

"What?" Lacey resumed glaring at him. "Why would he want restitution? We paid all the investors what they owed, Braden."

"My brother-in-law died in the collapse," Chase volunteered. "My sister, Laura, was left destitute. She didn't just lose the man she loved. She lost her home, too." *Or she would have, if I hadn't stepped in and made things right.*

"So that's why you've come to Hope Falls, full of suspicion?

You're looking for *revenge?*" Lacey looked at him as though he were a snake about to strike her down.

"No." He met her gaze, willing her to be as innocent as she looked now. "I came to Hope Falls looking for justice."

"Get out." She flung her arm toward the door. "The train just pulled up, Mr. Dunstan. Get on it and don't come back."

"Ever again," Miss Thompson added for good measure.

"We'll see that your sister is handsomely compensated." Braden sank back wearily. "I promise you that, Dunstan."

"I can take care of Laura," he told them. "I didn't come here for money or for revenge. I came to find the truth."

"Well, now you know it. Braden really did survive, we put out the ads to help hold the large size of the claim and get the sawmill underway, and there are no plots or impostors. *Now go.*" Lacey looked furious, but her voice cracked on the last words.

"I can't." Chase drew a deep breath and laid his cards on the table. "Not until I find out who sabotaged the mines."

The man has a bad habit of leveling me with shocking comments, Lacey decided. After this one, she could only gape at him. *Is it possible he's unbalanced?* No, that would be an easy explanation.

"What?" Unbelievably, Braden perked up. "What did you say?"

"I know how seriously you took safety," Dunstan clarified. "Surveyors, architects, extensive support systems. . . It made me wonder how Miracle Mining, of all the outfits, caved in."

"Didn't make sense to me either." Her brother leaned forward eagerly at the idea the collapse hadn't been his fault. "Do you have any proof, Dunstan? Anything concrete to go on?"

"Just Draxley's recollections," he admitted. "To hear him tell it, it sounds like an explosion started everything."

"That's what you're going on?" Lacey heard herself screech,

winced, and modulated her tone. "The impression of a cowardly little twitch when he wanted to look good in front of Arla?"

"He didn't say it sounded like an explosion," the hunter admitted. "And I don't doubt Draxley exaggerated for his audience. But he didn't describe rumbling or shaking. The first and most important recollection he had was of a great boom."

"So the telegraph operator says 'boom,' and you suspect sabotage?" Cora sounded as incredulous as Lacey. "The same way you saw our ad and decided we'd manufactured a fake Braden?"

Put that way, Dunstan's speculation looked as ludicrous as Lacey believed it to be. "We can only be thankful you haven't sought to use your investigative skills in law enforcement."

"He's right." Braden sounded full of wonder. "I hadn't thought about it. . . . It didn't seem important which aspect of my operation caused the collapse, since any of it was my fault. I signed off on the route, the tunnels, the supports—all of it."

"Anyone can make a mistake," Cora was quick to assure him. It looked as though Braden's newfound liveliness gave her hope.

"Oh, I made a mistake all right." Braden's expression turned grim. "By avoiding the memories. If I hadn't fought so hard not to relive it, I would've remembered the blast."

Lacey gasped. "You don't mean to say he's *right*?" For a moment she didn't know which to hope for. That Dunstan was proven a raving lunatic, seeing conspiracies everywhere—or that Dunstan's instincts were right, even if his theories were wrong. Because if he was right, then the cave-in wasn't Braden's fault, and her brother would really have a reason to start recovering.

"I know the sound of a blast when I hear it," he confirmed. "But I didn't realize it at the time. The world collapsed around me, everything buckling, the air impossibly thick with dust, and rocks crushing everything in their path. Then, when everything settled, men screaming in the dark. . . I couldn't think about it then, and I didn't want to think about any of it afterward."

Men screaming in the dark? For the first time, Lacey began to get a sense of the horror Braden endured. *All this time I've been impatient for him to move past it. How do you move past something like that? Even worse if you think it's your fault?*

"Will you keep searching, Dunstan?" Her brother looked to her accuser. "Can you find the proof we need to catch a killer?"

"He's been here for weeks on end." Cora seemed hesitant to voice her doubts, but pressed forward nevertheless. "If he's not found anything by now, I fear you'll have to look to your own memory for comfort, Braden. But now you know. *It wasn't your fault.* And I hope you know that we never thought it was."

"I've managed to search the town fairly well," Dunstan intervened. "But with everything else, I've yet to inspect the area around the mines, nor what's left of the tunnels."

" 'Everything else' meaning the job we hired you to do"—Lacey tried to vent some of her smoldering rage—"completely unaware that you were trying to prove your foul suspicions."

He didn't have the grace to look shamefaced as he nodded.

"So will you do it?" Braden's eyes lit with hope.

"I planned to try this afternoon," Dunstan admitted. "It's why Decoy's in the barn with a beef bone. I misinterpreted some things and have lost some time, but there's still daylight enough to get the job started as soon as I grab my supplies."

"You're going into the mines?" Cora looked aghast.

"No." Lacey didn't give him a chance to answer. "*We* are."

"Oh no you're not!" Her brother lapsed back into the scowling, yelling oaf they'd been stuck with for months. "I forbid you to step foot inside or even anywhere near my mines."

Lacey gave him a sweet smile. "I won't. We can just consider anywhere I happen to step foot a part of my half. I own equal shares of those mines, and it's my decision to make."

"You're not equipped to go down there," Dunstan refused.

"Of course I am." Lacey's smile grew even wider as she hitched her skirts to her ankle. "You see, I have new shoes."

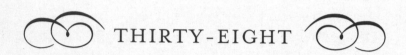

THIRTY-EIGHT

Go back inside." Once Chase managed to pull his jaw from the ground, he started issuing orders like a stern papa. "Right now. Before any of the men see you wearing that getup." *The woman has a bad habit of wearing outrageous, impractical outfits that look far too good on her. She's going to start a riot.*

"I'm not listening to you." Lacey Lyman stuck her nose in the air and walked on, her hips swaying hypnotically beneath the buff-colored, fitted *pants* she'd donned for the trip ahead. She showed enough sense to reach for her cloak and swing it on, concealing the all-too-revealing clothing. "They won't see a thing, and it's not sensible to try dragging a crinoline and skirts through a half-blocked mine. This is the safe choice."

"Only if none of the men catch sight of you." Chase didn't mince words. "If they do, I won't be able to fend them off."

"Careful, Dunstan." She pinned the cloak in place and gave him a tight smile. "You wouldn't want to give me a compliment."

"It wasn't a compliment," he growled, shouldering his pack and heading out. "It was a warning. With a getup like that, you

302

may well survive the mines only to be attacked here in town."

"After your baseless accusation, I've already been attacked here in town." The look she shot him could've frozen stew.

Each carrying a bag supplied with candles, torch material, some food, and a canteen, they cleared town and hit the woods. "I admitted I was wrong," Chase pointed out. "And I'm letting you come with me to search the mines." *What more does she want?*

"Admitting you're wrong is not the equivalent of apologizing for your spurious accusations," she sniffed.

"Would an apology take it all away? Make it better?" If she said it would, Chase would apologize here and now.

"No. It would indicate that you regret maligning my character." She gave a small, sad sigh. "And that you truly know you're wrong and maybe even that you're glad of it."

"I regret maligning your character," he offered. *Until I find the evidence and know for sure that you're not insisting on coming along to hide proof of your guilt, I can't say more.*

Lacey didn't accept his apology, maintaining stony silence until they reached the mouth of the mines. There she drew off her cloak and stuffed it into the bag then addressed him.

"Despite what you believe, Mr. Dunstan, I am neither a fool nor a criminal." Her lips compressed into a thin line, giving something for him to train his eyes on so they didn't wander down to her legs. "It's painfully clear to me, if no one else, your suspicions about Braden hint at much darker assumptions."

Chase looked at her for a long moment before nodding. "You're the person who stood to gain the most and who's gone to such extremes to ensure the sawmill gets off the ground." Even as he said it, something inside him withered at the words. All his instincts clamored that he'd gotten it wrong.

Some things cloud a man's instincts, he reminded himself. *Beautiful women top that list—particularly ones in pants.*

"That's what I thought." She pulled the strap of her bag tighter and lit her candle. "So here we are to find evidence to exonerate me of your speculation and Braden from his own guilt."

"I hope so." Chase lit his own candle. "You have no idea how much I've wanted to be wrong about all of this."

"Let's go then." Her expression softened infinitesimally. "I trusted you when you didn't truly deserve it. You don't trust me when I do. It's time for those two wrongs to come right."

Chase ventured toward the gaping maw in the mountainside first, holding his candle aloft to catch sight of the tunnels within. The left branch lay blocked by boulders, but the straight path had been cleared by the rescue party long ago.

He started in with a heightened awareness of the woman following at his heels. They picked their way over and around various rocks and clumps of earth strewn throughout the path. The farther they went, the darker it became. The air grew damp and heavy, smelling of dust and metal. Various offshoots branched away from the main canal, but Chase ignored them.

Once they'd gone through the mother tunnel, they'd go back and thread guide rope before exploring the rats' maze. Or what was left of it. Entire passageways were obscured by stone, remnants of splintered supports the only evidence that there'd once been paths. The ceiling bowed in places, cracked in others, and the deeper they went, the worse conditions became.

At length they reached a cavernous room—the main worksite of the mine. The hairs on the back of Chase's neck stood on end as they made their way around the perimeter of what space remained. Pockets of the room remained open, but here the destruction was most evident—an entire wall had buckled, making the roof slant down at a sharp angle to meet the ground.

"We can't go any farther, but this was once the hub of operations." Chase spoke for the first time since they'd left sunlight. "Used to be many more tunnels leading away from here, going deeper into the mountain where the silver ore waits."

"All gone." Her voice was somber as she peered into corners and nooks. "The supports I can see make me think the room collapsed in the very middle." She held her candle high, pointing to the ceiling, where the roof supports of the column-like supports branched toward the middle, making a half circle.

Chase bent down to where the floor met the ceiling, looking for any open spaces or seams to peek through. He came up empty. "Whatever happened in here, it was thorough."

"Wait!" she called. "Here's another passage. Much smaller."

At her words, dread pooled in Chase's stomach. *Danger.*

"No, Lacey!" He rolled away from the sloping roof and jumped to his feet, catching her arm before she continued farther. Chills coursed down his arms, a warning that had never been wrong before. "We're leaving."

He pulled her back the way they'd come, but she fought him. "Look! There! What is that?" She crouched down, poking a thin wire running along the ground. "Why isn't it covered in dirt?"

Fear curdled in Chase's gut as he grabbed her. He didn't bother trying to be gentle as he jerked her to her feet and headed back down the passage. "We have to get out of here."

"When we found something?" she cried. "What's wrong?"

"It's a fuse line, Lacey!" He broke into a run, half dragging her behind him. *"Run!"* Chase felt the moment she obeyed, her weight no longer pulling him backward. It seemed like years before he saw the faint glow of sunshine at the mouth of the tunnel, and he put on an extra burst of speed.

"Stop." A figure moved forward, blocking the light as he raised a pistol, grip firm as Chase and Lacey skidded to a halt.

"Mr. Draxley?" Lacey tried to push past Chase, but he held her behind him, out of aim of the gun she hadn't yet seen. "What are you doing? Why are you here?"

"Finishing what I started." Mustache twitching as much as ever, Draxley gave no other sign of nervousness. "Pity you two didn't wait another day—it would've all been hidden by then. Now you'll be part of the next tragic accident of Hope Falls."

"Why?" Chase couldn't move for his gun, couldn't launch himself at Draxley and protect Lacey at the same time. All he could do was keep the man talking as long as possible.

"Because you started poking your nose where it didn't belong," the telegraph operator snapped. "And because you"—he pointed the gun higher to indicate Lacey—"meddled where women don't belong at all. Hope Falls was supposed to be ours, you interfering witch. But you stepped in and ruined everything!"

"The other bid," Lacey gasped. "You're the buyer who made that abysmal offer for our half of the mine you destroyed?" She sounded both horrified and outraged at Draxley's daring.

"Start walking." Draxley waggled the gun. "I don't want to have to shoot you and drag your bodies far enough back they won't be found. You'll go there yourselves." He moved forward, forcing them back. "It would be most fitting to take you to the chamber where your brother was trapped, but I'm afraid that's too easy to get out of. Now drop your candles and go left. I don't want you able to light them later."

They didn't have a choice. Darkness surrounded them on all sides, save the flame of Draxley's candle and its pinpoint reflection on his glasses. "Now right." He barked directions until they'd wound themselves deep into the maze.

"Why?" Chase heard the sorrow in Lacey's voice as she asked. "What made you kill all those men? There's silver in other places where you might strike a claim. Why do this?"

"Didn't your brother tell you?" Surprise halted Draxley's progress, and they all came to a standstill. "This mountain, about to be so tragically wasted, holds more than silver."

"Your friend," Chase guessed. "The one who brought you here to man the telegraphs—it was Lyman's partner, wasn't it? Owen."

"A sentimental fool!" Draxley spat on the ground. "He knew the plan, but ran back when he realized Lyman was inside. Had some fool notion he could outrun the fuse and save his friend."

"But not the others?" Rage laced her words. "Not the men he hired on and brought here, in the bowels of the earth?"

"They might have guessed about the gold—we couldn't have them flapping their gums. I told Owen it'd be the same problem with your brother, but he had the fool idea Lyman would give up mining after the cave-in." Draxley shook his head. "As though any man would leave gold in the ground he owned. The investor we had lined up didn't want to leave Lyman as a loose end."

"What investor?" Lacey asked sharply. "If Owen didn't plan it and you were helping Owen, who put you up to this?"

"I'm not going to tell you." Smugness settled on Draxley's pallid features. "You won't have the mystery neatly solved. You'll go to your deaths with questions—not at peace."

"The fuse wasn't lit when Owen went in, was it?" Certainty settled over Chase. "You pushed down the detonator after."

"Doesn't matter," Draxley sneered. "You know, I could give you quick deaths. But you've cost me the mine and everything I worked so hard for, so I'm going to leave you to its mercy. You don't know the way—but I've haunted this place for weeks trying to find a way back in to the mother lode. Good-bye."

With that, he pinched the wick of his candle and plunged them into pitch-black darkness, his footsteps sounding the path of his retreat.

Chase wrapped his hand around Lacey's and, for the second time that day, dragged her through the tunnels. All his time as a tracker and hunter rose to the fore in those desperate moments as they fought to find a way out. Listening for footsteps and following his gut, he wound back the way they'd come—the air grew less stale.

"I see it!" Lacey gasped for breath as they caught a glimpse of light once more.

They sped for it, only to be thrown to the ground as the first blast echoed through the tunnels. Chase rolled atop her, sandwiching her between his body and the wall as daylight disappeared.

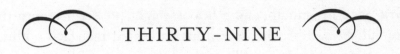

THIRTY-NINE

J ake felt the mountain lurch moments before the last train of the day pulled into Hope Falls. The car tilted on the tracks, but didn't tip over. His mouth went dry. *Evie!*

The moment they pulled to a stop, he vaulted over the edge of the iron guard, over the pull-down steps, and hit the ground running. He didn't stop until he reached the door of the diner. When he saw her, unharmed, Jake could breathe again.

"You're all right?" He wrapped his arms around her before she could even turn around. "No one's hurt?"

"Jake!" She shifted in his arms, gorgeous amber eyes bright with tears. "I'm so glad you're back!"

"Don't cry, sweetie." He thumbed a tear away from her cheek. "It's all going to be fine." *I'll make sure of it.*

"No it won't." Cora entered the kitchen, a bulging rucksack over her shoulder and a shovel in her hand. Miss Higgins followed close at her heels, similarly equipped.

"Lacey and Dunstan went to explore the mines." Evie's tears ran afresh. "Jake—they might still be inside the tunnels!"

No. He struggled to hide his horror as he extricated himself from her arms and swiped the shovel from her sister. "I'll send Lawson to get word to the men to come help. The sooner we get through, the sooner we'll find them."

Please, God, let them still be alive.

Lacey couldn't breathe, and for once it wasn't because of her corset. Grit filled her mouth, and a heavy weight pressed her into the ground. *Chase.* She tried to call his name, but managed nothing more than a dry wheeze. She took a breath and tried again.

"Chase?" When he didn't answer, the sour taste of panic filled the back of her throat. Lacey squeezed her hands under her and pushed upward, trying to jostle him. "Chase!"

He groaned and stirred, but then went still.

"Come on, Chase." Heart beating fast enough to race a train, Lacey pushed up again.

"Don't move," croaked a voice next to her ear. "Can't. . . breathe. . ."

She could have cried for joy at hearing him speak. *He's alive! Thank You, Lord. Please help him. . . . Help me help him. We have to get up and find a way out.*

"We're pinned." Still raspy, he sounded stronger as he shifted his weight. "The support's bowed over us."

"You can't move?" Panic began its slow creep again.

"A little." He strained, and Lacey felt some of the pressure ease off her. "Scoot to the right, Lacey."

Wiggling and sliding, ignoring sharp jabs from pieces of rock, Lacey moved over. Her bag halted her progress, making her stop everything to slip the strap over her head and push it away. Then she began to move again. It went slowly, agonizingly slowly, as Chase couldn't hold himself up indefinitely. Finally, she slid free and dragged air into her starved lungs. Dimly, she realized Chase was doing the same thing—he'd been compressed beneath the weight of the bowing beam. She crawled beside him.

"Can you move now?" Lacey pressed her hands against the wooden support, feeling the tension, knowing it wouldn't hold.

She heard the slide of rocks and a grunted breath as he tried to move and failed. "My coat's caught at the side and the bottom of my sleeve." He didn't say he couldn't take it off.

But he didn't have to. Lacey groped around for the bag she'd pushed aside, found it, and felt around the interior with trembling fingers. It seemed as though years went by before her hand closed around the slick wax of a candle, and she found the pocket holding her matches. It took five tries before she lit one properly then managed to light her candle.

The soft glow looked abnormally bright in the blackness, but Lacey held it forward to better see Chase. Sure enough, his jacket was pinched between the leaning wall and the floor, which pushed higher than the area mere feet away. From the looks of it, the beam must have pressed down on his back and ribs.

But he didn't complain.

"I can cut it away," she told him. "If you hold this." She pressed the candle into his outstretched hand, letting her fingers linger atop his. "It'll only be a moment."

"Thank you." A cough punctuated the words, and Lacey realized he'd probably breathed in far more dust than she had.

"Here." She took back the candle and pressed her uncapped canteen into his hand. "Take a drink before I get started."

It took some shifting, but he rolled slightly, tilting his head to drink. "Aaah. That's better." The difference in his voice astonished and pleased her as she withdrew her folding knife from the pocket of her pack and knelt over him.

"Hold still," she cautioned unnecessarily. The moment she

drew close, he'd stiffened as though bracing himself. Lacey reached out and felt the fabric, tugging slightly to get a sense of its weave and strength. Thick and somewhat stiff, it refused to pull free. Lacey lifted it as far from Chase as she could before puncturing the cloth then sawing to start a rip line. Soon the rip was long enough for her to grab both sides and tear the fabric down to the bottom seam. This she cut.

Slicing down the length of the sleeve made for trickier work, but she'd gotten a feel for the fabric by now. Chase held still as a stone until she finished. Taking back the candle, she scrambled backward, so he could move away from the wall.

He moved to the side before pushing himself into a sitting position, rolling his shoulders and pressing one hand against his ribs. "Thank you." Chase took the candle and held it aloft.

For the first time, Lacey saw their surroundings. Beyond the buckling wall, they had mere yards before the tunnel collapsed in a mammoth tangle of dirt and stone. She moved toward it and began pulling at the smaller rocks, pushing them away.

Please, God, she prayed. *I know I'm not worthy of Your grace, but we need help.*

Beside her Chase began working on larger rocks. Between the two of them, they cleared a good-sized heap off to one side before the sheer size and weight of the remaining rock defeated them. Lacey sank down, panting slightly from the work.

"They know we're in here." Again pressing his hand against his ribs, Chase settled beside her. "There's air coming in—I feel the draft on the right side of the pile. We'll be all right until they find us."

"Yes." Lacey stared at the small stub of candle they'd sandwiched between some rocks. "Do you have any of your candles?"

"No." He looked at her for a moment, dark eyes missing nothing. Then he slid his arm around her shoulders and tugged her closer. "But I'm here."

Somehow the warmth of his arm around her shoulders, the feel of his strength along her side, kept the fear at bay as her candle guttered. Now there was nothing but darkness. . .and Chase.

"Lacey?" His voice rumbled, low and reassuring.

"Yes, Chase?" She noticed they'd slipped into using first names, but liked it. *Besides,* she reasoned, *when you're wearing britches and sitting on the floor of a caved-in mine, the proprieties went out the window a long time before.*

"I was wrong, and I owe you an apology." Of all the things he might've said, he chose to remind her of their differences?

She brushed it aside. "You can apologize once we're out of this place." *For now I don't want anything to divide us.*

"Lacey?" He shifted closer. "What is it that makes you think God won't forgive you?"

"Does it matter?" Any other time she would have pulled away.

"Very much." Certainty underscored his words like bedrock. "Because I can't understand what a woman like you could have done to make her unworthy of God's mercy."

She thought about that for a long time and decided it was a compliment. *So now that he thinks the best of me, I'm supposed to tell him the worst?* Lacey sighed at the irony of it.

"I resented my brother." The words dropped like fellows of the stones around them. "When he came to Hope Falls, leaving me behind because women of quality weren't welcome in a mining town, I resented him. His freedom made me jealous. I could buy the mercantile and take part in Braden's plans, but I couldn't make my own. In his last letter, he told me to stop asking when I could come join him—he'd send for me when he wished, and until then I should keep myself busy. He suggested shopping. I wrote back that if the mines made it so Hope Falls would never be readied for us, I might begin to hope they failed. The next day we heard of the cave-in."

She heard him suck in a sharp breath and knew he was starting to understand. "It was a coincidence, Lacey."

"I know. But I still thought it, and then I heard he was dead. Gone forever, and the last words I'd written him were in anger. It was the second time I cried in the last ten years."

"When was the first?" His hand cupped her shoulder, rubbing up and down in a soothing motion.

"The day my father died. Before that," she rushed on even though he hadn't asked, "was the day my mother passed away. We were told she wouldn't make it, and I cried for a week straight until we lost her. Crying doesn't make a difference—it just keeps you from appreciating what you have while it's here."

"And it lets out some of your emotion, lessens how easily something can provoke your temper." He gave her shoulder a squeeze. "You couldn't have saved your parents or spared your brother, Lacey. As for envying Braden for his opportunities—it's understandable. It's human." Chase squeezed again. "It's *forgivable*, so long as you regret it and do better."

"That's what I thought, too." The hot prickling of tears warned Lacey to stop talking, but she couldn't keep it in anymore. "But then I found out Braden lived. I was so relieved, so happy. . . . I sold our family home and convinced the women to come here and find husbands to help protect us. What they really needed protection from was my planning." She gave a dry laugh.

"They're adults, Lacey. You were trying to take the burden off your brother and provide for your friends." He paused. "However misguided your attempt became."

"But. . ." Lacey gave a hard swallow and plunged into the worst of it. "When we arrived and Braden began raging and yelling and trying to kick us out, throwing my failures in my face every day. . .I began to think we would have done better without him, that if the brother I knew and admired couldn't have come back from the mines, I didn't want what was left over." The tears won, sliding down her cheeks and dripping off the tip of her nose. "How could I resent him all over again? It's a fatal flaw. I've tried to suppress it, tried to ignore it, tried to confess it and start again. But it didn't work, Chase."

"Repenting doesn't mean you never make the mistake again," he told her. "It means you fight your hardest not to. From the sounds of it, you've been fighting yourself and your brother for so long, you don't know the difference anymore."

"Maybe not." Lacey sniffed back more tears. "So long as I'm fighting all the time, I'm not at peace. I'm not gentle or patient or long-suffering like Cora. You were right when you said I lacked virtue, Chase. You knew it on the second day you met me! No matter how much I try, I'm not a good-enough Christian. I don't think I ever will be."

"Stop trying to be a good-enough Christian," Chase advised. "You're a believer in Christ, so focus on Him instead of on all the things you think you need to change about yourself. Maybe then you'll realize how brave and clever and caring He made you to be."

Lacey's breath hitched at the sweetness of the words and the conviction behind them. *If only he really believed that.* "You thought I was a murderer."

"I said I was wrong." He slid his hand down her arm. "Didn't you wonder why I didn't apologize, Lacey?"

"Men don't give apologies." She shrugged.

"They do when they mean them," he corrected. "You see, Lacey, there's a world of difference between being wrong"—his fingers twined with hers as he finished—"and being sorry about it."

FORTY

Chase sat in the dark, at least one rib broken, and smiled like a fool. The woman nestled against his side wasn't talking anymore, but she'd heard him—*and she's still holding my hand.*

"Chase?" She sounded hesitant, but he loved hearing her say his name.

"Yes, Lacey?" He liked the newfound freedom to say hers, too.

"Why don't you like people?" The question made his ribs hurt, as though she'd given him a hit to the midsection.

After everything they'd made it through today, she wanted to talk about how different they were? Chase drew in as deep a breath as he could without it hurting and squeezed her hand.

She squeezed back, and suddenly it didn't seem like a bad thing that she'd asked. Lacey snuggled closer, waiting.

"It's not that I don't like people." He eased into it. "It's more that I don't like very *many* people."

"Oh." She shifted a bit then settled. "Do you mean you don't like to have very many people around you at once or that there aren't many people you like in general?"

"Both, probably. Lots of people cause lots of problems."

"But you like Granger," she mused. "And my brother, when he was himself. And I think, maybe, after today. . .you might like me, too?"

"Sometimes we fight hardest against the things we want most." Chase found it hard to explain, even to himself. "I've never fought harder than when I met you, Lacey."

She went so still, he could barely hear her breathe. *She understands. I'm bad with words and worse with women, Lord, but here sits one who understands.* Something light fluttered in the vicinity of his heart, and Chase recognized it as hope.

"Why do you think you're unable to have a civil conversation when you can say sweet things like that?" She sounded perplexed and slightly put out, like she'd been fooled.

"Because being civil usually means two people who don't like each other pretend that they get along," he explained. "I don't like pretense, and I don't go in for games. It's better to say what you think and mean it."

Another, longer silence. For the first time, Chase began to understand why it worked so well on other people when he did it to them. He made it a rule not to break silence—but rules were meant to be broken. "What do you think?"

"I think that's surprisingly civilized." She surprised him. "And I'm thinking that this means you were sincere about what you said. . .about fighting hardest for what you want most."

"I meant it." He turned his torso to face her, even though he couldn't see her. Chase heard her breathe faster.

"Then tell me, Chase Dunstan. What is it, exactly, that you want?"

From beyond the wall of rock came the sound of scraping and chiseling and many men working hard to break through. *We're saved.* But for some reason, Chase wasn't as happy as he should have been.

"Lacey!" a woman shrieked from the other side, the cry mercifully muffled in their chamber. "Dunstan! Are you there?"

Lacey pulled her hand from his, and pain blossomed in his rib cage. Then she cupped her hands over his ears and screeched back, "Yes, Evie! We're in here!"

A flurry of shouts on the other side, and the sounds of work doubled. Chase wanted to ignore it for the short time they'd have left, but first he had to do some yelling of his own. He reached over, felt the softness of her hair, and clamped his hands over her ears to holler at the men.

"Don't let Draxley leave town! Some of you hunt him down if you have to!" He moved his hands to Lacey's shoulders, keeping his fingers in the silkiness of her loosened tresses.

"He won't go anywhere." Granger's grim promise came through loud and clear. "Draxley's just outside the mines, head crushed by a boulder from up the ridge."

Chase heard Lacey gasp just before she buried her face against his chest. He looped his arms around her and held her close. "It means he won't hurt anyone else, sweetheart."

"I know." She pushed away from him slightly, and Chase resisted the urge to pull her back. "Chase? Did you mean to call me sweetheart?" Lacey sounded almost shy.

She never sounded shy before. Chase started grinning. "Yep." He went ahead and pulled her close again. "Are you ready to hear what it is that I want most?"

He felt her nod even though she didn't say anything.

"Right now I want to kiss you." Chase waited for her answer, but he couldn't even hear her breathing anymore. Just as he started getting concerned, she took a great, gulping breath.

"And later?" came the shaky query. "What do you want later?"

Before he answered, Chase moved his hand to cup the side of her face. "When we get out of here, I want you to forget about your ad and say you'll be my wife."

He lowered his lips to hers before she could make a decision, hoping the kiss would convey the tenderness and longing he couldn't find the words for. She matched him, soft and sweet and passionate as she curled her hand around the nape of his neck.

When he pulled back, Chase tilted to rest his forehead against hers. "Do you know what it is that you want, Lacey?"

She nodded. "Right now I want you to kiss me again."

Chase's breath hitched, but he needed more. "And later?" He echoed her question. "Do you know what you want later?"

She threaded her fingers through his hair and ignored the calls of their rescuers as they began to break through the barrier. "I want to marry you, too." Enough light seeped through for him to see her smile as she moved closer to whisper, "And you know how I am when I set my mind on something. . . ."

Life doesn't wait, and neither does **Kelly Eileen Hake**. In her short twenty-eight years of life, she's achieved much. Her secret? Embracing opportunities and multitasking. Kelly received her first writing contract at the tender age of seventeen and arranged to wait three months until she was able to legally sign it. Since that first contract ten years ago, she's reached several life goals. Aside from fulfilling over twenty contracts ranging from short stories to novels, she's also attained her BA in English Literature and Composition and earned her credential to teach English in secondary schools. If that weren't enough, she's taken positions as a college preparation tutor, bookstore clerk, and in-classroom learning assistant to pay for the education she values so highly. Recently, she completed her MA in Writing Popular Fiction.

Writing for Barbour combines two of Kelly's great loves—history and reading. A CBA best-selling author and dedicated member of American Christian Fiction Writers, she's been privileged to earn numerous Heartsong Presents Reader's Choice Awards. No matter what goal she pursues, Kelly knows what it means to *work* for it! Please visit her website at www.kellyeileenhake.com to learn more.